MYSTICAL EMONA

RONESA AVEELA

BENDIDEIA
PUBLISHING

Cover Design by Nelinda, www.nelindaart.com

Cover images from Depositphotos.

"Silver Butterflies" poem and Carina's song were written by Noor Lek, especially for *Mystical Emona: Soul's Journey.*

Dedication

This book is dedicated to my father, whom I miss
every day. To my husband, for supporting me behind the
scenes and letting me be myself. Last, but not least,
to my children, whom I want to teach how to pursue
their dreams.

Contents

Authors' Notes

Ronesa Aveela is the pen name we have chosen for our collaborative work.

I visited Emona in 1998. The wild beauty of this mystical place located on the Black Sea, a land and its people and history hidden from the world, left a deep impression on me. It inspired me to use my pen and my brushes to unveil a story of love and mystery, and to depict the wonders of *Mystical Emona* through my characters, born from the imagination of my personal experience.

Emona opened a new world for me—time turned back thousands of years. I imagined the era when the great Thracians ruled the land, when King Rez defended his people and the cape. I imagined the time when the old lighthouse, now so lonely and forgotten, was once alive, and its light illuminated the way for sailors on the stormy Black Sea. I imagined the time when the now-ruined church was alive with generations of people marrying, baptizing their children, and praying to God for good health and luck.

I was amazed by the power, independent freedom, and strength of the wild horses galloping like a hurricane along the foothills of the Stara Planina.

I hope you enjoy reading the story of this magical land as much as I did writing it. —Nelly Toncheva

Although I've never travelled to Emona, I've experienced its beauty and wealth of history and magic through my journey that began when Anelia asked me to assist with this project. I've learned so much about the legends and culture of those living in the Balkans, that its people and places have become alive for me. I hope you feel the same way. —Rebecca Carter

"And when one of them meets with his other half ...
the pair are lost in an amazement of love
and friendship and intimacy, and would not be
out of the other's sight ...: these are the people
who pass their whole lives together;
yet they could not explain
what they desire of one another."

– Plato's *Symposium*, 360 B.C.E.

Silver Butterflies

Behold the silent beauties ruffling winds,
spelling purity of a love so bold,
goddesses of water, woods and land,
swish their dresses upon your pool.

Vedra's hands could raise the seas,
bring upon you draught or prosperity,
oh heaven behold, she was blessed,
with silky dresses and a voice so sleek.

Sweet Carina is laden with lands,
to hold the minds of all mankind,
her thoughts dance upon the sands,
meaning to show a man his heart.

Dear Morena burdened the most,
to see the loss of those she loves,
always hunted by the future,
she's to ever be your seer and guard.

Nymphs so pure, embrace the world,
call with golden songs to the skies,
listen as they guide you home,
listen as they hold your hand.

—Noor Lek

Together Forever

February 14, present year

OUR LOVE IS yesterday, today, and forever.

Sitting at an antique roll-top desk, Stefan Tarrant scrawled the words onto the handmade greeting card, depicting the view from the bedroom window—Boston Harbor, alive with the Tall Ships, their white sails unfurling in the breeze. He shook his head, laughing silently as he looked from the writing to his hands. How could he paint such breathtaking images, and yet write with such disgrace? He hoped Katherine could decipher the words their eight years of marriage had inspired.

He gazed at the bed where his wife lay, the curls of her shoulder-length blond hair tousled from the night's sleep. Her slow, steady breathing assured him she still slumbered. With the stealth of a cat, he tiptoed toward her to place the card on the nightstand. The heat of passion burned him as his eyes lingered on her figure, her chest rising and falling with each breath. The straps of her creamy, lacy nightgown had slipped, revealing her slender shoulders. Lower down, it had bunched up around her waist, exposing the belly button he loved to explore. He ran his fingers along her cheeks and down her throat.

Shifting her position, she turned on her side. Her eyes fluttered open. She smiled, placing her hand over his. "Happy anniversary. You're up early."

"Shh." He touched her lips. "It's bad luck to break tradition."

He returned to his side of the bed and crawled beneath the covers, scooting closer to her. "Why did the cookie go to the doctor?"

She groaned. "Can't you at least tell a new joke?"

With a shake of his head, he wiggled his fingers for her to answer.

"Because he felt crummy." She leaned closer to whisper into his ear, exaggerating the words with a French accent. "Let him kiss me with the kisses of his mouth: for thy love is better than wine."

He obliged her with the requested kisses, unlike the first time she had challenged him with those words. They had met at a beauty pageant in Paris years ago, where seventeen-year-old Katherine Armand was a contestant. He and his college friends watched from the back row. When she smiled at him, his stomach flip-flopped. Afterward, she sought him out to introduce herself. He'd been so tongue-tied, he responded with the stupid cookie joke. She giggled when she answered with the punchline, afterward reciting the beautiful verse from the Song of Solomon. Glancing over her shoulder several times as she walked away, she smiled, while he stared with his mouth agape. The whirlwind romance that followed led them to the altar a year later.

Stefan's lips and hands now traversed her body. He kissed her nose. "Katherine?"

"Mmmm." With dilated pupils and parted lips, she trailed her fingertips down his chest.

He leaned toward her and nibbled her earlobe. "Let's have another baby. Sonia's already in school. She needs a little brother."

Her breathing accelerated. "When?"

"I was thinking now."

Snuggling closer, she lifted her face, brushed her lips against his, and whispered, "Yes."

THE BELL ABOVE the door of the out-of-the-way antique shop in historic Salem jingled when Stefan opened it. A blast of warm air whooshed around him as he entered the dark, misty room, pungent from fragrant candles and incense. Dusty shelves overflowed with bizarre figurines and bottles containing strange, unidentifiable concoctions. This was his last hope to find a special gift for Katherine.

He picked up an hourglass. Two black-robed grim reapers stood opposite each other; their hands rested on a bar in the middle, while their scythes lay at their sides. He turned the glass over. The fine white sand trickled down, filling the bottom globe.

Raising his eyebrows, he chuckled, the corners of his mouth curling into a playful grin. "Certainly not a gift for Katherine."

A woman with white hair, peppered with black, appeared at his side. She lifted her soft-gray, catlike eyes to him. "Hello," she said with a thick Eastern European accent. "May I help you look for something?"

"I hope you can." He crammed the bizarre item back on the shelf in a hurry. "I'm looking for a bracelet or a ring, something unusual. My wife loves antiques."

"You've come to the right place." She reached out to reposition the hourglass, revealing a flower tattooed on her age-spotted hand. "The jewelry is at the back."

Hindered by the cramped aisles, he followed her at a snail's pace. From one of the shelves, he fingered a small glass bottle decorated with gold and pearls in the shape of a heart. The amber liquid inside sparkled. He laughed after reading the label: *Love Potion*. When he unscrewed the cover, the liquid remedy revealed its aphrodisiacs—vanilla, citrus, and something sweet-smelling, perhaps honey.

The woman looked over her shoulder. Her eyes glittered like the liquid. "Please look around; don't be afraid." An amused tone crept into her voice. "We have many love potions. That one is our most popular with women of all ages. It brings new desire into a relationship. One of its main ingredients is orange, which acts like a magnet to attract men and bring the wearer eternal love and happiness."

She removed the cap from another bottle. Spearmint and woodsy scents drifted out. "Or perhaps you'd be interested in a love potion designed for men. This one stimulates both body and mind. It produces a mood of creative playfulness."

Chuckling again, he put the bottle back on the shelf. Katherine would be amused when he told her about it. "I don't need it yet, but maybe for our fiftieth anniversary."

The woman continued to the back. "I have the perfect piece of jewelry for you. Let me see where I put it." She looked inside a few cupboards. "Here it is." After dusting the top of a blue velvet box, she opened it. "Yes, yes, this is it. I think this is what you've been searching for." She handed it to him.

The box held an exquisite golden ring with an unusual blue stone, a luminous star with six rays spreading out from its center. A golden crown, embedded with small blue chips, surrounded its outer edge. Stefan picked it up, holding it in his palm. It radiated warmth. *How unusual.* The image in the stone wavered while he examined it; black eyes stared back at him. He jerked his head up to look at the shopkeeper.

"Is something wrong?" A smile flitted across her face.

He glanced at the stone again. Only a blue star. "No. I thought I saw ... It was nothing." Stefan shook his head. Despite the warmth of the shop, the tiny hairs on his arms stood up.

I need to get more sleep. My eyes are playing tricks on me.

The woman spoke with soft words. "The ring is quite old. The gentleman who sold it to me claimed it'll guide its owner to his true love."

"I'll take it. It's the perfect gift for my true love, my wife."

THE CLOCK TOWER struck seven when the limo pulled up to Katherine's favorite French restaurant, situated by the waterfront in the Back Bay. The familiar cacophony of the city greeted Stefan as he got out. Scents of American, French, and Italian cuisine wafted around him in the brisk wintery air. Tiny snowflakes, driven by the wind gusts, shimmered in the headlights of the passing vehicles. He extended his hand to his wife. As she stretched her long legs from the vehicle, her black pumps clicked on the walkway. Wrapping his arm around her waist, he escorted her inside.

In the marble-tiled foyer, he relieved her of her coat, and handed it, along with his leather jacket, to the attendant, tipping the youth. While they waited to be seated, Stefan traced his finger along the heart cutout on the back of her chiffon dress, its red complementing her royal blue eyes.

"My lovely Valentine, such a perfect rose." He leaned closer, kissing her cheeks and tucking a stray strand of hair behind her ear.

The maître d' led them to the small, informal dining room. The steady rhythm of Katherine's heels softened as they moved from the dark hardwood floor to a periwinkle-blue area rug on the way to their window-side table. A bottle of champagne chilling on ice awaited them.

In the lounge next to the dining area, a musician played a saxophone. The lights of the sconces lining the walls reflected off the instrument. At other tables, couples laughed, conversed, or gazed into each other's eyes, celebrating the day dedicated to lovers.

After they placed their orders, Stefan stood and bowed to Katherine. "Dance with me, my beautiful wife. They're playing—"

"Don't say it." She laughed. "That's so cliché."

"A slow waltz."

Tapping him on the shoulder, she shook her head. "You're hopeless. That's not what you were going to say."

The notes of the saxophone sprinkled them like a gentle summer rain as they connected soul to soul. Katherine's sensual body moved in time with his, heating his blood. Amber light from the chandelier frolicked across her—a nymph dancing under the moon's glow. He breathed in the citrus scent of her perfume as the song ended.

"I'm ravished." He released her hand. Wrapping his arms around her waist, he drew her closer to him. "Maybe we should continue this dance at home."

"You're insatiable." She smiled as she pushed him away and dragged him back to the table where their food was being served. "I'm not leaving here without trying my grilled lobster and a taste of your cider-glazed duck."

"Perhaps I'll have some oyster stew to start." He winked. "It might work as well as the love potion the woman in the antique store wanted to sell me."

Katherine tilted her head. "A love potion in an antique shop?"

"Now that you mention it, that was rather strange." He pulled out her chair, and pushed it in as she sat.

After he seated himself, the waiter popped the cork and poured the champagne.

Stefan raised his glass. "A toast to the lovely lady I want to spend forever with."

"À ta santé." She clinked glasses with him, the sound melding with the notes of the jazz music. "To the love of my life. Thank you for bringing me so much happiness. I knew the moment I saw you that we were meant to be together."

Stefan reached across the table, took hold of her hand, and brought it to his lips. "I have a special gift for you." He released her hand, withdrew a box from his jacket pocket, and kneeled in front of her. "For the woman I would marry all over again." He opened the box and removed the ring.

Katherine blinked away a tear. "Mon cher, it's beautiful." She leaned forward to kiss him. "I'm sure if our next child is a son, he'll grow to be tall, dark, and handsome like his father."

"Now who's using clichés?" Stefan chuckled. "It's a mystical blue star, shining like your eyes. It even has some ancient writing on the band."

He placed it on her finger. It fit as if it had been made for her.

THE WIND HOWLED around the bay, blowing biting snow into their faces. Several inches had accumulated by the time Stefan and Katherine left the restaurant. A mixture of sand and rock salt covered the icy walkway, but drifts continued to grow. They hurried into the shelter of the warm limo. He wrapped his arm around her as she nestled close to him.

The wheels spun as the driver merged into the congested traffic.

Stefan grew drowsy and closed his eyes. As he listened to the soothing beat of the wipers thumping against the windshield, he counted the stops along Boylston Street. Now turn left onto Berkeley. More stop and go, until finally a right onto Storrow Drive.

He caressed Katherine's hair. *Not much longer now, love. We'll be home soon to continue our celebration.*

"Get out of my way!" The driver blasted the horn.

Stefan's eyes flew open as the car swerved, then skidded across the intersection like a bobsled racing down a hill. Katherine screamed. He tightened his arms around her. Twin beams of light shone through the window, growing larger. Metal crunched and glass shattered.

Katherine was wrenched away from him. The limo spun in circles, finally slamming into a guardrail.

He opened his eyes. "Katherine?"

Excruciating pain shot up his shoulder when he twisted his body. Her head, leaning against the smashed window, lay at a crooked angle. With the seatbelt restraining her body, her shoulders slumped forward.

"Katherine?" Stefan whispered. "Please say something."

He touched her cheek, as white as the snow outside. A red trickle flowed from her ear, matting her curls. Her eyes remained closed.

"Katherine!" He shouted her name until his voice grew hoarse. Then his lips mouthed the word over and over.

The blustery storm spread its arms around them, coating the vehicle white. Snowflakes drifted through the shattered windows, chilling him. A blue light, flashing like a beacon to guide weary travelers home, reflected off the ring, illuminating the darkness like a newborn star.

Road to Emona

March 25, one year later

GRAVEL AND TORN-UP asphalt pelted Stefan's car like a hailstorm as he drove along the narrow road that wound around the slope of the mountain toward his destination—Emona. The secluded village by the Black Sea, a summer haven for artists and actors, would soon be his new home. The arrangements having been made ahead of time, all that remained was his signature on the official documents. He had one final chance to back out of the deal if he didn't like the house. That wasn't likely. He had fallen in love with the charming cottage from its online pictures.

He glanced at the dashboard clock. Not late yet. He still had a few hours before the agent was scheduled to show him the property. After he checked into the hotel, he would call his daughter Sonia to let her know he had arrived.

After his wife died, he had been in no condition to take care of his seven-year-old. Thankful when Katherine's parents invited him and Sonia to live with them in Rouen, France, he agreed. Now, not wanting to disrupt his daughter's life after she had finally adjusted to being without her mother, he would let her stay there for the duration of the school year. She would join him as soon as he was settled here and found a reputable private school equal to the one she now attended. It was time for them to begin their own life.

He had already spent a year agonizing over Katherine's death. A year drinking to excess. A year isolating himself from everyone he knew. On what would have been their anniversary, in a fit of rage, he destroyed everything in his room. After he pulled out a drawer and hurled it, a golden ring bounced back toward him. The last gift he had bought for Katherine. He picked it up and slumped down the wall, crying the tears he had held back since her death. The ring began his healing. Now he hoped Emona would lighten the scars.

Engrossed in his thoughts, he paid little heed to his surroundings. A movement in the forest made him focus a moment too late. Something black darted across the road, and he slammed on the brakes. The car buckled, veered off course, and plunged into a deep rut. He cringed when metal scraped against rock.

"Damn animal," he muttered, his heart racing.

He looked out the side window. With a sharp intake of breath, he gripped the steering wheel. A rocky beach lay at the base of the cliff. The driver's side tires had missed careening over the edge by no more than a foot. Stefan exhaled slowly and released his death grip on the steering wheel, allowing color to return to his knuckles. With a shaky hand, he wiped away the sweat dripping down his brow.

Easing out of the rut, he pulled off to the side, a safe distance from the cliff. He got out and surveyed the damage to the car. One more dent creased the fender, but all else appeared intact. He continued his drive through the dense forest with greater caution. Small patches of light filtered through the branches hanging over the road, chasing away the shadows. When the tree line ended, he stopped to view the vista.

The brilliant sun shone in a sky so blue it merged with the cerulean waters. A lighthouse, perched like a seagull on a buoy, overlooked the rocky coast. The mountain range, still covered in snow, hugged the village nestled in the valley; no more than thirty or forty houses lay scattered like orange-capped, white mushrooms springing up among the brush in the surrounding wilderness.

Hope lit his spirit and chased away his shadows of doubt. *This is where I belong. Here I can find solitude and ... and perhaps inspiration.*

A dazzling white falcon sitting in a tree chanted, "Kak kak kak."

"Hello to you, too." Stefan grabbed his camera and snapped a few shots. Setting it down, he snatched up his sketchpad and charcoal from the seat beside him and drew the bird with a few quick strokes. He scrutinized the image. Not too bad after a year away from his hobby.

He sketched a few more images, tossed the booklet onto the passenger seat, and continued down the road. After a few sharp bends, the road straightened, and the village lay ahead. *Quaint* wasn't the first word he thought when he caught sight of the "Hotel Emona," more like *enchanting*. Dominating the center of the village, the four-story building demonstrated exquisite architecture, with its mix of balconies and windows, including curved walls sporting ceiling-to-floor glass.

Although modern, the hotel's décor mirrored the neighboring small houses—a white, cracked-daub façade and a brownish-red, terracotta-tiled roof, with bordering shrubs and flowers. The impressive structure lent the village a quaint character after all.

Stefan chuckled at the street signs attached to fences around some houses. Surely such a small village didn't require posted names to find its occupants. Shaking his head, he started toward the hotel, but the sun glinted off something on the opposite side of the street. A bronze statue of a young woman stood atop a fountain built into the terraced hill.

With time to spare, he walked over to inspect it. Curly hair tumbled around her face as she leaned forward under the weight of an amphora on her shoulders, her hands grasping its handles. Her face tilted downward, smiling at him, as if welcoming him home to Emona. The look on her face reminded him of Katherine. His eyes misted. He wished she was alive to share this adventure.

He sat on the fountain's low wall and ran his hands over the rough-hewn stones. Water gushing from three brass pipes that extended over a deep marble basin soothed his anxiety about leaving everything familiar to him for this remote spot.

The relief carvings on the front of the basin intrigued him as much as the statue. Small swags of flowers encircled a medallion, where two horses pranced beneath a crescent moon, with a three-headed snake coiling around a tree branch.

He leaned forward, cupped his palms under one of the pipes, and drank deeply of the sparkling water. His heart told him this was home. He never wanted to leave—again.

He jumped up. *What did I mean—again?*

THE FRAGRANCE OF expensive tobacco drifted around Nikola Karanov as he puffed on a cigar in his penthouse living room. Stretching out his legs on the green-motif Persian rug in front of the white leather couch, he leaned back to admire his favorite room. He had paid an interior designer well to oversee the details. All the furniture except his grand piano had been made in his own shop.

The drapes at the sides of the tall windows along one wall were pulled back, giving him a grand view of boats sailing in and out of the harbor. This evening, the calm water sparkled with reddish-violet colors. On many other occasions, the unpredictable sea could explode into a violent storm with no warning.

A light breeze through the open windows brought with it the salty smell of the seashore mixed with enticing aromas from bakeries and restaurants along the pedestrian street. The motion of the air against the stubble on his cheeks made them tingle, reminding him he needed to shave and make himself presentable before he met Elena for dinner.

Thinking about her flooded him with desire. He longed to run his fingers through her shoulder-length chocolate hair and gaze into her serious dark eyes. They shared a love of art and culture, and so much more—but as friends, and it wasn't enough for him.

He wanted to bring passion to her life, but he hadn't found the right way to express how much he loved everything about her. Her impeccable style of dressing that highlighted her body's slender build. Her passion for fashionable and sometimes outrageous hats. Most of all, her intellect, strong will, and dedication to her art gallery. She ran her life on a schedule, and business was a top priority. So much alike, they were perfect for each other.

Why couldn't she see that? Would she have shown a romantic interest in him if he was tall and handsome like his father, instead of only having his greenish-gray eyes? And if he didn't have that deep-red curly mop and those cursed freckles swarming his cheeks and nose? How he hated them. They didn't seem to bother other women, but Elena wouldn't allow anyone to make an emotional claim on her life.

Scowling, he recalled how everyone had called him "Carrot Top" his freshman year in college after students loaded his bed with the offending vegetable. He had never been able to eat them again.

Nikola put out his cigar and headed to the bathroom for a shower. The warm water calmed him, erasing the detestable taunts. He shaved and splashed on some Clive Christian X for Men cologne. Filled with spicy scents, including a touch of cinnamon, it had become his favorite indulgence, next to his special blend of cigars.

From his wardrobe, he pulled out a sophisticated linen suit he had bought during his last trip to Monaco. It wasn't quite right for the evening, so he replaced it. Instead, he chose an Armani, tailored in pale grays and soft whites, its light material perfect for Varna's warm spring weather.

He grabbed his car keys from the glass table and headed for the door, but stopped when the phone rang. His realtor. Nikola debated letting it go to voicemail, but decided he should answer.

"Mr. Karanov, good evening. The deal on the house in Emona has been finalized."

"Fantastic." Nikola set his keys down and grabbed a pen and paper. "I love the house, but with my busy schedule, I never have time to go there." He tapped the paper with the pen. "What do you need from me?"

"If you sign the documents releasing the property from the estate, you won't have to attend the closing tomorrow. I'll fax them over now."

Nikola hung up and glanced at his watch. If he didn't hurry, he'd be late meeting Elena. He poured himself a whiskey and paced the room until the fax spewed out pages. When he read the buyer's name, his breathing became shallow. He hurled the papers, scattering them across the room, then clutched the edge of the table until his knuckles turned white. Gulping the rest of his whiskey, he poured another one. Memories flashed by like frames of an old movie.

"Stefan. My old *friend* Stefan is the buyer." He spit the words out. The man who destroyed his happiness. The man who stole Katherine from him.

Katherine. Nikola's countenance softened when he thought of her dancing blue eyes and her beautiful smile. He would have another chance to see her soon.

Vortex in Blue

March 25

A STREAK OF light, like a dazzling comet, scorched a fading trail along the long corridor. Brief glimpses of drawings depicting momentous events in the lives of Carina and her sisters flickered in the glow of the torches as the young woman, her golden hair streaming behind her, flew past.

Excitement enflaming the blood coursing through her veins, Carina reached the first of three caverns, where they offered sacrifices to their goddess. She and her sisters had been blessed above the other samodivi when Bendis entrusted them with the guardianship of her temple.

She paused for the briefest moment, forever in awe of the room's splendors. Nature's jewels clinging to the ceiling winked their rosy, azure, and snowy eyes in the flickering torchlight, wishing her fortitude and fortune. The *aqua vitae* murmured in agreement as it traversed toward the waterfall, promising to wait there to ponder her fate with her.

Today, she mustn't tarry. Her destination waited below where she and Morena resided. She must deliver the long-awaited news.

He has the blue-star. The power of the ring drew me to him.

She burst into the chamber with the ferocity of a fire blazing out of control. One moment, the flash of her white robe gleamed off the thin layers of hammered gold that covered the fluted columns as she twirled around them with her hands outstretched.

The next instant, she dashed past the marble relief of the Bendideia, a torch-relay competition performed on horseback. She tossed a kiss to the lead athlete who reminded her of Dushan. So tall and muscular. Such an alluring smile. Her own race took her past sculptures and frescoes of Bendis. The vibrant reds, blacks, greens, and blues blurred as Carina sprinted past. This time she didn't stop to admire the blond, curly hair of the goddess that hung down her full figure, or the deep-set eyes, prominent cheek bones, and full lips that contributed to her regal beauty.

Once, twice, thrice, the whir of white flared up by the columns as Carina wove between them in her zealous dance. After spinning around the room several more times, she collapsed at her sister's feet.

Ceasing to pluck the strings of the *outi*, Morena laid the instrument down and smoothed Carina's unruly hair. "What excites you so much?"

She whispered with a ragged breath, "Dushan has returned. At last, we'll be together forever."

"How do you know?" A sea of flames as resplendent as Morena's auburn hair ignited in her black eyes. "Others have owned the ring and haven't been the chosen one."

Carina clutched her hands over her heart. "When I watched him arrive today, something deep within me stirred. I have no doubt the mortal who now carries the ring is my beloved. I haven't been so alive since Deyan stole the blue-star."

"Be careful." Morena's body tensed as she grasped Carina's arms. "I don't want to lose you to an ill-fated love as we did Vedra. She, too, spoke such words of certainty."

Morena had never been in love. She wouldn't understand how souls cried out to one another, how they healed each other with a single word or touch. Even so, remembering their elder sister's heartbreak, a flicker of doubt flashed through Carina's mind. The mortal Vedra loved had stolen her belt. Carina and Morena punished him, but the oracle of death and destruction held fast. The sisters had wept, holding each other in sorrow, knowing Vedra's power would drain as she aged.

Carina narrowed her eyes. She pushed away Morena. After scrambling to her feet, she threw back her shoulders and thrust her fists on her hips. "Vedra was deceived. *That* mortal wasn't her true love. I know the man who arrived today is my Dushan."

"Sister." Morena spoke softly, but said no more.

Tears welling in her eyes, Carina held her head high as she stormed away, retreating to the lowest of the three caverns. High above, a thin trail of sunlight streamed down by the waterfall. A torrent of *aqua vitae*, wending its way through the cave, cascaded with a deafening roar into the sparkling emerald and topaz pool. Where the falls collided with it, the waters churned with a force as strong as her impassioned emotions.

A misty spray soaked her while she sat on the boulders that had fallen over the eons, creating a place where she could kick her feet in the cool, life-restoring water. The colors swirling in the pool reminded her of her sapphire ring. She could visualize Dushan's face in it.

How happy they had been. One day, lying in the meadow, looking up at the clouds, they planned their wedding. They decided to build a home and raise children in that spot. It was there he had given her the ring. Would she ever be reunited with him to fulfill those dreams?

Saddened by her memories, Carina sang a love song to her *kamoles*, her beloved.

Dear sorrowful heart rejoice,
May 'morrow love prevail,
Answering your silent pleas,
Painting you with warmth.

I've silently prayed the moon,

Goddess of pearl white,
Guide my dear ashore.
May his heart never quiver,
Please, still his fearful core.

Dancing notes will break our silence,
Turn our yearning to songs.
May his ring find my finger,
And all our fears drown.

I've been searching for paradise.
He's been longing for my soul.

As the last note echoed over the pool, she looked around. Could she bear to leave this place so dear to her for so many millennia? With the arrival of spring today, the gate to the other side of the moon had opened. She was free to enter the mortal realm and remain there until the onset of winter when the gate closed. Yearning to be reunited with her love and feel the warmth of his embrace, she made her decision to go to him.

He would prove his love for her and end the ring's curse.

AFTER THE REALTOR showed him the house, Stefan signed the papers, asking if they could close the following day. The realtor informed him he would check with the owner, but he didn't anticipate any problems.

On the way out, Stefan gazed one more time at the single-story, wood-and-brick house. It resembled those in the village, with dark-wooden shuttered windows. A swing swayed in the breeze on the open porch. Countless women must have sat there, looking out to sea, anxiously waiting for their loved ones to return from fishing in the Black Sea.

He passed through an unkempt garden, desolate like an abandoned lover. Cranesbill overgrew the boxwoods, scraggly rose bushes skulked along the old wooden gate, and vines suffocated the stone wall. With its grout in need of repair, several stones had fallen unattended on the ground. Even the cement around the stones in the path leading from the gate to the house was fraught with cracks and holes.

It needed work, but it was perfect—remote, yet close to the village center; small, yet large enough for him to have a studio and a room for Sonia. And it came furnished, with even the tools in the shed. Well-worn items were better than nothing to start with.

He had already fallen in love with the studio. It reminded him of the family room in his grandfather's cottage in Vermont where he spent many of his childhood summers. Weathered exposed beams on the high ceiling and the dark-stained floors made a striking contrast to the white walls, appealing to his artistic eye. On a cold day, a fire blazing on the hearth of the large open fieldstone fireplace would inspire him while he worked into early morning hours creating paintings to place on the now-bare walls. He could set his family photos on the sturdy beam used as a mantel.

His stomach grumbled as he approached the hotel. He increased his pace, bounding onto the terrace, in a hurry to get lunch. Two elderly men sitting at a table glanced up from their game of backgammon. Smiles filled their sun-creased faces. He nodded to them as he entered the hotel.

"Mrs. Pavlova," he called to a plump, middle-aged woman walking around the reception area, holding what looked like a candle.

She paused to meet his eyes, as if searching his soul. "Yes, Mr. Tarrant?"

He sniffed the air. Incense? "I'm going to become your newest resident."

"Wonderful." The hotel owner set the object on the counter, wiped her fingers on her red apron, then clasped his hands. "But call me Maria, please."

"Maria it is. And call me Stefan."

"This is a perfect day to hear this. It's Blagovets, which means 'Good news.' It's the day the Archangel told Mary she would give birth to the Savior."

Stefan glanced at the burning candle.

Maria followed his gaze. "That's a *kandilo*. I'm purifying the hotel. It cleanses all the evil that settled in the rooms over the winter. Women have done this for generations. Later on we rake up leaves to burn them. People jump over the fires for protection."

Is she serious?

Her sides shook, and she covered her mouth. Finally losing the battle, she laughed with so much energy he thought it could be heard in the village square. "Please forgive me. I was imagining what you would have thought if you had arrived here earlier this morning."

"This morning?" He rubbed his forehead. "Why?"

"Right after sunrise, women walk around the outside of their houses banging pans." She turned her rosy face toward him. "To drive all the snakes from their dens. I'm sure you've never seen anything quite like that."

"You're right." He laughed. "You might have driven me away, too."

"I'm keeping you from lunch." She crooked her arm in his. "Let me introduce you to Todor, our barber. He's in the pub now."

They opened the door to the pub. The smell of cheap cigarettes drifted out, along with a blast of warm air from the cheery fire crackling on the hearth. A simple stencil of grapes and vines bordered the white walls. Beneath the design, baskets of dried flowers and herbs decorated the places between the light sconces.

Maria led him to the far side to a wooden table. The man sitting there wore a sailor hat over his pearly white hair. "Todor, this is Stefan Tarrant, our newest resident. He bought the Professor's house."

"Welcome to Emona." Todor reached out his wrinkled hand. He spoke with a thick accent. "Please sit."

"Thank you." Stefan pulled up a chair on the opposite side of the table. "I'll have a quick lunch."

"Today you must eat well and have money in your pocket."

"Why is it important to eat well today?"

"And have money in your pocket," Todor replied. "If cuckoo sings to you, you'll be well-fed and have money all year."

"Interesting. I do have money, so now I need to find a cuckoo after I eat." Stefan laughed as he examined the small feast laid out on the table, each dish in a colorful ceramic bowl. "This looks great. What is everything?"

"Stuffed grape leaves." Todor pointed to a plate stacked with small green rectangular-shaped items. "They have rice and spices inside." He identified the other items—yogurt, garlic and dill salad, cold cucumber soup, and bread.

The waitress came to the table, pad of paper and pen in hand.

"I'll have what Todor's having, plus a local red wine, please." He could take some food back to his room if he didn't eat it all.

"Please have some *pitka*." Todor passed the plate of bread. "And dip in *sharena sol,* colorful salt."

"It smells homemade. I think I will. Thank you." Stefan broke off a piece of the warm bread, dipped it into the bowl, and took a bite. "Mmm. This is wonderful. What kind of spices are these?"

"Summer savory, paprika, and sea salt."

Stefan leaned back in his chair. Great food, friendly people, quiet country. This was definitely the place he belonged.

LATER, STEFAN LEANED on the railing of his hotel room balcony, gazing at the sea fading into the horizon. It was too distant to hear the waves breaking against the shore, but its saltiness flavored the air, reminding him of his old house in Boston. Sad and happy events drifted through his mind. Tomorrow he would be in his home and create new memories.

He put his phone on speaker to listen to his messages. The realtor confirming the signing in Varna in the morning. Sonia giggling. "I love you and miss you. Tell me how pretty my house is."

The phone beeped. "End of new messages."

Stefan pressed a button and played the old recordings. Katherine's accented voice frolicked in the air, telling him to hurry home for a sexy surprise. Another reminded him not to forget an appointment. The final one bore three simple words, "I love you," spoken in a seductive whisper, sent to him on their anniversary.

He closed his eyes as he replayed her messages a second time. Then, resolving not to dwell on painful reminders, he called Sonia.

"Hello, sweetheart. How are you?"

"Daddy?" Her voice quivered. "What's wrong?"

Not realizing his grief had worked its way into his voice, he cleared his throat. "I miss you, darling. I hated leaving you."

"I miss you, too, but I like staying with Mémé and Pépé. They let me do all kinds of fun things." She giggled and whispered as if telling a secret. "I heard you talking to them about your 'crazy adventure,' your 'op-a-tune-i-ty of a lifetime,' your—"

He burst out laughing and held his palm out in front of him. "Stop, please. I know all the things I said."

It was true. The artist's life called to him since he was a child, but when he became a father, his priorities changed. He had already created his most beautiful masterpiece—Sonia. His mind turned through the pages of her life, remembering his and Katherine's high spirits at their child's birth. All his doubts about being a father melted away when he held his beautiful, tiny daughter. He cherished every moment of her life—her first steps, her every smile, the first time she said "Dada."

"Daddy? Are you still there?"

"Yes. I'm here. I was thinking about ..."

"I miss Mommy, too." She sniffled.

"I know, sweetheart. I'm sorry. I shouldn't make you sad again. Mommy would want you to be happy. She loved you. She loved us both." He took a deep breath, and exhaled slowly. "How is school? What did you learn today?"

"The teacher told us about a magic place with dragons and fairies."

"Was it called Emona?" Stefan whispered.

"Nooo." She gasped. "Do dragons and fairies live there, too?"

"Yes. I barely escaped with my life today." He looked toward the ridge where horses galloped. "A gigantic, black fire-breathing dragon tried to prevent me from reaching my castle. I jumped on a horse that came to my rescue. He galloped—"

"No. A mare. Mommy had one here. Remember?"

"You're so right. What was I thinking?" Moving away from the balcony, he sat on the lounge chair, stretching out his legs. "She galloped toward the beast, where I battled him on the edge of a cliff. The dragon lunged at me, but the horse side-stepped in time to avoid the blast of flames. I sliced the monster's neck with my magic sword."

"Where did you find that? What did it look like?"

"It was a beautiful sword with rubies, emeralds, and diamonds all along its golden hilt. It was lying on the ground—"

"No, I know. A fairy princess gave it to you."

"A beautiful blond fairy, but not one as lovely as my own princess ..." Stefan smiled listening to Sonia giggle. "Her hair flowed down to her ankles—"

"Oh, no! She could trip on it."

"Again, you're right. The sun must have blinded me. Her hair flowed down to her waist. She handed me a most magnificent sword. Her words were like music. 'You are the one destined to destroy the beast.' She flew away, disappearing into the clouds before I had a chance to thank her."

"Then what happened?"

"I thrust the sword into the dragon's neck. He threw back his head and screeched. His fiery eyes glared with hatred, knowing he had been defeated. Diving over the cliff, he flew to the mountains to recover from his wounds."

"Were you scared?" Sonia breathed rapidly.

"No. I thought of my beautiful princess waiting for me to get her castle ready. She made me brave."

"Is my castle pretty?"

"As lovely as my princess."

A pause, then she said, "Pépé wants to talk to you."

"Good-bye, sweetheart. I love you."

"Bye, Daddy. Love you, too."

Assured by Katherine's father that Sonia had adjusted to the separation, Stefan headed to the beach for a quick swim, hoping the brisk water would numb the recurring pain of his loss. The rays of the sun sparkled like stars on the emerald waters. As if to console him, the sea sang a mournful tune, and a strong, moaning wind joined in the melody while it assailed the tide, creating short, shallow waves.

His mind adrift in the depths of his thoughts, he closed his eyes as his carefree strokes brought him farther out to sea. After a while, he opened them. The sky had turned dark. The wind battered his face and arms from all directions. Wave after wave crashed over him, stinging his eyes. He labored to breathe as salty water flowed into his nose and mouth from the violent, churning water.

Reversing direction, he looked toward the shore. He was farther out than he had intended to swim. No need to panic. He had trained with professionals, who often swam in stormy weather in the frigid Atlantic. Although he had disobeyed the first rule by swimming alone, he would abide by the others. He held his breath and dove under the waves.

Breathe, dive, swim became his mantra as he fought his way toward safety.

The large boulders by the cliff loomed ahead. *Breathe, dive, swim.*

The rocky beach came into view. *Breathe, dive, swim.*

His arms and legs ached. *Breathe. Dive. Swim.*

Numbness set in. *Breathe ... Dive ... Swim.*

His feet brushed against sand. Crawling the remaining way, he doubled over at the edge of the shore, clutching his chest while he coughed out sea water. He inhaled long breaths through his nose and exhaled through his mouth until his breathing slowed to normal. Shivering, he staggered to the shelter of a large rock.

He clutched the ring he always wore on a chain around his neck. *Thank you, Katherine. I know you were looking out for me today.* Bringing the ring to his lips, he kissed it with the tenderness he once expressed for his wife. The sapphire stone warmed to his touch. Like a gentle massage, a tingling sensation spread out, easing his tension and anguish.

A gentle breeze replaced the storm. The scent of citrus floated in the air like perfume, the same as the one Katherine always wore. Splashing interrupted the rhythmic flow of the tide. A blond woman jogged along the shore toward him.

Katherine? His heart fluttered. *Did I die?*

She stopped and held her hand up, shading her eyes from the bright sunlight. Small drops of perspiration covered her pink cheeks. "Is it you, *kamoles*?"

Her sultry voice drew him to her, like sailors of old who couldn't resist the siren's song. He pushed himself up from the ground and held out his hand. "Hi, I'm Stefan Tarrant. I live nearby."

"Oh." She frowned and paused. "I thought you were someone I was waiting for." She extended her hand and shook his. "I'm Kalyna Doneva."

The scenery around him blurred, and he staggered. Faces flashed before him. Kalyna. Other women he didn't recognize. Katherine. A jumble of unfamiliar words whirled past his ears—laughter, shouting, murmuring. He pressed his hands to his temples.

Someone shook him. "Stefan?" A distant-sounding voice called him back. "Are you okay?"

His vision cleared, and the sounds of the sea returned. "Yes, sorry. I guess I blacked out."

She peered into his face. "Will you be okay?"

He nodded. "I got caught swimming in a storm earlier. I'm still a bit shaken."

"You shouldn't swim alone. The weather often changes without any warning along the coast."

"I know better now." He smiled at her with warmth. "Ka-ly-na, you said?" He pronounced each syllable of her name as if singing a melody. "What a pretty name. Do you live in Emona?"

"No, I'm visiting friends." She walked to the water's edge and kneeled where the ridges of a shell poked up. "I came to work on an article about the history of Cape Emine and Emona for the magazine I work for. I thought being here would inspire me to finish it sooner."

Digging around the sand, she uncovered a scalloped orange seashell trimmed in black. "Oh, how delightful!" Rinsing it off, she held it for him to see. "My sister will love this. She collects shells for her shop in Varna."

He joined her on the sand. "Have you discovered anything interesting about Emona? I've fallen in love with the village already. It's easy to forget about the outside world. It's so peaceful here."

The shadows of passing clouds darkened her eyes, giving her a haunted, mysterious look. "Today is the first day of the year *samodivi* ..." She paused. Her eyes darkened even more, and her words swirled around him. "Do you know who they are?"

He shook his head, unable to speak, unable to tear his eyes away from hers.

"They're nymphs. Today is the day they can return to the mortal world from their winter hiatus."

Stefan looked deep into the blackness of her eyes. *Why does she captivate me?*

"I'm researching a legend about them that originated in this area ..."

Is it the youthful innocence she paints with those strands of hair clinging to her face?

"It tells the story of Thracian lovers trying to find each other ..."

Or her mesmerizing eyes that speak of sorrow?

"One of them became immortal, and she waits for her lover's return ..."

Or the pain and longing in her voice that mirrors mine?

Kalyna stopped speaking. She kept her eyes glued to him as if waiting for his response. Opening his mouth to speak, he found no words. She finally looked away and twirled her finger in the water.

He gulped in air. "Kalyna?"

She looked at him, her green eyes unreadable.

"Forgive me. I'm not sure what happened. I couldn't speak."

"You're probably still suffering from the shock of being caught in the storm." Her fingertips brushed his upper arm. "I should go, but it was nice meeting you. Sorry for interrupting your solitude. You looked deep in thought when I arrived."

Stefan surprised himself by opening his mouth to ask her to stay. He hadn't thought about being with any other woman since Katherine had died. What was it about Kalyna that made him want to ask her to meet him for a swim, a walk along the beach, a sunrise breakfast on the rocks? Fear, not of rejection, but of betraying Katherine by moving on, kept him silent.

He stood and held out his hand to help her up. "That's quite all right. I welcomed the company."

Waving good-bye, she continued jogging along the shore, leaving behind a lingering scent of citrus. A gust of wind arose between them forming a violent whirlwind. He shut his eyes tight and covered his face with his hands to keep the stinging sand out of his mouth and nose. The sandstorm ended a moment later. When he looked down the beach, Kalyna had disappeared. The wind had even wiped away all traces of her footprints.

How strange. What was with the weather? Wind gusts twice on a beautiful sunny day? It certainly did change without warning. He shook the sand out of his hair and brushed it off his clothes. Sensing someone watching him, he whirled around.

What now?

A person disappeared behind a boulder, so he followed. In the hollow of a rock, someone had left a bouquet of flowers and a willow basket filled with fresh bread and a jar of honey.

I didn't think the day could get any stranger.

Prints in the sand headed toward the cliff. He looked up in time to glimpse a woman clothed in a black dress running away.

Sparks from the Past

March 26

A SLIVER OF pre-dawn light sidled past Nikola into the shadows of the secret room when he drew aside the thick curtain obscuring the tiny window to peer outside. The streetlights winked farewell, relinquishing their sentinel duty to the sun's superior reign. Only seagulls lingered on the pier. He smirked. No one would hear him. He let the curtain fall back into place to conceal his activities—and the room's stolen treasures.

Retrieving one of the numerous empty crates that lined the back wall, he brought it closer to the paintings and *objets d'art* stacked in the front of the room. He caressed the frame of a vibrant-colored acrylic depicting a ship battling a storm under a full moon. The bold signature of a well-known Italian artist shouted out across the bottom. Sighing, he placed the painting into the crate, but hesitated to secure the cover.

I would love this for my collection.

"Fool! You know you can't keep it." He ground his teeth, hammered the cover shut, and packed the remaining items in a hurry. His heart pounded from his zeal. When he finished, he sat on the final crate and held his head between his knees until the arteries in his neck stopped throbbing. Calm and rational again, he called his brother.

"The shipment for Switzerland is ready. Did you have any problems with the last one?"

"Brother, I've delivered everything as we planned. The paintings will be in Lugano in two days." Boyan breathed rapidly on the other end of the line. "I have a bad feeling something will go wrong this time."

"You worry too much." Nikola pushed his shoulders back, then tilted his head to the side, rolling it around his neck. It made a popping sound as it loosened the tight ligaments. "I've figured out everything to the last detail, and we haven't had any trouble before. Don't you have confidence I know what I'm doing now?"

"I do."

"Good. The Council won't let us down. They'd be foolish to jeopardize an operation that's been lucrative for more than twenty years." He walked over to the window and listened. Everything remained silent outside, so he returned to stand by the packed crates. "I wouldn't have been able to start my furniture business if they hadn't asked me to take over when Uncle Kamen disappeared."

"I know, but do you *trust* them?"

"No, I don't trust anyone except you. That's why we're the only ones who know about this room."

Nikola glanced at his watch. His voice quieted as he paced the room. "Do you want to get out of this? You can leave at any time. The Council doesn't know you're involved."

Two years ago, when Boyan was sixteen, he had stumbled across Nikola packing stolen art. Wide-eyed and wringing his hands as he looked from one object to the other, Boyan stammered, "Let me help you." The first time he delivered stolen goods to their fence, he returned to the apartment shaking and on the verge of collapsing. Nikola regretted giving Boyan a drink to calm him; it had been the first of many as they worked together.

Boyan spoke without hesitation. "No. I won't abandon you—ever."

Nikola smiled and ended the call. If Boyan left, it would be difficult to find anyone else to help—and he wasn't willing to give up the operation. Even though his furniture business, located among other high-end boutiques in Varna, was successful, the revenue from it alone wouldn't let him live in the luxury he had grown accustomed to.

Looking around the room one final time, he ensured everything was packed. He pulled out his keys to leave, running his thumb over the golden coin on the keychain. A symbol of edelweiss decorated one side, and a woman holding two javelins had been carved onto the other. It was a replica of a coin he had found when renovating his uncle's summer house in Emona, the one Stefan was buying.

I could give up dealing with stolen art if I found the Thracian treasure Uncle Kamen was on the verge of discovering. I'm sure it's hidden in the cave.

LATER THAT AFTERNOON, Nikola walked along the crowded pedestrian street toward his shop. The salty taste of the sea lingered on his lips as he whistled a lively tune, sure nothing could ruin the day. He entered his shop through the back door. The clerk spotted him, motioned for a client to sit, and headed toward Nikola.

"Mr. Karanov, this gentleman says he specializes in woodcarving and is looking for work." She clutched the catalogs to her stomach and stood motionless. "I asked him to leave his resume and portfolio. Do you want me to make an appointment for him to interview with you?"

Staring in the man's direction for a moment, Nikola smiled to himself, surprised by his fortune. Did chance or fate bring Stefan to his shop looking for work?

If I renew our friendship, *I'll be able to see Katherine again. Perhaps I can even win back her love.*

"No, I'll talk to him now." With a wave of his hand toward the counter, he dismissed her.

He straightened his tie and smoothed out his suit jacket. Grinning through clenched teeth, he walked over and extended his hand. "Stefan, is it you? How many years has it been?"

Stefan rose and stared for a moment. His eyes widened. "Nikola." He made a fist and tapped Nikola three times on the shoulder in rapid succession, a greeting from their college days. "This is a surprise. I haven't heard from you since I moved back to America after Katherine and I got married. What have you been up to?"

"School and work kept me busy." He opened the door and pointed across the street. "Let's grab a drink and catch up."

And you can tell me about Katherine.

He had resigned himself to losing her after she married Stefan, but the constant ache in his heart never subsided. It opened a rift, an emptiness he thought he managed to hide from the world and from himself, until now. With Stefan's arrival, the deep emotional pain surged to the surface to torment him.

Sitting at an outside table, they gave their orders to the waitress.

Nikola tightened his jaw as he fought to keep the bitterness out of his words. "How have you been? The last I remember, you were running your father's printing shop in America after he died."

Stefan gripped the edge of the table. "I was ... until my mother passed away. Then I sold it. I had kept the business for her sake because she couldn't let go of my father's memories."

"I remember how much you hated that place." Nikola grinned as he leaned back in his chair. "Wasn't your father angry and disappointed when you told him you wanted to 'sketch the wonders of nature,' rather than sit behind a desk?"

Stefan frowned. "Do we really need to talk about this? My father and I resolved our differences before he died."

"Isn't that why you left college after only a year?" Nikola leaned forward and rested his chin on his hand. "He died and you had to take over the family business?"

"Let's not talk about this. That's in the past." Stefan drummed his fingers on the table, his tone even.

The waitress returned with their drinks. "Would you like anything else?"

"No, thank you," they said in unison.

Nikola leaned closer and repressed a sneer. "What happened to your dreams? All I heard from you in college was how you were going to paint masterpieces on cathedrals in Italy."

"I was rather pretentious and optimistic those days, wasn't I?" Stefan took a sip of his wine. "I settled for working for a woodworking company in Boston after I sold the business. And painted as a hobby."

"My clerk said you're looking for work. What brought you to Varna?"

"I bought a house in Emona. I signed papers today."

"I ..." Did he want Stefan to know the house had belonged to his uncle? No. The less said about it and its circumstances, the better. "Did you know it was my shop when you stopped by?"

"No. I thought you had stayed in France."

"After college, I returned home. Varna has turned out to be a perfect spot to have a business. The sandy beaches, salt baths, and vineyards attract rich tourists. They like to spend money on unique local pieces. I've recently opened some international shops and a few more local ones." Nikola removed a case from his suit jacket pocket. He lit a cigar and let his success hang in the air like the puff of smoke he exhaled while he waited for Stefan to congratulate him.

"You're expanding. That's great. So, you must be hiring additional workers."

That's great? All he can say is "That's great"?

Nikola took a deep breath and held it. He released it slowly. "Hiring? No."

"Can you recommend someone?"

"Let me ask around. In the meantime, even though I can't hire you directly, I do contract custom orders from time to time." He couldn't resist toying with Stefan. Katherine would never forgive him if he denied her husband work. Besides, in the short time Stefan had been in school, he had won many awards, so Nikola's wealthy customers would pay handsomely for the quality of his craftsmanship. "In fact, a few days ago I received an order for a carved door. I can give you the details after lunch. Come back tomorrow to get it, and I'll help you with the paperwork so you can work here legally."

Stefan raised his glass in a toast. "Thank you. I'm free tomorrow. I appreciate your offer."

"Enough about business." He took a sip of his whiskey. "You moved to Emona, you say. What made you decide to move to that god-forsaken place? There's nothing there."

"Life can be unpredictable ... I thought the village would inspire me to get back to painting." Stefan looked away. "What have you been up to besides work? You always had so many things going on at a time. It was hard to keep up with you."

Nikola scowled. That wasn't what he wanted to hear. He wanted to know how life had been unfavorable to Stefan. How he'd never been able to achieve his goals— the way Nikola had. "I run a cultural society that focuses on the preservation of historical sites. The mayor and other high-profile politicians ask my advice for how to distribute funds for restorations." Taking another puff on his cigar, Nikola leaned back in his chair. *Look at what Katherine let slip away. What has Stefan accomplished with his life? A few woodcarvings and paintings?*

"Impressive. I'd—"

"And in my free time, I attend art exhibits to find new treasures for my collection. There's one next month you might be interested in attending."

"An art exhibit? I'd like that."

"Bring Katherine with you." Nikola took a sip, and motioned to the waitress for another drink. "How is she these days?" When Stefan didn't say anything, Nikola looked back at him.

Stefan slumped forward in his seat. "There was ... an accident ..."

An emotional storm exploded within Nikola. He tightened his jaw and narrowed his eyes to thin slits. Gulping the rest of his whiskey, he slammed the glass on the table, leaned forward, and put his face close to Stefan's. "What? What are you saying?"

But he already knew the truth even before Stefan moaned, "Katherine died."

Nikola narrowed his eyes. "How? When?"

"A year ago ... a car accident in Boston." Stefan held his head between his hands.

Nikola fumed. Now he would never have the chance to win back Katherine's love. His *friend* had destroyed the most precious thing that had ever belonged to him, shattering his happiness forever.

If she had been mine, that would never have happened! I would have protected her.

He laid one hand on Stefan's shoulder in a gesture of friendship and comfort, while clenching the other into a fist below the table so he wouldn't release his fury on Stefan.

You'll pay for this. I'll find a way to make you suffer for your neglect of Katherine, even if I have to rot in Hell.

He Knew Her Not

March 27

ONE BY ONE, straggling stars bade the forlorn maiden far below a good morrow, then closed their bright eyes. Aurora, bedecked in a flowing saffron robe, lazed her way toward them on her fiery chariot. The nocturnal serenade of the forest stilled, signaling the end of the evening's revelries. Soon, a sparrow, a lark, and then a dove rehearsed soprano and alto notes, until the full choir joined in the worship with their reverent songs.

Oblivious to the glorious dawn, Carina lay supine on the large flat stone in the meadow, her special place, looking at her finger, bereft of the blue-star. The sun rose higher, its heat warming the chill from the stone, but not from her heart. With the back of her hand, she wiped from her eyes droplets that sparkled like the morning dew. Brethren beads of moisture replaced them, shimmying down her cheek.

"Sister, where are you?" Morena's shout, emerging from the forest, held an anxious note.

She stepped into the meadow. The sun glinted off her auburn hair, braided beneath her fox-skin cap. Carina sat up and waved to get her attention.

In a flash, Morena was by her sister's side, wrapping her arms around Carina. "What happened? Why didn't you return?"

"Oh, Morena." She twisted her hair into a tight knot. "I've dreamed of my reunion with Dushan for so long, passionate memories buried like a relic deep within my heart. But he couldn't see his Carina."

Morena lifted her sister's chin. "Perhaps your heart deceived you." With the sleeve of her hooded hunting mantle, she wiped away the tears streaming from Carina's eyes. But still they flowed, sliding onto Morena's spotless high black boots.

"No, Dushan's soul lives. He reached out to me when I touched the mortal. A part of me, my lost breath, has returned, as if mine has been travelling through the centuries with his." She rested her head on Morena's shoulder. "Pain and disappointment obscure the path to his heart. I fear this makes my beloved weak."

"Even so, the time may not be nigh for Dushan to reunite with you." Morena ran her palm over Carina's tangled hair. "He may not have completed his journey yet."

"Surely this time he will. His soul has already travelled from one body to the next for three millennia." Even though this mortal resembled Dushan—so handsome, such dark, wavy hair, such intense blue eyes—he would die like all the others before him if her beloved wasn't strong enough to return by the time the Winter Moon faded. How long then would she have to wait for him to return again?

"Don't despair, sister. Your fate has been determined. All will go well."

Twisting away, Carina reached for Morena's hand and squeezed it. "The mare will know if Dushan is strong enough! If she recognizes him, then I have hope. I can restore his memories using the gift the Mother Goddess gave me."

Morena stood and smoothed her short white tunic. "Now that you know your way, dry your tears and cast off your melancholy face." She held out her hand and helped Carina up. "Come with me. Our forest reeks of danger. The Evil One has stolen a potion from our sworn sister. It poisons his blood, and he intends to injure innocent ones."

DESPITE THE COLD, Stefan opened the windows in his new home to air it out. He smiled at the thought. *Home.* Although uncertain about the challenges his journey to this new land would bring, he embraced the dawn full of hope. He looked outside. A clear blue sky. Chirping song-birds and squawking seagulls. Cool, salty sea air. And most important, the night had passed without his usual nightmare about Katherine's fatal accident. Emona had begun to heal his sorrow.

While he unpacked his few belongings—clothes, a computer, art tools and supplies, and some mementos—he thought about the previous day. All had gone well at the closing. His frustration hadn't begun until he ran into Nikola.

He and Katherine had tried to keep in touch with him. Phone calls, emails. They never heard back. So why had Nikola acted so angry? Did he actually take pleasure in bringing up Stefan's painful past? And Nikola's emotional outburst when he learned about Katherine's death surpassed grief. Granted they had been friends, but it didn't make sense. That had been nine years ago.

Stefan frowned and shook his head as he opened the last box containing an assortment of items that had once meant so much to him. Sifting through them, he spotted a medal he received for a triathlon in college. Nikola probably would have won it if he hadn't hurt his leg the night before the tryouts. He hadn't even made it onto the team. At the time, Nikola had been furious with Stefan. Could he still be holding a boyhood grudge because of that? Perhaps he'd like the award. He'd bring it to Nikola when he picked up work tomorrow.

After finishing unpacking, he took a sip of coffee. He grimaced. It had become cold like the room. Maybe he should start a fire. But was the chimney safe? It didn't look as if it had been used in years. He kneeled on the hearth, being careful to avoid the fine, dry ashes and charred remnants of logs. Poking his head inside, he looked up. It was too dark to see any defects. He patted along the side wall. His hand touched a handle to a small metal door. Opening it, he felt inside. The niche must have been used to keep food warm.

He backed out. "Ow." Scowling, he rubbed the spot on his head that had banged against the rusty kettle hanging on a chain. It was probably best not to tamper with the fireplace until someone could look at it.

Having spent enough time inside, he went onto the porch and looked around. A path at the edge of the woods could be exciting to explore. He headed down it, making slow progress, stopping often to disentangle his clothing from blackberry thorns reaching out and clinging to him like destitute souls seeking alms. In a short while, the underbrush cleared, and the trail opened to a creek. He crossed the round stepping stones. A little farther on, the trail ended at a grove.

A smaller version of the village fountain had been built into the side of the hill. Water poured out of a copper spout into a square basin. The walls extending out from the fountain reminded him of a chapel. Someone had even laid fresh flowers in its niche.

Moss had grown over a plate at the bottom of the basin. Using a stick, he scraped it off. An inscription was written in characters resembling those on the ring he had bought in Salem. He traced his fingers over it, curious to know what the symbols meant. Above the plate something had been carved into the stone. He cleared away the rest of the moss. The image looked like a flower with six petals.

An edelweiss, perhaps.

Ideas for paintings and carvings flooded Stefan's mind as he listened to nature converse around him—chirping birds, gurgling water in the fountain, and wind rustling through the trees. An ancient walnut grew alone next to the fountain. Its cracked bark looked like the wrinkled face of an elderly person. The branches had interwoven into a giant knot in the middle.

He sat in the tree's shade and dozed, lulled by the sounds around him. A strange thudding noise woke him as it shook the ground, blocking the babbling water and silencing the birds. A herd of wild horses rushed toward the creek. Bolting up to avoid being trampled, he clambered up a large boulder and watched from a safe distance.

A black mare, her sides bloated with the foal she carried, separated from the herd and walked a few feet closer, eyeing him as if trying to identify the intruder. He remained still, not knowing what to do. The mare stretched out her neck and edged her nose toward him. She whinnied and exhaled a couple blasts of air. He hoped she was either greeting him or was satisfied he posed no threat.

Stefan looked from the mare to a muscular horse, most likely the stallion, that paced by the creek. The horse, with his ears laid flat and his tail swishing, tossed his head and snapped his teeth. Advancing closer, the horse stamped his feet and turned sideways, flicking his hooves toward Stefan.

Keeping his eye on the stallion, Stefan relaxed only after the mare returned to the herd. The stallion came no closer, but flanked the mare, protecting her while she drank from the creek. Soon the mare led the herd back to the ridge. Lingering, the stallion took one final look at Stefan, snorted, shook his mane, and galloped away to join the others.

"Ne se strakhuvaĭ ot cherniya zhrebets."

The deep, thick-accented voice startled Stefan. A middle-aged man supported himself on a stick as he walked down the path.

Stefan jumped from the boulder and walked over to the man. "What? I'm sorry. I don't understand."

"Don't be afraid of the black stallion." The unsmiling man's fierce blue eyes peered out from beneath bushy eyebrows. A scar running from one eye down his cheek made him appear even more formidable.

"Are they wild? I didn't think wild horses got anywhere near humans."

"Wild? Yes." The man scratched his unshaven face. "But, they're used to us and roam near the village and the *cheshma*."

"Cheshma? What's that?"

"The fountain." The man pointed.

Stefan returned to it and kneeled by the plate. Touching it, he looked back at the man. "Can you tell me what this inscription says?"

"Samodivi Cheshma," the man replied without looking. He twirled the end of the stick in the dirt while he spoke.

"Samodivi?" Stefan came back to where the man stood. "I met a woman named Kalyna who told me about them. Has she spoken to you about a legend she's researching?"

The man looked up and raised his eyebrows. A brief smile flashed across his face. "No. I don't know any Kalyna."

"Oh." He pressed his lips together, then held out his hand. "I'm Stefan Tarrant, by the way. I moved to the village recently. The path behind my house led me here."

The man shook his hand. "Peter Kristof. I live next to the hotel with my niece, Neda."

"Nice to meet you." He nodded toward the inscription. "Do you know what language the plate is written in? I own a ring that has similar characters."

"Archaeologists say it was built in Thracian times."

"Thracian?" Stefan hadn't considered the ring would be quite so old.

Peter coughed. "Why'd you move to such a remote village?"

"I was looking for a quiet location along the coast to set up a studio. My realtor said a lot of artists live here in the summer." With a wide sweep of his arms, he encompassed the cheshma and the dense forest. "His description of the beaches and 'untamed nature' in Emona caught my attention. This seemed the perfect place."

"Yes. The village is quiet, especially after the artists return to Sofia and other cities in the fall." Peter scanned the forest. "I must go now. My goats are at the Old Beach. I came to set a few traps. A wolf's been seen around. I think that's what tore apart one of my goats this morning."

"Wolves?"

"They don't attack people. But don't wander into the forest." Peter held his hand out to shake again. "Welcome to Emona. Come to the pub later. I'll introduce you to others."

Stefan sat by the cheshma until his stomach growled. Then he headed to the pub, desiring both food and company. He looked forward to learning more of the village customs.

Having taken a wrong turn, he wound up near an old church surrounded by a fence. A black shape disappeared around the side of the building. He tried the wooden gate, but it was locked, so he walked along the fence to where the person had gone.

A bouquet of white flowers lay next to several lit candles that littered the ground, their flames dancing in the breeze. Had that been the same person who left flowers and bread at the beach?

All of a sudden, a strong gust of wind extinguished the candles.

Another wind squall? He shook his head and continued to the hotel pub. A galloping horse sounded as if it came from near the church, but when he turned to look, the only animals around were mules outside the gate. The wild horses were grazing on the ridge. Perhaps the sound had echoed from there.

"Wind. Candles. Horses." Stefan chuckled as he walked toward the hotel. "Must be the fairy princess I told Sonia about who's messing with me."

PETER HAILED STEFAN over to the table where he sat with Todor and a few others. "Come join us and have a beer and *tzatza*. We have one spot left."

Stefan pulled out a chair next to Peter. "I prefer wine. I had a superb Thracian one here the other night." When the waitress came by, he asked for the fried seafood dish the others were having, along with his drink.

Peter introduced him. "This is the person who bought the Professor's house. He's an artist, but he's going to live here year round."

"*Dobre doshul.*" Each person greeted him.

"*Dobre doshul.*" Stefan beamed at the welcome in the native language. He reached across the table, careful not to knock over the oil lamp, and shook hands with everyone. "Does anyone know someone who could check out my fireplace to make sure it's safe? I hesitated starting a fire since it's so old. I don't want to burn down the house my first day there."

Peter shook his head. "I'll come over tomorrow to look at it."

"Thank you, but will you be able to tell me if it's safe?"

"Yes." Peter shook his head again.

"I'm confused." Stefan scratched his cheek. "Do you know or not?"

"Yes, I said I did." Once again, he shook his head.

"Then why are you shaking your head when you say 'yes'?"

Peter stared at Stefan as if he was a child. "That means 'yes.' "

"So I suppose nodding means 'no'?" He twisted the fringe on the colorful hand-woven mat set at an angle in the center of the table.

Shaking his head again, Peter said, "Yes."

What a strange custom. They have it backward.

Maria patted Stefan's shoulder. "Dear, I was told you were here, so I brought your wine."

"Thank you." He took the glass and smiled at her. "I couldn't go an entire day without coming here for the fabulous cooking. My stomach's been scolding me all day to return."

Peter stood and pulled out a chair for her. "Join us, please."

"Thank you. I can spare a few moments to get to know our new resident."

"What's with the windy weather?" Stefan took a sip. "Does it always come and go so quickly?"

The people at the table grew quiet. Maria finally spoke. "That would mean the samodivi have returned, dear."

"The nymphs? Oh, that's right. They just returned from their winter vacation." These people were too serious. It was time to lighten the atmosphere. "What kind of horse goes out after dark?" Smiling, he looked around the table.

Blank stares looked back at him. The men he had met returned to their conversation in Bulgarian.

"Todor?" Stefan glanced across the table.

He shrugged.

Stefan swiveled around. "Peter?"

He nodded. In time, Stefan remembered that meant "no."

"Maria, do you have a guess?"

"I'm sorry, dear. The horses here sleep on the ridge when it gets dark."

"I'll tell you, then. A night mare." Stefan laughed—alone. Maybe they had trouble translating the punch line. Now what could he say to get past the awkwardness? He cleared his throat. "Can you tell me anything else about the wild horses? When I was at the cheshma, a black mare got so close I could almost reach out and touch her. I thought they didn't get too close to people."

The conversation at the table ceased. All eyes turned toward him for a moment. Then, three of the men tipped their heads and stood. One said, "We visit others now so you can chat. Nice meeting you." They walked over to another table.

"Did I say something wrong?" He looked at Maria.

Her face ashen and her lips trembling, she placed her palms on the table to push herself up. "The legend ... I-I should go, too, and get back to work. Enjoy your meal, dear." Her legs wobbled as she moved away.

Peter got up to help her.

"Maria, are you okay?" Stefan started to rise.

Peter put his palm out. "It is okay. I will help her."

Maria spoke to him in hushed tones as he helped her out of the room.

A waitress brought Stefan his meal. He picked at his food while he glanced toward the door where Peter and Maria had disappeared. "What happened? Do you think she's okay?"

"Yes, she is strong." Todor shook his head.

"What did she mean about a legend?"

"It is story about samodivi and horses. Black mare travel to heaven and underworld, looking for her master. She talk to God and dead. She ask, 'When will my master come back from long journey?' God tell her she will know him when he returns."

Stefan raised his eyebrows at the elderly man's serious expression. "Really? So the horse thinks I'm her master?" This was more interesting than the Blagovets customs. He'd have to tell Sonia about it.

"Yes. Horses powerful. If you ride one in forest or roads at night, you won't get sick or be attacked because they are protected from evil." Todor cleared his throat and took a sip of beer. "Let me tell you story about those horses. When I was young, I saw them by cheshma near Professor's house." He stopped and held his glass up toward Stefan. "I mean your house, Stefan. That black stallion scared me. Crazy eyes, full of fire. I thought he was going to attack me."

Peter returned before Todor could continue.

Stefan turned toward him. "Is Maria okay?"

"Yes, yes. She will be fine. Upset stomach."

"Because the horse thinks I'm her master?" Stefan laughed and shook his head.

Peter turned toward Todor and waved his fingers for him to continue. "Sorry to interrupt."

Todor took a long gulp of beer, then began again in a low voice. "My father told me why horses guard village. Deyan ruled mountain tribe when Thracians lived here. They had magnificent horses, you know. King Rez brought them to Trojan War. They were stolen by—"

"I know the story of the Trojan War." Stefan put his hand on Todor's shoulder. "What were you starting to say about the horses guarding the village? And about Deyan?"

"Deyan? Oh, yes. Let me think." Todor took another sip of his beer and squinted, as if thinking.

Stefan twisted the stem of his glass back and forth in his palms, waiting for the elderly man to continue.

Peter looked at Stefan, shrugged his shoulders, and took up the story. "Deyan stole all the gold from the villages and burned the houses to the ground. Nobody knows where he hid the gold."

Todor clapped his hands together. "Thank you, Peter. Now I remember. Deyan killed some young girls." Todor took another sip of beer. "Then they became samodivi. They live in a cave. Because Deyan and his soldiers were evil, when they died, they turned into horses. Now they guard village and cave."

"My grandfather told a similar story," Peter added. "But he said the horses are the soldiers of King Rez, not Deyan's."

Stefan laughed. "I love that story. So that's where the samodivi live. In a cave. Maybe the gold's hidden there. Does anyone know where it is?"

Todor's face paled and his hands shook. He clasped them together and held them on his lap. His voice trembled. "Nobody knows, maybe near Old Beach. Even if I did know, I wouldn't *ever* go near there. I'm old man, but I'm still afraid of what samodivi could do to me."

Stefan looked between the two men. "What do you mean? They're not real."

Todor drained his drink, and rose. "I have to go." He picked up his bag from the floor and shuffled toward the door. "Bye, Stefan. Nice seeing you again."

Peter rose as well.

Shaking his head, Stefan put his hand on Peter's arm. "Todor doesn't actually believe samodivi exist, does he?"

With a small smile, Peter looked down at Stefan. "Our beliefs and ways are not like your city life. Nature is mysterious. Don't be too quick to deny things that could be true."

Fountain of Love

March 28

A SECRET SMILE adorned her face. Stefan's beloved drifted along the beach as if driven by the wind, her golden hair fluttering behind. Her sheer silk robe, delicate like a moonbeam, billowed around her divine body. She glided past him as he swam to shore. Without a word, she beckoned him to follow. In her wake, she left only a trace of footprints in the sand.

My love, so wild and free. Where have you been? He longed to hold her in his arms again.

The waves pulled him back as he forced his way through the incoming tide. Arriving at the shore, he lost sight of her when she stepped backward into a mist, still extending her arms to him.

My beloved, don't hide from me. I've been seeking you for so long.

From above him, her melodic laughter sailed along the currents of the breeze. He looked up. She waited at the mouth of a cave.

The wind wrapped itself around her in a lover's caress, lifting the white silk from her shoulders, leaving the edelweiss tattoo on her shoulder her solitary covering. Her full lips curved upward in a triumphant smile as the garment floated away like a feather. A fire blazed within him, matching the flame in her black eyes. While he stared into them, they deepened into dark pools that engulfed him body and soul.

THE WOMAN IN Stefan's dream wove her way into the minute threads of his mind, the crazy yarns of the villagers unravelling in his unconsciousness. She must be a samo-diva.

Why did I call her "my love"? Katherine had been his love.

Yet still, passion poured through him as he sketched with charcoal, his fingers flying across the sheet of paper. He captured the moment when her white gown flowed over her shoulders and around the curve of her hips, while she extended her hands toward him. Tearing off that sheet, he filled another with the woman shrouded in mystery—her lips, her eyes, her hair, her body. Page after page of drawings lay strewn across the workbench.

Mid-stroke, the charcoal stub crumbled in his hand, scattering flakes across the image. He blew them away.

Kalyna! He stared at the drawing. *The woman in my dream was Kalyna!*

With the back of his hand, he wiped his brow. Was she even real? She had been with him one moment, then vanished the next, along with the wind. She must indeed be a samodiva playing tricks on him. He smiled. More likely he had conjured a vision of a beautiful woman on a deserted beach after his ordeal in the water. But, no, it had been too real to have been his imagination.

He fixed his eyes on a mahogany frame on the mantel—a photo of him, Katherine, and Sonia in a Boston park. Tree branches sprouted flowers and tender leaves. Katherine's face glowed with high spirits. He picked it up, rubbing his finger over the crack in the corner. It had been damaged the day she went for an ultrasound.

That morning, she ran down the stairs and into the kitchen like a storm. "Is the coffee pot off? Something's burning."

"It's off. Nothing's burning."

"I'm so sensitive to smells. They make me ill."

"Do you want a sip? You can hold your nose." Stefan laughed, extending his cup to her.

"I wish I could, but it's not good for the baby." She looked around the room, then headed toward a small table. "I'm ready to go. Let me check to make sure I have my insurance card."

Reaching for her purse, she sent several picture frames crashing to the floor. She bent to pick one up and started crying.

By her side in an instant, he wrapped his arms around her. "What's the matter, darling?" He glanced at what she held. "The frame's cracked? Is that the one your mother gave you? It can be fixed."

"The frame?" She leaned into his chest and sobbed. "No, not that ... I'm so afraid something will be wrong with our baby."

"Everything will be fine." Stefan kissed the top of her head. "It's time to go. This will be over soon, and you won't have to worry."

The waiting room was empty when they arrived, but soon filled with other expectant parents talking in hushed tones. Katherine shivered and nestled closer to Stefan while they waited for the receptionist to call her name.

Once inside the doctor's office, she lay on the examining table, while Stefan looked at pictures showing the week-by-week development of a baby. He went to her side after he heard her say "Oh, that's so cold."

The technician moved the ultrasound probe over her growing belly. The gray monitor displayed the image of their child, from the tiny head to the even smaller heart beating through the translucent skin.

"From what I can see, it's a healthy girl. Congratulations." The technician set aside the instruments.

Stefan squeezed Katherine's hand and leaned down to whisper, "See, she's fine."

She laughed and cried at the same time. "Look. Our baby's dancing."

And Sonia was a child who loved to dance around the house.

He set the frame back and looked at the sketches. Grabbing the pile of papers, he crumpled them and threw them into the fireplace.

What's wrong with me? I shouldn't be thinking about someone else.

He pulled out his cell phone and replayed Katherine's messages several times until his anger subsided. Then he called Sonia.

"Hello, sweetheart."

"Daddy! You didn't call me yesterday!"

"I know. I'm sorry, but I was on a mission to find the fairy princess."

"The one who helped you fight the dragon?" Sonia whispered. "Did you find her?"

"She found me when I was at the beach." Rubbing his hand on his chin, he walked over to the couch and stretched out on it. "She thinks ... I'm someone she knew a long time ago."

"Did you tell her your name?" Her words rushed out. "Fairies can play tricks on you if they know your name."

"I didn't know that." Speaking with a shaky voice, he pretended to be afraid. "I did tell her. What can I do now?"

She paused. "I think she has to fall in love with you. Did she tell you her name?"

"Yes. It's Kalyna." Despite his earlier anger at himself, his pulse raced.

"Oh, I like that. She's a nice fairy. They have pretty names."

"The people here call them samodivi. They live in a magical cave."

Someone tapped at the door. He pushed himself up and looked out the window. On the porch, Maria held a basket. He opened the door and waved her inside.

"Sonia, sweetheart, the nice lady from the hotel who feeds me so well stopped by." He smiled at Maria. "I'll call you again later, okay?"

"Okay. Bye, Daddy. Love you."

"Love you more." He sent her a kiss and hung up.

He gestured to the couch. "So nice to see you. Have a seat. How are you today?"

"Fine, thank you." She looked around the room. "Dear, I hope you don't mind company."

"Not at all. You're welcome here any time."

She held out the basket. "I wanted to officially welcome you to Emona and bring you some bread and cheese, the traditional welcome gift around here."

"Thank you. That's kind of you." He took it and peeked inside. "Mmm." The smell of homemade bread drifted out from beneath the cotton cloth, making his stomach growl.

"It's made with *sharena sol*, the spice you liked so much."

"It's sure to become part of my artist's diet." He laughed. "Red wine and melted butter on fresh bread with *sharena sol* sprinkled on top. I can't wait until I can use it when I barbeque this summer." He put two fingers to his lips, and moved them away in a gesture of a kiss.

"I also put a small icon and a *kandilo* in there." She pointed to the package tucked in the corner. "When you light the candle, it'll bring you good health and protection. A lot of the artists here have them. They say the flickering light and dancing shadows inspire them."

"Thank you for thinking of me. I'll definitely get healthy from your cooking, and be inspired by the light." He picked the icon up and laughed. "Do I need protection from the samodivi or the horses?"

She looked away. "I hope not."

"I'm sorry. I shouldn't tease. It's a nice gesture."

"Would you mind giving me a quick tour of the house? I've never been in here."

"Really? I thought everyone in a small community visited each other."

"The Professor and his wife were private people. They didn't invite anyone from the village over."

"You see most of it now." He swayed his hand around the open area. Wooden beams ran the length of the room. A recliner, couch, and small, low table occupied one side, and a kitchen with dark wooden cabinets and a table with four chairs, the other. A large fireplace dominated most of one wall. "Let me set this on the table, and I'll show you the rest. Would you like some fresh coffee?"

"No, thank you. I have to get back to my hotel soon."

He showed her the two bedrooms and small tiled bath, bringing her to his studio last. "This is where I'm going to be creative. I'll put the *kandilo* in here. What I like most about it is this old fireplace."

"It's called an *odiak*. They were popular in the early nineteenth century." She pointed to the small black-and-red rug in front of the fireplace. "These triangles represent trees. This particular design is called a *karakachka*, a black-eyed bride."

"That's a mouthful." Stefan laughed as Maria looked around the room.

She picked up a photo on the mantel. "Is this your family?"

"Yes. Katherine and Sonia."

"They're both so lovely. Your daughter looks like her mother. When are they joining you?"

He hesitated, then choked out his words. "My wife died in a car crash a year ago. My daughter will be here in the summer. She goes to private school in France and stays with her grandparents. For now."

"I'm so sorry, dear." Maria's hand shook a little as she touched him on the shoulder.

His phone rang. Nikola's shop. "Excuse me a moment, please. I need to take this call." He answered. "Hello."

"Mr. Tarrant, I'm calling from Karanov Fine Furniture. The panels are ready for you to pick up," the woman at the other end said.

"Thank you. I'll be there in a couple of hours." He ended the call. "That was the business I'm contracting for. They have some work ready for me."

"I should go back to the hotel now, anyway."

"Let me give you a ride back. I want to stop to see when Peter can come over to look at the fireplace." He glanced at the sketches he had crumpled. *I need to burn those.*

STEFAN DROVE PAST the cheshma in the village square.

The bronze statue. She looks like the woman in my dream, like Kalyna!

He parked in front of the hotel. After he opened the door for Maria, he headed to the cheshma. The face smiling down at him *was* that of Kalyna, from her high cheekbones and perfect nose, to lips curled into a mysterious smile. He touched the woman's face.

A shock jolted him. The day darkened to pitch black, then light seeped back. The scent of hot, melted wax overpowered his nose.

"Dushan," a soft voice called.

The cold metal of the statue softened to his touch. His fingers smoothed out a waxen face. But the hands weren't his. He had no control over them. The artist's thoughts entered Stefan's own mind as the man worked. He etched the playful curve of his beloved's lips and gingerly coaxed out the mass of curls in her hair, re-creating her image the way he remembered it from their wedding day. Molten brass bubbled in a cauldron over the fire. He would finish the statue tonight and begin work on the cheshma in her honor in the morning.

"Dushan." The voice spoke again, this time accompanied by creaking floorboards.

He turned his eyes toward the door. Near the threshold of the workshop, his mother held a *rhyton* and bowl of fruit. Her hands trembled, making the wine slosh over the edge of the golden cup.

She has something to tell me she doesn't want to say.

He motioned for her to enter. She walked closer and set the objects on a small wooden table. Her petite frame was thinner than he remembered, her eyes swollen from crying, and her long black hair disheveled. She managed a bittersweet smile, the one he recognized from his childhood when his father died.

She placed her hand on his forearm. "Dushan, it's getting late. You haven't eaten or slept for more than a week. Please come back with me. I worry about you."

"No, Mother." He bent over the image of his love once again to bring her to life. "I have to finish the statue so the shaman can bless it. It will lead me to my Carina."

"She's not going to return, my son." Tears spilled down her face. "You're young. You'll find another bride."

"No!" He whirled around. Although he glared at her, his anger was meant for the Goddess who had taken Carina from him. Brokenhearted, he was determined to find his bride. His love for her would prove him worthy, and the Goddess would return his Carina. The shaman had said destiny foretold they would be together. They shared everything—love, joy, passion.

She placed her hands on his shoulders again and shook him. "Please listen to me."

"Mother, stop! I love Carina. She alone will be my bride." He closed his eyes and touched the waxen face of his beloved, trying to recall her voice and not his mother's persistent pleas. He would never forget Carina. Neither in this lifetime, nor in any other.

"Can you hear me? Stefan!"

He opened his eyes, still envisioning his mother. Instead, someone else stood in front of him, shaking his shoulders. She was rather plump and wore a red, bibbed apron. Her hair was not black and long, but curly, cut close to her head, and graying, with a few strands of brown still peeking through.

The scene surrounding him had changed. He was outside, not inside his workshop. A strange, large building. A cheshma. A statue. No waxen image of his beloved lay beneath his fingers. No words were being spoken telling him to forget his love.

A violent trembling, starting in his fingers, crept through his entire being. Lowering himself to the edge of the cheshma, he cradled his head in his hands and moaned. "No, no, no. What's happening? Oh my god, what's happening to me?" *What strange language was this he spoke?*

The woman sat next to him and wrapped her arm around his shoulder. "Stefan, it's okay. It's Maria. You're in Emona."

Stefan? Maria? Emona? Yes, Emona. He remembered. Raising his head, he looked at her. "Maria? What happened?"

"I don't know. You walked over to the statue. I called to you, but you didn't answer. Your skin turned so pale, and your eyes glazed over. I got scared."

Stefan whipped his head up to look at the bronze woman. "I touched the statue, and I saw ... something. It seemed so real." He looked back at Maria and clutched her hand in his. "The statue? The cheshma? I don't understand. Do-do you know anything about them?"

She took a deep breath, then exhaled. "An excavation team the Professor was with found the statue near the Old Fortress."

"The Professor whose house I bought?"

"Yes. The archaeologists said the statue was as old as the cheshma, centuries old. The brass plate beneath it says 'Maiden's Cheshma,' so we think the statue originally belonged here."

"Any-anything else?"

"That's a short *history* of the cheshma." Maria's free hand dangled in the water. "There's also a legend."

Stefan leaned closer. "Please tell me."

"The brass pipes lead to an underground spring people say has magical powers. Anyone who drinks water from the cheshma will live in the village forever." Her eyes held a distant look. "Well, that part isn't a legend. I went to school in Varna, expecting to become a chef, but when I came here thirty years ago to visit my grandmother, I drank from the fountain. Then I met my late husband, and never left." Maria blushed and focused back on Stefan. "But you don't want to hear my story."

He smiled, but kept his eyes intent upon her. "Do you know anything else about the statue?"

"Legend says a youth built the cheshma and made a statue of his lost love."

"Dushan?" Stefan's lips trembled. "Was his name Dushan?"

"Yes," she whispered.

"And the woman's? Carina?"

"It was."

"Wh-what else do you know?" He gripped the cheshma wall to steady himself.

"A shaman performed a magic spell on the statue to keep the youth's love safe and to lead him to her." She spoke so low he had to lean forward to hear her. "The next morning, he discovered the edelweiss symbol on the statue's belt."

Stefan extended his hand toward the statue, but drew it back in a hurry. "The flower looks like part of the original statue. It's smooth all around. Not even a seam showing it was added later."

"Yes, I know." She spoke in a whisper. "That's all I know. Others may know more."

Stefan shook his head. It still didn't make sense. "How? Why?" He spoke more to himself than to Maria. He had seen the artist making the statue. But he didn't even know about the legend before Maria told him. How did he know their names?

Maria stood and straightened her apron. "Come with me, dear. You're still pale. Let me make you my special feta cheese *banitsa*."

"The statue reminds me of someone I met on the beach. Kalyna Doneva." He glanced at the bronze maiden again. Perhaps if he could find her, she could explain the mystery. "She said she was staying with friends in Emona. Do you know her?"

"Like the statue?" She gasped and stared at him with wide eyes. "N-no. The name doesn't sound familiar, and I know everyone who comes to the village."

Cliffhanger

BACK IN HIS studio, Stefan poured sunflower oil into the *kandilo* and placed it on the mantel. He laughed nervously as he lit it. It couldn't hurt, could it? Maybe it would protect him from any more strange things happening. Inexplicable gusts of wind, threatening wild horses, statues making him hallucinate, samodivi.

He chuckled. Animals running in front of his car, dragons, Nikola. Surely it was side effects from almost drowning. He blew out the flame. It would likely start a fire if he left it burning while he was in Varna.

The shopkeeper at Nikola's shop expected him to pick up the panel today. He should have been there by now, but the episode with the statue set him back. Then Peter came over to inspect the fireplace and visited for a while. Since the chimney was in good shape, Stefan wanted to build a fire when he returned. It would inspire him while he worked on this chilly day.

He looked at his resin-stained work shirt and patched-up jeans. Did he have time to change? He shook his head. Better not waste any more time. He slipped on his leather jacket. It would cover the worst spots.

Before leaving, he had one more thing to do. He retrieved the box of mementos from the studio cupboard and pulled out the award he had won for the triathlon. The sunlight glinted off the medal as it twirled around, tiny streaks of light flitting across the wall. Perhaps it would right whatever wrong Nikola thought he had done.

* * * *

STEFAN GLANCED INTO the shop through the display window. Nikola, dressed in a dark gray suit jacket, a spotless white shirt, and designer jeans, spoke with his attendant at the counter.

He turned toward the door when Stefan entered. "Late your first day."

"I'm sorry." Stefan tapped his fingers against his leg. "Something unexpected came up. I'll get the door panel and instructions now."

Pointing toward a door at the back, Nikola spoke to his attendant in Bulgarian. She responded, then left. Nikola headed toward the front door, but Stefan stepped in his path.

"Please, wait." Stefan thrust his hand inside his jacket pocket.

"What?" Nikola curled his lip.

"I have something you might like." Stefan held out the medal. "This really should have been yours." He rushed the words out before he changed his mind. "You probably would have won. I didn't acknowledge it at the time because I enjoyed the attention too much."

"Mr. Tarrant?" The attendant called from the counter. "I have the panel."

Stefan reached for Nikola's hand, dropped the medal into it, then hurried over to the counter. He returned a few moments later. Nikola hadn't moved, his head lowered, staring at his open palm.

"Nikola?" Stefan touched his shoulder.

He raised his head, his eyes glassy. Then he looked around the room. He cleared his throat. "Thank you. You're right. I should have won." He stuffed the medal into his pocket. "I'm on my way to Nessebar. Perhaps you'd like to join me, so you can get a taste of Bulgarian culture. It's one of our historical jewels."

"What about the panel?"

"That? You have plenty of time to finish it." Nikola held the door open. "We'll go in my car so we can ride in comfort. It'll be like our adventures in the old days. The town is on an island. It has an old fortress I'm sure you'll enjoy seeing."

"I don't want to interfere with your plans. I can always visit it another time."

"Nonsense. Now's as good a time as any." Nikola stepped into the pedestrian street. "You won't have time later. I'll keep you too busy with work. Besides, if you don't speak Bulgarian, the people will overcharge you for everything, especially at restaurants. And, it's better to go now than in the summer when the streets get hot and overcrowded with tourists."

"Okay. Sounds like fun." Stefan nodded. "Let me drop the panel off in my car and get my camera." He opened the passenger side door of his beat-up car, catching Nikola's sneer. When did he get to be such a snob? He came from a poor family.

Nikola talked about Nessebar while Stefan trudged next to him. "It's a three-thousand-year-old Thracian settlement that's survived many conquests—the Greeks, the Romans, the Slavs, and the Byzantines. You can still see the influence of all of them. When you stroll through the streets, you almost think you're back in ancient times."

They stopped at a shiny black Cadillac. "Here we are, my car." Nikola waved to the vehicle, a wide grin on his face. "Get in and buckle up. I wouldn't want anything to happen to you. Some of the country roads are quite bumpy."

Stefan dropped into the passenger's seat. The stench of cologne hung in the air, overpowering the pleasant smell of the leather seats. He gagged and held his hand over his nose and mouth. As soon as Nikola got in, Stefan removed his hand and held his breath, then rolled down the window when Nikola started the vehicle.

Looking in the mirror and then over his shoulder, Nikola put the car in drive and sped out of the parking spot.

Stefan clung to the seat, listening to honking horns and angry voices.

I guess it's no worse than Boston drivers. Stefan chuckled and relaxed, enjoying the fast pace as Nikola maneuvered the car through traffic, and finally onto the highway. "How long a drive is it?"

"An hour and a half usually." Nikola grinned. "But I can make it in an hour."

Stefan laughed. "Nothing's changed. You always were a daredevil." The old Nikola was returning.

Stefan admired the countryside as they zipped along the highway. It started to sprinkle, so Nikola put on the intermittent wipers. Stefan rolled the window halfway, the cologne still strong in the vehicle. He recognized familiar landmarks. He hadn't paid much attention at first, but they were travelling south, the same way he went to get home. "We just passed the cutoff to Emona. Have you ever been there?"

"I'm not sure. I don't know all the villages around here."

"Didn't you tell me it was a god-forsaken place? I thought you had a clue where it was."

"Did I? Bulgaria has a lot of small villages. I can't tell you where they all are."

They rode in silence for a while. Nikola braked suddenly after they passed a windmill, its web-like arms turning in the breeze. Stefan jerked forward a few inches and was stopped abruptly by the seat belt.

"A little warning next time?"

Nikola laughed. "Lighten up. We used to do that all the time to each other." He pointed in front of them. "Nessebar straight ahead."

Stefan held onto the seat as the car bumped along the creaky wooden bridge. "It's really not an island, is it? There's land under this bridge."

"It's a levee that's been built up. So, technically, it's a peninsula, if you want to argue about it."

Stefan remained quiet as Nikola slowed even more to drive through the stone gate into the town. He pulled into a spot along a narrow, cobblestoned street close to the entrance. The ruins of a fortress lay straight ahead.

The drizzle coming down didn't discourage Stefan. He jumped out and started snapping photos of the old ivy-covered stone houses, decorated with dark wooden flowerboxes. The place would be gorgeous when the flowers bloomed. "This is a great inspiration. Now I'm glad you invited me to come here. These houses are in wonderful condition for being so old."

"That's because the city is under UNESCO protection."

"Its protection? What does that mean?" Stefan put the camera down to look at Nikola.

"A country can have historic sites registered on the World Heritage List. It's quite prestigious to do that. They get financial assistance to protect and preserve sites from too much development."

"And are you on *that* committee also?" Stefan joked.

"Not yet." Nikola walked toward the fortress wall. "The lifestyle here is quite a bit different from what we saw in France, huh? And certainly not what you were used to in America."

"I feel like a toddler learning to walk when it comes to customs here. Maria, the owner of the hotel in Emona, has practically adopted me and taken me under her wing. A real mother hen, she is." Stefan lined up a shot of small boats moored along the pier. "The villagers certainly have a lot of strange beliefs. At first I thought they were joking, but they really seem to believe them. I almost got caught up in their stories."

"The rural people are rather primitive in their thinking. They have many superstitions that go back to

Thracian times. And even a lot of their remedies against evil powers date back to that era."

"I can add that to the stories I'm telling Sonia about Emona."

"Sonia?" Nikola stopped walking, and his voice tensed. "Who's that?"

"My daughter. She's eight and loves to hear about fairies and dragons. She's learning about them now in school."

"What did you do?" Nikola sneered. "Leave her alone in the house when you came to Varna today?"

"Of course not!" Stefan glared at Nikola. "She goes to private school in Rouen. The one Katherine went to. At least until I find her a good school here."

Nikola put his hand on Stefan's shoulder and laughed. "Calm down. It was a jest. You used to be able to take a joke."

"Real funny," Stefan sputtered. "I miss her a lot."

"Let's forget about it and enjoy the town." Nikola walked on ahead and pointed. "Look. That's an old Byzantine church. The arches are quite well preserved."

Stefan looked toward the church. "I'll be right there after I get a good shot of this house from the stone wall."

"Be—" Nikola stopped and looked around. "Well, hurry up."

Stefan pressed his back against the wall and pointed the camera. He wasn't high enough to get the shot he wanted. Craning his neck, he looked up the wall, and then twisted around to look at the house. From the top it would be perfect. The rain had tapered off. The rocks should be fine to stand on.

He hung the camera around his neck and grasped a massive block at the top. His hand slipped, so he wedged his fingers into a crevice, wrapping them around a rough rock. He found another spot farther up and grabbed hold of a sturdy rock. Stepping on a stone that had worked its way out, he pulled himself to the top.

The street below the other side of the wall ended abruptly at a cliff. Maybe this hadn't been such a great idea. He glanced at the house. On second thought, it offered a spectacular view. The rock he stood on tottered. He tested another one with his foot. It didn't move, so he slid over to it. Holding the camera in front of him, he positioned the house in the frame.

Something—a rock?—hit his neck, stinging like a bee. He swayed a bit, but regained his balance. Rubbing the spot with his free hand, he looked around. No one was anywhere close. Maybe it had been an insect after all.

He took a few pictures, then walked a little farther down the wall. Again, something struck him. This time in the back, pushing him forward. He swung his arms to regain his balance. A barrage of stones assaulted him. He dropped to his knees, but the wall was too narrow, and he tumbled off. Managing to grab hold of a stone, he hung there for a moment.

"Help!" he screamed.

His hand slid off the wet stone, then down the wall, scraping against the rough rocks. He grabbed at anything that passed within his grasp. Roots tore free as he slid past the wall to the embankment. Vine leaves tore away in his hand. He grabbed a protruding root. It held, and he clung on.

"Help!" he yelled again.

Red hair, then a face appeared over the edge of the wall, disappearing too rapidly to tell who it was.

"Nikola!" Stefan yelled. "Get help!"

He waited, but nobody came. Twisting his neck, he looked down at the rocks jutting up along the shore.

A "Kak kak kak" startled him, almost making him lose his grip on the root. He looked up. A white falcon flew above him. The bird landed on a large rock protruding from the stone wall. It tugged at the ivy grow-ing between the rocks. Maybe they were sturdy enough for him to grab onto so he could climb back up.

Keeping a grip on the root, he clutched some ivy with his other hand, tugging. It didn't tear away. He placed his foot in a knee-level gap. Steadying himself, he took a deep breath. He held onto some more ivy, pulling himself far-ther up the wall. He released the root and reached for an-other clump. With a slow, steady pace, he crawled up, fi-nally rolling onto the top. He let out a long breath and climbed down the other side.

The falcon flew in circles above him for a while. It landed on the wall and stared down at him when Nikola strutted over.

"What happened to you? You look a mess." Nikola helped Stefan up. "I thought you got lost when I didn't see you over at the church."

"What happened to me?" Stefan gritted his teeth. "Why didn't you get a rope or something to help me?"

"What are you talking about? Get a rope for what?"

"Someone was throwing rocks at me. I lost my foot-ing and fell." He stared at Nikola. "I yelled to you to get help when you looked over the wall."

"Me?" Nikola opened his eyes wide. "I've been over by the church waiting for you. It must have been a gypsy. They don't get involved in other people's problems."

"And I suppose a gypsy threw rocks at me, too." Stefan wiped the dirt and mud from his jacket, but it merely streaked.

"Who knows?" Nikola shrugged. "Why were you up there anyway? Danger signs are all over the place." He pointed to one in front of the wall.

"I don't read Bulgarian, remember? You could have told me."

"I guess I didn't think you'd be foolish enough to climb it." Nikola headed down the street. "You're fine now. Come on. Something is usually taking place in the plaza. Stick with me. The streets are narrow and twist around. It's easy to get disoriented, even though the town is small."

Although his legs wobbled, Stefan wanted to see more of the village, so he followed Nikola toward some lively music. "Is that a street show?"

"Probably the gypsies. They perform magic and bear dancing."

Stefan stopped. "What? They dance nude?"

Nikola burst out laughing. "No. B-e-a-r. The animal. They train them to dance."

A few people milled around the plaza watching a gray-haired man play a mandolina while a girl dressed in colorful clothing danced with a bear. Her dark hair swished as she moved.

"Amazing." Stefan took some pictures. "How do they train the bear to dance?"

"They place hot metal on their back paws," Nikola said.

Stefan stopped mid-click. "That's horrible! Can't anyone stop them?"

Nikola shrugged. "It's one of the livelihoods of the *Tsigani*, besides fortune-telling, music and dancing, and horse shows. The government has made an occasional effort to stop them, but they don't try very hard."

"I think I've seen enough. It's starting to get dark. We should head back to Varna now."

"It's over now, anyway." Nikola headed down the street, calling over his shoulder, "I have a boat. Let's go out to the islands and do some fishing when you drop off your next order."

Stefan looked over at the bear and his chest tightened. Such cruelty for the sake of entertainment. People should stop watching. Maybe it would put an end to this.

The gypsy girl walked around, holding out a hat to onlookers. Many tossed coins in. When she reached Stefan, he refused to contribute. She grabbed his hand, looked at his palm, then into his face. Her dark eyes opened wide. She put his hand over the place on his chest where the ring was and said, "*Amaya.*" She dropped his hand and backed away, not taking her eyes off him.

Stefan hurried to catch up with Nikola. "What does '*amaya*' mean?"

"Where'd you hear that? From one of those gypsies?"

"Yes. What does it mean?"

"Don't pay any attention to them. All they want is money."

Stefan grabbed Nikola's shoulder and stopped him. "What does it mean?"

Nikola looked at Stefan and smirked. "Curse."

A Thread of Hope

March 29

STEFAN STROLLED ALONG a path that meandered through a lush, green meadow with grass as soft as velvet. Pink and ruby strokes painted grooves through the pale blue of the morning sky, an alluring backdrop for birds chirping harmonious melodies. Sunflowers, swaying to the music, reached skyward in reverent rapture to touch the face of God. A warm breeze sashayed with poppies that promised sweet dreams to any who lingered. All the setting lacked was Kalyna by his side.

The fluttering of wings belonging to something larger than a songbird interrupted the serene moment. The gust of its movement tickled his cheeks. Looking toward the sound, he opened his eyes wide, and his jaw dropped.

An angel!

He rubbed his eyes to make sure they didn't deceive him. An exquisite being with wings danced close by, unaware of his presence. She wore a gown of fluffy white plumage, a purer white than he had ever seen. Curly blond hair, crowned by walnut leaves, flowed down her back and extended the length of her outstretched arms as she twirled in an unrestrained dance.

She frolicked around the meadow and giggled like an innocent child as she flapped her wings to a rhythm he couldn't hear. Something red and white wrapped around her foot danced along with her. Where her bare feet touched the grass, white flowers bloomed. A horse with a gleaming black coat and mane pranced along with her, while a powerful gray wolf guarded her like a sentinel, as if waiting to undertake her slightest command.

Stefan hid behind a boulder and watched, fascinated. Desiring to see her face, he crept closer. Lost in the ecstasy of her dance, she didn't notice his approach, but the wolf did. It bared its teeth and snarled a vicious warning. He stood still, not daring to move.

The woman ceased dancing and smiled. She motioned for him to come closer. He moved forward, but in the next instant, she whirled around and stared at something in the forest. Her deafening scream pounded in his ears. Wrapping her wings around her body, she spun like a whirlwind. Mist surrounded her, pouring out from her motion. He watched in fascination as she transformed into a white falcon and flew into the forest. The horse raced along the path after her, while the wolf remained, guarding the entrance.

The mist hovered over the ground, ever expanding, until it engulfed the creature. Only its constant growling assured Stefan the wolf remained at its post. Unsure where he should turn, his surroundings now a sea of hazy white, he waited for the heat from the sun to evaporate the moisture. Shadows of colors emerged. First gray, where the snarling continued, and then black. His blood froze.

A different beast!

A rangy, black wolf crouched on its haunches. Snarling at him, it crept closer, its sharp teeth bared. A thick branch lay a short distance out of Stefan's reach. Without taking his eyes off the wolf, he stepped toward it, but his legs, as heavy as concrete, moved in slow motion.

At his movement, the wolf lunged straight toward him. Stefan dove for the branch. An agonizing pain exploded through his thigh as sharp teeth tore into it. The creature's heavy body knocked him down, pinning him to the ground.

"Go away! Leave me alone!" He swung the branch at the wolf's face.

He thrust the branch into the wolf's mouth when it opened its jaws. Hot saliva dripped onto Stefan's throat. Rancid breaths gusted on his cheeks in rapid succession. He gripped the branch and shoved the beast's face away, but it pushed back. Stefan's arms wavered from the struggle. The branch curved closer to him from the strain until it cracked, and the wolf's face drew closer.

"God help me," Stefan whispered, his heart racing.

An ear-splitting screech pierced the air, interrupting the lethal dance. The white falcon swooped down and dug its claws into the wolf's back. It repeatedly jabbed its beak into the beast's neck. The wolf twisted its head away from Stefan, wrenching the branch out of his hands. While the bird kept the wolf engaged by its continued assault, Stefan shoved the beast off enough to crawl from beneath its deadly embrace. He clambered up a steep incline and located a sturdier branch.

Below him, the wolf snapped its jaw toward the falcon, but the bird flew out of reach. Again it dove to attack, pecking the animal in the head. The wolf, jerking its head around once more, caught the falcon's leg in its jaw, which shut tight like a vise. The shriek of the falcon penetrated the air, thickened with despair.

Stefan rushed down and swung the branch at the wolf's head. The startled animal opened its jaw, releasing the falcon. The bird fell to the ground in a limp heap and flapped over to a crevice in the rock. The wolf growled and looked between Stefan and the falcon. After snarling at him, the wolf leapt after the bird and tore at the crevice in a bloodthirsty rage. With a fury of his own, Stefan smashed the branch over the wolf's head. The beast yelped in pain and crouched, ready to attack. Stefan landed blow after blow on the wolf until it fled into the woods. Looking toward the crevice, he searched for the falcon to see how badly it had been injured, but the bird had flown away. He rested, trying to catch his breath.

Feathers and fur floated in the air and covered the ground like an early snowfall. A red-and-white object drifted down and landed on his chest, burning him with its touch.

STEFAN MOANED AS he awoke. "I have to learn not to stuff myself with the hotel's tasty cooking. It gives me nightmares."

Rubbing his burning chest, he brushed against the ring on the chain around his neck. Heat coming from the stone turned his heartburn to heartache. He longed to wake up next to Katherine again and tell a lame joke, while she responded by quoting a snippet of poetry, the way they did on their anniversary.

He squeezed the ring, trying to retain his memory of her, but heat pulsing through the stone like a beating heart denied him his desire. It drove away his cherished thoughts and replaced them with an all-consuming yearning for Kalyna, the mysterious woman haunting his dreams.

A cold breeze from the open window made him shiver. He released the ring, threw off his covers, and got out of bed. One leg buckled and he groaned. Sitting back on the mattress, he inspected his leg. Short gashes, still seeping blood, ran along his thigh exactly where the dream wolf had attacked him.

How did I get these?

Only surface cuts, they still stung. He limped to the bathroom to cleanse and dress them. After returning to his bedroom, he pulled off the blood-stained bed coverings. He patted the mattress for springs that might have poked through. Nothing. Not even a small tear. He had to be missing something.

A chilly breeze blew against his back while he flipped the mattress over. He gathered the soiled sheets into his arms, then dragged himself to the window. A pure white falcon sat perched on the sill with its head cocked, watching him.

First a bird assisted him in Nessebar. Then one came to his rescue in his dream. And now one was here. Could it be the same one? It had a thread of red and white yarn tied around its leg. Stefan stared at the bird and imagined it morphing into a woman with wings.

Stretching out his arm, he flicked his hand toward it. "Go away! I don't need any more reminders of that dream."

The bird bristled its plumage and chanted a harsh "Kak kak kak." Some seagulls resting on the fence took off, squawking. The falcon followed, soon disappearing among the clouds.

Stefan clutched the ring again. The stone no longer burned, nor did it cloud his thoughts. He released it and deposited the sheets in the washer. While they spun and churned, he turned on his laptop to search for *Thracian ring* and *curse*.

Several images resembled his, with similar ancient characters. Continuing his search through many websites, he was unable to find a ring that contained a sapphire stone. Neither did he discover its translation, nor even why such a ring would sometimes become warm to the touch. And absolutely nothing about a curse. He had to find another way to learn about it. Perhaps someone at a museum would know.

He walked around the room as he played Katherine's phone messages again, trying to picture her face. Her image faded. *No!* He ran into the studio and snatched the photo from the mantel, staring at it until her features became etched into his mind.

Please don't leave me ... again.

He closed his eyes, leaned against the fireplace, and pressed the picture to his chest.

Why did you die? I need you. Sonia needs you.

Opening his eyes, he caressed Katherine's face, then returned the photo to the mantel. He plopped down on the couch and called Sonia. She picked up on the first ring.

"Hello, my little princess. What are you up to this morning?"

"Waiting for you. I knew you'd call."

"You did?" Stefan gasped in mock surprise. "Did the fairy princess, I mean, the samodiva tell you that?"

"Noooo. Mémé did," Sonia said in her serious, grown-up voice. Then she whispered. "Did you see her again? The samodiva."

"I did. She saved me from the red dragon again."

"You said the dragon was black."

"He was when I first met him." Stefan stretched out on the couch. "The magic from the sword I cut him with turned him bright red." *The same color as Nikola's hair.* Stefan grinned. *He has become quite the dragon.*

"What happened?"

"The dragon captured me when I was ... walking past a magic fountain in the village."

"What kind of magic?"

"If you drink the water, you can find someone who's lost. I wanted to find the person the samodiva is looking for, so she won't think it's me. Then ..." He tapped his fingers against the back of the couch. "When I cupped my hands under the spout, a strong wind blew the water out of them. I looked around to see what caused it. The dragon flew above me, flapping his wings. He swooped down from the sky, snatched me in his claws, and carried me off to an island far out in the sea, where he dropped me into a deep, dark well."

"Oh, no, Daddy." She sounded close to tears.

"Fear not, my brave princess. All hope was not lost." The sniffles stopped and Stefan continued. "The samodiva flew to the edge of the well and threw me down a rope. She tied it around the black mare, and they pulled me to safety."

"What if the dragon comes back?" Sonia whispered. "He might hurt you again."

"Not so, my fair maiden." He sat up. "The mare's also magical. She lived long ago when people called Thracians lived here. I'm protected from evil when she's around. All I have to do is call to her, and she'll come to my rescue."

"Mémé says I have to eat breakfast now." Sonia sighed. "Will you tell me more about the samodiva next time you call?"

"Your wish is my command. You control my heart, most fair maiden."

Sonia giggled. "Bye. Love you more."

"Oh, you do? Love you, sweetheart."

He ended the call and got up from the couch. The mahogany door panel lay on the workbench next to his collection of chisels. He ran his fingers down the grain of the silky reddish-brown wood. It was a superb material for carving reliefs, but it tended to split if the strokes were too long. His tools had to be razor sharp to ensure a perfectly smooth cut.

Picking up a wide-edged chisel, he guided it down a test block of wood. A minuscule groove ran down the middle. He touched the tip of the tool with his finger. Yes, it had a small nick. He removed a leather strop from the cabinet. Holding the chisel at an angle, he dragged it over the leather toward him a couple of times, turned it to the other side and repeated the process. He tested the chisel again. This time the cut left no groove.

Stefan placed the panel in front of him. He guided the metal edge of the chisel parallel to the grain. The wood was soft so he didn't need to exert any force. With small cuts, he outlined the image of a majestic buck standing before a mountain range. He set the chisel down and picked up the next one to add more detail, but set it back on the workbench, unable to concentrate.

His strange dreams breathed within him a yearning to stroke a brush across canvas, rather than drag a chisel against wood. He had locked away the imagination of his soul, repressed by the unbearable pain of Katherine's loss. The mystery woman, Kalyna, the legends the villagers told, and Emona itself had inserted a key into that hidden niche and eased the door open.

His artistic nature awakened, he visualized wild horses prancing along the ridge, while samodivi performed ritual dances under the full moon. His mind travelled back thousands of years to the people who once inhabited this land. What had they been like? How could he capture their spirit and beliefs that still thrived among the villagers? He desired to unveil their stories, their mystery. Perhaps a series of paintings called "The Mystery of Emona."

Stefan looked around at the four bare walls of his studio. They stifled his creativity. He needed to be outdoors, where inspiration could seep into his pores. The Samodivi Cheshma was peaceful—when the horses weren't around. While there, he could sketch the flower symbol and inscription carved into the stone.

Grabbing his sketchpad and charcoal, he headed to the cheshma. A strong wind at his back had him almost running down the path. The branches of the willows, covered with tiny green buds, performed a wild dance.

At the cheshma, he stared at the old walnut tree. Amulets made from red and white threads of yarn covered the branches and swayed like graceful dancing girls. The whistling of the wind sounded like a reverent song drifting out of the forest. He moved toward it, stopped, and spun around. The tune came from every direction, as if the forest itself sang a hymn of praise to the arrival of spring. Riveted by the music, he remained immobile until the last note drifted away like mist evaporated by the sun. So unlike any song he had ever heard, it filled him with peace, and he experienced a oneness with nature.

The gurgling of the creek brought him back to his surroundings. He set his sketchpad down. Cupping his hands together under the cheshma's copper spout, he drank handfuls of the cold water. The music had built a fire of passion inside him, making him thirst for more. Wanting to immerse himself in the water, he unbuttoned and removed his shirt. His hand grazed the ring, its heat burning his chest. He yanked it off and set it on the cheshma wall.

He bent over the basin. A golden gleam reflected in the water a moment before something almost imperceptible brushed against his back. He whirled around, but no one was there. The sensation must have been the breeze.

Stefan filled the *cherpak*, the copper ladle hanging on a chain at the side of the cheshma, and splashed his face, shoulders, chest, and back with the refreshing water until he shivered from its chill. Something warm touched his cold back once again, and he spun around.

He gasped at the same time as the intruder. "Kalyna! Are you real?"

"Of course I'm real." She tilted her head to the side. "What a strange thing to say."

"I ..." Like a magical fairy, she tantalized him with her emerald eyes and her unbound hair flowing around her shoulders. A simple white dress made of fine silk clung to her, scarcely concealing her nakedness. He pried his eyes away from her body and lifted them to her shoulders, where a small flower had been tattooed. Had he seen it the day he met her? Is that what triggered his dream about the woman on the beach? She also had the same tattoo.

"I thought I might have been hallucinating. You disappeared so quickly on the beach the day I met you." He brought his glance upward and looked into her eyes. She was a sorceress, kindling a fire that burned him from the inside out.

"A path behind the boulder leads to my friend's house."

"The villagers have been feeding me legends about samodivi and horses. And then the statue. I ..." He forced himself to look away to break the spell she cast. She would think he was crazy if he said any more. "Why are you here? At the cheshma?"

"I came to look for flowers and herbs. My friend didn't have a basket, so I borrowed this to hold them." She handed him a white cotton towel embroidered with flowers. "But, I think you need it more. The water's freezing this time of year. You should dry off before you catch a cold."

He wiped the water from his face and torso, then wrapped the cloth over his shoulders. "Did you hear the music? It was surreal."

"No. Only the birds chirping and the wind whistling."

"Maybe it was the samodivi." He laughed as he brushed his fingertips against one of the amulets on the walnut tree. "What are these? I've never seen so many charms in one place. It's like a flowering garden."

"They're *martenitsi*. People start wearing them on the first of March. I have one on my ankle." She held out her leg to show him.

"Your ankle?" Stefan looked down. It was the same amulet from his dreams. Above it was a tiny scar.

What? No. Impossible. It was a dream.

He glanced at Kalyna's face, then back at her ankle. Lightening his tone, he asked, "You don't also have wings, do you?"

She laughed and spread out her arms. "Do these look like wings?"

Her movement distracted him, and he had a difficult time concentrating on her words. He looked away and touched one of the martenitsi again. "Do you know why they're on the tree?"

"People tie them on branches after they see a stork or buds on trees, to rejoice in the arrival of spring. I saw a stork yesterday on my way to the village, so the villagers must have put these on this tree."

Stefan looked back at Kalyna. "Why this tree and not the others?"

"The walnut tree is considered holy, a World Tree. It's held in deep veneration as a symbol of strength and protection from the evil forces of the world."

"World Tree?" He raised his eyebrows. "That sounds like a fairy tale Todor would tell me."

She touched her fingers to his lips. "You mustn't say such things. The tree is sacred. According to tradition, people are not supposed to cut one down or even break its branches. When they put a martenitsa on a branch, they pray for good health and fortune throughout the year."

"Does it work?" Stefan laughed as he fingered the amulet.

Kalyna gave him a half smile. She picked up a twig and sat under the tree and patted the ground for him to join her. "The World Tree has three parts symbolizing the nature of the universe, each encompassing its own supernatural beings."

She drew the crown of the tree in the dirt. "The top represents the heavens where divine spirits reside."

Then she outlined the trunk. "The middle signifies land, which is the home of men and preternatural creatures." She looked at him with a playful smile. "That's you and me."

He picked up another twig and sketched in the dirt. "And what do the roots represent?"

"The underworld and the dead who dwell there."

He grinned. "I've already learned horses can travel from one realm to the other."

"You jest, but it's more than symbols. All these beings exist and live in harmony with one another."

"Mankind and samodivi?"

She stared at him, her eyes darkened from the shade. Like a magnet, an invisible field surrounding her drew him nearer. He lowered his head to kiss her, but she placed her hands on his chest, giving him a gentle push. She scrambled to her feet and extended her hand. As he reached to grasp it, the air chilled, the wind whipped around them, and heavy, dark clouds gathered in the sky, blocking out the sun. A torrential rain poured down a moment later.

"Quick. We have to get out of this or we'll get soaked." She raced ahead, dragging him along. "I know a place we can hide. There's a cavern in the rocks by the cheshma. I think we can both fit in there."

The shelter had been carved out from the wind and rain. Dry hay covering the floor kept the chill from their bodies, but Stefan was content to sit snug against Kalyna for warmth as well.

She took the amulet off her ankle and wrapped it around his wrist. "The martenitsa is given to others as a sign of friendship. It has the power to protect people from evil. The two colors have special meanings. White is for purity, honesty, and clarity. Red is symbolic of blood, life, passion, and love."

Stefan glanced at the martenitsa, and raised his eyes to Kalyna's face. "How did this tradition start?"

She leaned closer to him and whispered. "There's a legend about Khan Asparuh and his sister Huba ..."

Only half listening, he touched a strand of wet hair clinging to her face and moved it behind her ear. Her cheeks, as rosy and as smooth as a peach, charmed him. The wet dress no longer hid her nakedness, making him tremble with passion and desire. A seed of hope grew in him; maybe he could overcome the sorrow of losing

Katherine and start life again. He pulled her closer to him in a tight embrace. This time, she didn't push him away.

In the darkness of the shelter, her eyes appeared black and brilliant like polished opals. He fell under her spell and kissed her with a fiery passion. The taste of raspberries was his last memory before darkness overtook him, and he became part of the tale she narrated.

STEFAN FLEW HIGH above the earth, the moisture from the clouds rolling off his wings; he was a falcon. Khan Asparuh, the first Bulgarian king, sent him to locate his sister Huba, who was being kept prisoner in another kingdom. He entrusted to Stefan the mission of leading her to a safe place where they could make their new home.

When Huba escaped, she galloped away on a horse and followed the falcon until they reached the Danube River. She looked around in desperation for a way across. Stefan flew down to her aid. She tied a long, white thread to his leg and beseeched him to find a safe way across. He flew high into the sky, searching along the banks, while she held onto the other end of the thread.

He found the passage, far below. As he flew back to guide her the rest of the way, a sharp pain exploded in his breast. An arrow had pierced him. He spun around and tumbled to the earth. His blood streamed down the thread, turning it red. He looked down. Huba still followed him. She reached the ford when he hit the ground. She would be safe now. He laid his head down to die with the satisfaction of knowing he had succeeded in his mission.

STEFAN WOKE WITH a start, shivering from the cold breeze. The rain had stopped, and a rainbow curved like an arc in the sky. He lay under the walnut tree; the martenitsi dancing above dripped droplets of water on him.

His shirt was on and buttoned, and the ring hung around his neck. Underneath him, his sketchpad was dry and opened to a page where someone had drawn a flower like the one on the towel. Edelweiss.

When he picked up the sketchpad, the amulet Kalyna had given him slid down his wrist.

What's going on here? He couldn't have dreamed everything if he had her gift.

He got up and walked to the cavern. Nothing but hay lay scattered inside. It appeared to have been undisturbed for years.

Bewitching Hour

April 3

TABLES LADEN WITH fruit and roasted game quivered from the incessant banging on the *tupans*. Stefan's eardrums vibrated from the loud notes pouring forth from the *zurlas*. The wine in his *rhyton* splashed over the brim as he twisted around, observing the festivities, spellbound and appalled at the same time. Torch flames flickered from the draft of lusty performances by barefoot girls, some naked and others clad in scanty fawn skins or sheer tunics. All wore wreaths of ivy and danced in an intoxicated frenzy. Some of them couldn't have been more than thirteen years old.

He slumped back on the round couch, covered with the skins of wild animals. Grasping his goblet with both hands to stop them from shaking, he drank a deep draught. Girls behind him leaned forward to pour more wine. Their breasts fell out of loose tunics inches from his face. He couldn't tear his eyes away.

What is this place? How did I get here?

Two beautiful young women, attired in gossamer garments more elegant than the others, danced over and clung to him. One curled up on his lap and wrapped her arms around his waist, pressing her buxom chest against him. As her warm body clung to his, a fire exploded within him. He pulled back horrified at his reaction.

She leaned closer, kissing his face, neck, and chest. Fluttering her charcoal-lined eyes, she pouted. "Dushan, why aren't you joining the celebration? Your wedding is tomorrow. Tonight, you're ours."

Why is she calling me Dushan? How can I even understand her? What language is this?

The other woman sat at his feet, leaned her head against his knees, and began to caress his thigh. She slid up his body. Catching hold of his hand, she splashed wine over his tunic as she tried to pull him up. "Come with me. You're the best dancer in the village."

The girl on his lap continued to molest him with kisses. She clutched his face and pressed her mouth hard against his, forcing her way in. The sour taste of her red wine remained on his tongue when she pulled away to breathe.

Two more girls, dressed in sheer tunics, danced with hips thrust toward him. They climbed onto the couch, kneeled by his side, and massaged his shoulders, one on each side. They leaned forward, laughing, their breasts exposed to him.

One of them ran her hand down his muscled arm. "Dushan, who will you choose for your companion tonight? Tell us, Master. We're here to please you."

More scantily clad and naked girls surrounded him, all offering carnal services. They giggled while they fondled him.

Stefan gulped down his wine. In an instant, a woman behind him refilled his goblet. He tried to push the girls away, but too many surrounded him.

"Who's Dushan?"

He struggled to be free of them. At the same time, he was aroused with lust as he drowned in a sea of naked bodies. They all wanted him, yet they called him Dushan.

"Let me go! Where's Kalyna?"

"Who's Kalyna?" The girl on his lap whispered into his ear, her words slurred and her breath hot against his skin.

The air filled with the noise of their pleas to be chosen. Some shouted, "Dushan," while others whispered it. The name floated on the air all around him. He couldn't tell where the sound originated as his body spun around like a top, the word becoming distorted in his ears.

The music stopped, the flames diminished, and the girls disappeared.

STEFAN GRIPPED HIS head as he rocked on the porch swing in the pitch black. This was madness. Why was the man from his vision haunting his sleep? Or rather why was he dreaming he was Dushan? That wasn't even it. He was himself, but those beautiful girls, like maenads, addressed him by that name. Rubbing his skin, still flushed from their caresses, he couldn't get their voices out of his mind.

No. The noise stemmed from somewhere else. He set his feet on the floor to stop the creaking of the swing. A discordant noise resonated through the air. He held his breath, concentrating on locating its source. The muffled moan broke the stillness again; it came from the direction of the creek.

He grabbed a lantern from the shed and headed down the trail that disappeared into the inky darkness. Blackberry bushes loomed ahead, indistinct from their shadows. Their merciless thorns stung him like angry bees when he brushed against them.

Near the creek, a large animal lay on the ground. A horse. It moaned again, thrashing on the ground. One of its hooves was caught in a trap. Stefan took a step toward it, wanting to assist, but unsure what to do. Maybe Peter could help; he had set the trap. As he started down the trail, the horse groaned again. His chest tightened when the moans quieted, still ringing loud in his mind. Turning around, he returned to the clearing.

He kneeled beside the mare, her bulky sides heaving with the foal she carried. Could it be the one who had approached him at the cheshma? He stroked her neck. As soon as his hand touched her coarse hair, night turned into day, and he was racing the black mare through a meadow teeming with poppies. A woman with a scarf wrapped around her head waved to him. The same woman from his vision. Again, she called him "son" in a language he didn't know, but somehow understood.

"Sine, sine. Dobre li si?" A woman spoke with a thick accent.

He opened his eyes. Once again darkness surrounded him. "What? What happened?"

"Oh, dear. Son, you okay? You be chosen one? Master of horse?" The petite woman, a hood shrouding her face, reached out from her black cloak and laid a wrinkled hand on his arm.

"Master of the horse?" Stefan had never owned a horse, never even ridden one. The only horse he had been near was Katherine's.

She motioned to the trap. "You strong. You help mare. You open." Kneeling, she murmured words that calmed the animal.

Stefan examined the trap to determine how to open it. He grasped the levers on the sides of the metal jaws and pushed down until every muscle in his arms and torso ached. The trap creaked opened a slight amount, but not enough to release the mare's hoof. It slipped from his grip and sprang back, provoking an eerie wail from the mare that made him cringe.

Positioning the device flush to the ground without twisting the mare's leg, he pressed against the levers with his feet until it opened. He reached down and released her hoof. As soon as he stepped off the trap, its jaws clanged shut, and the apparatus lurched into the air.

The woman slid toward the animal's injured leg, pulled out a small jar from one of her pockets, and applied a yellow jelly-like ointment to the wound. She patted the mare and offered it more gentle words. Standing, she smoothed out her cloak and replaced the jar. "Me think she be fine now. You do job good. Bleeding stop soon, and leg heal fast from me *pomada*. We let Nature care for her now, and be thankful for Her powers." The woman pointed toward the mare's neck. "See her martenitsa? She be protected by spirits."

The mare struggled to stand, her neigh weak. Once up, she limped to the end of the path, but turned back to look at Stefan. Tossing her head as if in thanks, she disappeared into the darkness. Stefan jumped when the woman grasped his hand and stepped closer to him.

She peered at him from under the hood. "What you do here by youself, son? You lost? These woods dangerous at night. Come to me place. Me make hot tea."

Contemplating the strange vision, he held back when she led him away.

"No be afraid. Me nearby."

Stefan smiled. *Afraid of an old woman?* He followed her, curious why she would be wandering around in a forest she said was dangerous, and wanting to protect her if it was.

All along the winding path, the moonlight's glow made the rocks resemble shiny, silver coins. After a long trek deep into the forest, they arrived at a small log cottage. Gray curtains covered the broken, dirty windows, and newspapers filled the holes. A dim light flickered inside, revealing a cat sitting like a sphinx in a window.

The woman clasped his hand. "Come in. Come in. Be me guest."

A blast of mixed aromas wafted out when she opened the door. The familiar smell of burning wood reminded him of pleasant summers at his grandfather's cottage. He also got a whiff of herbs; bouquets of them hung out of wooden bins all around the cottage.

The woman slid the hood away from her wrinkled, almost translucent face, and removed her black cloak. She hung it on a peg by the door, next to a birch broom. Stefan stared at her white curly hair full of knots, looking as if she hadn't brushed it for a long time.

"You be afraid of me?" She looked at him with a sympathetic and sad toothless smile.

He shook his head and felt his face flush for his rudeness.

"Me be Sultana. People no like me much around here, but they need me help. Now, who be you? And why you in woods at midnight?"

"I'm Stefan. I recently moved into the Professor's house down the road."

"Oh, *you* be stranger bought house." She gestured to a wooden chair, one of the few pieces of furniture in the room. "Please sit by fire and me bring some tea."

She shuffled away, and he headed to the massive stone fireplace that took up most of the back wall. An old black kettle, suspended on a chain above the hearth, swayed back and forth when he bumped into it as he reached for an icon behind a *kandilo*. The image was of two men holding vials and herbs. Healers perhaps?

After he placed it back on the mantel with care, he warmed his hands over the coals. He glanced around for more wood to get the fire started again, but the basket on the hearth contained only a few small twigs.

Stefan looked in the direction Sultana had disappeared, where the clatter of dishes and cutlery assured him she was still around. He sat on a small colorful rug, made with red, yellow, and green vertical patterns and drummed his fingers against the uneven clay floor. His hand touched one of the clay pots that formed a semicircle around the basket. Leaning over, he smelled the green leaves—more herbs. He looked into a wide, flat copper dish that stood on a low table; it was filled with water, maybe to water the herbs.

Sultana finally returned, carrying a tray with two steaming cups of tea, which she placed on a small wooden table. Stefan got up and straightened the rug.

"That be me *cherga*." She sat in her rocking chair. "Me make from old clothes." Pulling an afghan over her lap, she pointed to a chair. "Sit, sit."

He sat and picked up the cup. Wrapping his hands around it, he brought it close to his face. Cinnamon and cloves drifted out from the steam, but he didn't recognize the other scents. He took a sip.

"You like me tea?" Her chair creaked while she rocked.

He glanced over and saw her watching him. "It's delicious. The aroma is incredible."

"It me special tea, Bewitching Chai. Have thirty-two herbs."

Stefan raised his eyebrows. *Bewitching? She probably could pass for a witch.* His discomfort about the vision dissolved with the warmth of Sultana's hospitality. He set his tea down. "Do you think the mare will be okay?"

"No worry, son. She be fine. The Nature, She heal leg and help with birth. It the Nature job." She patted his arm in a comforting gesture, and then put her hands on the side of the rocker to push herself up. "You hungry? Want chicken soup and bread? Me make fresh bread. Special bread. It *dobra dusha*, kind soul. Make in *podnitza*. Me check. Me think it be ready." She cleared the ashes off the top of a round earthen dish sitting in the fireplace coals and lifted the cover.

Stefan's mouth watered when the aroma of baking bread drifted into the room. "It smells delightful."

Sultana removed the *podnitza* and placed the browned bread on a wooden tray, along with some butter. She broke off a piece and handed it to Stefan. "Here, son. Eat. Butter good on bread. Be careful to break bread, not cut. No want to hurt souls. Bread good for health. It drive out ills and demons. Clean you innocent soul. Help get mercy from samodivi."

Samodivi again? It didn't surprise him she believed in them.

He buttered the bread and took a bite. It was crunchy on the outside and soft in the middle. When Sultana went into another room to get the soup, Stefan got up to examine an old trunk similar to one he had seen at an antique shop in Salem. The painted flowers on this one had faded. Next to it some jars and bottles were stacked on a rickety bookcase. The labels were written with strange characters, but he recognized the images of flowers on several of them—lilac, cherry, pear, peony, primrose, geranium, and violet.

A small notebook on the shelf was opened to a well-worn page. It showed sketches of flowers, along with their descriptions in several languages. Surprised to see it in English, he read the text. *Primrose—young love.* Stefan smiled at the thought. It reminded him of the love potion he had seen in Salem. He read a few more entries: *Red peony—protect from spells and evil spirits*; *Geranium— health and strength.*

He set the book down and picked up a jar with no label, but cringed when the shriveled head of a snake with something growing out of it stared back at him. Replacing it on the shelf, he hurried back to his seat.

"That me medicine cabinet." Sultana carried the soup in on a tray and set it on the table. "No doctors close. Me use the Nature to heal ills. Me kill snake on holy day, Bla-govets. Snake and evil spirits play then. Loud noise drive snake to sun. Easy to catch. Garlic growing in head cure all ills." She sat back in her rocking chair and covered her lap with the afghan. "It not snake-guard. He live under house and protect house and hearth. Never hurt snake-guard or have bad luck."

She pointed to the steaming bowl of soup. "Eat. It hot."

Stefan picked up the spoon and held it over the bowl. Lowering it, he stirred the broth, seeing potatoes and chunks of meat.

He looked toward the shelf that held the snake head. She did say it was chicken. Bringing a small spoonful of broth to his mouth, he blew on it. The tantalizing smell of herbs tempted him. He looked at Sultana. She was watching him, so he took a tentative sip. Before he realized it, the bowl was empty. Leaning back in the chair, he stretched out his legs and sighed with contentment.

His mind had cleared, but his vision about his wild gallop on the black mare still confused him. He sat up in the chair and turned to look at his hostess. "What did you mean when you said I was the master of the horse?"

She continued rocking while speaking in a hushed voice. "It be old legend. Mare waiting for return of master. She recognize him, but he no remember her. You touch her. You see past?"

"How ... how did you know I saw ... something, someone."

"Me have gift to see."

He drummed his fingers against his leg. Dushan had to be the master of the horse everyone spoke about, but he wasn't that man. Wasn't anything like him. But then the mare had approached him at the cheshma. The thought was preposterous. "It was nothing that ever happened to me."

"Maybe. Maybe."

He stood and took a step toward the door. These people all believed in impossible things. "Sultana, it was nice to meet you. Thank you for the tea, soup, and bread. It's quite late. I think I should head home now."

"Come back and visit soon. Any time. Me sleep little. You find me when you need me. Need talk about loss of wife. Me listen."

"What?" This was getting stranger by the minute. "How do you know about my wife?"

"No be afraid. Me see much." She rose from her rocker and picked up a small paper bag. "Here some of me Bewitching Chai for you. It bring good sleep. No bad dreams. House have evil. This help you."

"It's evil? Why?"

"Bad thing happen there. Woman killed."

"What? No one told me. The realtor ..."

"Police have no proof. Evil man live there. Greed. Revenge. Bad spirit remain." She patted his arm. "Tea help you."

As he looked into her dark, friendly eyes, something touched his feet, and he jumped. The black cat that had been sitting in the window rubbed against his ankles.

"Milo, go away. Leave our guest be. Psst." She nudged the cat with her foot, and it scampered out of sight.

He said good-bye and walked a few steps away from the cottage before turning around. Sultana stood in the open doorway, the cat at her feet. The dancing light from the fire in the cottage cast a supernatural, yellowish-orange glow around them. His skin tingled.

Bewitching tea, a black cat, a broomstick. All this scene needs is a cauldron bubbling on the fire.

A twig broke behind him, alerting him to the possible dangers in the forest she had warned him about. He spun around toward the sound. The moonlight revealed the shadow of a horse and the outline of a woman rider. The hair on the back of his neck prickled.

A samodiva? My mystery dream woman? Kalyna again?

"Hello ... Kalyna?" His voice quivered.

He took an uncertain step toward her. Without another sound, horse and rider disappeared into the darkness.

Man's Fear

April 10

STORM CLOUDS FURTHER darkened the near-dusk sky as Nikola drove to Elena's apartment. A torrent of emotions washing over him, he snarled toward the heavens that threatened to rain. He ran his thumb over the medal Stefan had given him two weeks ago. His peace offering. A gesture of Stefan's sickening kindness. *Damn him!* Why did he always have to be so forgiving?

Nikola brewed over his plan. Stefan had agreed, however reluctantly, to sail out to the islands next week. This time Nikola would win the contest. He would finish what he had started. No one would ever doubt again that he was a champion.

Anger flooded his mind. Sonia, *Stefan's* child, should have been the child Nikola had with Katherine. He clenched his fist, the points on the award biting into his palm. A second-hand award. He rolled down the window and hurled it at a seagull. It struck the bird, sending it squawking into the air. His aim had always been accurate. The reminder of Stefan gone, he whistled. Tonight he was celebrating his birthday with Elena. He had to focus on moving their relationship forward, beyond friendship.

When she opened the door to her apartment, he greeted her with a polished smile. He kissed her cheeks, first right, then left. "As I promised, I have a surprise. We'll go in my car."

They walked down the drive toward a gleaming Rolls-Royce.

"That's quite a fancy car." She lingered before entering the vehicle, her image reflected in the flawlessness of the dark bronze hood.

"It's a Phantom, a birthday present to myself."

The leather scent filled his senses when he opened the door for her. She slid into the seat and ran her fingers over the soft cream-colored upholstery and along the oak veneer. "It's beautiful. You always did like to have the best of everything."

And soon I will have you, too, because you are the best.

His gaze lingered on her long legs before he closed the door. He strutted to the driver's side and sat behind the steering wheel. The engine started with a purr.

Elena buckled her seatbelt. "Where have you decided to celebrate your birthday?"

"At the Regatta. It's an old ship that's been converted into a restaurant. It's not far from here."

When they arrived, he opened her door and held her hand as she got out. "Welcome aboard." He bowed. "Captain Nikola at your service." He gestured toward the entrance. "The restaurant's cuisine has been unrivaled for years."

A string of lights lined the deck, shining on a faded pirate flag waving in the gentle sea breeze. The folded sailing canvas and rusty anchor hanging over the bow both added to the charm of the vessel. He hooked his arm into hers and guided her along the gangway.

The restaurant manager greeted them at the door. "Nikola, I'm so glad to see you again." They shook hands, and he smiled at Elena. "I have the perfect table waiting for you and your guest."

He motioned to the maître d', who led them down the stairs to a table overlooking the sea and the distant mountain range. A candle in a glass jar fluttered as the man pulled out their chairs to seat them. Uncorking the bottle of champagne chilling on the table, he poured their drinks, then handed them menus. He faded into the shadows, replaced by a waiter standing nearby for their order.

The rhythmic melody of water lapping against the hull was as soothing as the soft music from the band. The small dining area was filled to capacity with local fashion celebrities and artists, but Nikola had tipped the maître d' well to secure a secluded table, so their time together would be special.

Gazing at her as she watched the colorful harbor lights, he couldn't help remember the time he had been here with Katherine. She had sat across from him, twisting her ruby-studded silver cross. "Nikola, you know how much I love you." Her beautiful blue eyes never left his face. "You're my best friend. I want to stay close, but I'm getting married to Stefan."

His chest had tightened and he got up to leave. "I can't be just friends, Katherine. I love you too much."

Now he was here with someone else he loved.

Elena laid her menu down. "Nikola, what would you recommend? The choice is so large I can't decide what to order."

"The Captain's Special Platter is one of my favorites. It has a little of everything."

He lifted his gaze to the waiter. After they placed their orders, the waiter disappeared. Nikola raised a toast. "I have an announcement. The Council for Cultural Events has appropriated funds for renovating the St. Nicholas Church in Emona, and also approved the contest for the restoration of the iconostasis."

"*Nazdrave!*" Elena clinked glasses with him. "That's fabulous news. You've been nagging them about that for a long time."

"I have even better news. Since I'm the director, I can appoint the person who will choose the winner. And who better to do that than *you*—with all your contacts in the art world."

Her eyes lit up. "I'd be delighted. I know so many emerging artists. Such a project could make one of them famous. But, we're supposed to be here celebrating your birthday, so let's enjoy ourselves. We can talk about the contest later."

"You're right." He took a drink. "You look beautiful, my dear. I haven't seen this dress before and your hat. What can I say about your hats? They're always breathtaking."

Smiling in appreciation, Elena touched its brim. "This is from my last visit to Paris." Created from a dark purple satin and Brussels lace, it tilted over her forehead slightly, emphasizing her smooth olive complexion and complementing her stylish lavender dress. "You know me. I'm big on hats. If I didn't have the gallery, I might start a business designing hats."

"Why not do both? You're so talented. If you're ever serious about this idea, I can help you finance the business."

The waiter returned with their meals and a second bottle of champagne. Throughout the evening, Elena talked with excitement about the upcoming exhibitions in her art gallery. Nikola told her about his new shops opening in Italy and France. The second bottle emptied, and a third one arrived, while he garnered the courage to ask Elena to his penthouse.

The evening would be romantic. Candlelight. Soft music. They would sit on the couch, watching the sun rise. It would be so unlike his normal gatherings for the Varna elite that she attended. She was bound to be impressed, especially after he told her he had secured balcony tickets to view *Carmen* at the Varna Opera House. And they would meet the cast backstage after the performance. Surely she was waiting for him to express his feelings for her. He had no doubt he was desirable. So many other women pursued him.

He cleared his throat and took another sip, but she rose and placed her hand on his shoulder. "Excuse me for a moment." She returned shortly with two waiters who carried a chocolate cake, his favorite, with a single lit candle, and placed it in front of him.

"What a wonderful surprise." Seeing Elena's eyes sparkling with excitement, Nikola wanted to stop the moment and treasure it forever.

"Time to make a wish."

He closed his eyes. *I want to find the treasure. I want to find the cave and become immortal. I want to have Elena.*

He blew out the candle and opened his eyes. Her beautiful smile was all for him.

"This is for you. Happy birthday." She held out a small package tied with a stylish red bow.

"Oh, you're so sweet, as always." He opened the box and removed a gold-plated lighter, embossed with his initial. "Thank you so much. This is a great present. I'll treasure it and always keep it close to me." He made a show of placing it next to his heart.

She laughed. "It's only a lighter."

Nikola glanced at Elena between bites of dessert, trying to pluck up courage. When they finished the cake, he blurted out, "Ele—"

"It's been a great evening, but it's getting late." She got up to put her jacket on. "I'm sorry, what were you going to say?"

"I ... was going to say the same thing." He sighed. "I hate to see it end, though. But we should get going since we both have busy days tomorrow."

The night air was humid as they walked toward his car. Elena's hair shimmered under the soft glow of the streetlight. Overcome with longing for her, he caressed her hair. She turned toward him with a surprised look. Wrapping his strong arms around her, he pulled her close to his chest. He lowered his head to kiss her, but she pushed him away.

"No, Nikola!" Her voice was harsh. "Don't ruin our friendship. I'm not one of those women who cling to you."

She dashed away toward his car.

"Katherine—I mean, Elena, wait. I'm sorry."

Old Rivals

April 17

A BLUSTERY WIND drove menacing clouds across the re-splendent blue sky, blocking the sun's zealous rays. The Anemoi battled for possession of the land, Boreas blasting his icy winter breath, and Zephryos countering with a gentle spring breeze.

Sitting under the old walnut tree by the cheshma, Carina shivered, not from the chill in the air, but with desire for more of Stefan's kisses and the touch of his hands. Ever since she'd given him the martenitsa three weeks earlier, she couldn't stop thinking about him or dreaming of hearing his voice again. She held the embroidered, white cotton towel close to her face, inhaling the musky scent of his body, a trace of which still lingered. Her desire turned to shame, and she threw the towel on the ground.

How can I think such thoughts? Dushan is my love. But when she touched Stefan on the beach, hadn't Dushan called out to her?

Carina picked up the towel, once again caressing her face with it. What if she was wrong? Stefan's kiss was tender and sweet, but it wasn't Dushan's. And his spirit was soft and gentle, so different from Dushan's raw, wild one.

She vaulted up. With downcast eyes, she paced the grove, twisting the cloth in her hands. Her heart pounded and her body tingled, remembering exhilarating times spent here with Dushan. "Stefan *has* to be the one who will restore him to me. I need to hold my beloved again."

Morena entered the grove. "What troubles you that you speak to yourself?"

Rushing over, Carina wrapped her arms around her sister. Her voice quivered. "He still cannot remember me or who he is, even though I have used my gift to awaken Dushan's memories. I dare not enter his dreams too often for fear he'll go mad. What can I do?"

Morena took Carina's hand. She led her to the cheshma wall, sitting there with her. "You could do as I do. If you want him, use your power to force him to love you. He'll become a prisoner of your desires."

"No. I don't want an enslaved mortal." Carina stood to leave, but twirled around. "If I use my power to enchant him, I'd lose Dushan forever. My power would drain Stefan's energy, and he would die of a broken heart."

ENVISIONING HISTORY AND legends colliding with the elements, Stefan brought them to life on canvas and wood. Soldiers metamorphosed into wild horses. Beautiful mystical nymphs enchanted men, disappeared in whirlwinds, and turned into falcons. Wild, raging seas, like galloping horses, tore along the rocky shore.

He cured himself of his fanciful dreams and crazy thoughts by expressing himself through his art. Shaking his head, he chuckled. Or perhaps the bewitching brew truly appeased the demons of the night. More likely, he'd finally acclimated to his new surroundings and lifestyle.

After setting aside his latest painting, he put the finishing touches on the carved door ready for him to deliver to Varna. He scowled. Why had he let Nikola coerce him into another adventure? A boat ride this time, at least. No cliffs to fall down.

He called Sonia to put pleasant thoughts into his mind. The phone rang several times. He was ready to end the call and dial her grandparents' number when she picked up.

"Daddy!" Sonia squealed. "Pépé was pushing me on a swing, and my phone tickled me. I begged him to stop so I could talk with you."

"Hello, sweetheart." He went out to the porch and sat on the swing. "Did I tell you about the witch who lives in Emona?"

"A witch? Nooo." She took a sharp intake of breath. "Did she hurt you like the dragon?"

"No. She's a good witch. She gave me a magic potion to protect me from the dragon." He then whispered, "She even has a love potion."

She giggled and whispered back, "Maybe she can give some to the samodiva. I want her to fall in love with you."

He stopped swinging and sat straight. "You do? Why?"

"I don't want her to enchant you," she whimpered.

Stefan sighed. *She already has.* "She won't, sweetheart. She follows me on a black stallion so she can protect me."

"She ... she won't make you forget me?"

"Never!" His chest tightened. "No one will ever make me forget you."

AT THE MARINA, Stefan stared at the vessel the man told him belonged to Nikola. It wasn't the kind of *boat* he'd expected. The yacht was at least forty feet long. He ran the length of the pier and climbed aboard. An hour late, he anticipated Nikola's explosion.

"Stefan!" Nikola called out.

He cringed, waiting for the first barbed retort. "Sorry I'm late. I—"

"Welcome aboard, my friend." Nikola, bottle in hand, swayed as he walked forward and wrapped his arm around Stefan's shoulder. "Have some champagne." Pouring the last of it into a second glass, he slurred. "Ah, this bottle's empty. Let me get another."

Stefan put his hand out. "No, I'm fine. I don't want anything. Thank you."

Nikola pressed the glass into his hand. "Aw, c'mon. Have a drink with your old pal. Let's celebrate success. May we each get what we deserve."

Not wanting to start an argument, he took a sip.

Nikola watched, then swung his arm around and winked. "Ain't she a beauty?"

"Aye, captain. She is that." He relaxed his taut muscles and took another sip. Maybe this get-together wouldn't be so bad after all.

"She's my pride and joy." Nikola got up. "We are on our way to a wonderful day." He laughed and looked at Stefan. "Did you hear my rhyme?"

"Quite poetic." He looked down the pier. "When are the others arriving?"

"Today's party is for me and you." Nikola headed toward the controls. "Look around. Perfect weather. Gentle wind. Quiet sea. Now if you'll unhook the mooring rope, I'll start the engine, and we'll set sail."

"Do you think that's wise ... in your condition?"

"What? This?' Nikola held up the empty bottle. "A little alcohol won't hurt. Look out there. No traffic. No lines. I can sail this baby anywhere, any time. Just like my driving. You remember how crazy we drove in college, and nothing bad ever happened."

"We did have some fun adventures." He waved his hand. "Aye, aye, captain. Start 'er up."

Nikola turned the key and the engine roared to life. Steering the wheel and flipping a few switches, he maneuvered the vessel in expert fashion toward the open sea. He pressed more buttons, and the white sails rose, unfurling like a bird gliding on the currents of the wind. As the boat sliced its way through the gentle waves, it left a wake of white foam. Beneath the surface of the emerald sea, rocks and fish were clearly visible.

He fingered the ring with Thracian writing. "Do you know anyone in Varna, perhaps someone at a museum or university, who specializes in ancient languages?"

"Actually, I do. Lada. A friend of a friend." He glanced at Stefan and raised his eyebrows. "Why do you ask?"

"I ... there's some writing on a cheshma near my house. I was curious what it said."

"Remind me when we get back. I'll give you her number." Nikola returned his attention to the controls. "You should get out more and meet my clients, so they know who's working on their orders."

"I'm not really outgoing." Stefan gazed down at the churning water. "I moved to Emona to live a quiet country life."

"It would also benefit your career to meet people in the creative community. I have social gatherings often. I'll invite you to the next one."

"I don't—"

"The islands are just ahead." Nikola pointed them out.

The small dots on the horizon loomed closer more quickly than Stefan would have thought possible. In a short time, they reached the shore. Nikola made his way around the rocks, cut the engine, and released the anchor.

"The boat's secure. I'll let down the dinghy, and we can head to the shore to explore the island. Or ... here's a thought." Nikola grinned. "Let's have a triathlon, like in old times. Minus the bike ride, of course. We can swim to the island, run around it, and then swim back to the boat."

"Sure. I'm up to the challenge." Stefan finished his drink and leaned over the side of the vessel, but swung around. "Are you okay to swim after you've been drinking so much?"

"Never better." Nikola pranced around the deck without a hint of a stagger.

"What do you do with a boat that's under the weather?" Stefan removed his shirt and shoes.

Nikola groaned. "You still tell those stupid jokes?"

"Take it to the doc." Stefan laughed.

"That's bad." Nikola removed his shoes. "Now, show me you still have what it takes to compete. Unless you're afraid I'll show you up."

"I'll lend you a hand when I'm back first." Stefan jumped into the cold embrace of the water. A second splash followed.

The two swam toward the shore side by side, until Stefan pulled ahead. Soon, his stomach cramped and his vision blurred. "Nikola!" He looked around, but couldn't see him among the rocks.

He flailed in the waves, but his head kept dipping below the surface.

I can't hold on much longer.

Another cramp tightened his stomach. He bent his body, and the waves covered him. The pull of the sea drew him into its murky depths. Blond hair floated in the water above him, then below him.

I'm hallucinating.

Something pressed against his stomach, and a greenish glow illuminated the water. He rose toward the surface as if someone was pushing him. The water became clearer, and soon he could gulp air. He looked around, but no one else was nearby. The current had brought him close enough to shore that his feet touched sand. Nikola sat against a boulder, staring at him as he staggered to dry land.

"What happened to you? I've been around the island already." Nikola tapped him on the shoulder. "Out of shape, huh, old man?"

Stefan stared at him. "Once again, I almost died on an *adventure* with you."

"Don't be so melodramatic." Nikola scoffed. "It's wasn't *that* far to shore. If you're so bad off, I'll get the dinghy. You don't have to swim back."

"I got cramps and couldn't keep my head above water."

"And you worried about me drinking." Nikola laughed. "I guess you can't do that like you used to, either."

Stefan shook his head. He stood and stretched. Glancing toward the yacht, he gasped at what was emblazoned across the hull. He turned toward Nikola and said one word. "Katherine?"

"Well, she *was* once my best girl." He stared back with narrowed eyes. "Shall we head back?"

Best girl? What was he talking about? Katherine had told him she dated Nikola only a short time, and that was before Stefan had met either of them. It wasn't as if he had stolen her from Nikola.

He's lost his mind. He stared between Nikola and the vessel. "You first."

"Kak kak kak" sounded above him. On the branch of a dead tree a bird sat watching him and Nikola.

The white falcon ... again? Why is that bird always around when unexplainable things happen?

Among the Shadows

April 17

BACK IN THE safety of Emona, away from Nikola and his bizarre behavior, Stefan strolled along the shore, trying to figure out what had happened in his old friend's life that had put the look of contempt and hatred in his eyes. Was Nikola's obsession with Katherine the reason behind all the jabs he'd been throwing? It had been nine years since he had last seen her. Nikola had been the best man at their wedding. His toast at the reception had wished them love and happiness together. Surely any feelings he had for her would have, *should* have, become fond memories by now.

Frowning, he recalled his brief thought that Nikola might have been responsible for the cramps that almost made him drown. Was something in the champagne? No. That couldn't be possible. Nikola had been drinking from the same bottle, hadn't he? He might be holding a grudge, but he certainly didn't hate enough to kill. Right?

Better not tempt fate. He wouldn't go on any more adventures with Nikola.

A movement by the boulders set Stefan's heart racing, and thoughts of Nikola vanished. *Kalyna?* He hadn't seen her for three weeks. Even his dreams had stopped. He raced over to where the person had disappeared. Hadn't she said a path behind the boulders led to her friend's house?

He searched for footprints or disturbed seaweed along the edge of the forest. Instead of traces that anyone had passed by recently, he discovered a trail. Hiking along it, he ended up at the ruined church. Someone darted around the corner of the building. He hurried along the gate, but nobody was there.

Returning to the timeworn gate, he ran his fingers over the inscription on the brass patinated plate—Saint Nicholas the Wonderworker. How often had the church been destroyed and rebuilt? How many people had it housed during disasters and wars? How many weddings and christenings had been performed there?

His and Katherine's wedding had been in an old church, although not this ancient. Standing next to the pastor that day, Stefan fidgeted with the ring. His shirt and tie, tight around his neck, were uncomfortable, making him sweat. Everyone was looking at him. He concentrated on only one person. His mother, smiling at him. As soon as the organist began the wedding march and Katherine walked in on her father's arm, Stefan forgot his discomfort.

All eyes, including his, saw only Katherine. The light shining through the stained glass angels and saints enhanced her beautiful face with a rosy glow. She held a bouquet of pink and white roses, and looked like a perfect lily in her white silk gown. It reminded him of a verse from the Song of Solomon she loved to quote: "I am the rose of Sharon, and the lily of the valleys." Putting the ring on her finger had been one of the happiest moments of—

"It's quite amazing."

Stefan jumped and turned around. "Maria, hello." He took a deep breath, relinquishing his memory.

"Our church has been here for centuries. It's dedicated to sailors and fishermen because St. Nicholas, our patron saint, is their protector."

"It's a shame it's in such bad condition."

Layers of the cement had chipped and cracked in many places, revealing the red brick underneath. The four columns supporting three archways in the front and one on each side of the open area appeared sturdy enough. It wasn't likely they would collapse on anyone standing by the entrance.

"We received word today that the Council for Cultural Events in Varna has set aside money to restore the church." She handed him a paper and pointed to a paragraph. "They've been telling us this for twenty years. It's been a long, emotional road for us, but now thanks to the miracle of a donation, it's finally going to happen."

"I can't read Bulgarian." Smiling, he handed her back the paper.

"Sorry, dear." She patted his arm. "You're like an old friend. I forgot."

"Do you know who made the donation?"

"No, it was anonymous, but everyone in Emona is thrilled." A wide grin spread across her face. "I was heading inside now to take pictures to send to them. Would you like to join me?"

"Yes. I'd especially like to see any artwork."

She turned the key in the rusty lock.

"I stopped here a couple of days after I moved to Emona." Stefan looked around the yard. "Someone left lit candles and flowers outside a window. A person disappeared around the church again today."

"It must be Nona. She's always leaving her gifts. She's a strange creature, poor girl."

"Who's—?"

Maria grunted as she pushed against the gate. "It's heavy, and the hinges are covered with rust."

"Here, let me try." He shoved the gate with his shoulder until it squeaked open.

"Thank you, dear." She walked through.

"How could Nona get in if the gate was locked?"

"That girl manages somehow."

Maria looked at the dome where round, glassless windows had been carved out of stone in the shape of a ship's rudder. "Would you like to hear a story about Saint Nicholas?"

"Certainly. I love the stories people here tell."

They had reached the end of the short walkway, but remained outside, under the arches.

"Once when he was sailing to the burial place of Christ, a fierce storm developed and lightning hit the boat. It killed one of the sailors and blasted a hole in the hull." She made the sign of the cross. "Water poured in. Sailors ran around trying to plug it with anything they could find. Passengers prayed, thinking they were all going to die. Saint Nicholas got on his knees and raised his hands toward heaven. He called fish out of the sea to fill the hole. Then, he performed another miracle by bringing the sailor back to life."

"I've heard a lot of stories about the miracles saints have performed, but not that one." A few weeks ago, when he first came to Emona, he might have scoffed at her story. After all the strange happenings, he was less skeptical.

"Our Sea is secretive. You never know when She'll be angry." Maria gazed out at the water as if deep in memories of the past. "It's called the Black Sea because it's been a place of death. Sailors and fishermen caught in a violent storm often died because they couldn't swim to shore when their boats sank." Her eyes became misty. "My husband was one of them." She brought her hand up close to her face. With the fingers of her other hand, she traced a thin scar running the length of her palm. "I got this the day I learned he had disappeared. I fainted and cut my hand on a glass I dropped."

Stefan reached out to comfort her, rubbing her shoulder.

"But enough of that. Let's go look inside."

The massive wooden door creaked as he pushed against it. A few startled doves took flight and filled the air with dust. Maria followed him through. Inside a damp, musty odor mingled with the smell of wax.

She proceeded to the front, where she kneeled at the wooden altar, made the sign of the cross, and bowed her head. Not to intrude while she worshiped, he made his way around the church, his feet crunching bits of plaster that had crumbled from the walls.

Sparkling sunlight streamed through the ruined rafters and danced along the painted walls, revealing the building's massive devastation. A few of the beams were in danger of collapsing. He trailed his fingers along the panels of a wooden screen in front of the altar while he waited for Maria.

"A fire consumed so many things in the church several years ago." Her voice tearful, she stood and joined him. "All we could save was the altar and this iconostasis, although its doors were destroyed."

Stefan touched the carved frame with reverence. "The workmanship is exquisite, and the wood—it looks like walnut—is so smooth. I'm amazed it hasn't lost its natural color. It's unfortunate the paint on the panels has faded."

Maria bent over the image of a bearded man who wore a robe and a priest's shawl embellished with red crosses. A saintly yellow halo surrounded his head. He raised one hand in benediction and carried a Bible in the other.

"Is that St. Nicholas?"

"Yes." She looked at Stefan with pleading eyes, tears brimming on the edge of her lids. "Part of the restoration includes a contest to restore the iconostasis. With your skills as a painter and carver, you should enter, dear."

"To restore the iconostasis?" He raised his eyebrows. "That would certainly be challenging." After he thought for a moment, he smiled. "It would be an honor to be chosen to do the restoration. I'll come over later so you can tell me more."

Her tears now flowed like a river. She squeezed him in a big bear hug. "Blessed Saint Luke and Saint Joseph. I knew you were sent to us for a reason."

She released him, wiped her eyes on her apron, then looked up toward the dome. She closed her eyes, and her mouth moved in silent prayer.

Maria walked around the church, taking pictures of the destruction, then returned to Stefan's side. "That's all there is to see, dear. I would take you upstairs to the choir gallery and tower, but it's no longer safe. The four bells up there are quite old. The newest one dates back to 1804."

They started toward the front door to leave. Footsteps echoed near the altar. Stefan turned to look. A woman dressed in black stared at him from behind the iconostasis. Her eyes and mouth opened wide in alarm, and she ran out a side door.

He rushed through it after her. "Wait. I only want to talk with you."

Her long dress flapped in the wind as she ran away.

Maria came out of the church. "Stefan, stop!"

He hesitated. It was long enough for the woman in black to disappear down a path. Shaking his head, he walked back toward Maria.

"Don't mind her. That's Nona."

"I keep seeing someone around. I want to know if it's her stalking me."

"We call her 'The Black Shadow' because she follows everyone around, and then hides." She leaned in closer and whispered, "She's a little crazy. It won't do you any good to go after her."

"I'd like to speak with her anyway."

"She hasn't spoken since childhood. It's a strange and sad story." She took hold of his arm as they walked down the street. "She was a normal child before she disappeared twenty years ago."

"She disappeared?" He thought how terrified he and Katherine would have been if Sonia had ever disappeared, wondering if she was lost, hurt, or worse. "What happened?"

Maria's eyes glazed over with sadness. "She went to the Old Beach after school with a group of children to play hide and seek around the rocks and pick nuts from the trees. The other children ran back to the village, crying for help, saying she had disappeared. Many people went looking for her."

"Where did they find her? How long was she lost?"

She sighed. "We searched for more than a week without finding a trace of her. Everyone assumed the worst. But then one night, Todor discovered her at the door of the church. She was dressed in a white robe."

"Here, at the church? In a white robe? All alone?" Stefan stopped and looked back at the building, trying to picture the scene—a young child standing there at night, frightened and alone. Whatever had happened must have scarred her for life. No wonder she always ran away from people. "Do you know who brought her there dressed like that?"

"No, nobody knows. Ever since then, she hasn't spoken a word, and she started hiding from people." She hesitated and leaned in closer. "And people have been afraid to go to the Old Beach since then, as well."

Stefan raised his eyebrows. For the second time, someone mentioned fear and the Old Beach in the same breath. "The other day, Todor said he feared what some samodivi who live in a cave near the Old Beach could do to him. They're not real, so what would scare him?"

"Samodivi are real to us." Maria spoke in a hushed tone. "They protect our woodlands, mountains, and waters. They have power to control the weather, the sea, and animals." She looked around. "They can also enchant men to fall in love with them, and will drain their life. Or, if they prefer, they can make people go insane."

Shaking his head, he smiled at her with mischief. "Ah, to be enchanted by a beautiful woman. I can think of no worse punishment in life."

She stopped and looked around. "Let's go back. I don't like walking around here at night."

"You're right. I'll walk with you. Thank you for warning me about the samodivi." He grinned, but then a movement caught his eye, and he looked back.

"What is it?" Maria quivered. Her fingers dug into his arm, and her eyes flew open wide.

"I thought something white disappeared behind one of the trees." He started toward it.

"No. Don't go. Let's hurry back." She grabbed his arm.

"What are you afraid of? A samodiva?" He chuckled. "Don't they enchant only men?" He looked toward the trees again. "It's probably only Nona."

"Let's hurry. I'm expecting a small group of tourists from Italy. They'll be staying for a few days."

She dragged him along the path, her grip on his arm tight. Stefan had to stretch his legs to keep up with her. He turned to look once more when another flash of white appeared by a tree. Maria's fear had rubbed off on him. He had an uneasy feeling someone was watching him, with eyes penetrating into his soul.

Local Legends

April 24

"*THE PROTECTRESSES ARE here.*" The trees whispered their message, sending it gliding from limb to limb into the depths of the forest. Rustling their leaves, they welcomed Carina and Morena as the samodivi ran through the forest, swinging baskets laden with flowers, berries, and herbs. Finally, out of breath, the two sisters dropped to the ground and rested near the edge of the cliff.

Carina rested her chin in her hands. "Please play your *outi* for me to nourish my restless spirit. I've watched and guarded Stefan, waiting for a sign of his remembrance, but I see not, feel not Dushan in him any longer."

Withdrawing the instrument slung across her back, Morena cradled it in her arms. She leaned her head against a tree. Her nimble fingers caressed the strings, which responded with rich, mellow notes, as harmonious as the husky tune she hummed. She leaned forward to tighten a key. Her auburn hair cascaded over her shoulders, blending in with the woodsy hues of the instrument. Brushing the curls behind her, she twisted them into a knot.

Carina closed her eyes to listen with her heart to the tale of love and sorrow the *outi* cried out with each stroke of the strings. Morena poured forth her soul, the notes of her song fluttering above them like butterflies awakened from a deep sleep. The music soothed the ache etched deep within Carina's soul. The comforting embrace of Dushan's arms surrounded her waist. In her mind, they were galloping horses through the waves, the wind whistling a wild, unbridled melody. Everlasting love surrounded them.

The strings released their last mournful cry. It was then Dushan's warm breath whispered in Carina's ears like a gentle breeze, *"You know where to find me, my love."*

Her eyes flew open. She scrambled to her feet, looking around, hoping to catch a glimpse of the one she longed to embrace. No one was there except her sister. "Morena, your music has healed me. Dushan came to me through the passion of your song. I must go to him. I'm certain my beloved awaits me in my special place."

Morena reached out and grasped her sister's hand. "Wait. The time to meet him has not yet arrived. Sit with me awhile."

Trusting Morena's insight, she lay on the soft moss.

Morena brushed fingers along Carina's cheeks. "Your rosy countenance conveys more than the kisses of the breeze. Love blossoms on you like flowers welcoming the caress of the morning sun."

Closing her eyes, Carina crossed her arms over her chest. "Joy courses through my veins. Soon, our souls will be as one as the shaman foretold."

"I'm ecstatic for you, but continue to guide the mortal on his journey. He must cleanse his heart of pain before Dushan can awaken."

"What have you seen of his safety? I trust not the mortal he calls friend."

Before Morena could respond, a groan rose from below the cliff. Abandoning their baskets, the sisters rushed to look over the edge. A deer lay immobile, trapped between sharp rocks in the gorge.

Unable to climb down the sheer cliff, Carina spun around like a whirlwind, changing into a white falcon. She flew to the base and reverted to her samodiva form. Speaking soothing words, she moved her hand closer to the deer until it calmed and allowed her touch. Its eyes still stared at her in fright. She moved her other hand slowly, guiding it toward the animal's broken leg, where the bone poked through the flesh. The ground soaked up the blood like a sacrifice.

The deer looked beyond her and struggled to rise, its sides heaving. Carina turned around in time to see a white wolf disappear amidst twirling debris. Morena joined her sister, kneeling by the animal.

Carina's hand hovered above the wound. She closed her eyes and moved her hand in a circular motion while she spoke.

"Oh, Great Goddess of the Moon and Fate, protectress of the forests, waters, and mountains, bestow upon me your healing powers to remove the pain from this innocent being and restore its strength."

She opened her eyes. A green glow surrounded her and the deer. The animal's struggle subsided as the blood ceased to flow. The broken bone knit together, and new flesh covered the wound. Power still flowing through her, Carina set the weak animal on its feet in the cramped gully. It lowered its head, then leaped away, disappearing into the blackness of the forest.

The sisters smiled at each other. Fortune allowed them to reach the animal in time. They changed shape again and returned to the top of the ridge. Sticks crunched in the forest as a beast slunk away.

Morena shouted a deafening scream, "The Evil One is here. He has caused this unholy act against the innocent."

She sprinted after the fleeing wolf.

STEFAN RENDEZVOUSED WITH the morning sun, watching the rosy blush of its ascent. It caressed the sea with its long, slender fingers of light, stirring the waters with various hues of red, gold, and blue, bright sparkles dancing on the waves. The misty haze made the morning more enchanting and mysterious where the sun's rays settled on the trees and glided over the branches.

He sat on the porch swing, thinking about the trip to the island. Even after a week of brooding, he couldn't reconcile the fact that Nikola had christened his boat "Katherine." He shook his head. The morning was too magical to think about Nikola. He went inside to grab his camera. Timing was crucial to capture the beauty of the moment.

He took photos of the sunrise, then rushed toward the Samodivi Cheshma, where he captured more of the enchantment. Where else? Perhaps the hill where the wild horses often grazed. He hiked up the path. The white, smooth stones lining the way flowed down like a river. In the forest, shadows danced around the sunbeams that trailed down the tree limbs.

Near the crest of the hill, Stefan crept in the direction of the neighing horses, his camera ready to capture their majestic movements. The black stallion and a younger horse pranced next to each other. Their noses touched, and they both reared and nickered. For the briefest of seconds, their necks entwined in what looked like an embrace. They scuffled around a little. Then, to his surprise, a smaller black horse, followed by a colt, romped over. The stallion encircled them, maneuvering himself between them and the other horse while he edged them away.

It must be the mare he had found in the trap. Her leg had healed, and she once again ran with the herd. He named her Emona and her colt Crest. To him she symbolized this place—wild, strong, and free.

A flash of light whizzed past. In the next instant, a woman wearing a white hooded cloak strolled among the horses. Had she actually been there all along, perhaps hidden behind a horse?

A samodiva, no doubt. Stefan laughed nervously, his heart beating faster as he surveyed the forest.

He took a photo, fascinated when the horses bowed their heads to her. Tree branches blocked his view, so he stepped to the side to get a better shot. Dry branches cracked beneath his feet.

The horses snorted, their breath mixing with the misty air. They pranced around the woman, hiding her from his sight. She leaped onto the black stallion, and the two disappeared into the forest. The mare remained and looked toward Stefan, then shook her head and trotted away.

Before stepping into the meadow, he scanned the forest again. No one was around. He made his way to the spot where the horses had congregated around the woman. The moss showed the imprint of their hoofs. Something white lay among a circle of stones. He bent down to pick up a star-shaped flower covered with white felt hairs, six small yellow flower heads in the center. Edelweiss. He turned it around.

So perfect.

Stefan glanced in the direction the woman had fled. Who was she? He scrolled through the photos on his camera. When he reached the one he searched for, he scowled. Glare from the sun left a white streak right where she had been standing.

How had she been able to ride one of the wild horses? That couldn't have been Nona, could it? Each time he'd seen her, she'd been wearing black, not white.

Kalyna? No. She wouldn't have run away from him. Why would she even be here? She had been away for almost a month. He didn't know if or when she'd return. She was probably at home in ... Had she even told him where she lived? She said she wrote for a magazine, but which one? How could he find her? No one in the village seemed to know who she was. He had so many things he wanted to ask her. Did she know anything about the fountain and its legend? Was she an ancestor of the woman it was dedicated to?

He wouldn't learn anything else here. He headed back to the village.

Perhaps he could get some good pictures of the iconostasis for his contest proposal. The church meant so much to the villagers. It would be an honor to be part of its revival and in the process make his old dream come true—be involved in a church restoration. All the major newspapers carried the story, so competition would be fierce. Not only artists expressed interest, but also businessmen from as far away as Varna had contributed materials and funds in exchange for advertising.

STEFAN UNLOCKED THE church gate with the key Maria had given him. After he took photos of the iconostasis from several angles, he walked around the building. In a corner he discovered several wooden pillars he could use to replace the doors in order to keep the timeworn look of the iconostasis. He took a few more photos before leaving the church. As he was locking the gate, Nona hurried down an overgrown path. He set out after her, determined to talk with her.

The path ended at the beach. Nona had disappeared, but Peter sat on an old tree trunk, drinking from a bottle of water. His goats rested in the shade of a tree.

"Hello, Stefan." Peter waved to him, but remained seated. "What brings you to the Old Beach?"

"Hi, Peter." He waved back, but searched around the rocks for Nona, scanning the beach in frustration.

"What are you looking for?"

He looked around a moment longer, then headed toward Peter. "I followed Nona here, but she disappeared. She's as fast as a hound."

"Nona's crazy. She always runs away when she sees anyone." Peter nodded toward the large boulders. "She brings flowers, honey, and sweet breads to the beach every day and sits by the rocks for hours watching the sea.

People believe the guardians of the cave saved her life on the Old Beach."

"The guardians of the cave?" He raised his eyebrows. Coming closer, he sat next to Peter. "You mean the samodivi, the creatures everyone is afraid of?"

"Yes, the ones the cheshma behind your house is dedicated to."

"Do you know where their cave is supposed to be?"

"I've heard the entrance is somewhere around this beach, but I don't know for sure. I've searched for years, but I don't think most humans can see the entrance. Only those born on Christmas Eve, or the Saturday before Easter."

"I guess I'm out of luck, then. My birthday's in the summer." Stefan laughed. "Why were you looking for it? Did you want to find the lost Thracian treasure?"

"Treasure? No. I was looking for someone ..." Peter took a drink of water and stretched out his legs. "What a beautiful day. It's hot for this time of the year. Do you want some water? It's fresh from the Samodivi Cheshma."

"No, thank you." Stefan's shoulders slumped forward. "Will you tell me more about the samodivi?"

"Sure. I'll tell you what my grandmother told me." Peter got up. "Let's walk down the beach, so I can stretch my legs." He looked toward the cliffs. "The samodivi are beautiful women with light blond hair, pale blue eyes, and skin like marble. They dress in long white robes made from moonbeams."

"Moonbeams?" Stefan raised his eyebrows.

"Yes." Peter looked at him with a serious expression. "In the winter, they live in a place called Zmeykovo, which is located at the edge of the world. So you won't see them until spring arrives. Even while they're here, they come out only at night."

So I guess the woman in the field wasn't a samodiva. This is broad daylight.

"If a man steals a samodiva's clothing while she's bathing, she'll lose her power and become his slave."

"It must be difficult to pick up something made of moonbeams." Stefan shook his head. "Do you really believe this?"

"I'm telling you what I've been told." Peter stopped. "Do you want me to continue?"

"Yes, sorry."

"After a samodiva gives birth to the child of the man who enslaved her, she's no longer controlled by him." He started walking again. "They like to sing and dance in the forest. Magic flowers bloom where they walk."

Flowers? Stefan ran his finger over the one he still held.

"What's that?" Peter asked.

"Edelweiss." He held his palm out toward Peter. "I found it on the hill above the cheshma."

A brief smile broke Peter's expression. "Maybe a samodiva left it as a sign for you."

Stefan stopped running his fingers around the flower's petals. "A sign about what?"

He shrugged. "My grandmother told me many stories about how samodivi help people."

"I'd like to hear one."

"When I was a boy, many people visited the Samodivi Cheshma." Peter looked out to the sea. "One Easter a sick boy slept there because it made him happy and gave him energy. The next morning his parents were excited. The boy had gotten better, they said, because he drank water from the cheshma. Since then, people have made it a special holy day to the samodivi. Sick people often sleep there, holding the samodivi's flowers, believing the samodivi can cure them."

"Speaking about cures." Stefan turned his head to face Peter. "A few weeks ago, I met an elderly woman called Sultana, who brought me to her cottage in the woods. She certainly has strange remedies and uncanny knowledge. Do you know her?"

Peter glanced at Stefan with a somber look. "She's a *znahar*, a woman who heals with herbs. Some people are afraid of her and call her a witch, but she's never done any harm to anyone."

"Has she always been so skilled in healing?"

"Ever since I can remember, yes. When people don't understand things, they call them bad. Miracles still happen, but you need to believe deep in your heart before you can experience them."

Peter's brisk walk slowed. They stopped, and Stefan gazed out at the endlessness of the sea. The quiet water gleamed with blue and green hues. Gentle waves broke against the shore, washing the fine sand back and forth. The motion created ripples along the beach. Small pools formed before the water seeped down to return to its source, leaving rings of foam. A few seagulls squawked around the rocks, while others glided overhead in search of fish.

Finally Peter headed back in the direction they had started.

"What else do you know about the samodivi?" Stefan asked.

"Grandma told me that *aqua vitae*, the water of life, flows through the cave. If you drink it, you become immortal. Several years ago, a professor of archaeology, Professor Krum. That was his name." Peter turned to Stefan. "He's the one who lived in your house. He was looking for a tomb with hidden treasure at the Old Fortress. I think he also wanted to find the cave."

"Did he ever find anything?"

They had reached the grazing goats. Peter walked among them, talking to them, ensuring all was well, then sat on a log. "One night, Krum appeared at the pub drunk, boasting he had discovered the Thracian treasure. He said he had even found a way to the cave."

Stefan sat next to Peter. "Did he say where?"

"No." Peter wiped his face and took a long drink from the bottle of water. "He said the treasure wasn't at the cave. We asked him if he had seen the samodivi, and he laughed like a crazy man."

The hot sun bore down on the log. Peter moved to a shadier location. "When the Professor left the pub, he forgot a small silver key shaped like edelweiss. I picked it up and went after him. He took it and whispered, 'This is her power, *heeerrrr* power.' Then he rushed off before I could ask him what he meant."

Peter sighed and his eyes misted over. His voice choked on his next few words. "The next day someone found his wife murdered in the studio, and Krum had disappeared."

Stefan gasped. "Sultana said the house was evil and a woman was killed there. I ... I wasn't sure I believed her. So this Krum killed his wife?"

"Everyone thinks he did before he jumped off the cliff down by the Old Beach. The lighthouse keeper, Esinesi, told us the Professor was on the rocks that night, close to the Old Fortress."

"Why didn't anyone tell me this about the house?"

"Because ... it's never been proven Krum did it. Why accuse him if it's not true." Peter stopped speaking, seeming unable to continue. He folded his hands, and sat with his eyes unblinking.

"Did anyone ever find him?"

Peter coughed to clear his throat. "The police searched for him for about a month. They closed the case about five or six years ago because they never found his body. After this incident, people stopped going to the Old Beach. They were afraid of the strange things happening here. I still come from time to time with the goats because the grass is green and there's good shade."

"I want to find the cave to show people there's nothing to be afraid of. Will you help me?"

Peter looked at him and shrugged. "I'm getting older every day, so I should have nothing more to fear. I'll help you find it if I can, but I've looked for years and found nothing."

"Great! Now I'm going to take some more pictures. It's gorgeous here."

"Don't be too long. It'll be dusk soon. You don't want to stay here after dark."

Stefan took off his shoes. Tying the laces together, he draped them over his shoulder. He hung his camera around his neck and strolled to the shoreline. The cool water encircled his bare feet.

Up on the ridge, the herd of wild horses stood like guards at their post. He pointed the camera toward them. While adjusting the settings, he almost missed the neighing of a horse and the thundering of hooves. He spun his head toward the sound. The black stallion, teeth bared and nostrils flaring, raced straight at him, its mane gusting around it.

Stefan fell into the waves as the stallion raced past him like a whirlwind. A spray of sand and salty water erupted against his face and body like a volcano as the animal's hooves tore deep into the shoreline. The horse stopped a short distance up the beach, prancing around. It snorted and shook its head in a frenzy, before galloping away.

Mist of a Kiss

April 25

A MENACING WIND, howling as savagely as the beasts that preyed in the forest, conceded supremacy to the woman's shriek that shattered the air. Clouds, making a hasty retreat, jostled each other as they journeyed past the second Spring Moon, sending shadows scurrying across the meadow for shelter. Even the distant stars dimmed their light, deigning to be eclipsed by the fullness of the greater orb.

Why had Dushan spoken loving word that he waited here, in her sacred place? She had rushed out amidst the horses, her protectors, when his presence embraced her, thinking he had begun his journey of remembrance.

Her anguish tore the night asunder again. Stefan came to the meadow only to take photos, not to reunite with her. Even so, her heart was overwhelmed with joy at his—*Stefan's*—presence. Fearing her emotion, and her deceit, she fled.

She performed a frenzied *kolo* dance around the meadow. While she whirled, she recanted sacred songs learned long ago, melody and lyrics avowed to heal her soul. After a long while, she dropped to the ground, drew her knees up close to her face, and rested her chin on them.

What drew Stefan here? To her sacred place. Surely he knew what it meant. His spirit—*Dushan's*—must have stirred.

When dawn's rosy glow crept over the horizon several hours later, a shadow lengthened across the meadow, but Carina's forlorn pose remained unchanged.

"Sister, why are you so wretched?" Morena stroked Carina's hair with soft caresses. "You sit in such misery. What trouble weighs on your heart?"

"I fear I am falling in love with Stefan. I find myself thinking about him often."

Morena sat beside Carina, holding her trembling hand. "Why does that worry you, if he is your beloved?"

"My soul is divided. I shouldn't love him until he remembers he's Dushan." Carina wiped away her tears.

"Fate will guide you along its chosen path. Don't fear; your love will remain true to Dushan." Morena rose and extended her hand for Carina to pull herself up. "Embrace your fortune and rejoice in his return."

Carina paced the field, her white robe gracing the red poppies with its gentle touch. "Yet another thing troubles me. I'm not sure I want to return to the other side of the moon. I don't know if I could live in their world." She stopped and folded her hands over her chest. "But I do so desire to see him again."

"Fortune favors your meeting with him tonight, I've seen—" Morena began.

"He clutches his past as fervently as he holds the blue-star, *my* ring, to his chest." Carina clenched her hands together. "But I feel the desire for me that burns in him."

Grasping Carina's shoulders, Morena forced her to stop. "Listen to me, sister!"

She ran her fingers through her hair and looked at Morena, barely seeing her.

Morena shook her gently, until Carina's eyes focused. "My Astro Calendar has foretold that the stars of destiny will be aligned tonight, with the moon between them. This is a favorable sign."

Bendis, their beloved goddess of Fortune, had given Morena the gift of gifts to see into the future, but not to change it. As the reader of the stars, Morena had a connection to both the Sun and the Moon. Carina couldn't comprehend how her sister understood the meaning of the symbols, or how she made her predictions, but she trusted her words.

Morena took Carina's hand and led her away. "I have a plan that will appeal to him. You shall meet him tonight."

STEFAN LISTENED TO Katherine's messages on his cell phone again. The pain that had tugged at his heart for so long loosened its hold. He was torn between Katherine and Kalyna. Not wanting to let go of the one he had loved for so long, but desiring to understand the other. Why did Kalyna have such a command over his emotions? He craved to share her most secret thoughts, and tell her his. He yearned to heal the sorrows of her soul, and have her mend his.

He pressed his lips together into a tight line as he called the one person he loved unconditionally.

"Sonia, sweetheart," he said, "did your grandparents tell you my surprise?"

"Nooo. What?"

"I'm coming to visit you in two weeks."

"Really?" She spoke with a rush of words. "I have to tell you about school, my friends, Pépé, Mémé—"

"Slow down." He laughed, her excitement rubbing off on him. "You'll have plenty of time to tell me everything. I'll be there for six weeks."

"Yeah!" Sonia clapped her hands. "Now tell me more about the fairy princess, pleeeease."

"I haven't seen the samodiva for a few weeks." He paused, Sonia's heartfelt *"Oh, that's sad"* expressing his own sentiments. "But she sends her helpers to keep an eye on me."

"Does she have a unicorn?"

"No, sweetheart, not a unicorn, a white falcon ... and a human helper. She dresses all in black and constantly watches me to tell the samodiva what I'm doing."

"That's silly," Sonia said. "Why doesn't she talk to you herself?"

"I think she ... doesn't want to fall in love with me if I'm not the person she's looking for."

They talked a while longer, Stefan making up more tales about the falcon and Nona to amuse Sonia. After they hung up, he completed more door panels to drop off in Varna. Despite Nikola's antagonism, he had kept Stefan busy with work. He was thankful he had managed to avoid Nikola every time he dropped off orders and picked up new ones.

The studio smelled of resin, so he opened the windows to air it out while he swept up the wood chips and sawdust coating the floor. Returning to the living room to put the broom back in the closet, he stopped. A yellow paper lay in front of the door. He stooped to pick up a small envelope embellished with an edelweiss monogram. A citrus scent drifted out when he tore it open. He read the words written in elegant handwriting.

Dear Stefan,

I'd be delighted if you'd join me at a cocktail party and art exhibit. Young artists present their work and collect funds for a joint international project. This would be a great opportunity for you to meet other artists.

Troy Gallery
Luben Karavelov Street, Varna
Saturday, April 25
7:00 PM

—Kalyna

Kalyna! His pulse raced with desire. And yet his mind and heart both resisted.

How can I start a relationship when I can't let go of Katherine?

Stefan looked at the invitation again; the art show opened tonight. Anticipation he hadn't known for years consumed him. Like a teenager going on his first date, he imagined the touch of her lips on his. The blue-star ring radiated heat, igniting his body with passion. Desire defied his reason, and his heart won the battle.

"COME IN. WELCOME to the gallery."

The comely woman greeting Stefan exemplified success. Her powerful dark eyes and professional smile displayed confidence, as well as congeniality. Adorning her shoulder-length brown hair was a bonnet-style hat. From a white leaf at the side, two blue-and-white ribbons travelled out in the form of a V, one trimming the rim, and the other running over the crown.

"Is this your first visit?" She handed him a brochure. "We have a great exhibition of talented new artists. Please enjoy yourself. You can find refreshments in the back."

Stefan gave her a suggestion of a smile and a short nod. A rush of new visitors made their way into the room. He stepped to the side, looking at the crowd.

The woman at the door turned toward him. "Are you waiting for someone?"

"Yes, for Kalyna. Do you know if she's arrived?"

"Kalyna?" She thought for a moment. "I haven't met her, but I'm sure you'll find her if you mingle."

Taking her words as dismissal, he wandered among the items on display. The aesthetic arrangement of paintings, sculptures, ceramics, and jewelry placed throughout the spacious gallery impressed him as much as the collection of objects themselves. He picked up a bronze patina figurine of a woman astride a galloping horse. With the wind blowing her hair around her shoulders, it reminded him of Kalyna—beautiful, blissful, and carefree.

"That's a Thracian girl attempting to escape from the soldiers about to ravish her." The woman who spoke was dressed in a colorful hippie dress. Thin white ribbons, entwined within the strands of her French braid, set off its red and brown highlights. She held out her hand. "Hi, I'm Angelina."

"I'm Stefan." He set the object down and shook her hand. "It's exquisite."

She smiled in appreciation. "This is my first piece of a series called 'Three Maidens.' It's based on a legend about three sisters who were attacked on the youngest sister's wedding day. Since then she's been searching for her lost love."

Stefan stared at her. "Thracian lovers? I've heard that tale. Can you tell—"

"That's a great piece and a wonderful love story," a soft, melodious voice said behind him. "She looks like a goddess. What do you think?"

Taking a deep breath, Stefan inhaled her intoxicating perfume, scented with a hint of citrus. He turned to gaze at Kalyna's radiant, smiling face, and then his eyes travelled over her simple white dress that emphasized her graceful shoulders and slender figure. "You look beautiful. Thank you for the invitation. I needed to get out of my studio and meet new people."

"I see you've already met Angelina, a talented artist and a good friend of mine."

He turned his head, but the woman was speaking with someone else.

"Her work tells a wonderful story about how pure love survives through the ages." Kalyna put her hand on his shoulder. "Excuse me for one moment while I congratulate her." She sauntered away with the grace of a wild feline, her blond hair swishing across her back with each lithe step.

After a few minutes, Kalyna kissed Angelina on both cheeks, and sashayed her way back to him. "Let's walk around the exhibit. Angelina told me about some wood-carvings. I'm eager to see them."

Putting his hand on the small of her back, he guided her around the crowded room. "Do you do any kind of artwork yourself?"

"No." She sighed. "Angelina's the talented one. I used to dabble in jewelry when I was younger, but now I'm merely involved in supporting the arts."

"Have you and Angelina known each other long?"

"Yes. It seems like forever. We grew up in the same village." She stopped at one exhibit and looked at the display of glassware. "What about you? Are you an artist?"

Stefan chuckled. "I'm trying to be. That's one reason I moved to Emona."

"Why do you think that's funny?" Kalyna reached for his hand. "You have the fingers of an artist. Long, slender, capable of expressing ardor. I knew someone long ago with hands like yours. He worked miracles on wood, gold, and bronze. I still can visualize a statue he created ..."

"A statue?" He pulled his hand away and put it on her shoulder. "Do you know anything about the statue on the cheshma in Emona? She ... she looks exactly like you."

"Me?" Kalyna opened her eyes wide. "I must have a common face then."

About to move his hand toward her face to run his fingers along her cheekbone, he stopped and put it back at his side. "No. It's far from common." He cleared his throat and pointed. "I think the woodcarving exhibit is over there."

"What kind of artwork do you do?"

"I do woodcarving, like the exhibit we're looking for." He placed his hand on her back again and walked toward the next exhibit. "I work for a ... friend, doing custom work."

"Tell me about it. What's it like to feel the texture of the wood beneath your fingers?" She turned her head to look at him, excitement flashing in her eyes.

He took a deep breath, her enthusiasm stirring desire within him, and looked away. "Each wood is different. You have to understand them before you undertake a project. Basswood, for example, is plain, but you can create intricate carvings with it. This is a good wood for beginners. On the other hand, rosewood is quite colorful with its fiery reds and purples and its dark veins, but it's a hard wood, and tends to dull chisels quickly. It's better suited for professionals."

Stefan stopped talking and laughed. "I'm sorry. I could go on and on about this. You must be bored."

"No. It's fascinating." Her face was flushed.

"Maybe you can visit my studio the next time you're in Emona, and I can show you how to carve with the different types of wood."

She smiled at him. "I'd like that. Do you do any other type of art?"

"My real passion is painting." He turned his head away, remembering the frenzy with which he had drawn several sketches of his mystery woman, only to crumple and burn them. "I've finally been able to do that again, since I moved here. I think ... you've inspired me."

"Me? Why do you say that?"

He stopped and took hold of her hands. "You'll think I'm crazy." He paused, but she said nothing. "You haunt my dreams ... in strange, wonderful ways."

She raised her eyebrows. "Really?"

He laughed, the tension broken. They reached the artist's work they'd been searching for. Kalyna pointed to a carving of three women dancing under a full moon shaped like a flower, its petals swaying to the rhythm of the nocturnal melody. "I'm amazed by his work. Look how he's able to express the soul of the wood."

"The soul of the wood." Stefan closed his eyes and grazed his fingers over the carving, drifting off to the magical land where the women twirled in ecstasy, life's essence eddying around them like the carved whorls. "I feel the same way about each piece I carve. I'm not the one deciding what to create; the wood reaches out to the center of my being."

He opened his eyes, still lost in the magic of the women's world, and glanced at Kalyna. His body jerked as if jolted by electricity. Passion flowed from her while she examined other carvings, caressing them with her fingertips as if they were fragile artifacts.

Before he had a chance to think, he placed his hand over hers. The ring beneath his shirt began to burn. He ignored it, his passion for Kalyna more scorching. She looked up, her eyes raging with an intense hunger he thought he'd never share with a woman. Katherine had shown only a mild interest in art. Granted, she had praised his creations, but she hadn't understood it with the ardor of an artist, not even before Sonia was born and family matters took precedence.

A longing to share his life with her took root inside him, and he let himself sink under its control. His desire for Kalyna became urgent, passionate. He led her away from the crowd. Standing behind a column, he pulled her close to him.

"When are you coming to Emona again?" His voice desperate with longing, he talked to avoid kissing her with wild abandon.

She responded by running her fingers down the chain around his neck. His flesh tingled as her hand brushed against his skin. She withdrew the ring, her eyes sparkling like the sapphire stone she released from its hiding place.

"What an exquisite ring." Her short breaths turned low and sultry, and her cheeks rosy. "Is it a wedding ring or a family heirloom?"

"No." He spoke more severely than he intended as he relieved her of her newfound treasure to restore it beneath his shirt. "I'm not married. It's a memory from my past." Why was he upset Kalyna had discovered the ring? Why didn't he want to mention Katherine?

She didn't seem to notice his behavior, or chose to ignore his reaction. Instead, she pressed herself closer to him, closed her eyes, and kissed him. It lasted only a brief moment, but chills radiated throughout his body.

He looked around the room, but saw only her. "Let's go somewhere else, just the two of us."

"Would you mind getting me a glass of champagne first? I'm thirsty."

She wasn't by the column when he returned with the drink. He searched every corner of the gallery, but she had disappeared. Again. Listless and lonely, he left the gallery to sit in his car. He ran his fingers through his hair. Katherine was gone, so he wasn't deceiving her. Even so, the guilty pleasure of Kalyna's kiss lingered on his lips.

The Girl Is Mine

April 26

THE FULL MOON shone through the trees on an unnaturally quiet night. Even the owl watching Stefan from a dead limb remained silent. Trying to dodge the bird's stare, he wandered aimlessly in the endless forest, but the creature rotated its head to keep him in view. A thick fog crept in, blocking him from the bird's watchful eyes, but then he lost track of the path to his house. He ducked under low branches, swaying in the breeze like monsters attempting to grab him. A tingling on his skin and a tightness inside his chest alerted him to something evil lurking nearby; he could hear it breathing.

The uncanny silence magnified the breaking twigs and growling behind him. He swung around. A pack of wolves slunk toward him, their bodies almost indistinguishable from the fog. A huge black one broke away from the pack and crept closer. Stefan backed away step by step, trying not to alarm the beast, but stumbled over a log, landing in soft moss with a thud. The wolf, malice radiating from its eyes, leapt onto him, its hot breath inches from his face, and its claws digging into his cheek.

Those eyes! He had seen them somewhere. Where? He shuddered with the truth. They were Nikola's eyes!

Without any warning, the pack retreated. The black wolf stole away behind a tree, still glaring at him. Out of the fog, the mare Emona appeared, carrying a blond woman clothed in white.

Pain paralyzed his body as he rose to see her face. "Kalyna!"

She faded into the fog.

STEFAN DROVE TO Nikola's house to attend a gathering he would have preferred to avoid, especially tonight, after his horrible nightmare. Why had the dreams started again? He was still drinking Sultana's Bewitching Chai. He laughed nervously. Was it his loathing to be around Nikola? Still uncertain what had happened between them, he wanted to avoid another confrontation about Katherine, especially at a public gathering. But then, he had decided he wouldn't be alone with Nikola again ... just in case.

Stop it! He isn't trying to harm you.

He rubbed his cheek. For the second time, he had woken up with a wound after a dream about wolves. He must have hit his face on the bedside table. Either that, or a magic dream wolf was trying to kill him. He chided himself.

That's crazy thinking. I've been telling Sonia too many fairy tales.

Not wanting to think about Nikola or the dream, he contemplated his mixed feelings about Kalyna. She made him feel alive and confused at the same time. Why couldn't he let go of Katherine? She would have wanted him to be happy again.

The car dipped into a rut, so he concentrated on driving on what he called "that god-awful treacherous road," the only way into Emona.

Maria laughed when he had called it that. "Ah, yes, the road. It's a bit destroyed, isn't it?" She leaned forward and whispered. "The government wants to repair it, but we refuse to let them. The road doesn't keep the tourists out. They come here to enjoy the privacy and beauty of the beaches. But it *does* keep out developers who want to build one resort after another. Elenite and Irakli have plenty of those already. They can leave Emona alone. It's beautiful and peaceful here, and we want to keep it that way."

Stefan chuckled at Maria's intense dislike of the government. He, too, preferred the derelict road to Emona's development. He slowed as he approached the curve in the road so he could gaze at the Irakli beach. A black wolf dashed in front of his car, and he slammed on the brakes. The car veered close to the edge of the cliff.

"Damn wolf." He looked around. Sweat poured down his face. A black animal, possibly a wolf, had crossed in front of his car in the same location the day he arrived in Emona.

Had the dream been a premonition?

"STEFAN, YOU MADE it." Nikola stepped back with a surprised look on his face when he opened the door to his penthouse. "You're so late. I thought you decided not to come after all."

"I considered it." He had accepted the invitation because Nikola convinced him he needed to establish contacts. "*Varna is the summer capital of Bulgaria, the hub of the creative community*," Nikola had told him.

He found the influential people from the city who filled the room stiff and formal. After talking with a few to be polite, he broke away to study Nikola's collection of silk tapestries and modern paintings lining one wall.

"Do you like it? What do you see?" A strong and assertive, but warm voice spoke behind him.

He turned around. The woman who had admitted him into the art exhibit the previous night was behind him. "I see the strength and freedom of wild horses running through a field. It's a powerful image."

"This is one of the first paintings Nikola bought from me. Since then, he's become one of my best clients." With a sweep of her hand, she took in all the paintings on the wall. "All of these have come from my gallery, in fact. I even helped Nikola set up the lighting so they can be displayed to their best effect."

He opened his mouth to respond, but Nikola appeared, speaking first. "This is my favorite piece." He curled his arm around the woman's waist. "Elena has good taste and knows how to find talented artists."

Frowning, she removed his arm and took a small step to the side. "Yes, I've been fortunate to discover a lot of emerging artists. My next exhibit is a young woman I discovered a few years ago. Her name is well-known all over Europe now."

At the other side of the room, someone called to Nikola. With pursed lips and narrowed eyes, he hesitated, but the woman continued shouting. Nikola took a step away. "Please excuse me. I need to check on one of my other guests. I'll be back in a moment."

When he hurried away, Elena held out her hand to Stefan. "As Nikola said, I'm Elena Veleva. I didn't get a chance to introduce myself before."

"Stefan Tarrant." He shook her hand. She had a strong, firm grip. "I was at the exhibit last night. So that was your gallery?"

"Yes. That exhibition was a good example of the new talent I've found." She flashed him a confident smile.

"How long have you known Nikola?" Stefan looked over his shoulder. Nikola glared back at him. What was he angry about now?

"He came to an annual art event at my gallery about four years ago. We found we have a lot in common besides an appreciation of art. We both like history, and this area abounds in ancient culture." Pausing for effect, Elena whispered, "Dracula even sailed from here on the *Demeter*."

"Be careful of him. He's an old scoundrel." Stefan laughed. "Nikola, I mean. Not Dracula. He always has an entourage of pretty girls and knows how to get what he wants."

"I've noticed." Elena looked where Nikola had gone, then back at Stefan. "How do you know him?"

"We attended the same art college for a while. When I started looking for employment, I happened to go to his shop. He hired me to do custom woodcarving orders."

"That's wonderful. You must be quite talented." She moved closer. "Nikola is particular about his workers. Do you do any carving on your own or only for Nikola's shop."

"I've been working on a few pieces and also some paintings. The village where I live is quite inspiring with its wild, beautiful beaches. The locals also tell fanciful tales. They give me great ideas." He motioned for her to follow him toward the bar. "Have you ever heard of samodivi?"

"Yes, they're from our folklore." Elena pursed her lips. "People in the villages actually believe they exist, especially in the more remote locations that don't have electricity. When they got power to their homes, they said the samodivi went away."

"I saw one," he said, his face serious, "and the village I live in has electricity. I even took a photo of her." Stefan reached into his pocket to retrieve his camera. "See, right there. That white blur."

She laughed along with him. "That looks more like one of the creatures that comes down with lightning. Their energy sources run around even after the storm is over."

"The people in Emona never told me about them."

"Emona? If you live there, you must know about the contest to restore the iconostasis."

"Yes, I've submitted my proposal to the Council for review." He lifted the liquor bottles at the bar, inspecting the labels. All expensive brands. "Would you like a drink?"

"Yes, white wine, please."

He poured one for each of them.

Elena took a sip. "I'd love to visit and see your art."

"Of course. When you have time, I'd be happy to show it to you."

While she smiled at him, her voice warmed. "I have time this weekend, so be prepared for a visitor."

"It looks as if the two of you didn't miss my company." Nikola moved close to Elena, despite the stern look she gave him. He darted a glaring look toward Stefan. "I see you've already captured Elena's heart."

Simultaneously, Stefan and Elena stepped farther away from each other. Elena's complexion darkened to a rosy color.

Stefan shrugged. What was Nikola talking about? He and Elena were only having a friendly conversation.

"Nikola." The word came out a dry rasp. Elena tried again. "Stefan says you went to school together."

"Yes, we were inseparable." Nikola grinned, and punched Stefan three times in the shoulder, a little harder than necessary for the gesture from their college days.

"Nikola!" Elena stared at him.

Stefan rubbed his arm. "What was that for?"

Nikola leaned closer and hissed in his ear. "She was mine!" Holding out a small silver pin with the initial *K*, he smirked and clutched it in his fist. He stalked away, leaving Elena and Stefan to shake their heads.

Stefan remembered the pin. Katherine had given it to Nikola on his eighteenth birthday. It wasn't an expensive gift, merely a token of their friendship. First the yacht, now the pin. Why was Nikola so obsessed with Katherine? It didn't make sense.

Evil Eye

April 27

THE TUMULTUOUS CRASH of the waterfall into the pool echoed throughout the cavern. Spray from the downrush misted Carina's legs while she lay on her stomach, looking into the cool water. It flashed with sapphire sparkles, like her wedding ring. She had beseeched Bendis to curse the blue-star to harm Deyan. Now Stefan was caught in the grips of the ring's destruction. His true love alone could break the spell.

Sighing, she closed her eyes. The wind stirred, and a whisper of a kiss passed over her lips. Her eyelids fluttered open as Dushan's smiling face faded from the crystal clear pool. Gripping the edge of the boulder, she leaned forward, almost pressing her lips on the surface. Not daring to stir the water, she whispered, "Dushan, my love, are you here?"

His image didn't reappear. She scrambled to her knees and looked around. "Where are you? Come back." Her shout echoed through the cavern, but she received no reply.

She hurried to the temple and fell at Morena's feet. "I heard Dushan's voice. I saw his face. I felt his lips against mine. But he wasn't there."

"Sister, it's detrimental for you to punish yourself by worrying. It'll only break your heart." Morena looked at her with love. "Trust me. All will be well."

A SKY BEJEWELED with stars kept watch over Stefan, as his emotions, like the porch swing he sat on, swayed back and forth—first missing Katherine, then yearning for Kalyna. Both women tormented his mind during his waking hours, but when he slept, Kalyna, in the guise of the mysterious woman, held sway. A deep-rooted emotion, stronger than his self-control, pushed its way to the surface. Why did he feel that way? He had seen her only twice, and then for such a brief time.

He sat there until the sun's golden rays rose over the horizon. Taking a deep breath, he filled his lungs with the salty sea air. Peter would be here soon to bring over a saw to cut boards for the closet Stefan wanted in his studio.

STEFAN HAMMERED AT the plaster on the wall, pretending it was Nikola. After clearing away the pieces from the hole, he peered in. "There's something in here." He dropped his hammer, reached in, and removed a package wrapped with yellowed newspaper. Bringing it to his workbench, he removed the torn, moldy paper and uncovered a silver box with an intricate edelweiss monogram on its cover. "Peter, come look at this."

Peter turned off the saw and walked over. "What do you have there?"

"A jewelry box." Stefan tried to open it, but it was locked. He shook it, and something jingled inside. "Maybe it holds old coins. People used to hide valuables in walls because they didn't trust the banks."

Peter picked up a scrap of the old newspaper. "This is from twenty years ago when the Professor disappeared. He must have hidden it in the wall."

A car door slammed shut. Stefan put the box on the mantel and looked out the window. He arched his eyebrows in surprise when the gate opened and Elena, carrying a large wicker basket, headed down the walkway, a spring in her step and a slight blush on her cheeks.

He met her at the doorway.

"Hello, Stefan. I'm sure I'm your biggest surprise of the day. After our conversation last night, I couldn't wait to see this mystical place with my own eyes."

"What a pleasant surprise. How did you find my house?" He hadn't expected she would make the trip to Emona so soon, maybe in a week or two. She struck him as disciplined, a woman who scheduled her time, not one who made plans on the spur of the moment, and never one who'd arrive anywhere unannounced.

"Someone at the hotel gave me directions."

He held the door open and reached over the threshold. "May I carry the basket for you?"

Peter intervened. "No, no. You must let her come in first. The doorway is a holy place. The guardian snake lives under it. You have to treat it with respect. Never greet anyone until they enter your house, and never reach over the doorway to take anything from someone's hand. It'll bring you bad luck."

Stefan stepped aside and waved Elena into the house. He shrugged at her questioning look.

"I haven't heard that superstition." She smiled at Peter as she adjusted her blue lace hat.

Peter turned to Stefan. "Who is this pretty lady?"

"Peter, let me introduce Elena Veleva to you." Stefan gestured. "She has a gallery in Varna. I told her about Emona last night when we met at Nikola's dinner party. She was eager to see the village." He turned to Elena. "This is Peter Kristof."

She stretched out her hand to grasp Peter's. "It's so nice to meet you. This is a beautiful village. I never realized what a jewel it is."

He beamed with pride. "I'm glad you like Emona. A lot of visitors fall in love with it."

"What an awful road to travel on, though. Someone should get that fixed. It's dangerous." She set the basket on the floor, and a small whimper came from within.

Stefan kneeled down and put his hand on the cover. "What's in there? May I look?"

"Open it. It's a house-warming gift for you, my new friend."

When Stefan lifted the cover, out poked a white-and-black ball of fur.

Elena bent to scratch behind the puppy's rumpled ears. "His name is Balkan. He's a Karakachan, which some people call a Bulgarian Shepherd."

Balkan crawled out, shook himself, and smelled Stefan's shoes. Stefan held out his hand for Balkan to sniff.

"The Thracians bred them to guard their livestock and property," Peter informed them.

Balkan scurried over to Peter next. He barked out a greeting and scratched at Peter's leg. Peter picked him up and rubbed the puppy behind his ears. Balkan's pink tongue hung out, and his tail wagged like high-speed wipers.

"Yes. They're the oldest breed of dog in Europe." Elena dug through the basket and pulled out some dog treats, which she handed to Stefan. "They survived all these centuries because they could adapt to adverse conditions and cope even when food was scarce. He can be your bodyguard and companion. I hope you can keep him."

"Definitely. Thank you so much. Now I'll have someone to talk to all the time." Stefan smiled in bewilderment at Elena. Such a strange gift from someone he just met, but it would be nice to have a companion.

"I have puppy food, a crate, and some toys in my car to get you started."

"I'll go get them." Peter headed out the door. "And I'll take Balkan out for a bit."

"Where are my manners? Please have a seat." Stefan wiped off a chair with his hands, and then patted them on his pants. "I apologize; everything's a little dusty while I'm remodeling the studio."

"Don't worry. I have on work clothes." She pointed to her sports shirt and jeans. "I can help if you like."

They went into the studio, and Elena looked around in delight. "What a great room with all this light. It must be inspiring to work on your art here. I'd love to see your creations."

"I don't have a lot done yet, but I have a few paintings and wood carvings you can look at." He opened a cabinet, removed a plaque carved into an edelweiss, and handed it to her. "This is made from black oak. The wood's texture is soft, but it's hard enough to endure for generations."

"This is quite intricate." She ran her fingers over the smooth finish. "You're a master craftsman. I must show off your talent. What inspired you?"

"It's funny you ask. I almost felt like a bystander watching someone else carve it. When I started, I didn't even know what it would end up being."

"Amazing." Elena pored over the details, then set it down. "What else have you done?"

He pulled out some sketches depicting a variety of scenes with nature and humankind living in unison. A samodiva danced under a walnut tree, its branches swaying to the sounds of the universe. A woman turned into a falcon. Wild horses raced out of a raging sea. Wolves battled to the death, while a rider astride a rearing black stallion, cracked a whip above their heads.

"Your work shows so much expression and imagination. You're a natural storyteller." She pointed to the dancing samodiva. "This is so realistic. She's quite beautiful."

"The woman I used as the model is someone I met the day I arrived in Emona. Her name's Kalyna Doneva."

"The only Kalina I know is Bulgaria's princess." She looked at the picture again. "She's blond, but she doesn't look like this."

"She said she has a sister with a shop in Varna. I've been trying to find her again."

"I'm sure you can find other inspiration." Elena smiled at him.

"I've definitely found my muse here in Emona. I have so many images and stories in my head. I can't seem to find the time to get them all out."

"You have a unique style. I'd like to organize an art exhibit in my gallery to show your pieces to the community. What do you think?" She searched his eyes, waiting for his response.

"That would be great, but right now I'm quite busy working on orders for Nikola."

"It wouldn't happen right away anyway," she said. "I have three shows already planned, so I won't be able to do it until the fall. That would give you plenty of time to get some more pieces done."

"I've started a cycle called 'The Mystery of Emona.' I could exhibit that, perhaps."

"Thank you for agreeing to this." She gave him a gentle hug and kissed him on his cheek.

He looked away, rubbing the back of his neck, then went to the mantel and ran his finger along the picture frame of Katherine and Sonia.

She followed him. "Is that your ... wife?" Her cheeks flushed.

"Late wife. And my daughter Sonia."

"A pretty girl." Elena looked around the room. "Is she here?"

"No. She's in a private school in France."

"Good. You want children to receive a proper education." She picked up the jewelry box. "How beautiful. Did you make this as well?"

"No, Peter and I found it hidden in the wall."

She turned the box over. "Look. Something's attached to the bottom."

He removed the paper, browned with age, and unfolded it, hoping it wouldn't crumble at his touch. "It looks like someone drew a map, but the lines are unclear and worn in places." He opened his eyes wide and pointed to a spot on the paper. "This one seems to indicate some sort of path or waterway. It says 'cheshma' here and has a star next to the word 'cave' over here."

Stefan glanced toward Peter, who had rejoined them, then looked back at Elena. "I doubt it's anything important." He put the paper in a drawer. "It's time for lunch. We can finish up later. Elena, would you come to the pub with us? It has excellent food and homemade wine. Maria is one of the best cooks anywhere."

Her voice became warm and soft. "I'd love to join you."

"Peter, do you think Maria would mind if we brought Balkan? I'd hate to leave him alone in a new place."

"It will be fine. Maria will give him a treat."

The puppy walked in a circle, sniffing the floor around the fireplace.

"Balkan, what's there? Do you smell something?"

The puppy looked up at him, then sniffed at the floor again.

THE PUB WAS quiet, so Maria joined the group after they finished their meal. She called Elena "dear" and kept looking between him and Elena with rapt pleasure. She fussed over Elena, worried she ate too little and worked too hard. For a little while, he had a reprieve from Maria's motherly ministrations.

"Maria, you must ask Stefan to let you see his sketches." Elena's face flushed as she spoke. "They're all so alive; each one tells a wonderful tale. And his wood carvings are so intricate and expertly crafted. I've never seen anything like them. He has such a unique style. With his talent, I'm sure his art exhibit will be a colossal success."

Maria rapped on the wooden table, and frowned at Stefan and Elena. She put her finger to her lips. "My dear, you must stop praising Stefan so much. Don't you know a person can become ill from too much admiration? Someone who is jealous of him might give him the evil eye."

"I don't know about getting sick from the evil eye." Stefan laughed. "But, I'm not sure my work deserves such high praise." He looked at Elena and smiled in appreciation.

Elena huffed. "Well, I praise all my exhibitors. Not one has ever been struck down with an illness because of it. I don't believe that nonsense."

Maria opened her mouth to reply, but Stefan put his hand on her arm. "Do you have any more of this delicious wine? I'd like for everyone to have another glass before we go back to work."

While she was out, Stefan said to Elena, "Maria's obsessed about protecting me from evil. Don't mind her. She keeps giving me charms to keep me safe."

Stefan looked at Peter who had been quiet during the entire conversation. He was grinning from ear to ear. "What's so funny?"

Peter leaned closer. "People seldom get the last word in any conversation with Maria."

A moment later, Maria returned with the wine and a smug grin. She handed Stefan a small blue bead shaped like an eye. "Dear, take this charm to protect you from spells and the evil eye."

"Thank you. I'll certainly wear it for protection." He put it in his pocket.

He looked toward Elena to give her an I-told-you-so look, but she and Maria were conversing as if the spat had never happened. Stefan didn't think he would ever understand the mysterious interactions between women.

Maria started in on a tale. "When I was little, my grandmother told me a love story about a master craftsman who was famous in many countries. He had golden hands. Everything he built turned into a work of art. One day, when he was designing one of his now most-famous fountains, a lovely young woman with hair like ebony and a smile like the sunshine walked by. Stunned by her beauty, he dropped his chisel. She picked it up and held it out to him. He looked into her eyes sparkling like emeralds and fell in love. She captured his heart, the same as he had won hers."

Elena sighed and looked over at Stefan. He smiled at her, then turned his attention back to Maria, to wait for the supernatural part he was sure would come.

Maria cleared her throat. "He later discovered the girl was the only daughter of the ruling vizier. Even though the master builder had no noble blood, he asked the vizier for the girl's hand in marriage. The vizier realized his daughter loved the builder, but he didn't want to give her up to him, so he gave the craftsman what he thought would be an impossible task. 'If you can build me a tower so high I can see the Red Sea from its top, I'll let you marry my daughter.' The craftsman agreed and soon the tower began to rise. People gathered from faraway cities to watch it grow. Month after month the tower grew higher, and people praised his work.

"Afraid the craftsman would succeed with his task and take his daughter away, the vizier called in a *znahar* for help. The old sorceress agreed to help. 'Don't worry. I'll send my blue-eyed daughter to enchant the craftsman and his work with her evil eyes. He'll become deathly sick and won't be able to complete the tower.' "

Stefan smiled at Maria. *Here it comes now. She's making her point about praise and the evil eye.*

"The daughter of the vizier overheard her father's plans. She sent her favorite falcon with a charm and a warning to the craftsman. He painted the door to the tower blue, which had protective powers to ward off evil spirits. When the daughter of the *znahar* tried to bewitch him, he clutched the amulet his lover had sent to him, and thereby avoided looking into the eyes of the enchantress. The blue stone absorbed the evil the witch's daughter cast over him, and the blue door protected the tower from any misfortune. He finished the tower and married his love."

Maria looked at her captive audience with a satisfied grin. "To this day, people keep an evil-eye amulet on doors or necklaces to ward off evil forces."

"What a wonderful story." Elena, her eyes dreamy, leaned over and grasped Maria's hands. "So romantic. I love happy endings."

LATER THAT NIGHT, as Stefan drifted off to sleep, the curtains fluttered in the breeze. The room filled with the smell of citrus.

Come, let me dream of you, my mystery woman.

Someone touched his face, and a light caress brushed his lips, leaving a lingering taste of raspberries.

Friend or Foe?

May 1

NIKOLA SCOWLED AT the sky as he sat on the coffee shop terrace waiting for Elena. The gloomy morning remained unsure whether it wanted to rain or shine. Patches of sunlight played hide-and-seek with growing dark clouds, but the blackness soon overpowered the light and won the ill-fated game. He moved inside to avoid getting soaked when the unavoidable deluge burst from the heavens.

The clock tower struck ten as Elena arrived, her long, brisk strides more determined than usual. Her face was tense, as if something had agitated her and she wanted the unpleasant task completed in a hurry. Was she still angry about the dinner party the previous week? After the others left, she told him how shocked she'd been at his behavior. No. It must be something else. Not the type of person to dwell on problems, she spoke her mind, then let matters rest. Something else had to be bothering her.

He pulled out a chair for her. From behind, Nikola smiled at her hot-pink hat, fashioned in a ten-gallon style with a half-foot rim. A rose-colored, stiff netting covered the entire ensemble and flared out a foot all around. To add to the extravagance, a large, deep-pink gardenia embellished the front. A fluffy ruby feather—*plucked from a duster, no doubt,* he chuckled to himself—and three long tan and brown feathers jutted out the back. This was definitely one of her more outrageous hats.

"Thanks for suggesting we meet in this coffee shop. I've never been here before." She drew out a long, exhausted breath, then gasped when he sat next to her. "Are you okay? What happened to your face?"

He touched the bruises and deep scratches, wincing. "I must have cut myself shaving this morning. I was in a hurry, so I didn't even notice."

"It looks quite bad. I have something that might help." She searched in her purse and handed him a tube. "This cream works wonders."

"Thank you for taking care of me." Nikola gazed at her with undisguised admiration. "You look lovely, by the way. Such a stylish hat."

Elena smiled. "Yes, I do love this one. I get the strangest looks when I wear it."

The waitress brought them menus, but Nikola only glanced at his. "They make the best pancakes, covered with butter, syrup, and an assortment of fruit. I'm having the ones with strawberries and cream. You should try them."

"You know I'm on a diet." Her words were clipped. "I'll get a tea with honey instead. I know you think that's boring, but it's my choice."

Was she cross with him? What had he done now? He motioned to the waitress that they were ready to order and tapped his feet until she left.

She leaned closer to him. "Nikola, I'm hoping you can help me."

Reaching over, he caressed her hand briefly. "What do you need?"

She tightened her hand, then relaxed it. "I've been trying to insure the paintings for my exhibit at the end of next month, but I haven't been able to find anything affordable. You have so many acquaintances. Do you know someone I can call?"

"Yes." He searched through his wallet and pulled out a card. Elena had never asked for his help before. Perhaps her attitude toward him was changing. If she became less independent, she might rely on him more and accept his romantic intentions. "Here's someone. He's not local, so you might not recognize the name, but he's the best."

"You're so good to me. I was certain you knew someone." The flicker of relief in her eyes was replaced by her more rational, disciplined persona. "I've never exhibited for such a famous artist before. I'm afraid to open without insurance."

"He's a friend of mine. He'll give you a good rate. I'll call and explain your situation." His heart warmed with love for her, glad he could help her, pleased she trusted him enough to seek his assistance.

"After this show, I want to do some minor repairs before my next two exhibitions." Elena's eyes took on a faraway look, and they became soft and gentle. "Then I want to show Stefan's work. I talked to him about it; my intuition tells me he's going to be one of my finest discoveries. That's why I've chosen him to do the restoration of the iconostasis in the Emona church."

The mention of Stefan's name sent a violent shudder through him. Stefan had to win everything. The woman Nikola loved. The triathlon. And now the restoration. Everything came easy to Stefan, while Nikola had to struggle to achieve anything—girls, good grades, friends. He hated Stefan, hated him for his good luck. Now was the time to punish him for stealing everything Nikola had worked for, punish him for his luck, punish him for all the pain he had caused.

"That's wonderful news." He barely managed to keep his voice even. "I've told the Council I'll donate the materials."

"That's generous of you; that's why I like you so much." Elena squeezed Nikola's hand. "You're my best friend."

Friend! Only friend! I want to be more than friends.

Katherine had been his friend, too. Would Stefan steal Elena the way he had Katherine? He had needed only a little more time before Katherine would have been his. They were so close on his eighteenth birthday. After they had spent a wonderful evening at a rock concert, she gave him a small silver pin with the initial *K*. "I hope you think of me when you wear it," she had said. He preferred to think of it as *K* for "Katherine," rather than "Karanov."

Certain he would spend the rest of his life with her, he was devastated when they broke up a month before he started college. She said she wanted to remain friends. Reluctantly agreeing, he hoped she would change her mind.

But then she met Stefan, his roommate and best friend.

His hatred of Stefan began that day. He wouldn't let Stefan steal Elena from him, too. What could he do to stop him?

"Hello, Nikola? Where are you? What are you thinking about? Your face is so intent."

A light touch on his shoulder sent quakes through his body. He narrowed his eyes. Remembering he sat in the coffee shop with Elena, he relaxed as he touched the hand resting on his shoulder. "Forgive me. It's been a busy day already."

Looking at her watch, she sprang up from her chair. "Goodness, it's almost eleven. I must get back to the museum; I've been helping until they get a curator. I'll talk to you later." She picked up her purse and hurried away.

"Elena, wait. You forgot the business card." He retrieved it from the table and pursued her, catching her before she reached the street.

"Thank you. I'm usually not so forgetful. You're so good to take care of me." She kissed him on the cheek and rushed off.

He returned to his seat, wolfed down his stack of pancakes, then headed back to his office. His secretary handed him his messages.

"Call my accountant. And I need a strong cup of coffee, no sugar; I had too many pancakes." Food alone didn't cause his indigestion; it was the bitter taste of hatred. A plan simmered in his mind. He had no qualms about putting it into motion, rationalizing it would be another business transaction. His burning rage subsided into cool composure as he spoke on the phone.

"Nikola here. I want to schedule a meeting as soon as possible to review our financial statements. I'm considering an investment."

His lips curled into a bitter smirk. He made another call.

Faith, Hope, and Love

Early May

SITTING CROSS-LEGGED IN front of a column in the temple, Carina leaned back, her pounding heart echoing in her ears. Stefan's voice was music to her soul. Kissing him while he slept had made her as jubilant as on her wedding day. She had thought she had lost him the day that woman came to visit. When they left his house together, she sped away to the meadow and screamed, her jealousy raging. But Stefan came home alone. He didn't love the other woman.

She looked up when Morena walked toward her, in one hand carrying a golden *rhyton* shaped like a horse's head, and in the other, her Astro Calendar, a bronze medallion with seven rays embodying celestial bodies.

"Let me look into your future." Morena sat next to her and placed the medallion in front of them, positioning the sun at the top. The rays signified the duality of life, from Venus, for love and beginnings, to Mars for death and endings.

Carina concentrated on the two most positive lights, the sun and moon, day and night.

As Morena poured nectar into the *rhyton*, Carina closed her eyes tight and held her breath. Her sister hummed, and Carina shivered with excitement and dread. She opened her eyes to slits when Morena stopped humming and poured the libation onto the center of the disk. The liquid swirled around the rays, travelling to its fated destinations, the Moon and Venus.

She smiled at the favorable omen. Looking up, she clasped her hands, waiting while Morena peered at her reflection in the cup, her somber expression giving nothing away.

Finally, she handed the cup to Carina. "Drink the nectar. All will be well."

Carina took a sip while Morena gave her prediction. "The power of the Moon and Venus will guide you along your path. As the lunar cycles change, so, too, will you experience a deep transformation in your exploration of the unknown. Venus promises a provocative journey and personal revelations. Together, they will guide you to Dushan, and him to you, until your souls reconnect. Fear not, the time will come."

Frowning, Morena pointed to the Calendar. "But, look. The journey will not be easy. See how the offering has travelled to Mars?"

Carina opened her eyes wide and covered her mouth with her hands to stifle a gasp.

Hugging her, Morena said, "Don't be afraid. Go to him. Today he celebrates a holy day. But be advised not to give your belt to the mortal unless he remembers ... or you both will perish."

A COMMOTION IN the churchyard piqued Stefan's curiosity. He spotted Maria dressed in traditional Bulgarian attire—a bright-red sleeveless dress over a white shirt, both embroidered with flowers in a multitude of colors, complementing her bright, cheery face.

She waved at him with her free hand. In the other, she carried a large basket. "Stefan, dear. Happy Easter. *Christos Voskrese*, Christ is risen."

People at the table responded, "*Vo Istine Voskrese*. He is risen indeed."

"Easter? That's today? I thought it was last month." He had spent that day alone, longing to hear Katherine's merry tunes as she bustled around the kitchen in preparation for the holiday while he entertained Sonia.

"This is the Orthodox Easter, or Greek Easter. It goes by the Julian calendar, not the Gregorian one. Occasionally it falls on the same day as the Western church, but most often it occurs after your Easter." She set the basket on the table. "Come have a seat. We're about to color eggs."

He joined the villagers, smiling at Todor, Peter, and the others he had met. Thin candles and jars labelled oregano, nettle, sumac, and walnut leaves were scattered all around. Off to the side, eggs were boiling in a kettle over an open fire. Unsure how to color the eggs, he looked around at the others.

Peter raised his eyebrows. "Do you need help?"

Stefan nodded, then shook his head. He gave up on the gestures. "Yes, I've never colored eggs before. Katherine always did that."

Peter showed him how to apply wax to the hot shell, then apply the color to the area without wax, and last melt off the wax. Then repeat the process with the next color. Beautiful creations took shape all around him. Intricate geometric designs and elegant floral patterns put his effort to shame. He made slow progress, his egg a disappointment; it looked like something a child would draw on a wall. Sonia made more attractive eggs.

The Thursday before her first Easter, he had come home with his temples pounding from another stressful day. He grasped the doorknob so tight his knuckles turned white. On the other side of the door, Katherine was singing her favorite French song. Before going inside, he took a deep breath. He opened the door slowly and snuck up behind her while she twirled around the room with Sonia in her arms, but she saw him.

Gasping in mock surprise, Katherine opened her eyes wide. She peered into Sonia's eyes and whispered, "Who's come home? Daddy. Yeah, it's Daddy."

Tiny innocent hands reached out to him. He snatched Sonia away. Hugging her, he smelled her baby-powdered freshness. "Where's my little treasure? Where's my princess?"

Sonia giggled and patted herself.

"Daddy, see the new princess dress?" Katherine stood behind him and rubbed his lower back. "See how beautiful our little girl is?"

"She is indeed a princess."

Wearing a pale purple dress with small flowers and cream lace, Sonia looked like an angel doll with tiny blond curls framing her face. He held her up to the ceiling and made faces at her. She giggled again and reached her hands down to him.

"You look tired." Katherine continued to massage the tension out his back. "Your face is pale. Do you have another migraine?"

"It'll be fine. It's easy to forget about my job when I come home to two beautiful women." He turned around and bent to kiss her on her lips. Sonia shrieked, so he kissed her on the top of her head.

"I made roast chicken and a salad. And Sonia helped me make Mémé's cookie recipe and even decorated some Easter eggs."

Sonia squirmed in Stefan's hands and reached out to the eggs.

"Yes, you helped." Katherine tickled Sonia's nose and cheeks, making her squeal with laughter. "Yes, yes, Sonia helped Mommy color the Easter eggs."

"Ladies, you're wizards." He leaned over the glass bowl filled with colorful eggs. "Which one's my egg, Princess? What egg did you make for Daddy?"

She grabbed a blue egg covered with polka dots and looked at it in fascination, then peered at her father. Pushing the egg toward his face, she rubbed it on his nose. Stefan and Katherine both burst out laughing.

He was still chuckling when Maria patted him on the shoulder.

"It's not so bad for a first attempt. Try again, dear, and you might not laugh at the next one." Then, clearing her throat, she waited for everyone to finish dyeing their eggs.

Todor leaned over and whispered to Stefan. "Maria will tell story now. She does this every year."

She walked along the length of the table. "In the springtime, young gypsy girls often come through our village, dancing in colorful clothing. They ask to clean our brass pots. In exchange, we give them colored eggs, potatoes, and onions, and sometimes even money to bring us good luck."

Pausing at the end of the table, she waited until all eyes turned toward her. "I had an old, battered kettle hanging over my fireplace. The gypsy girl who came to my house took it away with her to repair it. After she had finished, it looked like new. She was a master at her craft."

She continued in a low, mellow tone. "The gypsies can see both the future and the past. One of them looked at my palm and told me I would receive 'the gift of gifts.' Then she shuddered and dropped my palm, refusing to continue my reading. Something in my future frightened her. Years later I realized what she saw. It was me grieving over my husband lost at sea."

Tears filled Maria's eyes, but everyone remained silent, waiting for her to finish her tale. "The gypsies still come to the village every spring, always camping in the woods near Sultana's house. There's an old superstition: don't close the door in the face of a gypsy and never turn your back on one. If you do, evil and bad luck will follow you."

EVERYONE HEADED TO the hotel for the Easter meal after coloring the rest of the eggs. While Maria supervised the cooking, people picked up red eggs from a table and began tapping them against an egg that Todor held against his forehead.

"What's going on?" Stefan asked Peter, who sat at the table with him.

"It's egg knocking."

"Why is everyone tapping their eggs against Todor's egg?"

"He's the eldest one here."

Stefan shook his head and watched, trying to figure out the custom. One by one, people tapped the tip of their eggs against Todor's. When one cracked, that person walked away. So far, Todor's remained intact. Maria came into the room and picked up a red egg from the table.

"Enlighten me, please." He inclined his head toward the table where Todor sat, his egg still unbroken. "What is this 'egg knocking'?"

She patted him on the shoulder. "You don't have this Easter tradition?"

"No. We hide eggs for the children to find."

"Eggs symbolize rebirth and victory over death. The person who has the strongest egg, the one that doesn't crack, is guaranteed the best health for the coming year." Maria held up her egg. "Red eggs have magical powers that can protect people from illness."

"More protection from evil." Stefan winked at her. "Maybe I should give it a try."

"Indeed you should." She grinned and handed him her egg, then gave him a gentle push toward Todor.

He looked at the egg, then shrugged. A little extra protection couldn't hurt. He might run into Nikola again.

Smiling, he tapped his egg against Todor's. The tip of his caved in.

"Maybe next year." Todor leaned back and grinned.

Stepping aside, Stefan let Maria try her luck. Tap tap. She let out a "Whoop." Todor's egg had cracked. Maria was the new winner. She left, full of smiles, and returned to the kitchen to check on the preparations.

A STRONG WIND pressed at Stefan's back, making him run down the street as he returned home after the traditional Easter meal of stuffed lamb covered with a spicy rice stuffing. As usual, he ate too much. He had been happy to spend the holiday with friends, but he wished it had been with family instead, or with Kalyna. A week had passed, and he hadn't found out anything about her, not even where she lived or worked. No one he had spoken with in the village or in Varna knew her.

The gusts made the willow branches sway in a wild dance. A whistling through the trees sounded like a reverent song. He stopped to listen, bracing himself from being blown over. It wasn't the wind at all. The melody came from the direction of the cheshma. He started down the path, but the wind died down and the melody ceased. Deciding he wouldn't find whoever it had been, he returned home.

He opened the gate and broke into a grin.

"Kalyna!" He ran up the steps to where she sat on the porch swing.

"I came to knock eggs with you, and I brought a *kozunak*." She stood and held out a basket with a braided sweet bread decorated with colored eggs, like the one Maria had made. "Now, may I come in? It's a little chilly out. Or are you going to keep staring at me?"

"Yes, of course. I'm sorry. Come in." He held open the door and looked around inside. "It's a little messy from my work. Balkan romps around in the studio while I work. He drags the wood chips everywhere."

"Balkan?" She tilted her head and gazed at Stefan.

Her inquiry went unanswered because the puppy scampered toward her. He put his nose to the floor at her feet as if bowing in homage, then he jumped on her legs, begging to be picked up.

"Oooooh, this is Balkan. He's so adorable, like a baby." Bending to pat him, she whispered in his ears. He barked his assent and licked her face.

"Balkan!" Stefan scolded and snatched the puppy away. "I'm sorry about that. He has no manners. Let me get you a towel."

He returned a moment later with it, having let the puppy out the back door.

Laughing, she took the towel and wiped off the drool. "Balkan told me he'd protect you from the big bad wolf."

"What? Wolf?" Stefan's heart raced again as he thought about his dream from the previous week. "Why do you say that?"

"What's wrong?"

"It's nothing. A bad dream." He held out his hand for the basket. "This looks scrumptious. We can have some in the kitchen. Would you like a glass of wine?"

"Yes, please." She followed him.

While he poured the wine, he indicated for her to sit. "I looked for you at the gallery. Where did you disappear?"

"I'm sorry. A friend needed to talk to me right away." She pulled out a chair. "I couldn't wait for your return to tell you."

He handed her the wine. "Your friend from Emona?"

"Yes, but she's not actually from the village."

Getting a knife, he sat next to her and reached for the bread, but stopped. "Is it okay to cut this bread?"

She laughed. "Of course."

They ate and drank in silence, Stefan uncertain what to say. Balkan barked at the door, so Stefan let him in.

He put the dishes in the sink. "Would you like to see some of the wood carvings I've been making? I could even teach you to carve if you'd like."

"Yes, please. I'd love to do both."

They walked to the studio, with Balkan trailing behind.

"Emona has opened the door of my soul. I've had so many crazy ideas buried deep in my mind. Now that I'm here, I can share my experiences with the world and express what I feel." He picked up a figure of a tunic-clad man riding a horse. Coiled in a tree above them, a snake twisted down and its forked tongue lashed out against the man. "This is my most recent carving."

"It's amazing. Such intricate detail. But it makes me cringe." She shivered and her face turned pale.

"Are you okay? Here sit down." Putting his arm around her waist, he walked over to the couch with her. He sat beside her, holding her until she stopped shaking.

She smiled at him. "I'm okay now. It was foolish to be scared of a piece of wood. Could you teach me to carve now?"

He showed her how to hold a chisel and use a mallet to chip away the wood. She hit it hard, and the chisel slipped and scraped his palm.

She gasped and took hold of his hand. "I'm so sorry. Let me see."

"It's nothing serious. I'll be fine."

"Let me fix it for you." She went into the kitchen and returned with an egg. "This is the first red egg I did this year, so it has healing powers." She stroked his forehead with the egg, then his left and right cheeks, and last of all, the wound on his hand.

Astonished when the pain disappeared and the bleeding stopped, he lifted her chin. He searched her eyes to see what mischief she was up to, but they were serious. "How did you do that? Is the egg shell coated with ointment?"

"No. I told you. The first red egg has healing power. Ask anyone. It's an old tradition." She smiled and held it out to him. "Now you need to keep this until next Easter. It's a symbol of luck and good health."

"Maria told me the same thing earlier today." Shaking his head, he placed the egg on the mantel. He picked up a paper he had left next to the picture frame. "Kalyna, I have wonderful news. I don't know if you heard from your friend who lives here, but the Council for Cultural Events in Varna put on a contest to restore the St. Nicholas Church iconostasis." He grinned and held the paper out for her to read. "And I won it."

She read the document. "That's wonderful. You should celebrate."

"I will if you'll come with me." He took her hands in his. "Let me take you out to a great restaurant in Varna that a friend recommended. It has live music and a view of the sea."

"That sounds delightful. I couldn't ask for better company. Give me a few minutes to change at my friend's house, and I'll be back."

"No, don't go." He grasped her hands tighter. "Your outfit is fine. You keep disappearing on me. I'm afraid you won't come back."

She laughed. "Maybe you haven't looked hard enough for me."

"Take a shower here if you want to. I put clean towels in there this morning."

He showed her where the bathroom was, then took Balkan outside. Remembering he had already used the towels, he hurried back in.

The water was running, so he knocked on the bathroom door. "Kalyna?"

When she didn't answer, he opened the door a crack. She was in the shower, so he set the clean towels on the rack and gathered up the dirty ones from the floor, along with her clothes lying on the ceramic tiles. Her belt glowed, and an energy surged through it into him, his mind and body becoming one with hers.

Her thoughts floated through the steamy air like the pine-scented soap she lathered on her body. *I can sense Stefan so close to me, on the other side of the door.* She wanted to call him to join her, but she didn't dare. *Not yet, but soon. When he remembers.*

She closed her eyes and slicked back her hair, letting the water cascade over her. *My love, when will you return to me?* As thoughts filled her mind, the soothing warm water flowed off her body and seeped through Stefan's pores to nourish his soul.

Kalyna imagined caressing his bronzed back with the soap in slow, fluid motions. First across his shoulders, then undulating like a wave farther downward along his spine until she reached his waist. She let the soap slip from her hand, and wrapped her arms around him. *My beloved, touching you gives me such pleasure.*

She feathered kisses across his shoulders while her fingers journeyed upward—gliding along his abdominal muscles, inching toward his chest, before trickling back to his waist along with the streaming water.

Humming as she trailed her hands along the small of his back up to his broad shoulders, she pressed her fingers against the taut muscles and massaged his back. Stefan moaned with pleasure, and Kalyna opened her eyes. She was alone. Her beloved was gone. She placed her face under the stream of water and let it wash away her tears.

She turned off the water and opened the shower door, her perfect body covered with droplets sparkling like tiny pearls. He stared, unable to think straight, his body taking control of his mind.

"What are you doing?" The fierceness in her voice cut through him.

He held her clothing out to her. Stammering, he pointed toward the rack. "I ... I picked your dress up off the floor when I brought you clean towels."

Her expression softened and she relieved him of the garments. "I'm sorry. I don't like anyone touching my clothes."

Stefan looked away so he wouldn't stare at her nakedness. He picked up a clean towel, and handed it to her without looking. When he turned to leave, she touched his arm, igniting a fire in him. He turned back. She smiled as she handed the towel back to him.

Unable to speak or think, he became a marionette, forced to play the role she chose for him, and he did her bidding. The idea of drying her body chased away all other thoughts. He caressed her face with the towel, and then kissed her moist lips. He continued down her body, drying and kissing her neck, her shoulders, all of her until she was dry. Then he held her close and kissed her again.

He met her gaze. A power glowed within her eyes, and he fell into them, spinning around. Lost in the depths of their blackness, he was unable to find his way out. Shadowy images began to materialize. Like a flower that twists and turns to seek the light, he saw nothing but Kalyna. A mirror of his own hunger reflected in her eyes.

This I Can't Deny

June 23

CARINA SAT ON the rocks by the entrance to the other side of the moon. Above her branches intertwined to form an arched doorway. Beyond her world lay the realm of the mortals. Only those who were soul mates of the samodivi could pass through the gateway. But would true love ever guide Stefan here now? He had been gone for a moon and a half. Would he return? Had she driven him away by her behavior at Easter?

She had wanted to tell him why he couldn't *take* her belt. She would lose her immortality and her power and become enslaved to him. His love for her could never be true. It would destroy him, and Dushan as well. She had to protect her belt until he was ready to know her, until his love was true and not caused by her power. Then she could *give* him the belt, and they could be together forever.

Joyous sounds of the other samodivi drifted up to her as they left the temple chambers to congregate on Litos beach for the torch relay-race on horseback. The others would soon choose their teams and mounts for the Bendideia festivities. Tomorrow they would all celebrate Eniovden to restore the power of their sisterhood.

Her sorrow prevented her from enjoying the event she normally looked forward to each year. Looking up at the sky, she wanted to pluck each bright orb and put them all in a basket like the edelweiss she and Morena often gathered. It was on a warm, starry night like tonight that she sat close to Dushan while they planned their wedding and talked about their future.

"Dushan, Dushan." Carina stretched her hands toward the sky. Tears slid down her face.

STEFAN SLEPT FITFULLY his first night back in Emona after his long visit with Sonia. Someone cried out, whispering indistinguishable words, whether in his dreams or in his mind he couldn't discern. Finally, he crawled out of bed and sat on the porch swing. He looked at the starry sky and thought about Kalyna.

While he was in Rouen, she had crossed his mind on many occasions. Being with family had made him wonder about hers. He had so many things he wanted to ask her. Where did she live? Hadn't she said she had a sister in Varna? What about friends? She had mentioned only two. One lived nearby. Was that Angelina? The other friend was the artist who had sculpted a statue, but she had been evasive about him.

Kalyna was such an enigma. Her reasons for disappearing were valid, but something about them seemed amiss. They were too convenient. Did she have something to hide? And what had happened at Easter? Her belt had ... what? Allowed him to read her thoughts? *That's crazy.* He must have imagined that, as well as the other things he thought he saw.

What about how the egg had healed his cut? Surely she must have put something on the shell. Maria had said red eggs had healing power, but that sounded like an old wives' tale. It must be they can heal only if the person holding them believes it to be true ... and only in Emona. The villagers' stories were coming to life. He laughed.

My own samodiva, except she has green eyes, not blue. She'll explain it when I see her again.

The sun's glow soon replaced the stars. Peter would be up soon, and bring over Balkan and any mail that came while Stefan was away.

BALKAN BARKED AND ran up to Stefan as soon as Peter opened the gate.

"Hey, buddy. I've missed you." Stefan leaned down and scratched the puppy behind the ears, getting licks on his face as his reward. "I hope you behaved."

Peter came up the walkway. "Yes." He held up a bag. "I brought fresh bread and ingredients to make onion-and-feta scrambled eggs."

"Thank you. We can have a little wine as well. Will you stay and have some with me?"

"Yes."

Stefan took the bag and brought it to the kitchen. When the food was ready, they sat at the kitchen table. Stefan passed the wine and looked at Peter.

"How many times can a person fall in love in his life?"

His face pensive, Peter reached for the bread. "You may think you've found your true love many times, but you really have only one great love in life. That love will suddenly land on your shoulder like a dove. People are afraid of love, but they wait for it anyway. If you miss that opportunity, you'll never find it again. You're unlikely to have a second chance to capture it."

Stefan stared at Peter, surprised by such a long speech. He slid his chair closer. "Have you ever found your great love?"

Peter's eyes misted and his hands quivered. "No. I've been alone all my life because I missed my chance. If I could turn back time, I'd make different choices. It's too late for me now. Listen to your heart. Don't allow others to decide for you. If you don't keep a relationship alive, you'll lose it forever."

Unsure what to say, Stefan opened his mail. He stared at the letter after he finished reading it. "This doesn't make sense. It can't be right." He read it again. Crumpling the page, he dropped it on the table.

"What's wrong?"

"The Council for Cultural Events *cancelled* the restoration project." He pounded the table.

Peter's jaw dropped, and he opened his eyes wide. "How is that possible? Everything was already carved in stone. What are you going to do now?"

"I don't know. I'll have to find out who's in charge of the Council." He ground his teeth.

"I'm sure it's a mistake. Try to calm down. People here like to say, 'The morning is wiser than the night.' We'll think of something. This project is important to the village."

When Peter left, Stefan re-read the letter. He took a deep breath. Maybe Elena knew someone. With her presence in the cultural world, she must have contacts. He dialed her number.

"Stefan, how nice to hear from you." Her voice turned warm and husky.

"I'm calling because I need your advice and help. The iconostasis project has been cancelled—"

"What? Are you sure?"

"Yes, I got the letter this morning. I need to find out why they cancelled it and what to do to get the project back." He paused. "Can you help me? Is there any chance I can meet with you today?"

"Certainly. What time can you be here? I'll alter my schedule."

ELENA MET HIM outside the city hall. She kissed him on both cheeks.

Still uncomfortable with the Bulgarian greeting, he stiffened. "Thank you for agreeing to help me. This is a dream project, not only for the village, but for me. With the stipend from it, I can build a future here for me and my little girl."

"I'll always make the time to help you." She waved toward the building. "Let's go in. I'll introduce you to the people who can give you the paperwork to file the appeal. Did you know Nikola is the director of the Council?"

"Nikola?" He stopped and stared at her. *Did Nikola cancel this? Why?*

"Yes, he was voted in as director last year." She took a step toward the door. "He's influential in Varna. He moved here only five years ago, but he's established a veritable reputation as an authority on art and culture. If he's not in the building today, you can call him to let him know you filed the paperwork."

"I'd rather not." Stefan shrugged. Should he mention his suspicion to Elena? How good friends were they? He laughed. "Nikola probably cancelled it himself ... as a joke. We used to do things like that to each other all the time in college."

"Nonsense. He's quite serious about such matters. Are you still angry at him for how he behaved at his dinner party?" Elena sighed. "He told me he's tried to apologize to you, but he always seems to miss you when you go to the shop."

Stefan followed her to Nikola's office. He wasn't there, but his secretary gave them the form. After he filled it out, they went to a restaurant to discuss plans for his exhibition. He pulled out her chair when they were ready to leave.

"Elena, I have another request to make."

"Certainly." Her face flushed as she smiled at him.

"Actually, a question. Do you know someone who translates ancient languages? Possibly Thracian?" He wasn't going to ask Nikola again.

Her smile faded. "Yes. My friend Lada at the museum." She looked at her watch. "I have to run to an appointment, but I can introduce you to her now."

ELENA SHOOK STEFAN'S hand in a businesslike manner and left after introducing him to Lada.

The young woman's round cheeks dimpled when she smiled at him. Her eyes sparkled as she adjusted her thick glasses. "So, you need a document translated?"

"Actually, no. I have a ring with an inscription. I think it might be Thracian." He removed it and laid it on the table. "Do you have any idea what it says?"

"I mostly translate ancient Greek, but let me look. I've worked on a few Thracian documents, as well." She lowered her glasses and brought the ring up close to her eyes, studying the characters. "This is amazing. I've never seen one with such a stone. Where did you get it?"

"In an antique shop in the U.S."

Setting the ring down, she went to a shelf and searched through a few books, finally taking one down.

"Is there anything in those books that might explain why the stone would become warm?"

"Warm? No. Not unless it's been sitting in the sun." She returned to the book and flipped through several pages. "Ah. I've found one word. *Kamoles.*"

Where had he heard that word? His heart beat faster, remembering Kalyna had used it the day she met him. "What does it mean?"

"Beloved."

Moonlit Interlude

June 24

WITH WILD AND angry eyes, he galloped after the girl, his long red hair whipping through the air. When she stumbled and fell to her knees, he jumped down from his mount, tore off her gown, and pinned her to the ground. She screamed as his hands molested her body, leaving a purple trail in their wake. Lowering his head, he stifled the sound by punishing her mouth with his kiss. She tore at his face with her fingers until blood dripped down his cheeks. Cursing, he rose to his knees, allowing her to scramble to her feet and made her escape. Up in a flash, he resumed the chase. Stronger and faster than her, he caught up and grabbed her long golden hair. She spun around and beat his chest. Slapping her across the face, he added more dark colors, then punched her in the stomach until she bent over, gasping for breath.

A golden ring with a blue stone shining like a star flashed on her hand. He grabbed her wrist, but the girl clutched her hand into a fist. Her strength failing, she couldn't resist him. He pried back her fingers and twisted the ring off.

One of his soldiers loomed nearby after having satisfied himself with the girl's sisters. The ruthless man shouted his command to the soldier. "Take this ring and put it with the rest of the gold. Bury all the treasure under the walnut tree by the creek. We'll dig it up before we return to our village."

The man turned his attention back to the girl and finished what he had started. He left her porcelain white face bruised and streaked with tears. Her eyes, filled with pain and hatred, fluttered once more, then closed. Her head lulled to the side, but she cried out, "Dushan!" before she lost consciousness.

STEFAN AWOKE WITH a startled cry. "My god, what's happening to me?"

He hadn't dreamed in two months, pleasant or otherwise, and now this nightmare invaded his mind. His heart thudded as if trying to escape. He clutched his chest, where the sapphire ring scorched him. The assault on the girl had been so real—her pain, her screams, her despair. Her face had been a blur, but the ring ... His hands shaking, he removed the one around his neck. It burned so hot, it formed a welt on his palm, but he kept it there to relieve the turmoil of his mind.

It's the same one. He shuddered.

Kamoles, beloved ... Dushan ... Kalyna ... All his strange dreams ...

Is there a connection?

Balkan stretched in his dog bed. He looked over at Stefan and whined.

"What is it, buddy? Did I wake you?" Stefan crawled out of bed, patted the puppy, then opened the window to get some fresh air.

In the beautiful starry night, the moon watched over the sea, its rays flitting across waves like resplendent fireflies. No dangerous stranger lurked outside. His disturbing nightmare had ceased, but it left him dizzy and his stomach ached. He dreaded falling asleep again, even if he could.

Sitting on the bed, he glanced at the clock. Three a.m. The Witching Hour.

Sultana. Maybe she could rid him of this madness with something stronger than her Bewitching Chai. He would go crazy thinking about the dream if he didn't get relief soon. He couldn't wait until dawn. Besides, she had said she slept little, and he could come any time.

In his haste to get to her cottage, he tripped on the porch steps and landed on a red peony. He tucked the bloom into his buttonhole. Maybe Sultana could add it to the collection in her medicine cabinet.

The bright moon lit up the path, but in the dark forest, branches cracked and leaves rustled as creatures scurried about. He glanced around every few moments, but nothing followed him.

A soft, slow music drifted toward him as he neared the cheshma. Several women held hands and danced in a circle around the ancient walnut tree, a blue light glowing at its base. Wreaths of flowers crowned their unbound hair, their locks gliding over their shoulders. Their long white robes fluttered like lustrous moths under the shimmering moon.

Were these the gypsies Maria spoke about at Easter? He hid behind a tree, not wanting to have contact with another one after his experience in Nessebar.

At the edge of the glade, a shadowy image, playing a long flute-like instrument, cast out eerie notes. They hung over the darkness like a delicate silk net, enfolding the women within its threads. The longer Stefan listened, the more the sound hypnotized him.

The tempo of the music quickened, and the women kept pace with it. Their feet danced through the dewy grass, while their bodies, bathed in silver and gold rays of moonlight, twirled closer together, narrowing the circle around the tree. Their dance became wild and erratic, their voices louder, filling the night with a chilling sound.

A final shrill note reverberated through the air. The women released hands, raised them to the sky, and began whirling in a frenzied torrent. The belts around their robes loosened and slid to the ground. As the note faded, the women lowered their hands. Their robes, too, slipped off and drifted away, leaving nothing on their gleaming bodies but the magical light of the moon. Stefan's sharp intake of breath caught in his throat at their loveliness. Unable to tear his eyes from them, he envisioned the scene captured on his canvas.

Then, the flutist played a soft melody. The women lifted their faces to the moon and sang strange words. Stefan listened in awe to the splendor of their voices, as their bodies, like exotic flowers gliding back and forth in the breeze, swayed to the rhythm of the trees. Their words encircled him, as if the women themselves surrounded him. He glanced around, but the night revealed nobody except the dancing women before him.

Aware he was intruding, but still captivated by the women, he took a slow step backward. Any sudden movement might alert them to his presence. The night air echoed with a crack as he stepped on a dry branch.

The women ceased dancing and singing. Gazing in his direction, some called out, "Come dance with us." Their seductive voices sent goose bumps racing up his arms to the base of his neck. It was too late to hide, too late to run.

One of the women walked toward him. Her hair flowed over her shoulders like a golden river, swirling around her body like a growing eddy. His lips went dry and his heart raced the closer she came. He squeezed his eyes tight, too afraid to look at her. She spoke, and her words floated through the air, echoing inside his head. *Stefan ... Stefan ... Stefan.*

How did she know his name?

Her body moved so close to his, and yet didn't touch him. Her breath, like a warm, gentle breeze, blew upon his neck, his cheek, his lips. He was certain she could hear his heart thumping in his chest. She remained a moment longer, surrounding him on all sides, embracing him with her essence, and then she departed without a sound.

His eyes refused to open to watch what was happening, and his legs denied him the ability to flee. Hearing the women's voices glide in and out of his consciousness, still taunting him to come to them, to dance with them, Stefan thought he would go mad.

Gradually the familiar sounds of the night returned—the gurgling of the stream, the hooting of an owl, the rustling of the wind through the trees. He opened his eyes and moved his limbs. Relief that the women were gone escaped him in the form of a deep sigh. He walked on shaky legs to where they had been dancing. The ground around the walnut tree was trampled in the form of a ring, and covered with edelweiss.

Is this another one of my weird dreams? Oh god! I'm losing my mind.

Stefan splashed his face with water from the cheshma. When the moon drifted behind a cloud, the not-too-distant howl of a wolf made his heart beat even faster. He sprinted the rest of the way to Sultana's cottage. A light shone from one of the windows. She must be awake. He pounded on the door and waited, pacing on the porch. Slow, heavy steps sounded inside.

"Who there? It late. What you want?" A slight tremble in her words whispered through the wooden door revealed her wariness.

"It's Stefan. I need to talk with you." What had been a dream? What had been real?

The door inched open with a creaking sound, revealing Sultana's face aglow with light from the fire crackling and blazing inside. "Come, come. Such surprise to see you. Everything okay? You in danger?" She opened the door wider, looked outside, and bolted it as soon as he stepped inside.

"Please help me. The Bewitching Chai isn't working. Do you have other herbs that might help my dreams?"

Sultana touched his shoulder. "You so pale. Sit by fire. Me look at you." Mumbling to herself, she hobbled over to the shelf at the back of the room.

He took a step toward the hearth. "Maria?"

She sat next to the fireplace, holding a basket of herbs. "Stefan dear, you scared us. What's wrong? Why are you out so late?"

"Terrible nightmares. Women dancing in the woods. I'm losing my mind." He sat next to her, then stood, rubbing his hands over the fire.

Sultana returned. "Me look at you. Sit." She patted the back of the chair. She touched the warmth and perspiration of his forehead when he was seated. "Me think you have *uroki*, bad evil eye. Me help you."

She picked up a green earthen pot filled with water and used a spatula to retrieve a few embers from the fire. Chanting in a strange language, she moved the embers in a circle over the pot. She made the sign of a cross over it three times, then dropped the embers into the water. It bubbled with a hiss. Bringing the pot over to Stefan, she made the sign of the cross on his forehead with her fingers. "Drink water and wash you face. It make bad spirits go."

He looked from Sultana to Maria. This wasn't quite what he had imagined for a cure.

Maria shook her head at him. "Stefan dear, listen to Sultana."

He did as she ordered, and the anxiety drained from him. "That's amazing! I do feel better."

Sultana reached into a pocket of her dress and handed him a small blue bottle. "Here something help you, son. Me find strong potion in grandma's book. Many spirits haunt you. Strong demon spirit want to harm you. Other spirits in you fight him. This drive evil out. Heal you soul. Take few drops before you sleep."

Placing the bottle in his hand, she closed hers around his. Her eyes turned white. "Me get message for you. Wife say time to let go. She happy. Let go, son."

"You talked with Katherine?" His chest burned where the ring touched it. He pulled it into view with his free hand. A light emanated from the blue stone, pulsing in a soft glow.

Still in a trancelike state, Sultana grasped the ring. Her body shook, and her hand tightened around it. "This belong to another ... It carry burden ... Bad thing happen ... Bury under old walnut by cheshma." She shuddered and her hand went limp. The ring fell back onto Stefan's chest. "Oh, oh, horrible."

"Stefan, let's get her to her rocking chair." Maria wrapped her arm around one side of Sultana, while Stefan supported her on the other.

He kneeled beside Sultana, holding her freezing hand. "Are you okay? What did you see?" He looked with concern into her dark brown eyes. Remembering his dream, his own hands shook.

"Ring hold great power ... and message for you." She put her hands to her temples. "Me no able hear message. Writing on ring give you answer. Ring link you past and future. You chosen. You need decide what real. What you want."

"What do you mean chosen? Chosen for what?" He stood and clenched his hands.

"You learn. Be patient." She patted his arm. "Believe in yourself. It fate."

He paced the room, then looked at Maria. "What am I supposed to do?"

"Trust in Sultana." She clasped his hands in hers, their warmth and calmness dispelling his anxiety again as if they had infused a sedative into him.

Sultana got up. "Me make tea. You need relax."

"You rest." Maria took hold of Sultana's arm. "I'll get it."

"No. No. He need special tea. Me make." She went to the kitchen.

Stefan turned to Maria. "Why are you here so late?"

"Tonight is Eniovden, Midsummer, a holy spiritual day, the rebirth of Mother Nature." She sat in a chair, picked up her basket, and began to twine herbs together. "Sultana's been teaching me how to find herbs and heal with them. They're more powerful when we gather them at dawn."

He sat next to her. "Are these the ones you've gathered? It's not dawn yet."

"No, these are from Sultana's garden. We'll go out soon." She tied some herbs into a bouquet, set it beside her, and gathered some more. "We have to collect exactly seventy-seven and a half herbs, one for each type of pain and half an herb for any unknown disease. Then we make a wreath out of them. If we leave the herbs under the stars overnight in the containers we gathered them in, it increases their healing power. It's a tradition Sultana and I have kept alive for years."

"Sultana has strange ways and knows things you wouldn't expect her to know. Do you know how she learned to do this?"

"Yes, I do."

Stefan laid a hand on her shoulder and fixed his gaze on her eyes. "Please tell me. I want to know."

She paused a moment longer. "Many years ago, when Sultana was a child, she got caught in a whirlwind. People searched everywhere for her, but couldn't find her. Everyone feared she'd been killed. She returned several months later with a vast knowledge of the healing power of herbs." Maria gave Stefan a sidewise glance.

"Please continue."

"People were frightened by the change in her because she told them things that would happen to them. They started avoiding her, and visited only when they were quite ill and had no other choice." She stopped, looked around, then whispered. "Sultana never told anyone what had happened, but she told me when she started teaching me."

He nodded, leaning closer. Her words were so soft he had to lean in even farther to hear what she said.

"Samodivi found Sultana and greeted her as a sister. They taught her how to heal and see into the unknown." Maria glanced toward the kitchen. "On a Sunday, right before sunrise, when the moon was full, the samodivi initiated Sultana into their sisterhood with a secret and sacred ritual performed in the woods."

Sultana came in at that moment and placed the steaming mug in his hands.

"Here, son. Drink. Help you relax. Me add honey to calm you."

"Thank you." He took a sip. Its warmth glided down his throat. Closing his eyes, he breathed deeply, allowing the herbs to ease his tension.

They sat in silence while Stefan finished his tea. "Thank you for all you did, Sultana. I should go home now."

"No, no." She put her hand on his arm. "You stay here. Spirits out in dark. Some evil. Dangerous out. You sleep in back room. No go out. Sleep. Keep door locked. Maria and me go for herbs. We protected. Not you." She touched the flower in his buttonhole. "Red peony protect you some, but not enough. Magic strong tonight. No leave until light."

"I'll be fine. I think the gypsy dancers are gone now." He took a step toward the door.

Maria's voice quavered when she spoke. "Please stay. Spirits and other creatures celebrate with rituals in the forest. It wasn't gypsies. You saw samodivi performing the *kolo*, a circle dance. Sultana and I will pay tribute to them for you. We'll leave them some honey so you don't become ill."

"I'll be ..." Stefan suppressed a yawn, the herbal tea making him drowsy.

"You sleep here." Sultana handed him a candle and led him to the back room.

His feet became wobbly, so he nodded. He sat on the bed, and placed the blue potion on the table next to it. The ring became warm against his skin again. He lifted it from under his shirt. This was his last tie to his wife. He had promised himself he would always keep it close to his heart. Weariness overtook him, and he drifted off to sleep.

The ring is the link.

Fire in Her Eyes

June 25

THE FIRST SUMMER Moon beamed down upon her cherished samodivi, bathing them with her glorious light, a reward for their devoted rites. From the meadow, the women gathered Rosen, *Samodivsko Tsvete*, the burning bush, their favorite flower, and wove wreaths from the long spikes of purple, pink, and white. They removed their belts and slid off their delicate garments, draping them over vines adorned with a plethora of exotic florae unknown to mortals. The women themselves were by far the loveliest flowers blooming in the night.

Beneath a walnut tree, the enchanted shepherd played soft notes on his *kaval*. One by one, the samodivi graced the pool of aqua vitae, which had the luxury of lingering over their celestial bodies. They sang hymns of praise to Bendis as they performed their ritual cleansing. Here, hidden deep within the sacred grove, the life-giving water began its long journey to the cavern beneath the temple.

With the ceremony complete, some delayed their sojourn home, speaking alluring words to the man who could not refuse their demands. He laid down his instrument and came to them. Stripping him of his clothing, they bade him join them amidst the lily pads in the sparkling water. A mist over his eyes, he did as they commanded. Kisses, caresses, and more pleasures they bestowed upon him.

Carina, not caring to indulge in the sport of the others, retired from the pool and dressed. Their trifling actions were to no avail. He would not remember come the morrow. She cast a passing glance at the unfortunate man, another mortal making her heart soar to unspeakable heights of joy. Stefan had returned.

Laughter erupted from the pool. Carina looked, already aware of what had happened. The shepherd, in a state of arousal, scanned his surroundings. The samodivi had tied him to a tree and now threw taunts at him, their own desires having been satisfied. His eyes darted all around, and his body trembled.

Thinking how the others had wanted to do the same to Stefan when he intruded on their ritual, Carina took pity on the shepherd. He cowered at her approach. Touching his temples, she chanted to lull him to a restful state. Then, closing her eyes, she continued with words that let her enter his mind. She erased the enchantment, replacing it with memories of a pleasant dream. Despite the protests of the others, she removed his bonds and led him away to the place where they had captured him.

Upon Carina's return, Morena was kissing their sister samodivi good-bye, before each headed back to her own homeland, leaving the two of them alone once again to guard the temple. When the last one faded into the distance, Carina grabbed Morena's hands and twirled around with her.

"I thought I'd lost Stefan when he disappeared for so long." She sang a song of praise they had chanted during the night. "I must go to him now. Tell him who I am. He will accept me."

"Wait!" Morena released Carina's hands. "See how the mortal trembled at us? Your beloved is not ready to understand our world. Be patient. Embrace each opportunity to guide him closer to fulfilling the prophecy."

Picking up the shepherd's *kaval*, Carina played a mournful tune. Morena was right. Stefan had feared the samodivi, had feared *her*. How could she begin to let him know who she was? Only by loving her, accepting her, could he break the curse.

Morena ran her fingers down Carina's wet hair. "I have a plan. We can show him a little of our power tonight at the beach."

Carina smiled, understanding. Then she twisted her golden belt. "I'm so afraid."

"Don't worry. I'll be with you." Morena hugged her. "He's your love alone, none other's. I've seen it."

STEFAN BOLTED UP in bed, trying to remember where he was. *Sultana's.* Outside the open window, frogs croaked a beat to the constant chirping of crickets. Something else had woken him, a voice barely above a whisper saying *"Darling, I want to talk with you."*

The voice didn't sound like Sultana's, though. Who could it be? He had slept so soundly he hadn't heard anyone come in. He looked around the room. The light of the moon gleamed onto a small flower in the woman's hand as she leaned against the windowsill. Her blond hair cascaded to her shoulders onto a dazzling white wedding gown.

It wasn't Sultana.

He rubbed his eyes as he set his feet on the ground. "Katherine?"

She placed the flower on the windowsill and floated toward him, her face as radiant as the day they married. "Before I go, I want to tell you one last time how much I loved you and how fortunate I was to have married you."

"I love you, too." He reached out to her, but grasped only chilly air. "No. This can't be real."

He closed his eyes and reopened them. Katherine was still there, making his heart race.

"Please listen. I can't stay long. I came to say you have my blessing if you fall in love again. I want you and Sonia to be happy."

She leaned over and kissed him, her touch passing over his lips like a draft. Although it sent chills throughout his body, it warmed his spirit.

"Katherine ..." Words failed him.

"Good-bye, darling. Remember, I'll always love you." Her last word hung in the air as she faded.

"Wait, Katherine." He wrapped his hands around her, but all that remained was mist. "Please come back. I've missed you so much. Sonia and I need you."

He stared at the spot where she had stood. All the emotions he had experienced over the past year swept through him like a torrent. Denial. Isolation. Anger. Vulnerability. Depression. Love. Passion.

Was this another dream?

When dawn broke over the horizon, he went to close the window. A white flower lay on the sill. Edelweiss. Was this Katherine's gift to him? Had she truly been here? He picked it up and brought the petals to his lips.

NOT HAVING FOUND Sultana when he searched the house and yard, Stefan left a note thanking her. Now that he was back home, he wanted to preserve the flower. But where? He looked around the studio. Maybe in Katherine's picture.

First he had to know what the flower meant. He turned on his computer and searched for "edelweiss symbolism." *Noble purity, courage, true love.* Giving someone edelweiss signified true affection because the person risked much to find the flower in rugged mountain terrain.

He picked up the photo. "I never doubted you loved me."

Her blessing set him free, fortified him to move on, to love again. But did he want that? He looked into her happy face. How could he let go? The pain had begun to diminish, but not the memories.

I want you to be happy. The words swirled around in the farthest reaches of his mind.

But I still love you, Katherine.

I love you, too. Always. Let go.

He listened again to the messages she had left him. As the last word spilled from the cell phone, his guilt about moving on withered. He hesitated, then deleted them.

Something new grew in its place. His feelings for Katherine became like a decaying flower nourishing the soil around it, bringing forth a blossom of new love, a sense of belonging, of being part of the existence of another, where one couldn't survive without the other.

Was what he felt for Kalyna love or obsession? Her mysterious ways enchanted his heart. When he was awake, she mesmerized his soul. When he slept, he fantasized about her tantalizing body. He wanted to see her again, and desire flowed through him.

Stefan placed a canvas on the easel. Under his hands, he brought to life Kalyna's likeness. He captured her beautiful emerald eyes, her slim white shoulders, and her curly blond hair. Then he began to paint her ruby lips.

LATER THAT MORNING, Stefan called Sonia. He wanted to tell her about her mother, but was unsure how.

"Sonia, sweet—"

"Daddy! Guess what? I talked to Mommy last night!"

"What?" He nearly dropped the phone.

"She kissed me good-night." Sonia giggled. "It tickled."

"Wh-what did Mommy say?" He plopped onto the couch.

"She told me she loved me and you." She paused. "And to be good if I get a new mommy, because she'll love me, too."

"A new mommy? Perhaps someday, sweetheart, with your approval."

"I only want the samodiva. She—" Sonia talked to someone in the background. "I have to go to school now. Call me tonight?"

He promised and hung up, his soul at peace. Katherine had given her blessing. And so had Sonia. He alone wasn't ready.

Packing some completed door panels into his car, he stopped by the hotel to see Maria.

"Dear, how are you feeling today?" She put down the papers she was examining.

"The herbal tea worked wonders. I slept all ... most of the night. It's better than any medicine a Boston doctor could have given me." He laughed. "I wanted to make sure you and Sultana made it back safely from your herb gathering. That the gypsies didn't bother you."

"Yes. I'm here as you can see, and Sultana is back at the cottage." She patted him on the arm. "Wait right here. I have something for you in the kitchen."

She returned with some sweet, sticky baklava.

"Mmmm. Thank you. I'll enjoy this on my way to Varna." He took a step toward the door, then stopped and faced Maria again. "Do you know any place in the city I could buy a gift that's made locally? I've looked in the shops on the pedestrian street, but haven't seen anything that interests me."

"The Sea Garden has many boutiques that make delightful gifts." Maria smiled and winked at him. "A gift for a special person, perhaps? Oh, by the way, have you heard from Elena recently?"

"I saw her a couple of days ago. She helped me file the petition to reinstate the restoration project."

Maria sighed. "This has been a blow to all of us, but we have faith it will be resolved."

WALKING AROUND THE Sea Garden, he glimpsed a turquoise hand-painted silk scarf in the window of a small boutique. The bell above the door jingled when he entered. A petite middle-aged woman at the counter looked up. She had soft-gray, catlike eyes and white hair, with a little black in it.

"Good morning. What a beautiful day." She greeted him with a thick Eastern European accent. "May I help you find something? Everything is handmade."

That voice sounded familiar. Had he met her before? "I'd like to see the scarf in the window, please."

While she retrieved it from the mannequin, he looked in the display case. A silver edelweiss necklace with tiny pearls sparkled below the glass. It would look stunning on Kalyna.

The woman returned and handed him the scarf. She had an edelweiss tattoo on her hand like the one on Kalyna's shoulder. He arched his eyebrows. "I'm curious. Where did you get that?"

Something flashed in her eyes, they darkened, before their soft grayness returned. "From the window display. You asked me for it."

"I'm sorry." He gestured toward her hand. "I meant the tattoo. I know someone who has one like it."

"It's been so long, I hardly remember. Young girls do foolish things sometimes." She walked behind the counter. "That scarf's a great choice for a gift."

"Did someone local make it?" Stefan ran the soft and silky material through his hands. Envisioning it against Kalyna's skin made his heart beat faster.

"I make all these things when I've had my muse, but it's becoming rare." Her voice became sad, and the light in her eyes dimmed.

"It's beautiful. I'll take it." He set it on the counter, then tapped on the display case. "Could I also see this necklace?"

"Good choice. It's on sale this week." She removed it and handed it to him.

Looking at the price, Stefan made his decision. "I'll take it as well as the scarf. Do you have something to wrap them in?"

Nodding, she put the gifts into a box decorated with shells. The cover had the same edelweiss monogram as the letter from Kalyna. He opened his eyes wide as she smiled and handed him his purchases.

He took the package, his heart racing. "Do you know a woman named Kalyna Doneva? She said she had a sister with a shop in Varna."

"I have two sisters, but my parents didn't name either one Kalyna."

UNABLE TO CONCENTRATE on work when he arrived home, Stefan leashed Balkan and headed to the beach. The waves rolled in with a soft, rhythmic melody as he walked up and down the shoreline. Cool drops of water splashed against his face from the salty breeze. He sat on a boulder and removed Balkan's leash to let him run free. The puppy chased some seagulls and sniffed at seaweed tossed onto the beach.

Stefan chastised himself for buying the gifts. Would he ever see Kalyna again? She appeared and vanished like a dream. They shared a passion for art, but could they grow closer without him knowing anything about her? An inkling told him, *Yes, there could be more; there was more already.*

As the sun began to set, the sea reflected the rosy streaks in the sky, merging the two into one. Like infinity. Forever.

Balkan barked and scampered over to the end of the path. A noise of falling stones made Stefan turn toward the sound. His expression changed in an instant from gloomy to fervent longing. Kalyna walked toward him, her beauty radiating in the fading light. Lipstick the color of raspberries enhanced her full lips. A white silk dress, accessorized by a golden belt, highlighted her perfect body. He stared in silence, his own unspeakable desire reflected in her sparkling green eyes.

She stopped. "I found you." Her voice came out barely a whisper.

Overcoming his fears and doubts, he stood and opened his arms to welcome her. She smiled, ran over, and jumped into them, making him stagger and fall. They both tumbled onto the wet sand and broke into hysterical laughter. Inhaling the citrus scent of her hair, he pulled her closer to kiss her lips, her neck, her shoulder, her tattoo.

He caressed it with his fingers. "I like your tattoo. Where did you get it? I saw a woman in Varna with one like it."

Kalyna smiled and pulled up her neckline to cover it. "I've had it for a long time." She kissed him, her face beaming, making her even more beautiful. "I can't believe this is happening."

"What's happening?"

When she didn't answer, he said, "I've been thinking about you and hoping you'd return soon. I wanted someone to talk to. My dog still refuses to learn human speech."

She laughed, breaking the awkwardness. Putting her head on his chest, she looked up at the sky. "I used to lie on the grass in a meadow with my sisters and watch the clouds float by. We talked about our futures."

"Where are they now? Do you see them often?"

"Yes, we're close. I see one more than the other because ... well, it's complicated." She pointed at the sky. "Look. That cloud looks like a galloping horse."

"You're right. It does. You have the eyes of an artist. Would you like to try painting? It's less hazardous than wood carving." He laughed.

"I might." She turned her head to look into his eyes. "I'd love to paint a portrait of your handsome eyes and your gallant smile."

Ominous black clouds blew in, and the sky opened in a sudden downpour. They scrambled up, hurrying along the path to Stefan's house. Balkan sat barking at the door when they arrived. They all rushed inside. Water pooled on the floor, dripping from their clothing.

"I wonder where it came from all of a sudden." Kalyna shivered. "Maybe the horse got mad and wanted to punish us."

He heard the words, but was too bewitched by the image of beauty in front of him to reply. Kalyna's hair sopping wet, the corkscrew ringlets dripped onto her already soaked dress. The garment clung to her, revealing the contours of her body. He stroked the canvas of her face, gliding over the rosy hue of her damp cheeks. With the tips of his fingers, he caressed the outline of her full lips. At his touch, they parted, and a sigh escaped.

He continued downward, traversing the length of her throat in a soft, fluid motion. She tilted her head back, offering him more. Feathering out, he defined the boundaries of her torso, along her collar, then down the slope of her shoulders.

Even farther they would have travelled, but breathless, she placed her hands on his cheeks. "I-I have to dry my dress."

Sighing, he went to his room, and returned with a shirt and a towel. "Kalyna?" Where had she gone?

"In the studio." She peeked out, holding the picture from the mantel. "Is this your daughter?"

"Yes, that's Sonia." He joined her in the room.

"She's as beautiful as her name. She must be a joy to have around."

"My little princess is a handful, but so sweet and loving. She's coming in a couple of weeks. Perhaps you'll be around to meet her."

"I'd like that." She set the photo back on the mantel.

Stefan handed her the shirt and towel, glancing at her once more. "You can change in the bathroom."

She pulled back the wet hair clinging to her cheeks and wiped the drops from her face. Then she twisted the long strands in the towel.

While she changed, he made coffee. He handed her a cup when she returned, and motioned to the couch in the living room. "Here's a hot drink to take away the chill. Please have a seat."

"Thanks."

He gazed at her a moment longer before joining her.

"What?" She asked as he continued to stare.

"Your visit is a wonderful surprise." He smiled at her, so sexy wearing his shirt, with her long legs sticking out underneath it.

"I came to invite you to a special event in Varna tonight." She looked at him with serious eyes. "As soon as my dress dries, we can go."

"Then you should have something new to wear to it." He got up and went into the studio. Returning, he handed her the box. "I bought some presents for you."

Kalyna's eyes teared when she pulled them out. "They're so beautiful. How did you know the colors in this scarf are my favorites?"

"I didn't. When I saw them, I thought of you."

She wrapped the scarf over her hair, the bright colors highlighting the blond. Then, she handed him the necklace, its pearls glittering. "Will you help me put it on?"

Catching up her hair, she turned her back to him. He placed the necklace around her neck, a strong desire to touch her overcoming him. Leaning closer, he brushed his lips against her neck. A small sigh escaped from her. She turned to face him, her lips half open, her eyes dilated. Wrapping his arms around her, he kissed her lips, savoring the taste of raspberries. Her body trembled, and he couldn't believe she was real. He feared it was a dream, and he would wake up alone.

She pulled away, her face flushed. "I should check my dress. It's wrapped in towels, so it shouldn't take long to dry."

She returned a moment later. Her hair was tied back into a small bun. A golden belt was wrapped around her silk dress. The scarf and necklace graced her throat.

"You look amazing, like a fairy princess." Stefan hugged her. "My own samodiva."

"Really?" She smiled, then twirled around. "You believe in those tales?"

"In Emona, anything seems possible now." He laughed as they walked to his car. "Where are we going, your majesty?"

"To a magical kingdom at the end of the world, where people can love each other without being afraid."

"Sounds fascinating." He held the door for her and closed it after she slid into the seat.

In the car, he grinned at her. "What did the zero say to the eight?"

"Excuse me?" She gave him a questioning look.

"What did the zero," he held his thumbs and forefingers together to form a circle, "say to the eight?" He pinched his fingers and thumbs together to form two circles.

Still she stared at him.

"Nice belt."

"Thank you."

He repeated the action. "Zero putting on a belt." He shook his head when she continued to stare at him. "Nobody here understands my jokes." He started the car and drove down the road.

When they passed by the cliff near Irakli, Kalyna looked at the sky and the dark sea. She rested her hand on Stefan's arm. "The moon is so beautiful tonight. Look at the path it's making on the sea. It seems to be made of silver and gold, like the beams a lighthouse makes." She looked at him. "I wonder if the old one on the cape is open. I've never been there."

"Do you want to go with me some day? I haven't gone there either. I heard it's closed to the public, but I can ask Peter to talk to the Keeper."

"That would be fun. I'd love to go with you."

IN VARNA, KALYNA told him which beach to drive to. The night buzzed with excited talk, blaring music, and waves breaking against the shore. The salty smell of the sea mingled with the aroma of food cooking on grills over open fires. They headed toward the pier hand in hand, passing a man roasting mussels, while a woman sat next to him drinking, several empty cans already scattered around her. They stopped to get a couple glasses of wine.

As they got closer to the bonfire, where many people had gathered, someone shouted, "Come on. I thought you got lost on your way here." Angelina, Kalyna's friend from the gallery, waved to them from the rock she sat on.

They joined her, and the two women embraced. Kalyna whispered something in Angelina's ear.

Stefan sat close to Kalyna. The flickering light from the fire made her face more beautiful than ever. They didn't talk. They merely held hands. He wanted to stop time and preserve the moment forever. Nothing else mattered but being with her.

As the fire died down to coals, people quieted. The smell of charcoal mingled with the salty air. Angelina looked at Kalyna, then put on a CD of bagpipes and kettle drum music. A heavy, slow folk song rose in the darkness.

Everyone stood and encircled the coals. Then a man on the other side played a long flute-like instrument.

Stefan started. "What's that instrument? I think I-I heard that music in my dreams once."

"It's called a *kaval*. Shepherds often play them." She wrapped her arm around his waist and nestled into his side. "The *nestinarstvo*, or fire dance, is fascinating. It's a famous tourist attraction. Not too many people can do it, but it fills those who can with energy. Watch."

Angelina loosened her hair and took off her sandals. With her eyes closed and her arms stretched out to the sky, she stepped onto the live coals. She danced to the slow rhythm of the music, her long white dress flowing around her.

There's something unearthly about this.

After gazing at the gleaming yellow moon, Kalyna glanced toward Stefan with a mysterious smile. She took his hand, put it over her heart, and spoke in a chant. "This is an ancient ritual to rejuvenate your soul and body. Walking on fire releases pains from your life. It cures sickness. We perform this dance for the poor, for my sisters, for Mother Bendis, and to better serve all mortals."

Her words made no sense to him. He opened his mouth to ask her what she meant, but she released his hand, shook her blond hair loose of its bun, and stepped bare-footed onto the hot coals. With Kalyna's and Angelina's faces as pale as snow and their eyes half closed, they reminded him of the women dancing in the woods.

That's crazy. Those other women had been gypsies.

The two women danced across the ruby embers in a trance, their feet barely touching the coals. Stefan watched the powerful ceremony in mute surprise. His heart raced when Angelina danced past him. The tattoo on her ankle was the same as Kalyna's. Three women with identical tattoos. This was too uncanny. They must have a connection, but the woman in the shop said she didn't know Kalyna. Angelina and Kalyna at least knew each other. Maybe some sorority thing.

He turned his attention back to Kalyna. Her thick blond hair obscured her face and eyes as she danced. Her scarf came loose and fell onto the coals, but she danced around it, unaware.

After a while, the music ended. She bent down to pick up her scarf and tied it around her neck. A long silence ensued. When the two women walked out of the coals, the watchers cheered, clapped, and whistled.

Kalyna's eyes were fiery. She grabbed the wine glass from his hand, draining it.

"Incredible. How can you do that without getting burned?" He touched her scarf. It wasn't even singed.

"It's not difficult if you concentrate. I'll teach you if you want." Her eyes were playful and as radiant as the live embers she had walked on.

Angelina tapped her on the shoulder and whispered something.

"Excuse me." Kalyna looked at him. "I'll be right back."

The two of them walked away. He sat on the stone and stared at the coals. *How did they do that?*

On the other side of the embers, a young woman started arguing with a man standing next to her. It was the couple he had seen roasting mussels on his way in. The woman staggered as she walked toward the coals. The man kept pointing at them and shaking his head. Shrugging off his grasp, she sat and removed her shoes. She tied her hair into a knot, closed her eyes, and raised her hands the way Kalyna and Angelina had. The man said something to her, threw his hands up in the air, then staggered away.

Stefan jumped up and shouted, "Stop her!" The groups of people talking, laughing, and drinking paid no attention to his plea. He ran around the outside of the coals to avert the tragedy, but was too late. With a smile on her face, the woman stepped onto the still-burning embers. Her face immediately distorted, and her high-pitched shriek split the air, silencing all conversations.

People looked around before several bystanders pointed to the coals. More shouting occurred. Although Stefan couldn't understand their words, the fear and urgency in their voices was clear. Several men hurried over to the scene. But before they could get to the woman, Kalyna, with Angelina close behind, sprang across the hot coals like a panther and snatched up the woman, who convulsed and screamed in anguish.

Kalyna laid her on a nearby blanket. Stefan shoved his way through the crowd, ready to offer assistance. He shuddered when he reached them. The woman's red, blistered feet had patches of flesh hanging from their soles. Kalyna leaned over, blocking his view.

She gestured toward the beach. "Angelina, hurry and get fresh seaweed. Quick. We have no time to waste."

In a flash, she disappeared into the darkness and returned within moments with a handful of algae, sea water dripping from its green leaves. Kalyna wrapped the seaweed around the woman's feet and leaned in closer, stroking her forehead and murmuring something he couldn't hear. A green halo of light pulsed around the two of them for a split second. The screams subsided, and the woman closed her eyes, drifting off to sleep.

The man who had been with her wrapped his arms around Kalyna's shoulders. "*Blagodarya!* Thank you for helping her."

"She'll be fine now, but make sure she doesn't drink so much at a *nestinarstvo* again."

The man hurried to the woman's side, cradling her in his lap and kissing her on her forehead. Kalyna turned toward Stefan. Her eyes reflected the fading glow of the coals.

He pulled her close to him, still shaken from the incident, not certain he could absorb everything that had happened. "You're amazing. How did you do that?"

"People have known for centuries that seaweed has healing powers, and can ease pain quickly."

"What created the halo around you and the girl?"

"Halo? The only halos around here are on the icons people are carrying." She clung to him. "I'm exhausted. Can we go back to your house?"

BALKAN BARKED AND ran back and forth on the porch when they arrived. The puppy jumped on Kalyna, his tongue darting out trying to give her enthusiastic kisses. He nuzzled his nose against her hand until she patted him. When Stefan and Kalyna sat on the porch steps, Balkan calmed down and lay at her feet.

They didn't speak for quite some time, gazing into the sky. The stars flickered on and off in the darkness, like fireflies sending a coded message to the universe beyond. It would be easy to surrender himself to the power of the vast, resplendent sky, and drift upward to be lost among the stars forever. With Kalyna by his side, he was alive and full of hope again; he could forget reality, his worries, and his past. She had become his muse, opening the door to his dreams and filling the world around him with light.

He wrapped his arms around her and kissed her. "Please don't leave again. I love you. I want you to stay."

She put her finger on his lips to hush him. As he looked into her eyes, they became deep, dark pools into which he fell. A power emanated from her, and something unworldly overcame him. Shadows began to take shape, but departed before he had a chance to grasp them and make them his own.

Judas Kiss

June 27

NIKOLA PACED ALONG the beach, watching the angry sea roar in a tantrum, tossing waves high and heaving them against the shore. It accepted such abuse without complaint. After a long time, its wrath at last abated. As if regretting such rash outbursts and condemnable treatment, it murmured soft apologies and sent gentle, caressing waves to massage the sandy shore. His own fury still raging, Nikola hurled a stone into the sea, then raised clenched fists to the sky.

"Curse him! He ruins everything!" What he was about to do was Stefan's fault. He plastered on a smile and headed to Elena's gallery for a brief appearance.

Sporting a conservative look, with a light blue dress and matching vintage hat, trimmed with white embroidery, she looked professional as she handed out brochures. A smile lit her face.

So happy—for now.

"You look fantastic, my dear." He hugged her and kissed her cheeks. "A big applaud for your hat. That white silk rose adds the right flair."

"Thank you for coming. It's busy already."

A steady buzz of chatter and laughter filled his ears. She was born for this. "As usual, opening day is a great success."

"I found it challenging. This exhibit required so much publicity." She greeted another guest, and then turned back to Nikola. "Without your help and that of a few other friends, I wouldn't have managed to pull everything together in time."

"Anything to help you." He grinned.

She handed out more brochures to new arrivals. "Your friend at the insurance company was so professional. He had everything ready within hours. It was such a relief."

"I'm glad to have been of service to you, m'lady." Nikola bowed in mock formality. "I wish I could stay, but I have an urgent meeting at my office. I stopped by to wish you success." He lifted her hand and kissed her fingers.

Her surprised and disappointed look pained him. He wanted to mingle with her guests and sing her praises the way he always did. Without offering any additional explanation, he left. A wedge existed between them, a rift caused by Stefan, one which Nikola hoped to remedy soon.

The clock tower struck seven by the time he arrived at his office. His secretary was filing papers in a cabinet in a slow, methodical manner. She turned toward him. Dark circles lined her eyes.

"The accountant is waiting." She pointed toward the room. "Do you want something to drink or anything else before I leave?"

"No, but make sure the phone is off. I don't want to get any calls." He started forward, but stopped. "I almost forgot. Tomorrow morning, schedule an appointment with my lawyer for some time in the next few days."

"Of course." She picked up her purse and left.

The accountant jumped from his chair when Nikola shut the door behind him. "I'm glad you're finally here. What happened? Why the rush to have a meeting? We're not due to go over your accounts for another several months."

"Everything is under control." He spoke matter-of-factly. "I hoped to review the accounts to check our cash flow. I'm thinking about making an investment. I want to buy a gallery." Putting his briefcase down on the table, he removed some papers with his preliminary objectives.

"A gallery?" The accountant drew his brows together. "Why?"

Nikola, unsmiling, motioned for the other man to sit. "To expand my business into the art community. I need to know how much cash is available so I can make the appropriate plans."

They scrutinized the financials for several hours. At the conclusion of the meeting, Nikola gave his directive. "Allocate the funds as we discussed. I want to make sure I can move on this the moment the gallery becomes available."

When the accountant left, he poured himself a drink and made a call.

A cheery voice boomed over the line. "Hello, Eagle Insurance, the best rates and service."

"Hello. This is Nikola."

"What a surprise. I want to thank you for referring your friend to me. I hope she's happy with my service. I gave her the best options available."

"I know, but I need a favor from you. Remember, you owe me." He squeezed the glass. The harshness in his tone dared the agent to deny him his forthcoming mandate.

"I do remember." The voice at the other end became cold and distant. "What do you need?"

"Cancel her insurance."

"What? Why should I do that? I've been in business for more than twenty years. I haven't cancelled anyone's insurance without a reason." The agent shouted at Nikola. "You asked me to help her, and now you want me to cancel it. That will jeopardize my reputation."

Hatred, like a tidal wave about to demolish everything in its wake, flooded through Nikola's veins. He would achieve Stefan's ruin, regardless of the cost to anyone else. He enunciated each word. "It doesn't matter why. Find a reason and do it. I'm sure you don't want me to send certain information about you to the mayor. *That* would definitely ruin your reputation—and your business."

He gulped down the last of his whiskey and poured another. His old friend and former business partner would play by his rules as always.

After a long pause came a deep sigh. "I do know a way to cancel her insurance. When do you need this done?"

"Now!" He slammed the glass down, then ended the call. After he lit a cigar, he opened a drawer and removed an engraved silver frame holding a picture of Katherine.

Echo of a Dream

June 29

STEFAN'S LANTERN SWAYED in the dark corridor of the cave, giving him a glimpse of a pictograph on the moss-covered walls. He lifted the light to see more details. A crowd of people surrounded three dancing women. Their unbound hair descended to the ground and turned into flames that ascended to great heights. When he reached out to touch the drawing, a bat took flight, frightening even more of the mammals. He crouched on the ground while hundreds of the silently screeching creatures melded into a single whirling mass above him, before disappearing into the blackness.

Staying alert to other likely hazards, he travelled deeper into the cave. His feet sank into mud hidden beneath leaves littered along the passageway. The muck made a sucking sound as he tugged at his feet, pulling them out. More scenes decorated the walls. A young woman pursuing a beast strung a bow while she rode a galloping horse. Her clothing streamed behind her, held in place by a belt. He looked closer at the sign on her buckle, edelweiss. His heart raced. This was the right place.

He observed more drawings as he continued down the passage. One showed three women holding hands while they danced around an altar. Flames flared high from its four corners. A three-headed snake lay coiled at the top, each head spitting out its forked tongue toward a large tray. Stefan groaned. It held the ghastly head of an animal.

On the other side of the wall, a horseman held a bow taut, while a snake in a tree slithered toward him. Next to that, a man held a drinking vessel in one hand and an eagle in the other.

Leaves crunched behind him. Stefan spun around, but the passageway remained empty. Voices and a muffled cry echoed deeper in the cave. Careful to remain silent, he crept toward the sound. It originated in a large circular chamber with lit torches lining the wall. In the middle, a pillar held a golden tray, the same as the scene in the drawing.

The voices drew nearer, so he hid behind a column. His curiosity piqued when three women dressed in long, sleeveless robes entered the room. Light from the torch flames shimmered against their pure-white garments, setting their golden belts aglow.

The tallest woman captured his attention. Her exotic beauty rivaled any goddess—luscious curves; aristocratic, prominent cheek bones; and deep-set, brilliant-blue eyes. White-and-yellow flowers interlaced her golden braids. On her glorious crown of curly hair, she wore a fascinating headband resembling an ancient artifact. Thin, gilded leaves twisted around the rim, and delicate golden chains dangled to her shoulders. Her robe, embroidered along the hem with intricate woodland scenes, added to her beauty.

He found it difficult to tear his eyes from her until a glint of light distracted him. Turning his head, he found himself looking at the other women. Full-faced masks, carved with identical designs as on the goddess's robe, obscured these women's visages preventing him from learning if their beauty compared to the former's.

His heart thudded against his chest, and countless drops of sweat cascaded down his back. One of the women brandished a sword with a jewel-encrusted hilt. The other woman disappeared, but soon returned dragging along a baby goat. It bleated non-stop and struggled against the rope. The woman lifted the kid with ease, restraining it as she positioned it on the altar.

A three-headed snake, the same as in the drawing, slithered along the ground toward the women. It coiled around the base of the pillar, making its way to the top, spitting at the kid. The women chanted as they poured a clear liquid into the four corners of the altar. "Bendis, our savior, please accept this sacrifice from us, your true followers..."

Flames shot up, and the animal struggled more.

Stefan's heart beat to the point of bursting when the woman with the sword swung it high. He tried shouting "Stop," but no words came out. His legs refused to move. Not wanting to watch the slaughter, he tried to squeeze his eyes tight, but they, too, disobeyed him.

The sword came down with a sickening thud, and the bleating ceased. Stefan covered his mouth, certain he would vomit. As the blood flowed into the holes, the women poured a red liquid—wine?—along with it. The flames shot to the ceiling.

"The goddess is pleased and has accepted the sacrifice," one of the women said to the other. "A prosperous fortune awaits you."

EXHAUSTED BY THE horrifying dream, Stefan preferred to return to sleep, but he had work to do. He forced himself out of bed. Mud and blood stains were splattered on his feet. Was he awake or still dreaming? Rushing to the bathroom, he stood under a hot shower, scrubbing his feet until the water turned cold. He managed to wash away the grime, but couldn't rid himself of the nightmare. Had the ritual been real?

He brewed a strong cup of coffee and went into his studio. Taking out his chisels, he carved the newest panel for Nikola's shop, but the bleating and chanting wouldn't stop. He put everything away and drove down the street toward Peter's house. Although the summer residents, mostly artists from Sofia, had been returning, he was grateful no one was about this early.

The sun's rays peeked over the horizon as he arrived and pounded on the door. A young college-aged woman with a scarf tied around her blond hair opened it, staring at him with a perplexed look. Why was she in Peter's house? He had seen her in Varna entering a restaurant with Nikola and a young man. Then he remembered. Peter had a niece who lived with him during the summer.

"Is Peter home? It's urgent."

She hesitated. "Let me go get him." She left him standing outside, while she disappeared.

Stefan spoke in a rush the moment Peter came out of his bedroom, stretching and yawning. "I need to talk with you."

Peter came wide awake. "Come in. What happened?"

Sitting on the couch, he thrust his fingers through his tangled hair, clenching them into fists. He choked on his words as he relayed his dream. "Please tell me nothing has happened to any of your goats, so I don't feel as if I'm going crazy."

Peter's face went ashen, and he held it with both hands. "They took my Moon. I knew it. I knew it." The rest of the words he muttered remained incoherent.

SCENES FROM THE bizarre dream floated through Stefan's brain and clouded his reasoning. The cave, the women, the strange ritual. All of it was crazy. None of them could exist. Yet, the experience had been so vivid. Even Peter's reaction made the nightmare seem a reality. Perhaps finding the cave would end his daydreams from being played out in such fantastical ways in his sleep.

He scoured through the drawer searching for the paper Elena had found attached to the jewelry box. Although quite simplistic and almost childlike, the hand-drawn map might provide the key to finding the cave. He laid it on the table. The lines had faded, but it appeared to show the area around the Samodivi Cheshma. The cave could be hidden among the rocks on the hill where the wild horses roamed. When Stefan picked up his jacket to leave, Balkan's tail wagged, and he scampered over to the door.

"Sorry, buddy. You have to stay here. You're too small to wander around rough terrain. I wouldn't want you to get lost or trampled by the horses."

Balkan whined and tried to squirm his way out the door, so Stefan picked him up and brought him into the kitchen to give him a treat. As soon as he snuck out of the kitchen, Balkan bolted after him. Stefan hurried out and closed the front door behind him. His heart constricted as he walked away, listening to Balkan howl and scratch with a frenzy.

At the cheshma, he pulled out the map to get his bearings. Finding a path that might lead to the crest of the hill, he trekked upward. The steep trail, overgrown with blackberry bushes, wound its way among the pine trees. When the bushes thinned, the way turned stony and soon ended at a wall of white boulders. They extended out into the woods on both sides like a fortress. He found a crevice large enough for him to pass through. On the other side, soft moss lay beneath his feet.

The deeper he ventured into the dense forest, the heavier the mist became, and less daylight filtered through the branches. An eerie quiet settled around him, the sticks crunching beneath his feet the only noise breaking the silence. He hurried along the trail until it turned into an even steeper incline. Gasping for breath, he stopped to rest on a fallen log and looked at the map.

Rocks and gravel rolled within the depths of the forest. His breath caught in his throat, and sweat coated his shirt. A large black wolf appeared from behind thick brush. The creature growled and crouched, ready to attack.

He looked around for something to defend himself. No branches lay within arm's reach, so he inched his way up from the log and backed away with tiny steps. All the while, the wolf slunk toward him, snarling and baring its sharp teeth. Stepping backward again, Stefan staggered when his foot caught in a bush.

The wolf jumped on him the moment he fell. He grabbed its jaws with both hands, pushing it away.

"Help!" Stefan hollered to the blackness.

Someone—or something—responded, and came crashing through the forest. He groaned when another wolf, a gray one, rushed toward him.

Glaring at him, the black wolf didn't attack. Its eyes froze on Stefan's chest. The black beast shook itself free of his grasp. It bit at the chain around his neck, tore off the ring, and darted into the dark, foreboding bowels of the forest. The gray wolf pursued it, snarling.

Why hadn't the beast torn him to shreds? Why had it taken the ring? The glitter of the gold must have attracted it. And why did the gray wolf chase the black one? Didn't wolves run in packs?

Stefan's legs shook when he stood. He was about to hurry down the path before one or both wolves returned, but something in a clearing ahead flashed in the sun. The cave? The growling had become distant. It should be safe to continue. Picking up a broken branch in case either wolf returned, he made his way up the path, spinning around at every noise.

An old can lay in front of a cluster of granite rocks. He kicked it, sending it clattering down the path. All this for a worthless, empty beer can? Walking around the rocks, he looked for a hidden entrance, but didn't find any. Pressing his lips into a thin line, he headed back toward the cheshma.

Before he got far, a sheet of fog rolled in behind him. He hurried down the path that disappeared into a dark void. Before he had gone too far, a streak of white appeared ahead of him. Perhaps it was a local. The person disappeared before he had a chance to call out.

The fog rolled in, obscuring the path. He tripped over a root and fell against a lichen-covered log. His head growing heavy, he lay on a carpet of moss. When he closed his eyes, Katherine's shadowy image appeared.

I thought you had left me forever.

Yes, my love, I have. She kissed his forehead and faded into the mist. *Sleep now. All will be well.*

SNAPPING TWIGS WOKE Stefan. He snatched a nearby branch. Waving it in front of him, he swung it around when the bushes parted.

"What's wrong? It's me." Peter cocked his eyebrows as he entered the clearing.

Stefan stared at him. "What happened to your hand and face? They're all scratched."

Peter touched his face and looked at his hand. "Blackberry bushes. Many around here."

"Thank god you found me, anyway." Stefan let out a whoosh of air. He stood from the wet ground, his body stiff and his hands numb. "I wandered off the path."

"What path?"

Stefan looked around. The old walnut tree next to the cheshma rose high above him. Shaking his head as if trying to clear out cobwebs on his brain, he looked one more time. "How did I end up here? I was in the forest and a wolf, no two wolves, attacked me. Then I fell asleep up there."

Peter stared at him for a long time. "I think you must have been dreaming. It's dangerous to fall asleep in the shade of a walnut tree. This is where the samodivi like to meet. If they find you here, they can play tricks on you or even cause you harm."

"It wasn't a dream." Stefan wiped the dirt off his clothes.

Peter's mouth formed a fleeting smile. "Next time, fall asleep under a sycamore tree. Its shade keeps evil spirits away."

"It *wasn't* a dream."

Peter glanced up the hill. "I haven't seen the wolves this year. They're the spirits of the woods, the guardians of the wild. They don't attack unless they're scared. Some people say the samodivi can become wolves or other animals."

"The one that attacked me didn't seem scared."

Peter started walking back. "Come back with me to the pub. I'm celebrating my name day today."

Walking back with Peter, Stefan chided himself. Surely it had been another bad dream. He reached under his shirt. The gold chain was gone ... along with the ring.

The Darkest Hour

June 29

CARINA TOUCHED THE Astro Calendar, feeling the cold metal and nothing more. "Have you found the ring the Evil One stole?"

"I cannot see it, but don't despair." Morena laid her hand over Carina's. "It's survived for centuries; it's fated to make its way back to you."

"What about tonight? What do you see in my future? Will I be successful?"

Looking down, Morena read the signs. "It's unwise for you to go. I cannot foretell what will happen during a lunar eclipse. The moon's energy clouds my reading."

Carina twisted the hem of her robe. She wanted to abide by Morena's guidance, but she could no longer bear to be away from Stefan. "Without the ring, my connection to him is severed. After the *nestinarstvo*, my power kindled a flame in his memory. If I look deep into his soul again, I'll know if his words of love were sincere."

"Yes, the potency of the eclipse can draw out the innermost feelings of lovers." Morena looked up and smoothed a wayward strand of Carina's hair. "You will discover the truth residing in your heart and his. But be aware, all your emotions will be magnified tonight."

"The power of fire and the magical Midsummer herbs will give me control." She twisted several of the flowering plants together into a bouquet. "I must go to him now."

Carina flew out into the night. The full moon illuminated the dark forest as she journeyed to the lighthouse. Before the night ended, she would reveal her true self.

CIGARETTE SMOKE IN the pub curled through the air, clinging to Stefan's clothing. Todor waved to him and Peter from a table near the fireplace. As they headed there, Stefan looked over his shoulder every few steps, still on edge from the wolf attack.

They sat at the table. Peter ordered a beer, while Stefan asked the waitress to bring him a glass of wine. Looking at Peter, he asked, "What's this name day you're celebrating?"

"It's like your birthday, but more important. You celebrate your name."

Stefan shook his head. "Your name?"

"Yes," Peter said, tapping his fingers on the table. "Not everyone knows when your birthday is, but everyone knows your name."

Leaning closer, Stefan rubbed his chin. "Wouldn't you still have to tell people the date?"

"No. Each day of the year we celebrate different names. We like to say, 'The name makes the man.' "

Stefan looked between Peter and Todor. "How do you know when to celebrate it, though?"

Todor set his beer down. "Long ago, many people didn't know their birthday, so they celebrated on feast days of saints."

Having arrived with their drinks, the waitress added more to the explanation. "Someone named Peter, Paul, or Paval observes his name day today, Petrovden, Saint Peter's Day. Anyone with similar names, such as Pejo, Petya, or Polina also celebrates on this day. Anyone can look at a calendar and know when your name day is."

"There's a calendar for this?" Stefan raised his eyebrows.

"Yes," the waitress replied. "Different names are associated to various days of the year, even if that day isn't a feast day, so everyone has a day their name is celebrated on." She handed Peter his drink. "Long live you and your name."

Peter raised his glass to her. Then she wandered off to bring drinks to other tables.

Stefan turned back to Peter and clinked glasses with him. "Happy name day." After taking a sip, he set down his glass. "Let me get this straight. A name day is similar to a birthday, but you celebrate it on a different date, quite often the feast of a saint you were named after."

Peter shook his head. Stefan frowned, but then remembered this meant "yes." He shook his own head, glad it finally made sense.

Although he normally enjoyed listening to tales, politics, and life's everyday problems the villagers told, tonight a tingling crept through his temples as music from a live band boomed in the corner. He scanned the room. All the seats had filled since he had arrived, and many more people lined the walls. He hadn't met the summer residents who returned to the village. Many of them were performing artists, as well as patrons of the arts.

He turned back to his friends. "Why is there a band tonight?"

"The village is celebrating the feast day," Peter replied. "In a little while, the theater group is going to perform a skit."

Wiping the sweat from his brow with a napkin, Stefan raised a final toast to Peter. He leaned closer and shouted above the noise. "I need some fresh air."

He shouldered his way through the boisterous crowd. Settling into a cold iron chair on the terrace, he slouched forward, doubting he'd ever see the ring again. Flashes flickering around the base of the lighthouse distracted him. Esinesi, the Keeper, must be making his rounds.

After a while, Maria came out and sat next to him. "It seems lonely in the distance, doesn't it? We call it 'The Old Emine Light.' "

"It's a great view from here." Stefan grinned. "How does the man on the moon cut his hair?"

"What, dear?"

"Eclipse it."

"Sometimes I don't understand you." She patted his arm. "The lighthouse was built in the eighteenth century, and was the first one in the Varna area. It closed a few years ago because it became too dangerous for anyone to walk around in it."

"I'm going there tonight to take pictures of the lunar eclipse."

She frowned. "You have no common sense, dear. You shouldn't go. Esinesi warns everyone that it's dangerous."

Shrugging, he looked back toward the lighthouse. "I haven't seen him around. Does he ever come into the village?"

"Hmph." She pursed her lips. "Every few months he comes to get supplies, but returns right away. He doesn't like to talk to anyone, but when he does, he's rude."

"Has he always been like that?"

"No. He used to visit people, but since the Professor disappeared, he's kept to himself in his small cottage. He always keeps it dark. We call it his 'cave.' "

"Doesn't anyone visit him?" Stefan leaned closer. What could have happened that made him prefer isolation?

"His sister used to, but she moved away many years ago. Esinesi stopped talking about her." Maria wrapped a shawl around her shoulders and spoke in a hushed tone. "Legend says ghosts haunt the lighthouse. Although the light has been turned off for a long time, people say Seraphim, Esinesi's father, lights the lamp."

Before seeing Katherine a few days ago, Stefan would have raised his eyebrows at Maria. Now, after experiencing so many bizarre events, he was willing to entertain the idea.

Maria glanced around and moved closer to Stefan. "Several years ago, a college girl exploring the tower saw the ghost. She told her parents she had talked to an old man in the lamp room. Later, at the marine museum in Varna, she pointed out the man in a photo of Seraphim."

Since he was going there tonight, he hoped it had been only Esinesi. One ghost in a lifetime was enough, even if it had been someone he loved.

"Another strange thing happened one day when Esinesi tried to leave the cottage to run an errand during a severe lightning storm." She peered at him. "He claimed some unusual force blocked the door at the moment lightning struck right outside the old cottage. To this day, Esinesi believes the spirit of his father kept him from being electrocuted."

"I think I would have moved from there by now." Stefan laughed. But then, hadn't Sultana told him his house was evil? And he was still there.

"He won't. Someone in his family has always been the lighthouse keeper since it was built." Maria shivered. "My grandfather told me the Old Fortress near the lighthouse is also haunted. People believe Deyan is buried in a tomb under it and comes to life every year on the day of his death." Maria crossed herself. "Now he rides around the village on a black horse, whose mane is on fire."

"Peter told me people think gold is buried in a tomb there."

"Professor Krum spent a lot of time excavating the Old Fortress. Rumors spread that he found the Thracian treasure."

Stefan stood, ready to return home to feed Balkan before he headed to the lighthouse. "I'd like to visit the excavation site. I'll ask the Keeper if he'll show me around. Maybe he could tell me more about the bronze statue, too. You did say it was discovered near the Old Fortress, didn't you?"

"Yes, but you'll be lucky if he even opens the door to talk with you." Maria grimaced.

LATER THAT NIGHT, Stefan trod past the pub. The outside tables, having long ago been vacated by tourists and locals, gave the terrace a forlorn look with their umbrellas gone and the chairs resting upside down on the glass. Darkness cloaked the village houses, and no lights flickered behind the curtains of any hotel room. Peter's lights were off, too. Stefan rubbed the back of his neck. He had hoped Peter would change his mind and go to the lighthouse.

Twigs broke behind him when he reached the outskirts of the village. He looked around, waving his lantern. A dead tree seemed to float like a ghost in the moonlight, but the path was deserted. He trudged on through the shrubs and tall grass.

From time to time, a flash appeared near the lighthouse. The path dipped sharply moments later, and he lost sight of the light. He picked up a stick to use as a cane down the slope. Soon the path veered upward. He leaned forward, climbing the steep incline. Closer to the crest, the building reappeared, but now no light shone around it.

A woman leaned against the railing at the top, facing the sea. Her long blond hair blew in the wind. Maybe Kalyna waited for him up there. They had spoken about going to the lighthouse together, but had never set a firm date. Or maybe she, too, had come to watch the lunar eclipse on her own.

He must have fallen asleep after they returned from the fire dance a few days ago. The last thing he remembered was talking to her, telling her he loved her and asking her to stay. A moment later, he woke up on the porch alone, having experienced a rapid sequence of unfamiliar images flashing through his mind. Had he frightened her away? Why had he said that anyway? He had never been so bold before.

The woman by the railing spread out her arms.

She's going to jump!

"No!" He was too far away for her to hear his scream.

His mouth dropped. They weren't arms, but wings, like the woman in his dream. He rubbed his eyes and looked again. The vision disappeared. Maybe the woman had gone inside. He wiped the sweat from his brow. The moon shining against the white building must have made her arms look like wings.

He hurried the rest of the way to catch up with her before she left. The rusty chain clanked in the breeze against the stone-and-brick structure. He stepped inside, his boots echoing in the room. A thick layer of gray dust shrouded the stairs. No one else had passed this way. How had the woman made it to the top?

Cobwebs hanging from the rafters stuck to his face and hair as he climbed the steep, narrow steps. He swatted at them, and his lantern banged against the railing. Wings fluttered above moments before a colony of frightened bats rushed toward him. Their mouths opened, but emitted a sound they alone could hear. He tucked his head close to his chest and wrapped his arms around his face until the bats flew into the night sky through the broken windows.

At the top, he stepped into a round white room, the watch room. He walked over to the single long, narrow window. Looking out, he imagined generations of lighthouse keepers staring toward the sea during raging storms, as the lighthouse signaled its warnings to approaching ships.

Leaving his camera bag on the floor under the window, he climbed the set of stairs to the lantern room.

Pieces of glass and sand covered the floor. Windows surrounding the small round room allowed light to shine out in all directions when the lighthouse had been operational. An article he had read described how lighthouses once used open fires, and later candles replaced the fires. Oil once fueled the lamp in this one, but its light had ceased to shine. The heart of the lighthouse had stopped beating.

He opened the door to the parapet and stepped onto the balcony. The sea's roaring pierced the night. The swaying of the metal railing enclosing the narrow walkway sent out a warning to stay back or fall to the rocky coast. Heeding its advice, Stefan stuck close to the lighthouse wall.

The night offered the perfect opportunity for taking photographs. The full moon reflected on the sea like a silver lane meandering off to eternity. In its wake, it illuminated the ruins of the Old Fortress and bathed the beach and rocks below with a soft glow. In the distance, the sleepy village lay nestled in the arms of the mountain.

Stefan looked at his watch. Half an hour until the eclipse. He re-entered the lantern room, and returned to the watch room to retrieve his camera. When he reached the bottom, light, almost indiscernible footsteps echoed from the metal stairs.

"Hello, Peter, is that you?" Maybe he couldn't sleep and had decided to come after all.

No answer, but the footsteps continued.

"Esinesi, I'm in here. The door was open, and I came in." Perhaps the Keeper wanted to check on him.

All stayed silent. The footsteps began again. He peered down the stairs, watching as a shadowy figure emerged from the darkness.

"No. It's me." Kalyna stepped into the room. The light of the moon made her blond hair luminous and her earrings glimmer like small flames.

"Kalyna." He embraced her and kissed her. The night breeze had chilled her body. Her face, as white as marble, glowed in the pearly moonlight. He picked her up and twirled her around. "What a wonderful surprise. You weren't up here earlier were you? I thought I saw a woman near the railing."

"No, I just arrived." She leaned her head against his shoulder. "I stopped by your house. Since you weren't there, I went to the shore to watch the eclipse. When I saw the light coming from the lighthouse, I thought you might be here."

He set her down and held her hands. "You're so lovely tonight. I could look at you for hours. And paint your lips, your smile ... all of you."

"Some day." She smiled and a flush colored her face. Leading him to the window, she looked out. "It's magical; I love to peer into the night sky. Who knows what's out there." She turned her head to look at him. In the darkness, her eyes twinkled like the stars above, and her face shown with an unearthly radiance. "Did you know a new star appears in the sky every time someone is born?"

He raised his eyebrows. "You, too?"

"It's true." She opened her eyes wide. "The more powerful or fortunate you are, the brighter your star shines. When misfortune befalls you, your star shines less brightly." She waved her hand toward the vast expanse. "A starry sky contains the energy of all those people whose lights we can see. It's able to empower people, especially those whose stars shine with the most intensity."

Cupping her face, he turned it toward his. "Well, the moon is what interests me tonight, not the stars. I came here so I could photograph the eclipse." He looked at his watch. "It's almost time for it now."

He kissed her again, then bent to pick up his camera. A light flickered, followed by another and another, until hundreds of candles covered the floor. He stared, unblinking. It had to be another dream.

The aroma of herbs and wild flowers filled his senses. He gazed at Kalyna, but she only smiled. When he looked again, a pile of hay, shaped like a nest, had appeared in the midst of the candles. Yes, definitely a dream.

She took his hand and led him to the bed of hay. Drowsiness overcame him, and he lay down, reaching up to her. He felt the beat of her heart and the warmth of her body as she wrapped her arms around him. She kissed him on the lips, gently at first, then more fervently. He savored the familiar taste of raspberries. His feelings burst forth from the depths of his soul. He kissed her with a mad passion, his mouth crushing hers until her lips were swollen. His lips travelled the length of her throat, along her cheeks, then her ears. "I love you."

Outside the window, the moon turned bright orange, then blood red, and finally brown. It disappeared while Stefan became hypnotized by Kalyna's deep black eyes. Tumbling farther into her soul, he experienced her joy, love, and pain. He saw her battered and bruised, her life ebbing out of her. His own soul screamed at the injustice of what had been done to her. Then peace overflowed his spirit as she drank of the *aqua vitae*—and he looked into her immortal face.

The Time Is Now

July 1

LEANING BACK IN the chair, with his legs stretched out, Nikola puffed a cigar on the terrace, watching the calm sea. Before long, the warm, gentle breeze became a cold, howling wind, distorting the circular wisps of smoke he had learned to perfect. The squalls always proved to signal a tempest of great magnitude brewing off the coast.

His landline rang. Since he could no longer see the sea because of the growing mist, he stood to answer it. Pain shot up his legs. "Damn." He rubbed them, then limped inside. The phone display showed *Elena*.

The moment had arrived to carry forward his long-anticipated revenge against Stefan. Once he set sail on this perilous journey, he could never charter another course, regardless of how turbulent the sea of his despair became. *But, there's a time and a season for everything.* Although it weighed on his mind he would hurt Elena in the process, he rationalized that the innocent sometimes had to suffer in order for the guilty to be punished.

He let the phone ring twice more, then answered in as casual and cordial a tone as he could muster. "It's nice to hear from you. How's the exhibit going?"

"It-it's fine. Are you busy?" Her voice trembled. "I need to talk with you."

"What can I do for you?"

She let out a long sigh. "I hate to bother you with this, but my insurance has been cancelled. I don't want to complain since he's your friend, but he isn't returning my calls, and his letter didn't explain why he terminated the policy."

"Don't worry. I'll talk with him and make sure the problem gets resolved. I'm sure it's a simple clerical mistake."

He rejoiced. She needed him again. It was enough for now. The rest would come with time. She was the most important thing in his life. Soon she'd realize he was better for her than Stefan was.

I don't want to lose you. I love you, Katherine ... Elena.

RESURRECTED GHOSTS FROM the past taunted Nikola, keeping him awake well after midnight. He refused to turn on the lights, revenge driving him onward into an ever darker abyss from which he couldn't return. Rising from the couch, he opened the curtains, staring into the night for a long time, contemplating what to do.

He poured himself a glass of whiskey. The burning bite of the alcohol numbed the pain, drowning his demons. Still restless, he pulled a photo album out of a cupboard and sat back on the couch. Flipping through old, yellowed photographs, he gazed at a picture of his birthday, the day Katherine gave him the pin. Someone at the next booth in the fast-food restaurant had taken the photo. Cheek-to-cheek with her, grins stretching across both their faces, he held up the present. That had been the happiest moment of his life.

He turned the page. Another photo showed her first beauty pageant. She had turned her head to him as she walked back along the runway. With her hand held at her side, she had waved to him. "Gone forever." He caressed her face. "I miss you, Katherine. I didn't even get to say good-bye."

How happy they had been. *Before Stefan stole her away.* He always took what belonged to Nikola. Slamming the album shut, he dialed Boyan's number and waited while the phone rang several times.

"Hellooo? Who is this?" The hoarse, groggy voice on the other side coughed to clear his throat.

"It's Nikola." He slurred his words.

"How long have you been drinking?" Boyan admonished him. "What's the matter?"

"I need to calm my conscience." Nikola filled his glass and took another gulp before he pronounced the words determined to seal his fate. "I have a special request to make. At the end of the month, I want you to pick up a large collection of paintings worth millions. After you get them, I'll give you instructions about what to do with them."

"Give me the address."

Nikola told him and waited for Boyan's response.

"But this is Elena's gallery."

"Just do it." He slammed the phone down.

Warning Signs

July 8

IN THE CHURCHYARD, Nona waved at Stefan to come closer. Her mouth moved, but he was too far away to hear what she said. At last, she was going to tell him what she'd been hiding for so long. He hurried over before she changed her mind and ran away again.

She held a jar of honey out to him. Every time he reached for it, she snatched it away and backed a few steps farther from him until he was beneath the old oak. The dry, brittle-looking tree limbs were devoid of all leaves. What happened to it? It was only mid-summer. The tree had been healthy yesterday.

Buzzing grew louder overhead, and he looked up. A black cloud of bees swarmed around the crown of the tree. Some alit on the branches, while others plummeted toward him. Nona waved her hands back and forth from a window in the church. He sprinted toward its safety, covering his head to avoid being stung.

Once inside, he slammed the door closed. He scanned the room to see if any bees had made it in with him. He gasped. Even more angry bees filled the church, coming in from the broken windows and ruined rafters. They all surged toward him. He ran out the door, hurrying to anywhere as fast as he could.

STEFAN SHOOK HIS head free of the dream and glanced out the studio window once more. Green branches covered the old oak tree by the church, not dead ones. What could it have meant? Nona had never entered his nighttime thoughts before. He hadn't even seen her around Emona much, only glimpses every now and then.

She continued to disappear, with a look of fear on her face, every time he came upon her by the church or the Old Beach.

He looked beyond the churchyard to the lighthouse at the end of the cape. He had woken up there the week before on the hard floor, his back stiff, after another fanciful dream. But what a pleasant one. He touched his lips, remembering Kalyna's kisses. Was it a dream, though? She must have been there part of the time. He had found one of her earrings by his backpack. Where had she disappeared to this time? She was like the wild horses, free and unpredictable.

He had to find her again, had to know about the other dream that night in the lighthouse. The horrifying one. Had he projected the rape of his previous nightmare onto Kalyna? In the first one, he hadn't seen the woman's face clearly, but the night in the lighthouse, he had experienced the assault again, and so much more, as if those things had happened to Kalyna. Were the stories the villagers telling him distorting his sense of reality? It *had* been only a dream after all, hadn't it? None of it could have happened. It wasn't Kalyna's memory. She couldn't possibly be the woman who called out to Dushan in his dream. That was absurd.

Finding Kalyna would have to wait. He looked at his watch, then scrambled to feed Balkan. Putting food and fresh water on the porch, he let the puppy out. He was running late to pick up Sonia. She was coming today to stay with him for a month.

SONIA CLUTCHED BLUEI, her favorite white bear, its name reflecting the color of the animal's nose. Stefan had given it to her for her birthday. She hugged the stuffed animal tight to her chest, while she held onto the flight attendant's hand. When she looked Stefan's way, she squealed, "Daddy!" Releasing the woman's hand, she rushed over.

Snatching her up, he hugged her as hard as he could and swung her around. "Hello, sweetheart, my little princess. No, let me greet you the proper way. *Dobre doshla.*"

"What does that mean?"

"It means 'Welcome.' "

She giggled. "You said that already." Snuggling closer, she kissed him on his nose. "I love you, Daddy. I really, really missed you."

"Even though I saw you two weeks ago?"

"Yes, yes, yes." She kissed him all over his face. With a rush of words, she said, "I want to see my castle, the samodiva, her helper, the witch ..." She stopped and put her mouth close to his ear. "But not the dragon."

Sonia bounced in her seat on the way home, pointing and chattering. "Daddy, look at that pretty bird. What's it called?" Then a moment later, "See all those flowers. They have such long stems. What are they?" Quickly followed by, "Those trees look funny. Why don't they grow at home?"

By the time they reached the house, his eardrums hurt. He hadn't known he could say "I don't know" so many times.

As soon as Stefan opened the gate, Balkan bounded off the porch and jumped on Sonia, almost knocking her down, trying to lick her face.

"Balkan, no." He pulled him off Sonia. "Down."

She wrapped her arms around him. "Oh, a dog! You didn't tell me about him."

"I wanted to surprise you. He's still a puppy, but he's growing fast."

"He's so cute. I love him." She nuzzled her face in his fur.

Stefan chuckled, patting Balkan. "He's my bodyguard. Now he can protect you, too." He removed her suitcase from the car trunk. "Let's go in, and I'll show you another surprise."

The moment he unlocked and opened the door, Sonia ran through the house, peeking into every room. "Which one's mine?" She screamed with excitement and rushed out of one, colliding with him as he followed her. Wrapping her arms around his waist, she jumped up and down. "I love my room! It's blue. My favorite color. And you painted a mermaid on the wall!"

Stefan looked at his watch. "If you're not too tired from your flight, let's go to the hotel for a traditional Bulgarian meal. They're quite tasty as you can see from my growing belly."

Giggling, she patted his belly, then laid her head against it. "I like it. It's not fat."

He set her suitcase down on the bed. After feeding Balkan, and letting him outside, he walked back to the car with her, and they drove to the hotel.

Sonia rushed out the moment Stefan turned off the engine. "Look, more pretty flowers! What are they?"

"That one I know. Those are geraniums."

"Umbrellas on the table. Like the cafés in Rouen." She skipped over to him, and clung on his arm, looking up with eyes wide open. "Can we sit outside?"

"Of course." He patted her head. "But, let's go in first. I'll introduce you to my friend, Maria. She's the owner."

"I thought she was the cook." Hands on hips, she frowned at him.

"Well, they're her recipes." He leaned down and whispered. "She cooks for me, though."

"Ohhh." She pressed her nose to his. "Is she the samodiva?"

"No." He laughed. Taking her hand, he walked inside. "Just a friend."

At the front desk, Maria looked up when they entered. She spoke a few words to the desk attendant, then walked over, smiling.

Stefan beamed with pride. "This is my daughter, Sonia. She's visiting for a few weeks."

Maria bent down and kissed her on her cheeks. "She's even more beautiful than her picture with your wife."

Sonia backed away. Clinging to Stefan, she whispered. "You have a picture of me and Mommy?"

"Yes, sweetheart. It's in the studio. I'll show you when we get back." He wrapped his arm around her, then looked back at Maria. "We came to try your daily specialty."

They went back outside, and soon the waitress brought them colorful glazed earthenware bowls filled with *Emonska kavarma.*

Stefan's stomach growled at the tantalizing aromas. He took a bite. "Mmmmmm. It's delicious." He closed his eyes and indulged in the meal with his other senses, breathing in its appetizing aroma and feeling the tingle of the spices on his tongue.

Sonia didn't touch hers.

"Sweetheart, what's the matter? Don't you want to try the stew?" He reached over and stirred it for her. "It has things you like. See? Pork, onions, carrots, peppers, tomatoes, parsley."

She shook her head. "It reminds me of stuff Mémé makes in a crock pot." Her eyes fluttered and her head drooped.

Stefan motioned for the waitress, paid the bill, and had her package up the meals. He picked Sonia up and carried her to the car. She was asleep before he got home.

Someone had placed a basket on the doorstep. He glanced around the yard, but it looked deserted. After bringing Sonia into her room, he retrieved the basket and brought it into the kitchen. Close on Stefan's heels, Balkan wagged his tail in anticipation of a treat.

"Something smells good in there, doesn't it, buddy." He uncovered the white cloth. The aroma of warm, homemade baked bread drifted out and made his stomach growl and his mouth salivate. Two loaves, decorated with images of beehives, had been smeared with honey. Alongside them was a jar full of the sticky substance.

Who could have left them? Was it a gift to welcome Sonia?

A COUPLE OF hours later, Sonia came bouncing out of her room, with Balkan at her side. "Daddy, I'm starving. Oh, what's in the basket?" She uncovered it, removed one of the loaves, and brought it close to her nose. "Can I have some?"

He nodded. "A small slice for now. I made batter for your favorite meal, chocolate chip pancakes. After that, if you're not too tired, I want to visit my friend, the witch, to bring her the second loaf of bread. She lives by herself in the woods, and I'm sure she'd enjoy your company."

Sonia's eyes grew big. "She's a good witch?"

"Yes, sweetheart." He kissed the top of her head. "She's a good witch."

After she ate, they headed out, with Balkan tagging along. Sonia skipped along the way, picking handfuls of plump blackberries overflowing on the vines. She was still eating them when they arrived at the cottage.

Sultana sat on a rocking chair on her porch with Milo sleeping in her lap. "Stefan, so nice see you. Who be this with you?"

"This is Sonia, my daughter. She came for a visit."

Sonia plopped another blackberry into her mouth, then wiped her berry-stained hand on her shorts.

Sultana groaned as she pushed herself up from the rocking chair. "You be eating blackberries, child?"

"Uh-huh." Sonia cowered behind her father.

He bent down and wrapped his arm around her. "It's okay. She won't hurt you." Then he whispered so only Sonia could hear, "Remember, she's a good witch."

Sonia nodded, but her eyes remained wide open.

"You eat grape before you eat blackberry?"

"N-n-no." Sonia moved even closer to Stefan.

"Bad, very bad. Must always eat grape before black-berry. Grape holy food. Blackberry evil food. You eat evil food and Devil harm you." Sultana started muttering. "Come, come. Me get you what you need to protect from evil." She left the door open and walked inside.

Sonia hesitated outside, tears brimming in her eyes. "Daddy, I don't understand. Why is she saying that?"

Stefan kissed her cheeks and wiped away the tears. "I'm sorry, sweetheart. I didn't mean to scare you with my stories. Sultana's really not a witch. She's my friend." He leaned in closer. "She and Maria give me all kinds of things to protect me from bad things, too. I'll show them to you when we get back."

"What bad things? I'm scared. Does the dragon live here, too?"

"No, there's no dragon here." He took her hand. "Let's go inside for a little bit. It'll be okay. I'm right here. I won't leave you."

She sniffed and nodded. Clutching his hand, she walked into the cottage. Milo sat on the window like a statue, his yellow eyes staring at them. Sonia snuggled closer to her father.

When Sultana returned, she handed Sonia a martenitsa with an evil eye stone attached to it. "Take this, child. It protect you from evil."

Sonia swung the red-and-white amulet in the air. "Thank you. It's adorable."

Stefan held out the bread and honey to Sultana.

"What this?" She took the items.

"Someone left bread on my porch today, and a jar of honey. I wanted to share them with you."

"This special ritual bread. Nona leave for friends. She take care of bees when mother and father die." She walked farther into the room and set them down at the table. "Today *Prokopi Pchelar*, golden honey day. Beekeepers celebrate. Leave sacred bread at hives and church before sunrise. Honey on bread encourage bees make more honey."

As Sultana headed to the kitchen, Stefan looked for Sonia. He smiled. She was playing with Milo, swinging the martenitsa around while the cat jumped after it. Sultana returned with some colorful ceramic bowls and poured milk from the kettle over the fireplace into them. She handed one to Stefan, then broke the bread and handed him a piece.

She pointed to the honey. "This magical. See comb inside? It heal pain and ills and human soul. You take back with you. Meant for you. Help you." She sat in her rocker. "Now, why you come here today? What on you soul, son? Look like you shadow built in wall."

He told her about his dream. When he finished, she hobbled away to the trunk by her medicine cabinet. Rummaging around for something, she returned a moment later carrying an agate gemstone amulet. She handed it to Stefan.

"This protect you from evil. You dream of bees bad omen. Beware red hair. Evil want to hurt you and you daughter."

Red hair? Nikola? Surely he wouldn't try to hurt Sonia.

Age of Innocence

July 20

CARINA LOVED STEFAN, but now she had awakened Dushan's memories in him. In time, her *kamoles* would return. This was her desire, but she didn't want to lose Stefan. Connected to both, a part of her would be torn away if she lost either one. When Dushan returned, would Stefan remember those he now loved? She couldn't take that away from him. His pure love for his daughter came from the heart. Sonia's visit filled him with life.

Closing her eyes, she called on the powers of the white light to provide her guidance. She stretched out her palms toward the ceiling and began a low chant, drifting away until stillness engulfed her. Her body tingled as its rays descended to the tips of her fingers. The power travelled down her arms and through her body, encompassing her mind and soul, bringing her peace.

Morena's cry shattered the serenity. "Carina, come quickly!"

She ran to her sister's side.

Rocking back and forth, Morena clutched the Astro Calendar. "The Evil One's wicked intent is known to me. The Goddess didn't give him the gift, so he infects his blood each time he uses our sworn sister's potion. It makes him angry, and a craving to kill consumes him." Her complexion pale, she turned to Carina, whispering, "The girl is in danger."

Shaking with anger and fear, Carina rushed toward the exit, shouting over her shoulder. "I must guard her against him. She is the child of the one I love."

SONIA FLITTED ACROSS the cobbled stones like a bird, peering in the boutique windows while Stefan unloaded door panels from the trunk of his car, where he parked at the edge of the pedestrian street. "We'll drop these off first, then go see a friend of mine to talk about my art exhibit. After that, my princess, I am at your service."

She giggled and curtseyed to his bow, the white daisies on her blue dress swaying with her movement. Taking her hand so she wouldn't run off again, he walked into the shop. Nikola was running his fingers through his red hair while he leaned against a counter.

"Damn, he's here." Stefan covered his mouth, but Sonia had left his side to look at a wooden rocker.

Hands in his pockets, Nikola strutted over. "Stefan, so nice to see you." He grinned, but his eyes remained cold.

"Sorry, I can't stay and chat. I have a meeting with Elena." He dropped the panels off at the desk and called to his daughter. "Sweetheart, let's go. We can stop at another shop later to look for things."

She skipped over and stopped, looking up at Nikola. "Hello, are you Daddy's friend?"

"You must be Sonia." He crouched down. Catching one of her curls, he wrapped it around his forefinger, tugging at it. "You look like your mother."

Stefan drew her closer to him. "I'll pick up the new work on my way back."

Outside, Sonia whispered. "He scares me. I think he's the red dragon. He doesn't live in Emona, does he?"

"No, sweetheart." He squeezed her hand. "Don't think about him. Let's go meet my friend in the café across the street. Afterwards, we can go shopping."

He grabbed his sketchpad from the car. Sonia hopped from one cobblestone to the next. "This is like the shopping places in Rouen."

Stefan spotted Elena right away at one of the outside tables, and waved to her.

"This must be your daughter." She glanced at Sonia, then turned her attention to Stefan. "I thought you were going to leave her with a babysitter."

"I didn't think you'd mind since our meeting shouldn't take too long. I wanted to show my little angel the Sea Gardens."

"I like your hat." Sonia pointed to the leopard-skin, pill-box. "A shop where I go to school sells funny ones like that."

"Hmph."

"I know a joke." Sonia peered up at Elena. "What did one hat say to the other? You stay here. I'll go on a head." Sonia giggled, holding her side.

Stefan smiled. "Sorry. She gets the bad jokes from me."

Elena extended a gloved hand to Sonia. "Nice to meet you."

Sonia shook it and ran her fingers over the material. "Oh, I really like these. They match your hat and they're so soft."

Stefan laid his sketchpad on the table, and opened it. "Here's an idea—"

"Daddy." Sonia squirmed in her seat. "I have to go to the bathroom."

Elena frowned. "The waitress can show her where it is so we can discuss the exhibit."

Stefan stood and held out his hand to Sonia. "I'd rather go with her. We'll be right back. If the waitress comes by while we're gone, would you please order lemonade for Sonia and black coffee for me?"

When they returned a few moments later, Elena was looking through the sketchbook. "These are wonderful ideas, but you've done so little. Will you have more by the end of the week?"

"I'll get some done by Friday. I've wanted to spend time with Sonia while she's here."

"Daddy, look. A mermaid doll." Sonia swung her arm around to point, knocking over her drink. As the lemonade splashed onto Elena's gloves, Sonia covered her mouth. "Oh, I'm so sorry. It was an accident."

Elena looked at the growing stain. She stood and adjusted her hat. "Perhaps we can meet later, when you have more time to devote to your art. The exhibit is important to your career."

"Yes, I'm sorry. That sounds good. I should have rescheduled." He stood and patted Sonia on her head. "I have so little time with my daughter, but I'll work on more ideas when I get home." He pointed to the gloves. "Let me get those cleaned for you."

Elena waved her hand in front of her. "No, it's fine. Call me when you want to reschedule."

When Elena had disappeared into the crowd, Sonia tugged on her father's sleeve. "Daddy?"

"Yes, sweetheart."

"I didn't mean to make your friend leave."

He kneeled next to her. "I know. It was an accident." He stood and took her hand. "Do you want to look at that doll?"

"No. Let's go home." She lowered her head.

They returned to Nikola's shop. After picking up the panels, Stefan buckled Sonia in and started the car.

She twisted the edge of her dress, then looked over at him. "Daddy, that wasn't your samodiva was it?"

"No." He smiled. "Only a friend who has an art gallery. She's helping me with an exhibit."

Sonia remained quiet the entire drive home. When Stefan unlocked the front door, she dashed past him toward the studio.

"Sonia?" He tossed his keys onto the table by the couch and hurried after her.

She held the family photo, tears streaming down her face. "Mommy, I'm so glad *she's* not the one you told me about."

"Sonia, honey? What's wrong?" His heart ached from the pain reflected in her face. Each night when he tucked her in, she said good-night to her mother, too. What did she really understand about death?

She looked over, and he held his arms out to her. Rushing over to wrap hers around him, she banged the picture against his back. She sobbed, squeezing her eyes tight. "I miss Mommy."

He did too. The ache he had thought had subsided once again overwhelmed him. The mother of his child should be here to make their family whole. He held her for a while longer, stroking her hair, until she calmed.

She stepped back and wiped her eyes with her sleeve. "Oh, what a beautiful flower." Setting the picture on the floor, she stooped to pick up the blossom. "What is it? Where did you find it?"

"That's edelweiss. Your—" He bent down closer to her. "Do you remember when you said Mommy talked to you?"

She nodded.

"That same night, she talked to me and left me that flower."

"Where did she get it?" Sonia looked up, her eyes bright with new tears.

"Maybe on the hill behind the cheshma. I saw one there before."

Someone knocked at the door. Stefan hugged Sonia and picked up the picture. "Maybe that's Neda coming by to—"

"Neda!" She rushed over to the door, where Balkan already sat wagging his tail. Throwing it open, Sonia yelled, "Are you really going to take me to the beach?"

"I am, little mermaid. Go get your swimsuit on."

Sonia rushed to her room, and was back in no time, clutching Bluei. She ran over to Neda, jumping so the sundress covering her bathing suit billowed out. "I'm going to swim, and find seashells, and look for the samodiva!"

Stefan tilted his head toward Sonia. "Are you sure you're up for this, Neda? As you can see, she's a live wire."

Looking at the still-bouncing girl, she smiled. "She's a darling."

"Keep a constant eye on her so she doesn't wander off."

"I will." She headed to the door, Balkan trotting after her. "Let's go, little mermaid."

Alone for the first time in two weeks, Stefan stood by the door watching the girls disappear down the path. The silence was disquieting. He headed to the studio to do some sketches for Elena's approval. He soon lost interest, preferring to work on Kalyna's portrait. Since he'd met her, his life had become an endless dream. She made him feel the joy of being loved again.

If she's a dream, I don't want to wake up.

Something new and exciting flourished within him. A love like he had never hoped to experience again. Would Sonia accept another woman in Katherine's place? He wanted her to meet Kalyna, but she had disappeared again after the night of the eclipse. Would Kalyna even welcome his child?

After he'd been painting for a couple of hours, thunder rumbled in the distance. Setting aside his brushes, he covered the portrait with a white sheet and moved it to the back of the studio. He looked out the window. Dark clouds blotted out the sun, and drops of rain peppered the stone path.

The house was too quiet. Had Neda worked a miracle, and the two of them come back without making any noise? "Sonia? Neda? Are you here?"

He looked around for them, but they weren't inside. He opened the door and walked out onto the porch. Neda came rushing up the steps, out of breath—and alone.

"Stefan! Help! Sonia's missing." She wiped her fingers across her swollen, red eyes.

His heart raced. He grabbed her arms and held on none too gently. "What do you mean, missing? I told you to keep a close eye on her."

"Balkan barked at something in the woods, and I looked. When I turned back, Sonia had disappeared." She twisted her hair into a tight knot. "I don't know what happened. Oh god, she's lost. I looked all around, but couldn't find her."

"Go find your Uncle Peter. Tell him to get people together to help me search for her." He rushed down the path, yelling over his shoulder. "Then come back here and wait in case she returns."

As soon as he reached the beach, Stefan followed footprints to the boulders, but found only a basket filled with flowers. He combed the shoreline, dashing from one rock to the other, calling for Sonia and looking for traces of clothing or shoes. Peter and some others appeared and spread out the search.

Balkan barked and howled from farther down the coast. Stefan sprinted there and spotted the puppy sitting next to something on the sand. It was only a crab.

Seagulls screeched as they flew in the sky that darkened by the minute. The rumbling thunder grew louder, and thick masses of ominous gray clouds spat out fat drops of rain. A flash of light lit up the sky, and a deafening crack of thunder boomed. In a rush, sheets of rain came down. Wild gusts of wind whipped through the air, nearly knocking him over.

Balkan growled and crouched. Stefan froze when a black wolf ran past, dashing into the woods. It held Bluei clenched in its teeth. Chills went through his body, and dread pierced his heart.

Please let this be another crazy dream.

Another bright bolt of lightning split the sky, followed by a resounding clap of thunder.

He sprinted over to where the wolf had disappeared. Bluei lay on the ground. He picked the bear up and crushed it to his chest. Peering into the forest, he couldn't see farther than a foot. He needed a lantern. Stefan rushed home, his lungs constricting with pain at his speed. He couldn't lose Sonia.

The porch light beamed like a beacon. Balkan was already scratching at the door when Stefan raced up the steps two at a time. He wrenched the door open and bolted inside, water streaming off him, pooling on the floor. He stopped short, gasping for breath.

Sonia sat on the living room couch next to Neda.

Relief swept through him. Dropping Bluei, he grabbed his daughter, squeezing her tight. "You scared me to death. I thought I'd lost you."

"She just got back. I called my uncle and told him she was safe." Neda's voice trembled. "I waited on the porch. A woman walked up the street with her, holding her hand. I ran and got Sonia, but the woman disappeared before I could ask her anything."

"Daddy, I was so scared." Sonia laid her head on his shoulder and wrapped her cold arms around his neck. Tears streamed down her face, and her body trembled. "Th-there was a wolf."

Stefan's legs wobbled. He sat on the couch, still holding her. He felt her heart racing. Tilting her head up, he looked into her face. "You saw a wolf?"

She nodded. "A huge black wolf."

He tightened his embrace and stroked her hair for several minutes until the trembling ceased. "Shh. It's okay. You're safe now."

"I screamed and he jumped on me."

He held her away from him, looking her over. "Did he hurt you?"

She shook her head, sniffled some more, and wiped her eyes. "The samodiva saved me. She's my friend. I see her in my dreams."

Neda gasped. Stefan swiveled his head toward her. Her face had blanched.

He turned back to his daughter. "Why do you think it was the samodiva, sweetheart?"

"She was beautiful like you told me, and she rode a magic black horse."

The woman from the meadow? She was the only one he had seen get near the wild horses. Who was she? One of the gypsies?

"She whipped the wolf, and he ran away. Then she brought me back to the village."

Stefan stroked her hair. "We'll have to try to find her and thank her. But, sweetheart, why did you wander off alone? You worried us."

"I wanted to find the place where the edelweiss grows." She sniffled. "I thought I might see Mommy there."

"She can always find you. Please don't go looking for her, especially not in the woods." Stefan kissed the top of her head.

Sonia yawned, so Stefan stood and carried her to her room. He tucked her in and walked away.

"Daddy, please tell me another story about the samo-diva."

He sat on the edge of the bed. "Once upon a time in a mystical land called Emona, there lived a beautiful samo-diva ..."

As he continued talking, Sonia's breathing became steady and even. Her hand opened and an edelweiss fell onto the blanket.

Something Wicked

STEFAN INSERTED A silver key into the jewelry box's lock. He turned it until it clicked and opened a crack. Something glowing inside hissed. His fingers grazed the lid, but it flew open on its own. A three-headed black snake with red eyes sprang toward him, its tongues darting in and out, striking his face. He turned away, but the snake slithered from the jewelry box and coiled tight over Stefan's torso. Then across his shoulders. Around his throat. He couldn't breathe.

He gripped the snake's body, yanking on it, trying to escape from its embrace, but it constricted even more. The eyes from each head glared at him. Then they merged into one, and the visage became Nikola's, wearing an evil smile, his red eyes blazing like a demon's.

Sinister laughter erupted from this throat, but it turned into a cry of anguish. "Why did you kill Katherine?" Nikola screamed at him. "You'll pay for that."

The face changed once again, this time into a wild beast that opened its savage mouth. Stefan tried to scream, but the creature's body still gripped his throat.

WIPING THE SWEAT off his face, Stefan continued to paint. He shook his head to chase away the bad memory of last night's dream playing before his eyes. Sultana's warning and Nikola's attitude yesterday had come to a head in his sleep. The potion no longer worked, if it ever had.

Outside the window, the sun had reached the horizon, covering the sea with dark violet colors. He had to show Sonia. She'd played quietly in her room all day, claiming to be tired. He hoped she wasn't getting a summer cold. As he put away his brushes, Balkan bounded in, circling Stefan's feet and barking with a deafening racket.

"What's the matter, buddy? Are you hungry?" He patted the dog. "Let me check on Sonia first, then I'll feed you."

Balkan nearly tripped him as he headed to Sonia's room, all the while persistently barking.

"Well, you certainly can't wait, can you?" Stefan chuckled as he opened the bedroom door.

He looked at the empty bed where Sonia should be lying. When he stepped into the room, his body shook. He found her crumpled on the floor, mumbling.

"Sonia!" He rushed to kneel by her, feeling her pulse. It was racing. He touched her face. It burned with a fever. He patted her cheeks. "Sonia, can you hear me?"

He lifted her from the floor onto the bed, then rushed to the bathroom, soaked a washcloth in cold water, and hurried back to place it on her forehead.

Now what?

His fingers brushed the phone in his pocket. Maria could help him get Sonia to a hospital in Varna. He dialed her number. "Please come quickly. Sonia's feverish and unconscious. Hurry, please." He hung up without waiting for a response.

Sitting on the bed next to her, he held her burning hands in his. "You're going to be fine, sweetheart." He smoothed her hair, then brushed his fingers over her cheeks as he continued to murmur comforting words. Every once in a while Sonia shrieked, struggling as if trying to escape someone's grasp, and finally falling back onto the bed, mumbling.

Beads of sweat poured off him, drenching his shirt. He looked at his watch. "Where's Maria?"

She knocked, then came in. Peter was with her. Sonia opened her eyes. A white film covered them. She struggled against Stefan's hold and screamed again, her words unrecognizable.

Maria groaned. "We have to bring her to Sultana. This is no ordinary illness. It's an *uroki*. She's possessed by a bad spirit."

Shaking his head, Stefan squeezed his eyes shut and let out a long breath. "We don't have time for such nonsense." He opened his eyes and pointed to Sonia. "Look at her! This is the twenty-first century. She needs immediate medical attention."

Peter grasped Stefan's shoulders, turning him away from Sonia. "A doctor won't be able to save her. Maria's right. Sultana can help. We have to hurry."

"Fine!" Stefan clenched his teeth. "We've wasted enough time. Let's go ... *somewhere* to get her help." He picked up Sonia and headed toward the door.

Darting back and forth between Peter and Stefan's feet, Balkan barked and looked at Stefan with earnest eyes.

"Come along." Stefan glanced down, then headed out the door Maria held open. "Who knows how long this will take."

Sonia mumbled while they rushed down the path. Every once in a while she screeched with laughter. At other times she screamed in terror. As they neared Sultana's, Sonia's body shook. She thrust her arms and legs out straight. Then her eyes opened wide. With one final yell, she went limp, her eyes open in stark terror.

"Sonia!" Stefan held her tighter as he ran the last few steps toward the cottage, Balkan and the others right behind him.

Sultana met them on the steps, holding the door open. "Put her on floor, next to fire!"

Shooing Milo off the old rug, Maria straightened it as the cat scampered off, peering at them from behind a trunk. Balkan went over to sniff the cat while Stefan placed Sonia down. Clenching his fists, he moved to the side when Sultana and Peter came closer.

Sultana kneeled and grasped Sonia's swollen hand. "How she get scratch?"

"I don't know." Stefan clasped his finger to his head and shook it back and forth. "A wolf attacked her yesterday. Maybe it scratched her. I-I didn't even notice it."

Taking hold of Sonia's face, Sultana opened the girl's eyes. She shook her head, grunted when she stood, and shuffled over to her medicine cabinet. A moment later, she returned with an assortment of odd items—bells, a white flag, a clove of garlic, a bouquet of herbs, white caps, a colorful stick decorated with strange symbols, and a ceramic pitcher full of vinegar.

Maria touched his shoulder. "Don't worry. Sultana has the power and knowledge to heal Sonia."

He swept his sweaty palm over the objects Sultana had laid out. "With *those*?" How were all of those things going to make Sonia well? He should have taken her to Varna, but he wouldn't make it there in time now. He had to let them perform their strange ritual and pray for the best.

"Yes. With those. Have faith." She patted his arm.

Their actions played out in front of Stefan like a bad dream. Maria gathered the herbs and attached them to the flag. Sultana placed the jug of vinegar on a three-legged stool. She ground the clove of garlic and added it to the vinegar. Peter handed each of them a cap and bells. Next, the three of them placed the caps on their heads and attached the bells to their ankles.

When Sonia began to convulse, Stefan paced the room, whispering, "Please help her."

In a low tone, Sultana said, "We ready."

She picked up the flag and chanted in a strange language. Peter and Maria followed her lead, dancing around Sonia, slow at first, but soon in a wild frenzy. The vinegar in the copper jug began to boil. Sultana dipped herbs into it and sprinkled the liquid on Sonia's head. Shaking even more, Sonia's body twisted on the floor. Foam poured out of her mouth.

Stefan's chest tightened. Sonia couldn't die.

Balkan growled at the door. Stefan walked over to the open window to see what was out there. His breath caught. A huge black wolf crouched near the cottage. Was it the same one?

A screech from the sky filled the night air. The white falcon hovered overhead. It descended toward the wolf, attacking with its beak and claws, forcing the animal to withdraw into the underbrush. The falcon circled the cottage a few times, then disappeared. Stefan shook his head. It had all been so sudden. Had it happened at all?

When he turned his attention back to the ritual, the dancing had ceased. Peter and Maria lifted the rug Sonia lay on. Sultana massaged Sonia's forehead with the vinegar mixture and lifted her chin to make her swallow some of the liquid.

Peter and Maria lowered Sonia to the ground, and Sultana began another chant. When she finished, she picked up the jug and smashed it with the colorful stick. The liquid flew all around, landing on them all. Peter and Sultana moved out of the way, leaving Maria to be covered with most of it. Within moments, Maria groaned and dropped to the floor and twisted in agony.

Stefan opened his mouth to scream.

"Daddy?" The weak voice drew his attention from Maria. Sonia struggled to get up, her face pale and her eyes wide open.

"Oh, sweetheart. I'm here." He hurried to her and squeezed her tight. "Everything's going to be fine now."

Her body shook as she wrapped her hands around his neck. "Where am I?"

"You're at Sultana's. You had a fever, but it's gone now." He looked at her hand, still a little swollen. "How are you feeling?"

"Dizzy and scared. I dreamed two black wolves with big red eyes wouldn't let me out of a cave." She looked around. "Where's Bluei?"

"At home on your bed. We'll go get him soon." He hugged her and kissed her forehead.

While Stefan sat with Sonia, Peter and Sultana repeated their ritual over Maria.

"It done now." Sultana wiped her brow. "We leave them rest. Come." She motioned to Stefan.

First checking on Maria, Stefan followed Sultana to the medicine cabinet.

She handed him an ointment. "Take. It heal child's hand."

"Thank you." He glanced at the items scattered on the floor. "For all of this. I don't know what I'd have done if I lost Sonia."

She patted his hand. "She be fine. *Uroki* gone."

He returned and sat next to Sonia on the hearth. Balkan had his head on her lap. "Sweetheart, do you feel strong enough to go home? It's already dark."

She nodded.

Stefan turned to Maria. "How about you? Are you okay to leave now?"

"I'll wait for Peter, thank you."

Stefan looked around. "Where is he?"

"No worry. He fine." Sultana walked to the door and opened it, peering around. "He return soon."

Stefan stood, and held his hand to help Sonia up.

She hugged Sultana. "Thank you. You are a good witch."

Smiling, Sultana patted Sonia's hand. "No witch, child. *Znahar*. Heal with herbs."

The sun had dipped below the horizon by the time they reached the cheshma. The howling of wolves filled the night air, so Stefan pulled Sonia closer to him and rushed home.

252

Bittersweet Revenge

July 28

NIKOLA'S BLOOD SURGED hot through his veins. Boyan carried out his task without incident and stored the paintings in the secret room. Nikola wouldn't send this art abroad. When his plan served its purpose, he'd find a way to restore Elena's reputation.

In spite of his success, he'd slept and eaten little recently. A mounting emotional strain boiled beneath the surface of his consciousness, ready to erupt. It filled him with self-loathing; the fallout of his revenge against Stefan would bury Elena as well.

Certain his plan would work, he prepared to put act two into motion. He placed a call to his lawyer. "Get the paperwork ready. I want to move on this immediately."

He hung up. His phone showed a missed call from Elena. Humming while he called her back, he told himself he wouldn't give in to her anguish. He could hold on and force her to need him, to depend on him, to love him.

"I've been robbed!" She could hardly get the words out through her sobbing. "I don't know what to do. Please help me."

"What happened?" A pang of anguish tore through him. She'd understand in time why he had to do this. His plan would bring them closer together.

"My gallery. It's been ransacked. All the paintings are gone. " She drew in deep breaths, interrupted by hiccupping. "Lord, what am I going to do now?"

"I'm coming over there right now. Call the police if you haven't already. I'll take care of everything." A smug smile of satisfaction spread across his face.

Payback time had begun. Stefan wouldn't be so eager to show him mercy this time.

NIKOLA'S HEART ACHED when he approached Elena. Her shoulders, normally so straight, sagged while she paced the walkway outside her gallery. She looked so small, frail, and vulnerable. He longed to hold her with tenderness, to love her and have his love returned. As soon as he got Stefan out of the way, everything would be right again, and Elena would be his.

She jumped when he came near. "I'm devastated. How could this have happened? The worst part is my insurance never got reinstated." Her chest heaved and uncontrollable sobs escaped. She wiped away the tears, but more welled in her eyes.

"Don't worry." Nikola wrapped his arm around her shoulder. "I'm sure the police will find the paintings, and everything will be okay."

"I still can't believe it." Her eyes were wild, and her voice wavered. "What am I going to do now?"

"You're resourceful. You'll find a way to survive." With his fingers, he wiped away the black streaks coursing down her cheeks. "I have so many contacts in town who can help you. Together we'll think of something."

"Strong, dependable Nikola. What would I do without you?" She rested her head on his shoulder.

"It's getting late. Let me drive you home." He took her hands in his. "If you give me your car keys, I'll send someone over to drive your vehicle back. I'll stay with you until you fall asleep. You're too upset to be alone."

"Yes, thank you." She shuddered as she looked back at the gallery. "Why did they cancel my insurance? Who would want to do this to me?"

* * *

BACK AT ELENA'S apartment. Nikola took the key from her trembling hand and unlocked the door. He led her to the couch, fluffing a pillow and placing it behind her.

"Let me make you some tea with honey." He squeezed her palm and rubbed the thumb of his other hand across her cheek. "It'll relax you so you can sleep."

"Thank you." She yawned and leaned her head back. "You're such a good friend."

Her eyes were closed when he returned a few moments later, holding a steaming cup for her and a glass of whiskey for himself. She flinched when he sat close to her on the sofa.

"Shh. It's only me." He handed her the tea, wrapping his hands around her shaking ones.

She took a sip and let out a long breath, then leaned against him. "What am I going to do? I have so many commitments, so many events I'll have to reschedule."

"It'll be fine, my dear. Trust me." He kissed her on the cheek.

She sat up with a start and clasped her hands over her mouth. "What am I going to tell Stefan?" Looking at Nikola, she opened her eyes wide. "He's been working so hard getting ready for his exhibit. I don't know if I'll be able to reopen in time for that. He's such a brilliant artist and bound to be successful if he doesn't let his daughter distract him."

Gripping his glass, Nikola rose and refilled it. "Don't worry about him. He'll manage." He drained the whiskey and poured another. "Let's think about you and your gallery right now."

"The gallery." The words were soft, spoken through quivering lips. The cup rattled in the saucer as she picked it up.

Nikola rejoined her. He steadied her hand as she took another sip. When her head drooped, he set the drink on the table and wrapped his arm around her shoulder. "You should get to bed now."

"Yes." She jerked her head up, then started to doze again.

He helped her stand and brought her to her room. After he removed her shoes, he laid her down, covering her with a blanket. He pulled a chair next to the bed and held her hand until she fell asleep.

Tip-toeing out of the room, he returned to the living room to pour another glass of whiskey. He shook with anger, his pulse hammering with rage. *Stefan's manipulating her, but all she still thinks about is him!* He swallowed the drink, then slammed the glass down.

He stalked outside. The fresh air slapped his face and chilled his body, but didn't cool the wrath swelling within. He wanted revenge *now*, before he lost Elena completely. There might be another way, something quicker, one that didn't mean ruining Elena, too.

Nikola walked over to his car. Wrenching a ticket off the windshield, he lost his last shred of control. He crumpled it and threw it on the street, then stormed off into the night, howling in agony.

If Wishes Were Horses

August 5

LEANING AGAINST THE ivy-covered walls in the lowest cavern, Carina hugged her legs close to her face. Her eyes closed, she listened to Morena play a song about the seduction of shepherds on her *outi*, with the waterfall humming a background harmony. The melody shimmered on her soul like the mist glittering on her skin from the glow of the torches. Legends had arisen decreeing Carina the most talented of the sisters, their writers unaware of the jewel hidden in Morena, known to them only as the huntress. She alone could quench Carina's emotional fires with the sweetness of her voice, embodied with the spirit of the Muse Aoide.

Carina lowered her head, her hair draping over her bare feet. She pondered Sonia, so like a delicate flower. Last night, while she patrolled the woods, Carina projected her mind toward Stefan's house, which she was guarding, then into the room where the child lay sleeping. Her heart reached out to the sweet, innocent being.

The next moment she crossed the threshold of space, passing into the girl's dream. It was as if Sonia herself had pulled Carina there. The girl must possess special powers that only a samodiva should have. How was that possible?

Sonia had looked up from her drawing. "You came!" She smiled at Carina, then bit her lower lip. "You are my daddy's samodiva, aren't you?"

"Yes, sweet child." She sat next to her. "Is this me?" She pointed to a woman with golden hair.

"Morena!" A screech from above wrenched Carina out of her memory.

Laying her *outi* down, Morena dashed away to the path leading to the temple above them.

Carina jumped up and followed. Leaning against the rocks that formed an archway at the beginning of the passage, she listened to the angry words choked out through bouts of crying. Another samodiva had fallen prey to a mortal while she bathed. That meant they must prepare a sacrifice to appease Bendis. She covered her ears. Why did this now bother her? They had performed these rites before. She dashed around to the other side of the pool, clambering up the boulders, and disappearing into the shelter behind the waterfall. Its deafening roar drowned the shouts from above.

Sitting on a stone bench, she returned to musing about Sonia. The child had accepted Carina in the dream, but would she in reality? Could she fit into his world, their world?

"Carina!" Morena's shout echoed over the waterfall's roar.

She opened her eyes, returning to the turmoil that churned around her. Passing along the path behind the waterfall, she hastened to her sister's side. "When must we prepare the sacrifice?"

"Tonight." Morena grasped her shoulders. "But, sister, that's not why I returned. Misfortune awaits your beloved soon. The signs were cloudy. I cannot tell you when. We must be diligent and keep watch together."

AT THE AIRPORT in Sofia, Stefan held in his sadness as he hugged Sonia good-bye. The month had flown by. He caved in to her grandparents' pleas to let her spend the rest of the summer with them. They had been wonderful to him and Sonia, taking them in and caring for his daughter when he retreated from the world after Katherine died.

He didn't begrudge them spending the time with her. Sonia would live with him permanently as soon as he found a reputable private school, or possibly a tutor, who could home-school her.

"I'll miss you, sweetheart." He kissed her forehead and stood. He glanced at the flight attendant, who frowned while she waited to escort Sonia onto the plane. "Call me as soon as you get back."

"I will." Sonia giggled while she clutched Bluei to her chest.

"What's so funny?"

Bouncing from one foot to the other, she gestured with her finger for him to come closer. When he leaned over, she whispered in his ear, "I saw the samodiva last night."

"You did?" His breath caught in his throat. "Where?"

"She talks to me in my dreams."

"Sir." The flight attendant came closer. "She has to come with me now." Taking Sonia's hand, she walked away.

"Wait!" Stefan held out his palm.

Sonia looked over her shoulder, grinning, though tears formed in her eyes. In a sing-songy voice, she said, "The samodiva told me she has a present for you."

He exhaled a long breath as she disappeared into the tunnel. She had called the woman who rescued her from the wolf a samodiva, so it was likely she'd dreamed about her. It couldn't have been Kalyna, Stefan's own mystery woman, whom he used as the model for the stories he told Sonia. His daughter had never met her.

A lady sitting by the window near him rocked a crying infant, rubbing her finger over the baby's gums. The man next to her grumbled while he looked through a carry-on bag, finally pulling out a pacifier and thrusting it at the woman. They soon boarded, as did the others on the flight. With the waiting area nearly empty, Stefan stared out the window. Airport personnel loaded luggage onto a conveyor, while others fueled the plane. Another hour passed before the plane backed out and rolled down the runway.

Even after it had taken flight, he focused on it until it became a spec in the sky. The place where it crossed the path of another plane formed an image that looked like an angel, her wings unfolding. He concentrated on the clouds, squinting at them and turning his head. That one was a bearded man's profile. Another one resembled a dog. Even an ornate picture frame in a gallery.

Elena! He looked at his watch and frowned. Nine-twenty. He wouldn't make it back to Varna for their one o'clock meeting. Surely she would understand he couldn't leave Sonia until her plane departed. He'd call her on the way.

AN INCREDIBLE VOID filled Stefan's heart. His ride to Varna without Sonia seemed endless, and too quiet, without her constant exclamations of delight. He turned on his phone, dialing Elena. Hearing nothing, he looked at the screen. A low-battery warning flashed.

Several hours later, when he finally walked through the glass doors at the gallery main entrance, he found Elena speaking to one of her attendants. She met his gaze and held up her index finger. Resuming her conversation, she pointed at a wall where others were hanging paintings on wires, then handed her clipboard to the woman. Un-smiling, she made her way toward him.

"I see you made it." She crossed her arms at her waist. "I thought you got lost."

He took a step back. "I'm sorry. Sonia's flight was delayed."

"Well, I don't have time today to go over your show. I expected you two hours ago." She waved around at the bustle of people positioning pedestals, arranging flowers, and carrying in paintings and sculptures. "As you can see, I'm setting up for my next exhibit now."

"I'm sorry I upset your agenda. We can reschedule." He touched her shoulder. "Is everything else okay?"

"Isn't this enough?" She shrugged him off. "Look at this place! Peeling paint, stained cushions, scuffed-up floors."

Stefan touched the base of his neck as he looked at the pristine white walls with large picture windows, the immaculate love seat in the alcove, the seal-coated hardwood floor. Nothing was out of place or marred.

"Elena." He paused until she looked at him again. "Tell me what's bothering you."

Her shoulders drooping, she sighed. "It's about the gallery ..." She looked around the room. "The ugly truth is I'm being sued by the artist whose paintings were stolen. I-I think I'll have to sell this place to pay for the loss."

"That's terrible." He put his palm on the small of her back. "Let's sit over by the window. Then you can tell me more about it if you want."

She leaned into his shoulder as he guided her to the seat. "This has been my dream since I was a child. Now it's gone because of a clerical error. It's been a difficult time for me."

Sitting next to her, Stefan rubbed her shoulder. "I'm sorry you might have to sell it. I know how much you love this place. What will you do?"

"I'll work for the museum. They've offered me a fantastic job as the curator." She blinked away the tears welling in her eyes. "I-I might not be able to organize your exhibit."

"Don't worry about me." He leaned back onto the loveseat. "Take care of what you need to do."

She reached into her purse for a tissue and wiped away the tears. "I *want* to promote you. You have a special talent."

"I've made contacts from working with Nikola." Stefan shifted his position again, leaning forward. "Some of them have expressed an interest in my art."

"I have an idea." Now smiling, she placed her hand on top of his. "Let's meet on the fifteenth to discuss your exhibit. It's the beginning of Varna Days."

"What's that?"

"It's an important holiday. We celebrate it over four days." She peered out the window. "Signs are posted everywhere telling about all the activities—live music, theater productions, volleyball, lots of food vendors, and fireworks."

"That's a great idea. I'd love to learn more about your culture."

"That's settled then. I'll meet you at the entrance to the Sea Gardens at ten thirty." She stood and smoothed out her dress. "I should have talked to my lawyer about the gallery by then. I'm sure I'll be able to hold your exhibit."

WHEN STEFAN ARRIVED back in Emona, nature echoed his feelings. The wind moaned through the trees, their branches waving as if in sad farewell. He sat on the porch, staring at the sea. Along the coast, waves crested high and came crashing down in the turbulent sea. Balkan crawled out from under the steps, stretched, and rubbed his nose against Stefan's leg.

"At least you're still here." He patted the puppy. "You hungry?"

As he pushed the door open, Balkan squeezed past, headed toward the kitchen. Stefan picked up a crumpled napkin Sonia must have dropped on their way out this morning. After filling Balkan's water dish and feeding him, Stefan washed the dishes, swept the kitchen, and emptied the trash. He sat at the table and picked up the paper he'd been reading that morning. The words made no sense. He folded it, staring at the headlines.

Balkan trotted off, his toenails clacking against the wooden floors. Returning a few moments later, he whined and trotted off again. Once more, he came back. Plopping at Stefan's feet, he heaved a sigh.

"I miss her, too." Leaning over, Stefan scratched the puppy behind the ears. "It's much too quiet." Placing his hands on the table, he pushed himself up. His sketches for Elena weren't going to get done by themselves.

He entered the studio to do some work he had put off for too long. The cloth on Kalyna's portrait hung askew. Had someone been in the house while he was gone? Glancing around the room, he didn't find anything else out of place. Maybe Balkan had knocked the cloth off. Stefan lifted it to set it straight.

The picture Sonia had drawn that morning was there. She had covered it when he tried to look, saying it was a surprise. It showed her holding hands with him and a woman with long blond hair. They all were outside next to a house, with Balkan standing next to Sonia.

Why had she placed it in front of the portrait? She had never met Kalyna.

Portent of Death

August 12

CLANGING BELLS SOUNDED outside Stefan's house while he carved some door panels. A crowd of people, dressed in costumes and wearing daunting masks painted in vivid colors, paraded by his house. He had forgotten about the *kukeri* celebration. Sonia would have enjoyed this. He wished she had stayed for another week.

Peter walked among the costumed men. Like the others, a massive wooden mask, twice the size of his head, obscured his features. With the addition of the layers of animal pelts they wore, none of the men were recognizable.

After the last person passed, Stefan followed them to the village center where the procession made its way past the cheshma to the cheers of the crowd. He joined Maria at a table on the hotel terrace. Like most of the others attending the event, she was dressed in colorful Bulgarian attire similar to what she had worn at Easter.

"It's amazing how many people are here tonight." He scanned those congregating around the fountain and on the terraced hill behind it. "Emona's so empty during the day. It looks like more than a hundred people are here now."

"They've come from the nearby towns to watch the parade and festivities on the beach afterwards." She waved to a group of people.

"The *kukeri* look like Abominable Snowmen, except for the masks." He laughed. "They must be roasting in those costumes."

"The ritual's usually observed at the beginning of Lent, but we celebrate in the summer because more tourists and residents are here."

"I can't pick out Peter. He told me his mask was a goat's face, but I've spotted several of those with 'gaping jaws and wild, fierce eyes and teeth.' " Stefan made quote marks in the air.

As the men danced past he pointed at one. "Why do some of the masks have two faces?"

"The scary face represents evil, and the pleasant face, goodness." Maria twisted her head toward him. "These are two forces existing together in the world."

"Let me guess." Stefan exchanged a knowing look with her. "They have something to do with evil spirits."

She laughed loud enough to be heard over the huge cow bells the *kukeri* wore around their waists. "Yes, they do. The masks protect the people who wear them from evil spirits. I'll have to find a costume for you to wear next year."

"I think you've given me plenty of charms to protect me already." He chuckled. "Look, Todor is waving at us. Are you ready to go to the beach?"

"Yes, dear."

He helped her up from her chair. "What happens at the shore?"

"The *kukeri* perform a *horo* circle dance around a bonfire. And we've set up a huge feast."

"Count me in for the food, especially if you did any of the cooking."

Smiling, she patted his arm. "Thank you, dear."

When Todor arrived, they headed down the gravel road with the rest of the crowd. The *kukeri* continued to dance along the way. Some people banged on drums, while others played flutes and stringed instruments.

A bonfire and torches positioned up and down the coastline lit up the night sky. The smoke curled in the air.

They passed tables laden with fruit, sweets, fish, and much more he didn't recognize.

"Stefan, Todor and I have to set up for the start of the celebration." She scanned the revelers. "Peter is around here somewhere, if you can find him. He's probably still in his costume."

He waved her away. "I'll be fine."

As Maria and Todor headed to the shoreline, Stefan walked around looking at the *kukeri* masks. He imagined them as paintings and regretted he hadn't brought his sketchbook. One man dancing around the bonfire had taken off his costume, but still wore his mask. It resembled a woolly mammoth, with horns protruding from the top of its head, and a long snout with tuffs of hair dangling from its nostrils.

Over by the food table, another man's mask had a huge red mouth. It gaped open, showing sharp wooden teeth, some of which were missing. Above the mouth, nostrils the size of a fist flared on each side of the pug nose. The eyes were deep set below a conic forehead. Scraggly strands of spun sheep's wool hung down on all sides.

Someone banged a gong. All those assembled quieted, shifting their gazes toward the sound. Maria and Todor stood by a small rowboat.

Clearing her throat, Maria recited a protection incantation.

Accept these gifts with gratitude and praise.
That we offer all our days.
Bless us, gracious spirits in the mountains high.
Till ills and woes naught be nigh.
Guard us, divine nymphs of the forests vast.
By your might, keep evil bound at last.
Protect us, lovely maidens of the waters deep.
Guide our kinfolk home while in your keep.

With each line she spoke, she held an object above her head, then placed it into a small wooden boat. Stefan walked around some people and craned his neck to see what they were, but the torchlight Todor held flickered, creating shadows, making it difficult. When she finished, she stepped aside.

Todor faced the gathering. "We now send off presents with light to guide their way."

Walking completely around the boat three times, he held the torch high. He placed it upright in the middle of the gifts, attaching ropes to secure it on all sides. He lifted his hands toward the mountains, then lower pointing to the forest, and finally turning again to face the sea.

He bowed. "Accept these gifts with gratitude and praise."

Each grasping a side of the boat, Todor and Maria pushed it out into the water. "That we offer all our days," they repeated together.

Stefan held his breath as the boat wobbled with each surge of the waves, until it finally steadied. Cheers erupted all around him. Cameras flashed as the vessel drifted out to sea. He released his breath.

Nona sat alone on the rocks. He walked toward her. Would she talk to him today? He at least wanted to thank her for the bread and honey. When she caught sight of him, she ran away again. He shook his head and rejoined the crowd.

Some *kukeri* jumped over a fire. Others pantomimed the planting season. One man used a giant branch, pretending to beat two other men pushing a plow. Most, however, performed wild, frenzied dances around the bonfire, their heavy copper bells ringing over the folk music.

Staying close to the shoreline, Stefan followed the torchlight from Todor's boat until it disappeared into the blackness. Sonia would have loved the celebration. She would have fawned over every costume and begged to participate in each activity. But her grandparents deserved time with her.

"Stefan dear," Maria's booming voice shouted above the uproar of the crowd. "Are you enjoying the festivities?"

He nodded when she joined him. "Lovely protection spell. Were all those spirits, nymphs, and maidens the samodivi?"

"Yes," she hooked her arm in his. "We offer them gifts to give us health and happiness. The boat we sent off has honey, sweet rolls, healing herbs, and flowers to appease them."

"They like sweet rolls and honey?"

"They do. Nona leaves them gifts all the time." She headed back toward the bonfire. "Come join the celebration. The dancing is supposed to scare away evil spirits. But it's also a lot of fun."

"All the noise has given me a headache. I think I'll call it a night."

"No, don't go home, dear." She hung onto his arm. "Some of us are going back to the hotel to have coffee and dessert. I made your favorite, baklava. Won't you join us?"

"Not this time, thank you. It's getting late. I'm rather tired. Besides, I need to feed Balkan. Maybe I'll stop by tomorrow to see if you have leftovers." He patted her arm, then waved to Peter, who appeared too caught up in the dance to notice.

"I'll save you some dessert," Maria called after his retreating figure.

Stefan took the shortcut to his house, thankful for the moonlight, which helped him dodge the overgrown blackberry bushes crowding the path. When he had gone far enough from the festivities so the intensity of the bells had become faint, the crunching of twigs behind him became distinct.

"Peter, is that you?" He stopped and turned around. A figure with a goat mask followed him. "I didn't know you were going to leave also, or I would have waited for you."

The person didn't answer, but continued to advance.

"I thought you were going to go with everyone else to the hotel for baklava."

The man in the costume still didn't say anything.

Perhaps it wasn't Peter. Stefan took a step back, looking along the path for a stick.

The man reached under his costume, retrieving an object that glinted in the moonlight. Stefan squinted. Metal? A knife? He raised his fists to attack. With the quickness of a cat, the man leaped toward him, knocking him to the ground. He winced from the sharp rocks digging into his back. The man's gloved hand clamped tight over Stefan's mouth before he had a chance to yell. Fibers from the furry mask scratched his neck as the man's hot, rancid breaths assaulted his throat in rapid gusts. Hatred glared from the eyes behind the mask.

Stefan grabbed for the knife, but the man was quicker, forcing the cold blade of the dagger against his throat. A trickle of blood inched down his neck. His muscles tensing and his heart racing, Stefan latched onto the man's hand with both of his, forcing the knife away. Who was trying to kill him? Why? Thankful now that Sonia wasn't here, he struggled against the solid grip of his unknown assailant, but the muscular adversary restrained him.

The man wrenched his hand away from Stefan and lifted the dagger high over his head. Pinned down by the man's broad, muscular body, Stefan grabbed the mask and pushed. His attacker groaned, and the weight lifted from Stefan. The body above him bent like an arc and fell with a thud farther along the path. How was that possible? He couldn't have done that.

Scrambling to his feet, Stefan sought his savior. A figure on a horse galloped into the darkness. Branches rustled behind him. He spun around. His assailant had disappeared.

Legs shaking, Stefan stumbled along the path until he reached the cheshma. He sank to his knees by the basin and splashed water on his face. Branches rustled, and he leaped up, his feet at a wide stance and his hands fisted in front of him. The mare Emona snorted at him, shook her head, and trotted off. A quick, high-pitched laugh escaped his lips. He put his hand over his racing heart and breathed in deeply to slow his rapid breath.

A shadow passed through the woods.

"Hello?" Stefan's voice quivered.

"Hello."

His heart skipped a beat. He turned toward the soft, musical voice. "Kalyna."

When she stepped out of the darkness, he ran toward her and wrapped his arms around her, his body still shaking. "What are you doing here so late? This is a dangerous place for a lady." Keeping a firm grip on her, he scanned the area, listening for his assailant.

"It's okay. I have a knife to protect me." She patted the leather pouch at her side. Too large for her small frame, it hung low on her hips.

"Wh-where did you get that?"

"It belongs to my friend. She likes to hunt." She peered up at him.

"Why are you out here in the woods alone?" He scanned the shadows again.

"I arrived late to the *kukeri* dance. When I didn't see you there, I took the shortcut to your house and found you here."

Although the attack left him unnerved, his fears withered away, and tranquility and joy bloomed in their place. "It's so nice to see you again. You vanished from the lighthouse." He looked at her. "You were there with me, weren't you?"

She laughed. "Of course. We were going to watch the eclipse, but you had other plans."

"I had such a crazy dream about you. Candles and hay all over the place, and ... horrible things I don't want to think about again." He ran his fingers down her cheeks.

"Well, you are an artist. I imagine you would have creative dreams."

"I'd hoped you'd have been able to meet my daughter, but she flew back last week."

"I would have liked that. She seemed sweet from her picture." Sighing, she leaned against him. "I'm sorry I missed her. I was away until today."

With his arm still wrapped around her waist, he headed down the path, with quick looks in all directions. "Let's get out of here and go back to my house."

"I'd like that." She snuggled up close to him and lifted her dark eyes to his.

THE LOGS IN the studio fireplace burned down to embers, so Stefan stepped outside to get more wood. The moon had disappeared behind the ridge, and the night had become chilly. He shivered, sensing something watching him. Glancing around, he listened for any footsteps. Nothing besides normal sounds disturbed the night. Balkan crept up beside him, growling. A black cat on the stone wall arched its back and hissed. Crossing himself, he laughed for behaving like Maria. He stacked some wood in his arms and walked back to the porch.

"Come on, buddy. Let's go inside now. Leave the cat alone."

Balkan kept his focus trained on the cat and continued growling. When Kalyna's shadow moved across the window, Stefan gave up. Balkan would bark at the door when he was ready to come in.

Inside, Stefan loaded the fireplace with dry wood. It crackled, sending sparks flying up the chimney. Soon the roaring flames cast dancing lights along the walls. He opened a bottle of wine, cut up some cheese, and set them on the hearth. Lighting a few candles, he placed them on the mantel.

He glanced across the room where Kalyna put on romantic music to complete the setting. Her cheeks flushed when she met his gaze. She lay by the fireplace, leaning on one elbow, with her legs crossed.

When he joined her on the rug, she undid the blue ribbon tying back her hair. Love shone from her eyes as she wrapped it around his wrist like a bracelet. He kissed her with unrestrained ardor, reveling in the taste of raspberries on her full lips, and inhaling the citrus scent of her hair. He drank from her fountain of pleasure, never wanting to stop.

"Kalyna, I love you." He leaned forward and kissed her again.

With a sharp intake of breath, she clasped his face in her palms. He barely heard her whispered words. "I love you, too."

"My life has been torn into two worlds since I met you. One where the two of us alone exist and I can love you and be with you forever." He outlined the curves of her lips with his fingertips. "The other one where thoughts of you torment me night and day, but you always remain out of my reach. What kind of magic power do you hold over me?"

She breathed soft words into his ear. "Only the power of love."

"What are you doing to me? Are you real or is nature playing tricks on me?" He ran his fingers down the length of her silky hair, twirling it into a curl at the end.

Leaning closer, she kissed his face, his shoulders, and his chest. "Does this feel real?"

It ignited a passion that burned within his body and soul. He unbuttoned her white silk shirt, kissing each patch of warm skin as it became exposed. He thirsted with a sweet, mad passion, savoring the moment.

The flames from the fireplace illuminated their entwined bodies, while the fire danced within to the rhythm of the music. Nothing existed but the world he saw through her eyes. His body and soul merged into one with Kalyna's, their budding love destined to be ardent, passionate—and permanent.

Touch of Truth

August 15

THE BLACK STALLION galloped through the incoming tide across the sandy beach. The woman bent low on its back, clinging to the horse's mane, trying to outrace Stefan. Her hair streamed behind her like sea foam from a receding wave. Steam burst forth from the animal's nostrils, its breathing labored and its flanks heaving. Its hooves threw up a spray of sand and salt water, stinging his face. He urged his own mare on to the breaking point, getting closer with each stride until they rode side by side.

A wreath of flowers encircled her blond hair. Looking at his rival's pale face, he smiled. Kalyna! Wild and free, her eyes black as charcoal. He spurred his horse on, pulling ahead of her, but she came up level to him once more.

With one last glance at him, she raced the horse ahead to the boulder, leaving only hoof prints in the sand. She jumped down and twirled, her hair streaming around, hiding her face. Stefan dismounted, the warm sand coating his wet feet. She stopped her dance and rushed toward him with arms outstretched, a radiant smile setting her face aglow.

He reached for her, but she laughed and backed away toward the sea. When he took another step forward, she stepped backward. He moved forward two steps, and she retreated again, still laughing at him. When he reached the water's edge, he rushed toward her, grabbing her around the waist before she had a chance to escape. She shrieked with laughter, pushing at his chest until they both tumbled into the waves.

Pulling her on top of him, he kissed her passionately under the heat of the sun, overcome by the intoxicating citrus smell of her hair. He ran his hand down the back of her off-the-shoulder white dress. In a flash, the dress, as well as his own clothing, rose and fell on the waves a foot away. The two of them were soon lost in the eternity of their moment together.

SOMEONE TAPPED STEFAN'S shoulder interrupting his pleasant dream. He opened his eyes and rubbed his stiff neck. "Elena, sorry, I must have nodded off in the warm sun." He tucked his sketchpad under his arm and stood.

"I apologize for being so late." She smiled. Classy as always, she resembled a sunflower with her furry black hat with its yellow pearl petals.

"Don't worry about it." He turned toward the swan-shaped sundial at the Sea Garden entrance. Eleven-fifteen. Forty-five minutes late. Being even a minute late was quite unlike her. He grinned. "It's your turn."

The overpowering scent of familiar cologne gave him a clue to her tardiness even before a man behind him cleared his throat.

"Nikola." Stefan turned around.

"It's my fault. I stopped by." He glared at Stefan. "We started talking and lost track of time."

Nikola's phone rang before Stefan could reply.

"Excuse me." He walked off a short distance, but returned a moment later, scowling. "I'm sorry, Elena, my dear. I have an unscheduled meeting I have to attend." He lifted her hand and kissed her fingers. Without another word to Stefan, he disappeared into the crowd.

Elena crooked her arm in his. "Let's move to the amphitheater. A new folk band is playing. I think you'll like the music. Later, we can visit Yuzhen Beach to watch a volleyball tournament if you want."

They walked in silence for a while. A woman with long blond hair passed by. Stefan released Elena's arm.

"Excuse me one moment." He rushed after the woman. "Kalyna?"

She turned at his touch.

"Sorry." He smiled. "I thought you were someone else."

"You still haven't found your muse?" Elena frowned. "With all the wonderful drawings you've done, I wouldn't think you'd still need her for inspiration."

"I've found her. She's my own samodiva." Stefan's voice deepened. "But she keeps disappearing on me."

"Certainly you don't believe in that." Elena walked away. "Well, that wasn't her, so let's get to the amphitheater before we miss the concert."

Stefan hurried to catch up. "No, of course, I didn't mean for real. But so many strange things happen when she's around."

"What things?" Elena stopped, her lips drawn in a tight line.

"For one, I keep seeing vivid events, like memories, when I look in her eyes. Even though I know I've never experienced them, they're so real." He paused. "You'll think I'm crazy. But, it's like we've lived a life together before."

"You're right. That is crazy."

Someone grabbed his hand and traced the lines on his palm. "*Preroden otnovo.*"

"What are you doing?" He wrenched his hand free from the gypsy.

Elena pulled him to the side. "Don't pay any attention to her. They want money for their fortune telling."

"What did she say?"

"Reborn or something like that."

"What?"

She waved her hand in the air as if dismissing the matter. "Ignore her. They always talk nonsense. Let me talk to her and give her some leva, so she'll stop bothering you."

She walked over to the cart where the woman sold bottles of colorful liquids. Elena gestured toward Stefan. The gypsy handed her a blue bottle in exchange for the currency.

When Elena returned, he glanced back at the gypsy, who pushed her cart away. "What did she give you?"

Her face colored, and she walked away. "I'm not sure. She insisted I take something for the money."

STEFAN AND ELENA managed to squeeze into two adjoining seats in the packed open-air theater. All around them, various shades of green-leafed trees and shrubbery encircled the platform where the band played and other performers danced. At center stage behind the musicians, yellow-green vines twisted down the curved pillars, in stark contrast to the colorful red, yellow, black, and white of the costumes the entertainers wore.

Stefan soon tapped his feet and clapped his hands to the lively beat of the reeds, stringed instruments, and tambourines. Dancers twirled on the stage in two lines that swung back and forth like an accordion. Elena, her eyes transfixed on the performance, leaned forward, swaying to the magic of the music.

At the end of the song, she turned toward him and waved her hand in front of her flushed face. "It's a bit hot. I saw a refreshment stand nearby. I'll be right back."

Stefan stood. "Let me get it."

"No, no. They overcharge foreigners, especially the ones who don't speak the language." She stood before he could object.

She returned a moment later with two cups and something wrapped in paper. "Some wine and *banitsa* to enjoy while we discuss your exhibit." Handing him the food and a drink, she sat next to him.

"Thanks. Maria makes this for me, too. Wonderful stuff." He took a bite. "So, what did your lawyer tell you about the exhibits? Can you still hold them?"

"Yes." She took a sip of her drink, her hand shaking a little. "I even have a buyer for the gallery. He offered me a price that would cover all my losses from the lawsuit."

"That's wonderful." Stefan touched her shoulder, and she leaned closer to him. "It's still a shame you have to sell it."

"My one requirement was to be able to keep my remaining commitments. They assured me this was acceptable." She raised her cup. "*Nazdrave*. To success."

"Cheers." He touched his cup to hers and took a sip. "Hmm. That has a different flavor. It's rather sweet."

"A honey-wine. It goes well with the *banitsa*." She looked down at her purse. "We should discuss your exhibit while the band is taking a break."

Stefan opened his sketchbook. "These are what I have so far for the 'Mystery of Emona' series. I'm sorry it's not more. Most of them are still in my head, waiting for me to start them." He turned through more pages. "I wanted to spend as much time as possible with Sonia while she was here. I haven't even looked into local private schools yet. I want her to get a good education, but be able to stay with me."

"Emona is such a remote place. Great for an artist's retreat, but I don't think it's somewhere you should raise a child. Leave her where she is. She'll get the best possible education." She leaned closer, placing her hand on his. "You need to make more friends and find someone else to fill that gap in your life, someone who'll help you with your career. Having a child around will make that difficult."

Stefan leaned back and withdrew his hand from under hers. "A career is important only so I can have her here with me. I was hoping the iconostasis restoration project would give me the exposure in the art world that I needed to kick-start my career."

Frowning, Elena tilted her hat forward a bit. "Have you heard anything about it yet?"

"No." He tightened his hand into a fist. "It's so frustrating. I've called and have been told it's being reviewed. No one will give me any more information than that."

"I can help you with that. I'm going to see Nikola tomorrow. I'll ask him if he can speed up the process." She took another sip. "For now, relax and enjoy the music. Don't let your wine go to waste. It'll get too warm in this hot sun if you don't drink it soon."

STEFAN PULLED IN front of the hotel when he returned to Emona. Maria was singing while she swept sand from the terrace. Her face shone with its normal cheerfulness.

He stopped and got out of the car. "*Zdravei*, Maria."

"Hello to you, too, dear. Where have you been today?"

"In the city celebrating Varna Day."

"It's also the Assumption of Mary, an important church day, *and* my name day." She wrapped her arms around the broom handle and held her hands at the top while she leaned on it. "When my husband was alive, we visited the city and attended the church service in The Little Virgin Mary."

"It is a lovely church. Elena and I went there after the volleyball tournament."

"I haven't seen her around recently. You should invite her over." Her face shining, Maria offered him a questioning look. "She's so beautiful. You could use a woman like her around. She'd be good for your career, too."

He arched his eyebrows. "She's been too busy to come to Emona, so I met her in Varna today to discuss my exhibit. She's going to talk to Nikola about the restoration, so perhaps we'll have good news soon."

Maria crossed herself and smiled at him. "I'm sure it's in God's plan to honor his place of worship. Why don't you come back later tonight, dear? Peter, Todor, and some others will be celebrating with me."

"I'd like that. It's also my birthday today. Twenty-nine. We can celebrate together."

"Congratulations, dear. I'll make you something special."

"Thank you. Right now, though, I'm feeling a little queasy." He placed his hand over his stomach. "I think it was the honey wine. A little too sweet for my taste."

Stefan waved as he pulled away. When he arrived home, Balkan raced around the yard, wagging his tail and barking out his greeting. Stefan stepped onto the porch and picked up the empty water bowl.

"Sorry I'm so late, buddy. I'll get you some more water."

He set the bowl on the kitchen counter and turned on the faucet. A few brown drops dripped out, then nothing else. Balkan's tail thumped against the floor as he sat waiting, his eyes glued to Stefan.

"Damn." Why was the water off? Had someone been messing around his house? He inspected all the rooms. Nothing else seemed out of place. Maybe something was clogged in the pump. He'd look at it later, but first he'd go to the Samodivi Cheshma to get some fresh water.

He retrieved a pitcher from a cupboard. Then he bent down to attach a leash to Balkan. "Let's go for a walk. Stay close to me so you don't get hurt or lost."

Balkan pushed his wet nose into Stefan's hand, then raced toward the door. When Stefan opened it, the puppy shot away like an arrow, tearing the leash out of Stefan's hand. Balkan bolted through the gate Stefan had forgotten to close.

He ran after the puppy. "Come back!"

Balkan chased birds and sniffed bushes along the path. Stefan caught up at the creek, where the puppy slurped the water.

Scratching him behind the ears, Stefan said, "Don't do that again. You could get lost out here."

"Kak kak kak," a falcon chanted from the walnut tree. Balkan dashed off toward the bird before Stefan had a chance to grab the leash. The bird peered down at him, flapped its wings, and headed up the hill. Balkan chased after it as if in pursuit of a rabbit.

"Where are you going?" Stefan ran along the path, following the barking. He caught a glimpse of the puppy disappearing behind a boulder. Panting by the time he reached it himself, he stopped to rest.

A meadow lay ahead of him. Balkan's barking seemed to come from there. At the edge of the tree line on the other side of the meadow, the puppy trotted behind a figure leading a horse. His breath caught in his throat. Could it be the woman who had ridden the horse here months ago? Stefan walked toward them along the soft moss, hoping she wouldn't disappear again.

He smiled. "Kalyna! What are you doing way out here?" Without waiting for an answer, he rushed toward her, wrapped his arms around her waist, and drew her close to kiss her. "Why do your lips always taste like rasp-berries and your hair smell like citrus, my mysterious nymph who keeps disappearing on me?"

The horse next to Kalyna snorted, then returned to eating grass. Stefan looked at the mare, then back at Kalyna, his eyes wide open. "That's Emona. She's wild. Why does she let you touch her? Have you ridden her before?"

"Don't be afraid. She's tamer than the others. Why don't you pat her?"

The mare pricked up its ears and whinnied when Kalyna took Stefan's hand. He looked into the mare's large brown eyes. Remembering the vision he had when he had touched the mare before, he hesitated.

"Go ahead. It's okay." Kalyna coaxed him. "She won't hurt you."

He stretched out his hand to stroke the mare's mane. In an instant, the meadow disappeared. He and a woman were racing horses, splashing through the water along the shore. The salty spray slammed into his face.

"I'll catch up, Carina. You can't win."

"No, you won't. I'm a better rider." She laughed and heel-tapped her horse forward.

They raced onward toward the boulders. Looking back at him, she laughed with delight. She arrived first, seconds before him, and vaulted from her horse onto the wet sand. While she flittered like a butterfly in the breeze, with her white robe rippling around her divine body, she shouted, "I won. I won."

"Okay. I admit defeat." He jumped from his mare and snatched her up. Before she had a chance to gloat anymore, he closed his eyes and kissed her with fierce passion. "I love you, my sunshine."

"I love you, too, Dushan." Her gentle hands caressed his forehead.

His mare neighed and nudged him, so he opened his eyes. But it wasn't his mare neighing. It was Balkan barking. Stefan glanced around. He was lying on a blanket next to Kalyna. The wild horses grazed at the farther end of the meadow.

"Kalyna?" He sat up.

"Yes, Stefan?"

"What? Where?" He opened his mouth to say more, but no words came out.

"I'm glad you didn't nap too long. We should go back soon before it starts getting dark." She packed the picnic basket next to her.

He shook his head, trying to rid himself of the tangled web of confusion. He stood and reached down to help her to her feet. "How did I get here? Weren't we standing next to Emona a moment ago?"

"Emona?"

"The black mare. You-you had me touch her." He looked again toward the horses. "Didn't you?"

"I think you dreamed that. You don't remember I met you at your house and we came here?"

"No, not at all." He shook his head.

"I suppose you don't remember the birthday present I gave you, either." She put her hands on her hips.

"Birthday present?" He scratched his head. "You knew it was my birthday?"

She tilted her head. "Yes, you don't remember telling me that, either?"

He shook his head again.

"You put it in your pocket."

Reaching in, he removed an antique bronze key shaped like a key of life. It had writing similar to that at the Samodivi Cheshma.

"Stefan?" Kalyna reached over and grasped his shaking hand. "It's going to be okay."

He clutched his stomach, which ached again, and bent over, groaning.

"What's wrong?" She helped him back onto the blanket.

"I think the honey wine I had today didn't agree with me." He laid his head on her lap.

"Close your eyes and rest a while longer." She rubbed her hand over his stomach. "I'm sure it will be better when you wake again."

A soft green glow shone from the sun, reflecting off the grass as he closed his eyes.

Dirty Deal

August 16

THE NEXT DAY, Nikola and Elena strolled in silence down the tree-lined promenade in Primorski Park, while seagulls squawked above, looking for signs of discarded food. All around lovers held hands, laughing at secret jokes, while children ran around, shouting at their families to hurry so they could get a good spot at the beach.

Two elderly women sitting on a sunny bench knitting some lace looked up as they passed. Elena smiled at them. Stopping to adjust her floppy hat, she sighed. "I love this garden." Her eyes lowered to the flowers in the center of the walkway, the reds, purples, and yellows arranged in alternating circle and diamond patterns. "When I was a girl, I came here with my nanny to play and listen to the afternoon concerts."

"We've spent many pleasant afternoons here together as well." *And we will soon again. Maybe we can make even more sweet memories as soon as Stefan is out of the way.* He put his hand on her arm. "Any word on the recovery of the paintings?"

She spun to face him, her words spilling out. "No. I still have to sell the gallery to pay for the loss." Her eyes showed a hardness he had never seen before.

He stepped back at her crossness. His plan had been to comfort her after the robbery, but she acted distant and irritated with him all the time now. "But the gallery has been your dream, your life. You've invested so much into it. Don't rush and make this decision now. Let's explore other options."

"No, it's too late." Elena snapped, her words a whip against his soul. "I called my lawyer and told him to start the papers. I'm going to sign a contract next week."

"Who's the buyer? Someone local?" Nikola tensed. Was she on to him?

Her shoulders slumped and her voice lost its normal confidence and vitality. "I don't know who's buying it. He has a lawyer representing him because he wanted to remain anonymous." She looked away. "I don't want to know. This has all been so stressful. I want it over."

She strolled down the boulevard in silence for a while, Nikola close at her side. "I've negotiated with them so I can proceed with the exhibits I've already scheduled, including Stefan's." Stopping suddenly, she turned toward him, a spark lighting her eyes. "I'd love to help him succeed. He's so talented."

Nikola's blood boiled. *Still Stefan. Always Stefan.* Couldn't she see he needed her more, wanted her more, loved her more? Stefan would neglect her the way he had Katherine.

He had to talk about something else. "Since you're selling the gallery, this might be your chance to start your hat-design business. Life's full of challenges and surprises you can turn into great opportunities." He laid his hand on her shoulder. "Let me help you start over."

"You're such a good friend. After this is all settled, I might consider it." Then she leaned closer, talking in a hushed tone. "I think Stefan's house is full of secrets. When I visited him the first time, he found a jewelry box hidden in the wall. It appears to have belonged to the previous owner."

"What was inside?" He focused on her.

"I don't know. It was locked, and we couldn't find a way to open it. It seemed quite old. We also found a map to some cave."

"Interesting." Nikola's mind raced. *This might be the key to the mysterious cave and the Thracian gold.*

"He put it in a cabinet in the studio. He's been so busy getting ready for the exhibit I think he must have forgotten about it. I'm curious to see what's inside." Elena's face held a dreamy look. "It's all so romantic. Maybe it holds love letters."

She turned around and headed back toward the city. "Oh, yes. I almost forgot. Have you and the Council reviewed Stefan's petition to restore the iconostasis project? This is a great opportunity for him."

His jaw tensed. "Let me check with my secretary when I get back. I don't recall her giving me the paperwork for that."

They reached the exit to the park. Elena kissed his cheeks. "I'm glad I had the chance to talk with you, but I have to go now. I have so many things to settle today. I'm not sure what to do first."

When she departed, Nikola grimaced. *Well, I know what I need to do.*

NIKOLA ENTERED THE empty office. A smile crossed his face when he smelled the new leather furniture, but a scowl soon replaced it. He opened a cupboard, removing a decanter. Pouring some whiskey, he took a gulp. The fire burned his throat. He unlocked his desk drawer, pulled out a folder, and looked through the contents to refresh his memory. The air around him sparked with malice. He picked up the phone to call his lawyer.

"Get a pen and listen. I don't want to repeat myself. Make sure to follow my orders *exactly*." His revenge would not, could not, be prevented now. "Review the documents and ensure we have nothing in writing to obligate us to let the previous owner of the gallery host exhibits."

"Part of the initial deal entailed allowing the seller to hold her remaining exhibits for a fee. Do you want to meet tomorrow and discuss different options?" His lawyer spoke in a businesslike manner.

"I don't want to *discuss* anything. I told you what I want. We're changing the deal. Do we have this clause in writing in the contract?"

"No, we don't."

"Then what's the problem? We can say *no* without any implications."

Nikola hung up. Pouring another whiskey, he tossed it down. Despite being the director of the Council, he had only one vote. He wouldn't be able to thwart the Council's decision much longer. It was time to make additional plans. Nothing was going to stop him from achieving his goal. He made one more call. Boyan answered immediately.

"I need your help again," Nikola whispered.

* * *
** ** **

STEFAN TOSSED AROUND papers looking for his phone. It stopped ringing before he could answer it. Finally recovering it from under some sketches, he looked at the number. *Sonia*. He pressed auto-redial.

"Hello, sweetheart."

"Daddy, Daddy! Did you get your present?"

"Yes, your card and the keychain with your school picture arrived yesterday. You are quite the artist yourself."

"No. Not what I sent you." Her voice became low. "The one the *samodiva* gave you."

Stefan tightened his grip on the phone. "What do you mean?"

"The samodiva said she was giving you a present because you were ready. Sometimes she talks funny."

Stefan sat on the couch and exhaled the breath he'd been holding. "When did you see her ... again."

"She visits me in my dreams. Tell me, please. What did she give you?"

Had Sonia seen Kalyna in her dreams? Had he himself only dreamed about being in the meadow yesterday? He awoke to Balkan licking his face, but Kalyna wasn't there. Had his stomach cramps made him hallucinate? Had any of it been real? He fingered the key in his pocket. Someone had to have given it to him. Perhaps the gypsy in Varna had managed to sneak it in there.

"Daddy! What did she give you?"

"Sorry, sweetheart. A key. She gave me a key."

"That's all? That's not exciting." She giggled. "Or romantic. You can put it on the keychain I gave you, I guess."

"It's a lovely old key, shaped like a cross, but the top is a circle. It has something written on it in an ancient language."

"Oh. Sounds pretty, but still not romantic. I thought she was in love with you."

His phone beeped. *Nikola. What did he want?* "Sonia, sweetheart, I have another call. Can I talk to you later?"

"Yes, but please don't forget to tell me more about the samodiva."

"I won't forget." He hung up and answered the incoming call. "Hello."

"Stefan, I'm calling to follow up on the appeal process. I looked at your documents this morning. To change the decision, the Council requires that the majority of the local residents sign a petition supporting the project. When I get that, I'll authorize it."

"Thank you for helping. I'll get the signatures and send the documents as soon as I can."

"You have to submit it by today. It has to be within two weeks of the original paperwork being processed."

Stefan clenched his fist. "I filed that almost two months ago."

"Your petition must have been misplaced. I can try to persuade the other Council members, but I can't force them to reconsider. We have to follow standard procedures."

"Understood." Stefan ended the call. After typing the petition and printing out several copies, he headed to the hotel to talk with Maria. She was cleaning the outside tables, and welcomed him with her radiant smile.

"I was thinking of you, dear. You didn't stop by yesterday."

"I'm sorry. I was ill." Sighing, he plopped down in a chair. "Maria, I need your help. It's about the iconostasis project."

"You're so pale. Let me get you some herbal tea first." She entered the hotel and returned shortly with the drink. "Here. This is good for your body and soul. It has seven herbs including 'The Samodiva Hearth' found only locally." She placed it in front of him and sat at the table. "Drink it first to calm yourself, then tell me what you need."

Stefan took a sip, letting the warm liquid glide down his throat. He put the cup down and opened his mouth to speak. Maria wagged her finger at him, pointing at the cup. He finished it, then looked to her for approval.

"Okay. Now I'm listening." She folded her hands on the table.

He handed her the petition. "I have to get the villagers to sign this today so the Council will restore the project. Can you help me get to everyone?"

"Of course. We've waited for years for someone to restore our church." Standing, she patted his arm. "God sent you to us. Let's go visit Peter. People listen to him."

They walked to his house together. Maria pounded on the door.

Peter threw it open at the persistent knocking. "What happened? Is everything okay?"

"Stefan needs our support to sign this petition today."

Peter read and signed it. Stefan gave them each a copy. They headed in different directions to get signatures. By noon, almost the entire village had signed the petition, enough to reinstate the project.

"I'll go with you to the Council," Peter said.

"Thank you. Let's go now, before he changes his mind."

AFTER SUBMITTING THE petition, they returned to the car. Peter pointed to a person walking into the city hall. "That's Professor Krum's nephew. I haven't seen him since he was fixing the house."

"Who's his nephew? I see only Nikola, the director of the Council."

"Right, Nikola. He came to the village several times and spent a lot of time at the excavation site by the Old Fortress. People said he was looking for the Thracian treasure."

Stefan stared at Peter, then back at the city hall. *Nikola was Krum's nephew!* Stefan remembered he talked about his rich uncle when they were in college, but he had never met the man. That meant it was Nikola who sold Stefan the house. Why had he kept that a secret? Because of the stories about his uncle? Or something more?

Pillar of Fire, Pillar of Truth

August 24

FIERCE TONGUES OF flames burned his face, and clouds of smoke choked him, making it difficult to breathe. Beams collapsed and roof tiles broke and crackled as fire like a hungry *lamia* swallowed one house after the other. Moans and desperate cries for help filled the smoldering village. Children and women, their faces plastered with soot and fear, hid behind the remnants of houses, but couldn't escape the horror of burning bodies and blood-soaked streets.

How had so much destruction happened in such a short time? Only moments ago, he galloped toward Aemon when the smoke began to rise.

His eyes watered, blurring his vision, as he wandered around the village calling to his beloved. "Carina, where are you?" His voice vanished among the moans.

Blond hair on a mud- and blood-splattered body lay in the doorway of a house on the verge of collapsing. His heart raced with dread. *Not my Carina, please, dear Goddess.* Kneeling beside the still warm body, he turned the girl over with a gentle touch and sighed with relief and anguish. *Not Carina, but someone else's love.* He said a silent prayer for the child who ceased to suffer.

He had to forego his hopeless search. Galloping horses and clashing swords were at the other end of the village. It was his duty to fight.

An arrow flew over his head. He spun around to face an enemy youth no older than his beloved Carina. The boy's eyes shone fierce with hatred as his hand reached toward another arrow.

The youth must die. He could have been the one who murdered the child.

Covering his body with his shield, he grasped his sword. He would fight for the village until his dying breath. As he advanced toward the youth, he swung his sword. Spraying blood drenched his clothing and dripped down his face and hair. The boy fell, his haughty gaze forever now an empty stare, no longer free to express love or hate.

STEFAN WOKE TO Balkan's wild howling and a steady thumping. His heart raced. He could still smell smoke. Jumping out of bed, he scanned the room. No, his house wasn't on fire. What was going on?

"Stefan! Stefan! Are you asleep? Wake up! Please help!" Peter pounded on the door, his voice urgent.

He hurried to open it. Peter's eyes were frantic with fear and anxiety, his face covered with soot. *A real fire, not a dream?* "What is it? What's happened?"

"Fire! Fire at the church! I'm trying to get everyone from the village to help."

"Let's go! We don't have time to talk. Go!" Stefan pulled on his shoes and ran after Peter. Balkan bounded out after him.

At the church, dozens of people had gathered, a bucket brigade extending to the cheshma. Thick, black smoke billowed through the broken windows. Stefan took his place in line next to Maria.

Bits of conversation from unknown speakers filled the night air.

"The fire's burning our beautiful altar. It was almost the only thing left in the church. Now it's destroyed."

"Who started this fire?"

"Nobody knows."

"Probably St. Nicholas sent it to us. The church has been locked for so many years."

"Yes, but it's been unsafe."

"And people let their mules roam in the church yard."

"Move faster! It'll burn the iconostasis, too."

"God's punishing us. Oh why is God punishing us again?"

Stefan's arms ached, passing bucket after bucket of water down the line. Eventually, the fire subsided. People collapsed on the ground, tired and haggard as much from emotion as smoke. Peter attended to an old woman who clutched her burned hand. Maria entered the church, and Stefan followed. Smoke curled around the mass of charred wood where the altar once stood. The iconostasis, too, had been further marred, the wood closest to the altar still smoldering, the paintings thick with soot.

"Oh, oh, oh!" She crossed herself, tears mixing with the grime on her face. "Our beautiful altar is destroyed. The iconostasis is damaged. Nothing's left! Nothing!"

Stefan wrapped his arm around her shoulder. "What happened? How did the fire start?"

"I don't know. Nona knocked on my door like crazy. She dragged me to the church. I shouted for help and started waking up people. I grabbed a bucket, but it was too late." She wiped away tears, leaving a streak of soot in their place. "Flames were everywhere. The smoke was too thick to even get inside the church."

"Let's go back outside. We can't do anything in here right now." With his arm still around her shoulder, he guided her toward the door.

At the entrance, Nona, her eyes wide, pointed toward the lighthouse, then skittered away. Once outside, Stefan walked to the side of the church. The area around the lighthouse was dark, but then two small pinpricks shone, making their way along the path away from the building. They blinked out a moment later.

Maria joined him. "What are you watching?"

"It looked like someone driving a car away from the lighthouse."

"A car? Who would be there at this hour?"

"Nona pointed to something or someone. We should let the police know when they finally get here. Maybe the Keeper saw what it was. It could have been the person who started the fire."

"I doubt the Keeper will talk to anyone, even the police. Besides, I'm not sure how reliable Nona is. She might be the one who accidentally started the fire. She's always around the church lighting candles and leaving flowers."

The wailing of sirens grew as the sun's light crept over the horizon. People drifted away to their homes.

"The Varna police and firefighters are finally here. I'm surprised they even made the trip down that torn-up road. I should go over and talk with them." Maria hurried off. She gestured to the police toward the church, then the lighthouse. Firefighters poked around the church. Soon, they all left.

Maria returned and took hold of Stefan's hand. "Please come have a cup of coffee with me at the hotel. I-I'd rather not be alone right now."

Stefan nodded.

She leaned against him, sobbing. "Now what are we going to do? Where can we get money for an altar? We don't even know if they'll restore the iconostasis."

"We'll figure it out." He squeezed her hand. "I'll go back to the Council tomorrow and submit a petition to request additional aid. I'll do the work for free. It would be an honor for me."

Maria looked at him with hopeful eyes as they walked to the hotel. "That would be wonderful, dear."

Balkan trotted along behind them, sniffing the air, still heavy with the acrid smell of burnt wood. He nosed around a bush and picked up something shiny from the ground. When they arrived at the hotel, Maria indicated for Stefan to sit at the outside table, while she went to make coffee. Balkan lay at Stefan's feet, his new treasure still in his mouth.

"What'd you find, buddy?" He held his hand down to pat the puppy.

Balkan dropped the shiny object, his tail wagging. Stefan picked it up. It was a small gold-plated lighter, engraved with a stylized "N."

Nikola? Could it possibly be his? He had to be behind the cancellation of the restoration project. But would he stoop so low as to destroy a centuries-old church important to Emona, merely to ... what? Prevent him from getting recognition in the historical and art communities? For what purpose? To get back at him for marrying Katherine?

The Shadow Knows

September 3

CARINA, LYING ON her stomach, trailed her fingers through the *aqua vitae* by the waterfall. Rosy cheeks and eyes sparkling with love reflected back at her. Cherished memories of the night of the *kukeri* dance a month ago still made her heart race. Stefan loved her. Not through her power over him, but from his very soul. His words and touch made her skin tingle as if he were bestowing his affections on her all over again. She had never known freely given intimacy with a mortal could be more powerful than any control a samodiva could wield.

She had wanted to hand him the key of life then, but the child, the sweet child with her mysterious power, had called to her in the night from so far away. Her father's birthday, she had said. Give him a present then. He had told Sonia a samodiva loved him. The girl hugged her and whispered, "I want you to love me, too."

Wiping her tears away, Carina had kissed the girl. "Yes, my child, I love you as well."

Carina devised a plan. The Goddess had given the mare the power to recognize her master. Carina brought the horse to the meadow on Stefan's birthday. The *zmei*, the dragon spirit who lived under the village fountain along with his sister, the *lamia*, offered a solution. He would stop the water from flowing to Stefan's house, but for a price, one that he would collect at a later date. Carina insisted on knowing the payment now, but he declined to tell her. With reluctance and fear, she agreed. For anyone to approach the *zmei* and deny him his request guaranteed disaster for the seeker. From there, it was easy to get

Stefan to the cheshma, and then to the meadow. The puppy had been eager to assist.

Her plan worked. She saw the same vision as Stefan when he touched the mare. Dushan's power and love flowed from him, growing stronger. With Dushan's memories set free, he would know how to use the key to find his way to her. Fearing he could not yet understand, she turned the memories into dreams. She sighed. All she had to do now was wait.

She sat up with a start. Someone had used a love potion on him. Who? That woman who came to see him? Her plan had failed because he had already given his love to Carina. All she had done was cause him great pain.

Fuming, Carina returned to the temple, seeking out Morena. "Sister, how long must I wait? The Autumn Moon is almost upon us. Another is trying to steal him away."

"Fear not. The Astro Calendar predicts the mortal will find where the token awaits him before the second Autumn Moon. With it, he can open the door to the temple."

"Did you see anything else? What does it say about the child?"

"I see trouble ahead, but the exact path to her future is not set." Morena reached out and held her sister's hand. "Her Fate, too, is sealed. All will turn out well."

STEFAN WAVED TO the postman as he drove away on his motor scooter. He had brought the weekly newspaper and two letters, one of them from Sonia. He tore it open immediately. She had written in cursive, each stroke and curve drawn with precision.

Dear Daddy,

The samodiva visits me a lot. She is very nice and very pretty. I love her and she loves me. She told me she did. She loves you too. She says you will find her soon. That's silly. You already know her. She doesn't make sense.

I love you and miss you. I am being good for Mémé and Pépé.

Love you most.

Sonia

At the end of the letter, she had drawn a flower. It reminded him of edelweiss, like the one she had clasped in her hand after the wolf attack. He kissed the paper, missing his little girl.

Reading the letter again, he smiled. Sonia must be thinking about Kalyna because of the painting he had done of her. He hoped that was the "samodiva" in her dreams. Kalyna had seemed eager to meet Sonia, but would they like each other? Sonia was such a lively child, and Kalyna ... He hadn't seen her since the night they made love a month ago. Except for the strange dream in the meadow. It was only a dream, wasn't it? He sighed. Why hadn't she returned? Would he ever understand her?

He looked down at his mail. The other letter was from the Council. He held his breath while he opened it. A wide grin spread across his face as he read the words. They had reinstated the iconostasis restoration project after the support from the villagers. The letter went on to say they were also appropriating funds for the altar. They provided him with a generous stipend for labor, as well as all materials.

"Yes! Yes! This is wonderful!" He waved the letter over his head like a flag, a signal of his victory.

Rushing inside, he grabbed his camera. He would share his news with Peter and Maria later. Right now, he wanted to take a few more photos before he built the pro-totypes for the iconostasis and the altar.

The lush grass in the churchyard had overgrown, blocking the gate. The hinges screeched as Stefan shoved against it and squeezed through the narrow opening. When he entered the church, several frightened doves flew through the broken windows. Nona, too, was there. She stared at him wide-eyed for a moment, then dropped her bouquet of white flowers and scurried through a half-open door.

Maybe now he could find out why she kept following him. He walked over to where she had disappeared. Stairs led to a dark basement. The stagnant air drifting up smelled of candle wax. He searched the church until he found some candles and matches scattered on the floor. The faint light barely lit the stairs. The dry wooden step creaked when he set his foot on it. He put his other foot on it, hoping it would withstand his full weight. It appeared safe enough, so he continued down.

At the bottom, he swayed the candle back and forth. Dusty wooden benches lined the wall, and an old chest stood in one corner. Nona appeared once again to have vanished. The candle had nearly burned out. As he headed back up the stairs, someone touched his hand from behind the railing. He jerked his head to the side. It was Nona.

She peered at him with her eyes wide open. Biting her lower lip, she formed a shy smile.

"Nona! Why—"

She put her finger to her lips. Directing her eyes to the chest, she walked there and dug to the bottom through some maroon material. She pulled out an object wrapped in a white cloth and tied with a red ribbon. With her head lowered, she handed him the bundle.

"What's this?"

She disappeared up the steps in a flash. He followed, making his way back up the creaky steps to the church sanctuary. Nona wasn't around when he reached the top.

Eager to open the package, Stefan extinguished the candle and left the church. He sat on a bench under the old oak tree and untied the red ribbon. A small journal with a black leather cover had been wrapped inside the cloth. The name on the cover said "Krum."

He looked toward the church. As still as a statue, Nona leaned against the window, her eyes fixed on him, a mysterious smile on her face. How had she known it was there? And why had she given it to him?

STEFAN PROPPED A pillow on the headboard of his bed and stretched out. He opened the frayed cover of the journal, prying apart several of the stuck pages. The blurry ink and small handwriting made it difficult to decipher in places, but with much concentration, he made out the words.

> Today the keeper of the lighthouse and I dug around the walls of the Old Fortress. In the Middle Ages, the fortress was called Emona; now the town alone bears that name. It's derived from Aemon, the ancient name for the Stara Planina, or "Old Mountain," the mountain range beginning in Emona. The fortress walls were built using stone taken from these mountains.
>
> From legends and other documents, I'm sure the tomb of Deyan lies here somewhere. Based on ancient rituals, scholars believe he was buried with his favorite horse, his faithful dog, his most-loved wife, and his servants. They were all sacrificed to accompany him to

the next life. It was assumed many gold and ritualistic materials were entombed with him as well.

And the secret location of the cave lies buried with him.

⁎⁎

Last night on my way home from the excavation site, I met a beautiful woman. She seemed to be a vision at first, but when I got closer, I realized she was flesh and blood.

Her name is Leana. She's staying with friends in the village and is a history student at the University of Varna. She said she likes studying the Old Fortress and is doing a school project on it. I suggested we work together because I needed help. The Keeper, Esinesi, has been helping me, but he doesn't know anything about historical artifacts, and he could damage the items we might discover. It would be better to work with an archaeological student. We agreed to meet at the fortress the next day.

Leana said she had heard of the tomb, and it would be a great experience if we could find it.

⁎⁎

Lora has been upset and unhappy lately. Peter has stopped coming to the house. He said he's too busy helping his brother Pavel build a new house because Pavel's wife, Rosa, is expecting a child.

Lora threatened to stay with her mother so she could get away from me, but I want to keep her here. This marriage was a mistake. I don't love her. She knows it, but without her money it would be impossible for me to work on my research and support my adventures. From my room, I often hear her crying, even though she thinks she's hiding it from me. When I find the Thracian treasure, I won't need her anymore. I can divorce her and find a new love, maybe Leana. She doesn't know I'm already married.

**

Leana comes every morning and evening to the fortress. She seems to know every inch of this land. She's a strange woman. She appears and disappears like a shadow.

I think we're about to discover the tomb.

Stefan turned several pages, his curiosity growing.

I've never felt like this before. When Leana is next to me, I feel my chest burning, my heart beating fast; I can't stop thinking about her. I dream about her every night. My dreams are so strange. I feel as if I'm going crazy.

Last night Lora wanted to talk to me. I think she wants to leave me, but I won't allow it.

**

Earlier tonight, Leana and I hurried to finish the excavation at an end wall of the fort when my pick hit something metallic. I struck the spot several times more. It was a large stone plate.

Leana's beauty excited me almost as much as the discovery did. She stood beside me and watched, a pink tinge on her face and her ebony hair falling on her shoulders and over her beautiful breasts. I turned to kiss her.

"Not now. Let's see what's inside."

I refrained from any further advances and proceeded to clear away the thick ivy to expose the black stone plate. It covered an area about three feet by three feet. I tried to move it, but it was too heavy.

Leana surprised me by lifting it with ease. I started to ask her how, but she had already lit a torch and hurried into the tomb. Not wanting to waste another minute, I followed her.

We walked down a corridor about forty feet long. A fire had blackened the granite walls. At the end, we passed through an archway into a small, round anteroom.

On the floor, the skeleton of a human lay curled up like an embryo—to immortalize her soul. It was probably the wife of the man buried in the tomb. Thracian women considered it an honor to be chosen as the most-favored wife and sacrificed to accompany their husband. The room also contained the bones of what appeared to be a horse and a dog. Golden ornaments decorated all three skeletons.

This room led us into the massive burial chamber, which had been carved out of a single block of stone. In the middle of the room, a skeleton had been placed on a stone table. Deyan, I'm certain of it. A finely woven cloth with an intricate design lay beneath his torso. A golden wreath adorned with images of oak leaves and acorns garlanded his head. At his side lay a magnificent sword, its handle gold-plated and encrusted with jewels.

Many other golden artifacts and ornaments had been placed throughout the room, along with bronze mirrors, weapons, and clay figures—everything necessary for him in the afterlife.

"We found the tomb. We're rich." My hands started shaking from my excitement about the discovery.

Leana ignored me and appeared captivated by a silver box she held.

I grabbed it away from her. "Don't touch anything."

She lunged forward to reclaim it.

"What's wrong with you?" I tried to open it, but it was locked. "What's in here?"

"I don't know, but I like it. May I keep it? I want to use it for my jewelry. It's so beautiful."

"No. What I'm looking for might be inside. We'll return tomorrow with my car and take the gold. I have a friend in Germany who'll help me sell it. We'll have plenty of money, and you can buy as many jewelry boxes as you desire." I grabbed her by the shoulders and shook her. "We need to keep this a secret."

She agreed, and we made arrangements to return the next night to remove the treasure. We covered the entrance to the tomb with sticks and dry shrubs. The windows of the Keeper's house were dark when we passed by.

Back at home, Lora waited for me in the kitchen.

"I want to talk with you." The serious tone of her voice annoyed me.

"I want a divorce, Kamen. I'm leaving you."

I didn't love her, but her declaration surprised me.

"I love Peter, and I can't lie to you or myself about it anymore."

The thought of her and Peter angered me, but I didn't let her know. I laughed instead. "Peter, the peasant fisherman? Lora, you're nuts."

I had to stop her any way I could. I needed her money to get to Germany and sell the gold.

*
**

I couldn't sleep because the treasure danced before my eyes. I thought Leana might go back and rob me. At two in the morning, I got out of bed. Since Lora slept in the next room, she didn't hear me leave. I grabbed a burlap bag and headed back to the Old Fortress. I wanted to take as much of the gold as I could and hide it in my house.

When I arrived, the plate had been moved. Leana must have returned. As I suspected, I found her in the chamber. She looked like a goddess in her long white dress with a beautiful golden belt around her waist.

* * *
** ** **

The rest of the pages were blank. *What a strange ending.*

Stefan flipped through some more pages and found a folded paper near the end. He opened it.

305

Dear sister,

I know I've made a lot of promises to you over the years, but this time it's real. I found the treasure. It's hidden under the Old Fortress. I'm planning to hide it and sell some of the artifacts. This will enable me to move to Germany. From there, I can arrange to sell the rest of the treasure. I'll send you money as soon as I can to help you. After I'm established in Germany, I'll come back for you.

Stefan put the journal on his night stand and turned off the light. He tried to sleep, but the words he read swam around in his head. Why had Nona given him the journal? Had she wanted him to find the Thracian treasure? Where could it be hidden? The Professor had lived in this house, but Stefan hadn't found any gold. The journal said the Keeper had worked with the Professor. Perhaps he knew something more. Stefan would speak with Esinesi to see if he knew the rest of the story.

Throwing Bones

September 17

A TORCH LIT Stefan's way down the musty corridor that was scented with fragrant candles. Soot from a massive fire coated the ceiling and granite-block walls. The crunching of broken pottery beneath his feet broke the silence of the tomb. He coughed from the dust he disturbed. At the end of the corridor, he stooped to enter a small, rectangular room with a sloping ceiling. In one corner, animal skeletons were strewn across the floor. Next to them lay a woman resembling an ancient goddess. A golden tiara of galloping horses and small flowers rested on her dark, braided hair. She wore a long white garment embroidered with a series of alternating lines and circles. A leather belt was tied around her waist. Her hands folded on her stomach held edelweiss.

He kneeled beside the woman and touched her cold body. She jerked, and her flesh withered before him. Moaning, she turned her mummified face toward him and opened her eyes. Bloody, black sockets stared at him. He fell backward onto shards of pottery, sending them scattering across the floor. When she reached a withered hand out toward him, he scrambled to his feet and backed out of the room.

He rushed down the corridor, her cries still reaching him. A shadow coming from the room lengthened along the wall, as if chasing him. The passageway narrowed the farther he went, forcing him to return when it became impassible. The chamber might have another exit.

The woman was now standing, extending her hand, in which she held a silver key. He reached for it, but she turned to ashes, the key clattering to the floor. As he bent to retrieve it, the floor beneath it dissolved, sending him tumbling down a dark tunnel. He spun around, the key forever out of his reach.

STEFAN RETURNED FROM Varna, after delivering his final proposal and detailed sketches of the iconostasis restoration to the Council. They approved the design, telling him he could begin as soon as the materials were delivered. That gave him time to pursue other matters. The most pressing was to visit Esinesi. His dream had cemented his decision to see the tomb. He put on a jacket and headed out into the brisk autumn evening.

Arriving at the lighthouse, he found two paths. Unsure which led to the Keeper's cottage, he took the more-travelled one that wound along the edge of the cliff. A panoramic view of the ocean lay at the end, but he hadn't passed the abode, so he returned to try the other way. It led to the Old Fortress and an observation area. Where was the house? On his return, he nearly missed the small structure with a black-stone roof. Overgrown shrubs hid it from both directions. Only a wisp of smoke coming from the chimney indicated it wasn't deserted.

He knocked on the door, listening for any noise from inside. Waiting a moment, he knocked louder. Still no one came. He walked down the porch steps and glanced around the yard. No one was about. A tattered curtain on a dirty window opened a crack, but fell back into place.

Returning to the porch, Stefan knocked again. "Hello? Please, I only want to ask you—"

"Go away!" a deep, gruff voice on the other side said.

"Esinesi? I've heard some fascinating things about the Old Fortress. Someone—"

"I don't give tours anymore."

"Someone gave me a journal. I wanted to ask you about it."

The door creaked open a crack. "A journal?" The Keeper's wrinkled, sun-weathered face peeked out. A black patch covered one eye, the band stretching across his snow-white hair.

"It mentions you worked with Professor Krum. I bought—"

"Krum?" His eyes darted around before he banged the door closed.

"—his house."

The door flew open, and Stefan took a step back.

"You bought the Professor's house?" Esinesi's mouth formed a snarl, revealing yellowed teeth. "Wh-what else do you know?"

"Krum said he found Thracian treasure."

"Why do you care? It's gone." The man pulled his head inside. "Go away before you get hurt."

"Wait!" Stefan reached out to hold the door open. "I'm not looking for the gold. I was wondering if you knew what happened to him. People said you were the last person to see him."

"Maybe. I already told the police everything I knew." He pushed at the door, but Stefan held it open with his foot.

"Please listen. You'll think I'm crazy, but Nona gave me the journal for a reason, but I don't know why. I don't know who else to get answers from."

"Nona?" Esinesi released the door.

"Yes. I thought if you could explain what happened, some of the other things that have been happening to me—dreams, visions—might make sense."

The Keeper scratched his tangled beard, while waving a cigar with his free hand. He came out onto the porch and eased himself into a chair. "I have to tell someone. I can't keep the secret of my sin in my soul anymore."

"Your sin?" Stefan stared at him. Maria said he'd kept to himself ever since the Professor disappeared. What could have happened?

He pointed to a chair for Stefan to sit on. "I met the Professor one summer twenty years ago. A lot of college students were camping in tents around the Old Fortress." He paused to puff out circles of smoke on his cigar. "One day a stranger dressed in city clothes knocked on my door. He introduced himself as Professor Krum, an archaeologist. He said he had moved to the village two weeks earlier and needed an assistant. I needed money, so I agreed to help."

Stefan leaned closer. "The journal said you were excavating the Old Fortress."

"Yes. We worked there every day. The Professor arrived early in the morning before dawn and left well after dusk." The Keeper coughed for a while, then continued. "One day he told me he no longer needed my help because he had found a student to assist him."

"Leana?"

"Such a beautiful girl, but I didn't meet her until later." The Keeper slumped forward in his chair, silent.

"Esinesi, are you okay? Do you need a doctor? A glass of water?" Stefan reached out to touch the older man's shoulder.

"I'm fine." He pushed away Stefan's hand. "As the weeks went on, the Professor stayed at the excavation site all the time. One night when I made my rounds, I came across an opening in the fortress wall. Ivy and dirt lay on the ground around it."

"His journal said he found the entrance to the tomb."

The Keeper's hands shook. "I walked through the entrance into a dark corridor. A low light shone ahead, so I headed toward it. I dimmed my lantern and crept closer when I heard someone crying."

"Who was it?"

Esinesi flicked the ashes onto the porch. "I peeked into the room at the end of the passage. No one was there, but it was full of gold and skeletons. Then a man started talking in the next room. His words were slurred. 'Princess, my fairy, have you decided what you'll do? I have your poweeeerr.' I snuck closer. The Professor held a sword up to a woman's throat. Her hands and feet were tied. He stroked her hair while she cried."

Stefan gasped. "What did you do?" Peter had told him the story about the Professor being drunk and saying he had someone's power.

"I wasn't sure what to do. I looked around the room. A shovel was on the floor near the entrance. I crept closer and picked it up." The Keeper's hands moved as if re-enacting the event. "The woman saw me, so I put my finger to my mouth. I snuck up behind him and swung the shovel at him. But, I lost my balance, and fell to the ground. Something sharp jabbed my eye. The Professor grabbed my throat and choked me. That was the last thing I remembered."

Stefan clasped his hands together to keep them still. "Was the woman his wife? Peter told me she was murdered."

"No. It was Leana, his assistant."

"What happened? Did he kill her?"

"No. When I came to, I was in my bed. My eye hurt terribly." He pointed to the patch. "As you can see, I lost it."

"What happened to Leana? And the Professor?"

"She told me her sisters found her and untied her. When I asked her about the Professor, she said, 'My sisters have taken care of him. Don't worry. He's where he wanted to be—with his bags of gold.' "

"Where is she now?"

"I don't know. She stayed with me until I could manage on my own, calling me her hero. I only did what anyone would have done. She was so sad when she learned ... No, that's not a story I can share."

Stefan leaned closer. "I had a strange dream about the tomb. Would you show it to me?"

The Keeper looked at him for a long time. At length he groaned. "Yes, I'll take you there. The gold is gone, but I'll show you the tomb." He went into the house and came back with a flashlight. He pointed to a shed to the side of the cottage. "Get something to clear away the vines and move the cover."

Stefan picked up a machete and a crowbar. He proceeded down the path toward the Old Fortress, stopping often to wait for Esinesi. With each shaky, careful step, the Keeper wheezed. At the edge of the ruins, they wove around large stones fallen from the walls, until they arrived at the tomb's entrance on the opposite side. Stefan chopped away the vines, then lifted the heavy cover with the crowbar, sliding it to the side enough so he could crawl through.

"Don't stay too long. I'll wait for you out here." Esinesi sat on the stone wall. "I never want to go in there again. I still have nightmares about what happened."

Stefan disappeared into the darkness. He flicked on the flashlight and walked down a musty corridor. Large blocks of rough granite. Blackened walls. Everything the same as in his dream. When he reached a room, he shuddered. Human bones lay scattered on the floor. He picked up a skull and placed it where it belonged with the rest of the person's remains. Kneeling by the skeleton, he said a silent prayer.

As he started to stand, something wedged under the remnants of the clothing glinted in the flashlight beam. He retrieved the object. A silver key shaped like edelweiss. Again, the same as in his dream. Would it fit in the jewelry box he found in the Professor's house? If so, it now belonged to him, didn't it? He put the key into his pocket and hurried outside.

A VIOLENT WIND beat at Stefan's face as he trudged home, his shoulders hunched. He kicked a stone, sending it hurtling over the cliff. The waves far below, foaming like a rabid animal, surged high and came crashing down. They pounded the rocky shore, hurling seaweed against the ledges, then wrenched the algae back into the black, murky depths. Beside him, shadows in the bushes swayed, the wind's muffled groan of discontent sounding almost human. He looked around, but no one else was in sight. Who else would be out on a night like this?

Balkan crawled out from under the porch when Stefan opened the gate. The puppy jumped around his legs, barking. They both rushed into the house to get out of the wind.

Stefan hurried into the studio to get the jewelry box. He opened the cupboard, but the shelf was empty. Setting the key on the counter, he searched the others. Balkan whined, then barked. He trotted over to the fireplace. With a low growl, he sniffed around the room.

"I'm sorry, buddy. I should feed you first. Come along."

Someone tapped at the door while he was in the kitchen. A broad smile lit up his face when he opened it. "Kalyna! Come in, beautiful."

The wind rustled her braided hair, loose strands flying across her rosy cheeks.

"Where have you been?" He wrapped his arms around her, drawing her into the house. "I haven't seen you since my birthday ... or perhaps the *kukeri* dance. I don't even know anymore if I've ever seen you at all."

She laughed. "What an absurd thing to say."

"You show up and disappear like an apparition. I can't tell if you're real or a beautiful figment of my imagination. If you're merely a dream, I don't want to ever wake up."

"Stefan, *for you* I'm quite real. Can't you feel me, kiss me, hug me?" She pressed her lips, cold from the night air, against his.

He kissed her back with pent-up longing. Balkan barked and growled again. Stefan released Kalyna and ran a finger across her cheek and over her now-swollen lips. "Please don't leave. I-I have to check on him."

Balkan wasn't in the kitchen, so Stefan returned to the studio. Kalyna followed. The puppy was by the fireplace, growling.

"Balkan, what's the matter? Does the howling wind coming down the chimney remind you of a cat?"

Balkan continued to growl, and nosed around the ashes.

"Hey, buddy. You're making a mess." Stefan dragged him away.

Kalyna picked up the silver key, her eyes wide with excitement. "This is a fascinating design. What does it open?"

"I found a jewelry box in the wall several months ago, but it was locked. It has the same design, so I thought the key might fit it." He scanned the room. "Unfortunately, I've misplaced it. I was searching for it right before you arrived." He stroked his fingers down her cheeks. "I was excited about it until you showed up."

"Let me help you search for it." Her breathing accelerated as she spoke the words out in a rush. "I'd like to know what's inside."

"I've already looked in this room." He tugged on Balkan to move him away from the fireplace, but he wouldn't budge. "Let's close the door, so Balkan doesn't make any more of a mess." Stefan patted his leg. "Come on, buddy. I'll give you a treat."

Still growling, Balkan followed Stefan out of the room.

Stefan and Kalyna looked through the cupboards in the living room and kitchen, still unable to find the jewelry box. Then they headed to his bedroom, where she opened drawers.

"Kalyna." His voice deepened. Moving aside her hair, he ran light kisses down her neck. "Please stay with me tonight."

She turned around, her lips slightly parted and her breathing ragged. "Yes, b-but I have to leave early."

"I don't care. You're here now." Stefan led her to the bed. Sitting next to her, he unravelled her hair, caressing the soft, silky tresses. Sliding off her dress, he kissed her bare, beautiful shoulders.

"Kalyna, I love you."

"I love you, too."

They made love feverishly, becoming one in body and soul until Stefan succumbed to a sweet sleep, hugging Kalyna in his embrace.

Thief in the Night

September 18

NIKOLA WAITED UNTIL the house quieted and the breathing in the next room steadied, hoping its occupants slept. He opened the closet door a crack. Where was the dog? Not seeing it, he tiptoed down the hallway to the studio. The dog barked from Stefan's room, and scratched at the door.

A woman's sleepy voice mumbled, "What was that?"

Who was she? He scowled. How could Elena be interested in Stefan? He was sleeping with someone else, merely using Elena to spite Nikola and deprive him of everything he wanted.

He hurried to the studio, ducked into the fireplace, and squeezed through an opening at the back. Something fell to the floor. Maybe a button from his shirt. He couldn't waste time looking for it. His muscles strained as he inched a metal cover over the hidden passage, trying to avoid making any noise.

"I don't know. I'm going to check it out," Stefan said.

The studio door creaked. Footsteps made their way around the room. The dog growled right outside the metal cover.

"Must be mice. I hope you're not afraid of them." Stefan laughed. "I have to get a cat. Come on, buddy. Let's go back to sleep."

It was already well after midnight, but Nikola waited another half hour, not daring to move. The voices having quieted, he crept down the steps to the cavern below the house. He and Boyan had made the discovery the previous summer while making renovations.

When he removed the cover that day, dank air drifted up from a dark hole. He fetched a lantern and crawled down the steps into a murky cavern. A tunnel led from it to a cracked wooden door that daylight seeped through. No amount of pushing against the panels would open it.

He returned to the steps. "Boyan, there's a room down here. Come and see."

Over the years, their uncle had written to his sister, Boyan and Nikola's mother, saying he was on the verge of finding the Thracian treasure. This *had* to be where he had hidden it if he found it. Nikola craned his neck and ducked as he walked around, looking for any crevice where the treasure might be hidden.

A shadow. He swung the lantern back in a slow arc. *A hidden niche.* His heart pumped faster. "The treasure's here. I know it."

He rushed over to the opening and shone the light in. Empty except for some straw and a few old newspapers. He shook them, tossing them aside, to make sure nothing was hidden there. Running his fingers along the walls, he searched for a door. *Nothing.*

"Did you find it?" Boyan whispered behind him.

"No." He stumbled over a rock as he backed out of the space.

Something glinted in the light. He kneeled to pick up the object and rubbed the dirt off. It was a small coin. He set the lantern down. "Come help me. I found something." He dug into the hardened soil with his fingers.

"Brother, stop!" Boyan shook him. "See what you're doing to yourself."

He examined his cracked nails and bloody pads.

They both left, returning moments later with shovels to search the tunnel, but discovered no more gold coins. If his uncle hadn't hidden the treasure here, where did he stash it? He said it would be somewhere safe until he could find a way to sell it to his contacts.

They might never know. The secret could be buried with him, if he *was* even dead. The authorities had never found his body.

Nikola began his own investigation when the police told him they presumed his uncle drowned. His inquiries in the village revealed a solitary fact. The old lighthouse keeper had been the last person known to speak with his uncle. When Esinesi refused to talk to him, Nikola hired a private detective, who discovered the authorities thought his uncle had murdered his wife, then slipped out of the country. Nikola hadn't found any other clue the entire time he continued his search.

Before he found the coin, he had planned to pay Esinesi another visit. Now that might not be necessary. The jewelry box he had taken from Stefan's house could hold the answer to the location of the Thracian treasure.

He retrieved his lantern in the cavern. Crouching, he hurried down the narrow corridor to the exit. The fresh air and his successful search invigorated him. All his meticulous planning and investigations had fallen into place.

Broken shells crunched under his feet as he hurried along the rocky path to where he had hidden his car. The moon's glow created eerie shadows along the way. At the beating of wings, he spun around. A falcon landed on a branch of an old dead tree.

Not paying attention, he slipped, cursing when he fell. Kervanka, the portent of disaster, shone above. His heart beat faster. Legends told of travelers killed by evil spirits after they beheld this star.

His foot tingled from the fall, making him limp. When he finally reached his car, he slammed the door, locking it as fast as his trembling hands allowed. He revved the engine, then sped away.

Relax. Don't rush. You got what you came for. Don't be afraid of fairytales.

He slowed when thick fog rolled in, obscuring the narrow, rutted road that veered close to a sheer cliff.

All of a sudden, the car shook as if a stampede approached. It stilled just as quickly. He looked in his rearview mirror. Nothing moved. His imagination was running away with him.

Eyes back on the road, he drove ahead another few feet. The car vibrated again, this time accompanied by thudding. He leaned forward as he drove, searching the growing mist.

A dark shape darted past his car. Then another. Nikola slammed on the brakes, gripping the steering wheel so tight his knuckles whitened. Sweat dripped down his brow. He unclenched his clammy hands, wiping them on his pant legs.

Two black horses pranced in front of his car. Alongside them crouched a snarling gray wolf. The animals drew closer. From the fog, two more images appeared. Women, wearing white, sleeveless robes, with golden masks covering their faces, rode the horses. Wreaths of flowers encircled their hair, one blond, one auburn.

They looked like goddesses ... or demons. Could samodivi, the guardians of the cave, be real? Wasn't that part of the legend about the treasure only folklore? His body trembled. He mustn't look in their eyes or he'd be doomed.

The blond one brandished a sword. Jumping to the ground, she hurtled toward the car, her hair like a rocket's smoke trailing behind.

Nikola removed a small bottle from his pocket. He gulped the few remaining drops of the magic potion he had stolen from Sultana. As its power burst through his veins, he jumped from the car with the strength of a wild animal. His face lengthened, his jaw developed long, sharp teeth, and his body and limbs strengthened. Black, shaggy fur sprouted from this flesh.

Bounding forward, Nikola challenged his adversary to a battle of strength and endurance. As Nikola hurdled over the other wolf, his teeth snapped shut inches from his enemy's throat. Then, the other wolf struck. Its feral breath tinted the air a moment before its sharp teeth tore into Nikola's neck. Twisting his body, he rolled on the ground to dislodge the attacker. The gray wolf lost its grip, but landed on its paws. Bloody white foam poured from its mouth, as its cold blue eyes glared at Nikola with defiance. It crouched, preparing for a new assault.

Nikola leaped forward first, and the gray wolf fought back, slashing the air with its claws and snapping its teeth. Mid-air, Nikola's legs tingled as power drained from him. Slumping to the ground, he howled as his bones crunched and his body reshaped, leaving him lying exhausted on the cold ground. The gray wolf hovered over him, its hot saliva dripping onto his shivering, naked body.

The woman with the sword headed toward his car.

"No! It's mine!" He leaned on his elbows to rise, but his body wouldn't move.

She turned to glare at him. Her fiery eyes, blazing like flames from the depths of Hell, froze him. After she removed the jewelry box from the front seat, she handed it to the other woman, then sprang to his side. She pressed the cold blade of the sword against his throat.

Frigid air wrapped itself around him, making him gasp for breath. A sharp pain cut across his neck.

"This doesn't belong to you." Her words hissed as she severed a golden chain holding the ring he had stolen from Stefan, its stone blazing black, instead of blue.

He grabbed for it. "It does! I loved her."

Leaning close to his face, she whispered, "I could punish you for all the evil you've done. You should die, mortal."

The other woman spoke. "Carina, it's almost dawn. Leave him here to suffer his own fate. We have what we came for."

Narrowing her eyes at Nikola, Carina pointed the sword at his throat again, trailing it down his chest. Then, both women jumped on the horses and vanished. The gray wolf, too, disappeared into the dark night.

Nikola stumbled back to his car and leaned against it. Forming a fist, he punched the palm of his other hand with it, then shook it in the direction they had gone. "I'll find the cave and the treasure. Then I'll be rich and live forever."

He bent to recover his torn clothing. Chills went through him as blood dripped from his chest. His heart beat so fast he thought it would burst. He covered himself as best he could, then flopped into the car. Twisting the key in the ignition, he cursed. The engine wouldn't turn over. Again and again he tried, until it coughed and roared to life. He revved the engine to make sure it didn't fail him.

Putting it into gear, he sped away. His hands shaking so much he couldn't keep the steering wheel steady, he weaved all over the road. The gray wolf reappeared, jumping in front of the car. Nikola raced toward it, trying to run it over, but the wolf bounded out of the way. Nikola spun the steering wheel around. Too late. The vehicle skidded close to the cliff. Out of control, it plunged over the edge.

No! This can't be happening! I have to find the treasure.

The last thing he saw in the rearview mirror was the wolf grinning as it looked over the edge of the cliff.

Puzzling Pieces

September 18

AT THE FAR side of the lowest cavern where the samodivi performed ritual cleansings, the waterfall's roar was a mere murmur. Carina, sitting cross-legged, with her back against the ivy-covered wall, hummed while she wove a wreath of herbs—sage for immortality, lavender for tranquility, chamomile to attract love, and rosemary for fidelity of lovers. She held it up to inspect it. Perhaps a little peppermint, too, not only for purification, but so Vedra would feel refreshed after the ritual. She still couldn't believe her sister was rejoining them after twenty years living as a mortal.

Upon recovering the silver jewelry box, she and Morena sped to Vedra's boutique in Varna. Vedra's eyes flew wide open when they placed it into her hands. Fumbling with the key that Carina passed to her, Vedra finally opened the box and removed her stolen belt. The three sisters wept as loudly as when they had last been together, but this time with joy. Vedra vowed to never be foolish enough to trust another mortal man with her love. She tried to dissuade Carina when she proclaimed her own love for a mortal, but Carina eventually won her over.

Now, tonight, Vedra would be restored to the sisterhood of the samodivi.

The wreath complete, Carina stood. She placed it on her own head and danced around the flat rock where the ceremony would take place. Voices and laughter above made her stop short. The preparations weren't complete. She laid the wreath on the stone and hurried up the pathway meeting her sisters coming down.

Unable to hug them, because each carried ceremonial objects, she kissed their cheeks. "I must hurry. The candles. Bendis will arrive soon."

In the temple room, she swooped up an armful of scented candles, and passed her sisters once again. She placed a candle at each of the eight points of the star shaped like edelweiss carved into the stone. Along the edges, she sprinkled more herbs and sandalwood. Her sisters walked in as she finished. Vedra laid a basin by the water's edge, and Morena placed a white robe and silver box alongside the star.

"Vedra!" Carina hugged her. "You look lovely."

"Not yet." Vedra laughed. She ran her fingers through her graying hair, then pointed to the lines that had formed around her eyes. "But soon."

"Let us begin." Bendis clapped her hands twice.

Along with her sisters, Carina fell silent at the arrival of the goddess. She looked so frightful wearing the sacred mask, carved like a snarling wolf, with a collar of feathers and sharp teeth hanging around her throat. At her side, she held a sword, the jewels along its hilt gleaming in the torchlight. Her pleated robe, embellished with nature scenes, brushed aside the scattered herbs as Bendis strode forward.

She extended her hand toward Vedra. "It is time to prepare for your rebirth."

Vedra approached, bowing low. Retrieving the herbal wreath, Carina handed it to Bendis, who placed it on Vedra's head. Carina retreated to light the candles.

Bendis led Vedra to the pool, motioned for her to kneel, then held the sword above her head. "Under the silver light of the moon, cast off the remnants of your mortal life. Absorb the celestial power to rejuvenate your body."

Vedra held up the basin. Its thick red liquid sloshed over the edge, coating her fingers. It slid down toward her wrists, finally dripping onto the stone.

The goddess dipped the sword into the sacrificial blood. With the flat edge of the blade, she tapped each of Vedra's cheeks. "From the life of the offering, you shall become whole."

With the substance dripping down her face, Vedra set aside the basin, stood, and disrobed.

Morena began the purification chant. "Immerse yourself in the sacred pool."

With her hands raised toward the sky, Vedra stepped into the emerald water.

"Clear your mind and relax your body." Carina continued the rite.

Tiny drops of water sparkled on Vedra's body as she stepped into the glow of the moon. The water rose to her shoulders.

"Feel the healing energy envelop you." Morena placed her palms together, then extended her arms toward the pool, her hands pushing the restorative power toward her sister.

Carina scattered more sage, sandalwood, and peppermint around Vedra. "Breathe deeply. Inhale the herbal scents."

"Close your eyes." Morena held her hands fast in front of her. "Let the rhythms of your body guide you."

Stepping farther into the pool, Vedra sank beneath the water. Her silver and black hair floated amidst the white petals of the lily pads, then disappeared.

"Release your negative energy." Carina tossed more herbs over the place where Vedra had been. "Let it seep out of your pores."

Throwing her hands toward the sky, Morena shouted, "Let the water rejuvenate your body, your spirit, your soul."

Bendis extended the sword over the water. "Arise, Vedra."

The pool stirred. Black hair emerged, then a youthful countenance. Vedra walked onto the stone, water cascading off her slender, seductive body. She stepped into the center of the star, the candles sizzling from the drops falling on them.

Carina and Morena positioned themselves outside the star, on opposite sides of Vedra. Carina picked up the white robe. Holding it open, she stepped into the inner circle with Vedra.

The goddess spoke. "Clothe yourself with the attire of your sisters."

Vedra slid into the robe. Then Carina retreated from the circle.

Morena opened the silver box, and Bendis removed the golden belt.

With a solemn face, the goddess entered the circle. "Rejoin the sisterhood, my daughter." She wrapped the belt around Vedra's waist and kissed her. "This time guard your belt well."

DAWN REVEALED ITS golden tendrils of light. The warmth of its sunbeams danced across Stefan's face. He reached out to the space next to him, hoping Kalyna had lingered, but the spot was empty. After letting Balkan out, he decided to continue his search for the jewelry box. He glanced at the counter in the studio where he had left the silver key. Nothing. He was sure he had left it there.

Getting down on his knees, he searched under the counter. It hadn't fallen. He got up to look in the cupboard. The jewelry box, with the key inserted in the lock, sat on the shelf. His hands trembled as he removed it, setting it on the table. He turned the key, holding his breath. The lock clicked open—and nothing hissed as it had in his dream. Letting out a deep breath, he lifted the cover to peer inside. He removed a yellowed manuscript written in an ancient language. It had a map drawn on it. He didn't know Lada's phone number at the museum, so he called Elena instead.

"Stefan, how nice to hear from you." Her voice deepened. "I've been meaning to call you, but I was hoping for better news first." She sighed, then continued talking with a rush of words. "When I signed the papers to sell the gallery, they reneged on letting me hold my exhibits. I considered not going through with the deal, but I'm in such a bind with the lawsuit, I didn't have much of a choice. I've been trying to get in touch with the buyer's lawyer, but I haven't had much luck. Anyway," she took a breath, "I'm still hoping I can do your exhibit. So, how are your pieces for it coming along?"

"I haven't had much time to work on them. I've been busy with the iconostasis and orders for Nikola." He paused. "Elena, I'm calling to ask a favor. I've found an old manuscript. Do you think you could arrange a meeting with Lada to see if she could translate it?"

"I'm sure she'd love to. She's away, working at another museum until the middle of October, so you'll have to wait until she gets back. I'll contact her and see what we can schedule."

"That's a whole month!" He thanked her and ended the call.

He set the map aside and removed another paper from the box. This one written in English.

Fear the wrath of Bendis, the goddess of destiny ...

"Some sort of fairy tale, I guess. I'll have to read it to Sonia."

Going to the kitchen, he removed a glass from the cupboard, then a lemon from the refrigerator. He cut it and squeezed the juice into the glass, filling the rest with water.

Wait a minute. Didn't something in the jewelry box rattle when I first found it?

He returned to the studio, put the glass on the table. Nothing else was in the box. He shook it. No rattle, so no hidden compartment. He had been certain it contained coins.

His phone rang, startling him. He knocked over his glass of water onto the paper. He rushed to the bathroom to get a towel and a hair dryer.

The ringing had stopped by the time he dried the manuscript. The caller ID showed Elena's name. He called her back. Maybe she had been in touch with Lada already.

Her words came out in short spasms. "The police found Nikola's car at the bottom of a cliff in Irakli."

"What? When? Take a deep breath and tell me what happened."

"I don't know." She moaned. "I've been so busy lately, I haven't seen him much. Now he's gone. Oh my god. They can't find his body. Why is this happening?"

"When did this happen?"

"Last night or early this morning. Someone in Irakli told the police they heard a loud noise during the night, but they weren't sure of the time."

"Do you want me to come over?"

"No, no. Don't worry about me." She let out a long sigh. "I'm going to the police station to see if I can find out any more. Maybe I can tell them something that will help them find him. I'll call you when I have more information."

The pain in her words made Stefan's heart ache. She gave so much, yet wasn't willing to let anyone give her anything in return. Not sure what else he could do, he picked up the manuscript again and began reading.

Hear now the tale of the samodivi and learn the fate of Deyan.

"Samodivi and Deyan." Yes, this had to be the legend the villagers had been telling him. He leaned back, propping his feet on the table, ready to enjoy the tale.

... three maidens, Vedra, Morena, and Carina

"Carina?" He sat straight. What did she have to do with the samodivi or Deyan? Were all those tales part of the same legend?

He continued reading.

... the honor of marrying Dushan

Yes, that part made sense. Carina and Dushan were connected in his dreams and visions.

He read about Carina's wedding day.

... glowed as bright as the blue-star ring she wore

Stefan reached for the ring around his neck, forgetting the wolf had taken it. What else did the legend say? *Deyan burned the village and raped the girls.*

He had dreamed of both events. And he had seen the rape through Kalyna's eyes the night of the eclipse. No. It wasn't possible Kalyna was Carina. Sweat dampened his shirt. Putting the paper down, he got up and paced the room. What kind of madness was this?

Not wanting to read more, but finding not knowing a worse option, he sat and picked up the paper again.

Afflict the defilers with calamity. Curse the ring so it brings misfortune to all who possess it.

Katherine had died the day he bought the ring. *No!* It couldn't be the same ring. Her death was an accident, not a result of a curse. But, what if it wasn't? Then it was his fault she had died.

The paper shook as he read on. *Bendis saved the girls and gave them a drink from the water of life.* He had seen these images in the lighthouse the night of the eclipse when he had looked into Kalyna's eyes.

Unable to resist, he continued reading. *Bendis made a belt with a golden edelweiss.* Kalyna has a similar belt. She wore it to the *nestinarstvo,* the same belt he picked up from the floor at Easter. *No! No! No!* This was crazy. That would mean Kalyna was a samodiva. They didn't exist.

Bendis placed the souls of the soldiers into the wild horses.

Dushan had a black mare. Stefan had ridden a black horse in his visions after he touched the mare.

The mare would recognize her master when he returned. The mare acted as if she remembered him the first day he saw her at the cheshma.

He was losing his mind. This was a legend. It wasn't real. As impossible as it was for Kalyna to be Carina, it was even more impossible that he was Dushan.

He reached the end of the legend, sweat dripping from his forehead. Professor Krum had translated the document. Peter said Krum had been looking for the gold and the cave.

He had to find the cave to prove this wasn't true.

He read the legend once more.

Thrace, 1197 B.C.

Fear the wrath of Bendis, the goddess of destiny, the protectress of nature, the patroness of lovers. Seek not to kindle her anger, lest she smite you.

Hear now the tale of the *samodivi* and learn the fate of Deyan, the once-mighty chieftain of the mountain tribes, whose vile deeds begat his ruin.

In the land of Thracia, during the reign of King Rez, before the war in Ilion, three maidens, Vedra, Morena, and Carina—beloved daughters of Tarbus, chieftain of the valley people—excelled in music, poetry, and artistry. All the lands praised them for their exceptional beauty, but the loveliest and most talented of the three was Carina, with eyes the color of emeralds, hair soft and golden like corn silk, and a voice to serenade birds and beasts alike. Because she so resembled her long-departed mother, the most-favored wife of Tarbus, he bestowed upon her, his youngest, the honor of marrying Dushan, the son of a neighboring chieftain. This privilege by right belonged to the eldest, Vedra. The sisters rejoiced in their fortune, for Vedra desired another and Carina loved Dushan.

On that glorious wedding day, festivities abounded in the village. The aroma of roasting game from the magnificent feast mingled with the fragrance of flowers decorating the streets and houses. Joyous, mellow notes of *zurlas* joined wailing skirls of *gaidas* and the steady beat of sticks against *tupans*. Music vibrated through the air, drowning the clamor of the multitudes.

Meanwhile, Carina, Morena, and, Vedra, their countenances as vibrant as the flowers overflowing their baskets, journeyed home from Mount Aemon, having spent the morning paying homage to Bendis, their patron deity. Lovely like goddesses themselves, the sisters wove wreaths of edelweiss. The small white flowers, dazzling like stars fallen from the heavens, garlanded their long, flowing tresses, each as diverse as their spirits—one blazing like the radiant sun, another gleaming like the earthy coat of a deer, and the last as dark as the blackest night.

Sweet melodies of laughter perfumed the air as Carina twirled around with outstretched hands. She glowed as bright as the blue-star ring she wore, a gift from Dushan. "Today, my wedding day, I begin my lifelong journey with my beloved, my betrothed."

She danced her way down the mountain path, into the meadow atop the ridge. Her long, pleated robe frolicked along with her. Golden ornaments, sparkling around the frills of the garment's neckline, sang their praises to her comeliness. The linen belt surrounding her graceful waist hugged her with love, while the bronze ankle bracelet, embellished with fertility symbols, promised her happiness and lifelong joy.

"Carina!" A startled cry from Vedra and Morena shattered her idyllic moment. "The village is on fire."

Bewildered, she looked toward her home and gasped. Pillars of black smoke coiled toward them like an evil, slithering snake, warning of doom. A river of tears flooded their faces, drowning their joy. The sisters rent their clothing, their moment of celebration blackened by anguish.

"Dushan! Dushan!" Carina wept on the day she was meant to rejoice.

Vedra wailed in anguish. "What vile evil has befallen us today?"

"Hurry, sisters," Morena urged. "Away to the village. We must save those we can."

Stinging sand lashed at their faces as dogs, goats, sheep, and horses, having escaped the carnage, fled past. The howling of wind and beasts alike failed to drown out the wailing of women and children, and the clashing of weapons. Nor could the fragrant flowers disguise the stench of blood and burning flesh. The sisters lifted their hands and voices in prayer to Bendis to keep their loved ones safe, but deep in their hearts knew they were too late.

In the valley, Deyan, the ruthless and haughty chief of a mountain tribe, spied the girls hurrying home. With the fervor of his conquest as yet unquenched, he lusted after them with an intensity fiercer than his yearning for the pillaged gold. Signaling to nearby combatants to finish the valiant youth he battled, he left the waning battle to his fearsome forces.

He gathered his mightiest warriors. "Follow me. More treasure awaits us on the ridge."

With his flaming red hair raging around his shoulders like the fires he had ignited in the village, Deyan urged his mighty chestnut steed forward. His men, howling like feral wolves, pursued their terrified prey. The maidens scattered at the approach of the blood-stained horses and the wild-eyed marauders riding upon them.

The sisters, exhausted from the relentless chase, found no refuge. They collapsed by the creek like flowers wilting from the merciless summer sun. The savage men ravished them and thrashed them to within a breath of their lives. The wreaths of edelweiss, like the maidens, lay ruined, their remnants tangled amidst disheveled hair. Flower petals, having fallen from the baskets as the sisters fled, were strewn along the way like autumn leaves wrenched from the shelter of branches by a vicious coastal storm. Others were crushed deep into the soil, defiled by the boots of the invading hordes.

Their stolen virtue failed to suffice as plunder; their ornaments, too, Deyan claimed as the victor's spoils. Carina, struggling against her captor, having lost one treasure, clung in desperation to her cherished ring. As Deyan tore it from her finger, she cried out to her goddess with her last conscious breath. "Bendis, protectress of the innocent, spare me, my sisters, and our land. Afflict the defilers with calamity. Curse the ring so it brings misfortune to all who possess it."

The forlorn cry echoed across the skies, borne by the winds to the farthest regions of the heavens, where it murmured in the ears of the Great Goddess Bendis. She looked down from her lofty throne to the slaughter below. Her wrath split the sky with fire and thunder.

Crowned with a crescent moon, she raced her silver chariot to the vanquished village, urging the triad of white, winged horses onward. They galloped across the stormy sea, rising and falling with each crest and trough. Foaming like the waves breaking against the shore, the mares raced along the beach, where bodies lay strewn across the sand. Some writhed in the dance of death; others remained forever motionless, their agony over.

Bendis bellowed, "Enough!"

She hurled her javelin at the invaders, slashing them with her sword until their blood soaked into the sand, from whence the unquenchable tide drank deep.

The battle over, yet still the fires blazed. The goddess hastened to the ridge to rescue the maidens who had honored her that morning with their worship. Gathering them up into her chariot, she carried them away. In her sacred temple deep within a cave, she restored their beauty and lives with a drink from the springs of the *aqua vitae*. Embracing them with a mother's grace, she bestowed upon them the distinction of becoming her daughters.

She clothed her new offspring in flowing white robes and golden belts. From the edelweiss in their hair, she molded an ornate buckle. She spoke a warning oracle. "Guard your belts well. They hold your power, and are the key to love and life. When given by free will in exchange for true love, your belt will beget eternal happiness. If given with a foolish heart or taken by force, it will lead to death and destruction."

The goddess obscured the path to the cave. Entrusting the guardianship of her temple and its sacred rites to the maidens, she marked them with the symbol of edelweiss.

Touching Vedra on the hand, Bendis said, "You are now '*Voda*,' the keeper of the waters. I grant you power over the elements, to cause or withhold storms."

Touching Morena on the ankle, she said, "You are now '*Gora*,' the keeper of the woodlands. I bestow upon you the gift of sight, to know what is to come."

And touching Carina on the shoulder, she said, "You are now '*Planina*,' the keeper of the mountains. You shall have the gift of illusion, to reach into the minds of men."

Tears welled again in Carina's eyes. Her body shook as she tried to restrain her sobs.

Bendis consoled her. "Weep not, my precious child. One day you shall be reunited with your beloved Dushan. When the ring is returned to you, its curse will be fulfilled. If his love is true, it will lead him to find you at the temple."

Vedra, Morena, and Carina, to express the anguish of their ordeal, depicted the events of their attack and restoration on the walls of the cave. The tale of their violation filled the goddess full of wrath.

The pillars shook when she thundered, "Death is the destiny meted out to those who injure the innocent."

Under the light of a full moon, riding astride a giant stag, with a quiver slung across her back, Bendis hunted Deyan and his warriors to avenge her daughters. Finding the evil men by the dying embers of a fire, drunk and spent from the celebration of their violence and destruction, she cursed them.

"For the dishonor you have brought upon my land, you will be forever doomed to roam the ridges and beaches of Thracia, protecting the sanctuary of those you have violated." Saying thus, the goddess slew the dumbstruck men, entrapping their spirits inside a herd of magnificent wild horses grazing nearby.

One horse alone, the faithful black mare of Dushan, who fought by her master's side, retained her own soul. Bendis laid her hand upon the creature's neck, blessing her. "For your valiant loyalty to your master, you shall live to see his return. You will recognize him, but he will know you not. Protect him again, for evil will seek him out until at last he fulfills the destiny of the ring—the reunion with his everlasting true love."

"The Legend of the Samodivi"
Translated by Professor Kamen Krum

Still shaking, Stefan put the legend and the ancient text back into the jewelry box. He looked for a hiding place, so it wouldn't disappear again. The fireplace had a niche with a metal door. When he went to put it there, something shiny shone in the fireplace ashes. He picked it up, turning it over between his fingers. A silver pin. The letter K. Could it be Nikola's? That didn't make any sense. Nikola had never been at the house.

A Hint of Mystery

October 16

CHAOS REIGNED IN the village. Houses burned, and charred, bloodied bodies lay everywhere. The attack came as a surprise; the treaty had been broken. No one had time to prepare for the fight. Screaming women held wailing infants tight against their bosoms. They pulled small children along as they fled in search of a safe haven. Goats and sheep ran bleating down the streets in confusion, with dogs barking after them. The clashing of swords against wooden implements had replaced the festive wedding music and dancing. The villagers tried in vain to defend themselves against the invading horsemen. The temple had been ransacked and all the gold seized. The holy day, the day of his wedding celebration, had been desecrated.

Hope was all but lost. The mountain men left the village bereft of its youth and treasures. He alone held a sword, ready to defend himself and those around him. His muscles strained as he slashed upward at the invaders mounted on horses. With each thrust of his jewel-encrusted sword, he struck the mountain dwellers. The golden hilt, flashing bright in the glow of the setting sun, ran red with the blood of the attackers. But one man, no matter how valiant, fighting against hundreds could not win.

He got a reprieve when his faithful black mare galloped toward him. Swinging himself astride her without her slowing pace, he pursued the leader of the hoard, a man with bright red hair. The battle between them grew fierce, both bleeding and sporting long gashes.

Failing to see those conspiring behind him until it was too late, he swung around the moment a sword pierced his body. He grimaced and screamed with agony. His body fell forward, limp, while his sword clattered to the ground. Embracing his mare's neck, he urged her to gallop away from the battle.

He uttered one word, "Carina," then slid from the horse and lay bleeding on the ground.

The mare pranced around him, then fled to the forest. A free spirit, she had bonded with him alone. No other could tame or ride her. Her blurry form fleeing was the last image he beheld before darkness overtook him. She would survive on her own or with others of her kind who had escaped.

"Dushan, awaken." Like a command from the gods, the words drifted into his brain.

Pain wracked his body. "Carina?" His dry, cracked lips uttered the word with a croak.

"Lie still. Be content you are still alive while many others are not."

He opened his eyes. It wasn't Carina, his love, but Slava, his sister.

Days later when he recovered, he searched for his love everywhere—the forest, the mountains, and the sea. The days turned into weeks, then into months. And still all he found on the hillside was a scrap from her wedding gown, crushed into the soil along with flowers she must have been carrying. He could still smell her perfumed skin, feel the warmth of her body, and see her radiant smile and playful green eyes.

Life without Carina held no meaning. As part of the ceremony to connect him to his beloved, he ordered master builders to enclose his shadow in the wall of the house he had been building for her. This would ensure the house would be strong. With his shadow separated from his breath, his soul could begin its long journey. At the end of his forty days, he would choose neither to remain in paradise, nor return to his body. He would reunite his breath with his shadow in the walls of the house to await the return of his lost bride, his eternal love.

LATE IN THE afternoon, Stefan drove to Varna for the scheduled meeting with Lada, hoping she could translate the document, providing some clue to what all this recent insanity meant. Every night for the past four weeks, ever since he had read the legend, his dreams became more vivid, more real. It wasn't possible he had lived them.

Kalyna looked so much like Carina, the woman in his dreams. She had a belt like the one described in the legend. Surely she must know *something* about what all this meant. He had searched for her, along the beach, in Varna, everywhere he went. But she remained elusive.

And what, if anything, did Nikola have to do with this? Was it merely a coincidence he disappeared the day Stefan discovered the legend? The same day he found a pin identical to the one Katherine had given Nikola? The last Stefan had heard, the police still hadn't discovered a body or his whereabouts—if he was still alive.

Yet another mystery. How had the jewelry box made its way into the studio cupboard—with the key inserted? Kalyna had been the only one around, but she had helped him search.

He shook his head as he pulled up to the café where he was meeting Elena and Lada. Maybe something in the document would help him find the cave. It seemed to be at the center of this mystery.

Elena waved to him from the table in front of the window. Pulling up a chair, he asked, "Any news about Nikola?"

"Not a thing." She clutched her hands around her cup. "The police refuse to talk to me. It's so frustrating. I've spoken with his brother and all his acquaintances. No one's heard from him."

"They'll have news soon, I'm sure." He looked around. "Is Lada here?"

Elena pointed to the counter. Lada was walking back with a steaming cup of tea.

Stefan rose. "Nice to see you again. Thank you for taking the time to look at this document." He pulled out a chair for her and sat next to her.

She smiled at him, her dimples growing. "Elena told me you found a manuscript and wanted to see if I could translate it. I'm always excited to see old documents."

"Yes, here it is." He slid the folder with the sheet of paper toward her.

Her face glowed with interest. She pulled a magnifying glass out of her purse and studied the document. "The paper itself isn't that old. Someone has copied it from the original, I'm sure. But the writing is ancient Greek."

Looking at it for a moment longer, she began the translation. "The cave will be protected and invisible to mortals. Only one who has true love will be able to see the entrance. In order to open the sacred door to our temple, he must find the golden edelweiss, our symbol. It's hidden in the maiden carrying the ..." She looked up, moving her glasses farther up her nose. "Sorry, that's where it ends."

Stefan leaned closer and pointed to the map. "What do the words down here say? Do you know where this is?"

She looked it over. "I think I do. It looks like a map of Cape Emine. See, here's the end of Mountain Aemon, the ancient name of Old Mountain. And here's the Old Fortress. This symbol here looks like a cave. It says 'Temple of Bendis.' And—"

"A cave? Where?"

"Right here." She pointed to the spot. "It appears to be near Litos Beach. That's a Greek word meaning stone, rock, or magnet. The place is maybe five miles from the Old Fortress."

"Thank you for your help." He exploded out of the chair almost overturning it. "I think I have everything I need to know."

"Stefan, do you have to go so soon?" Elena swiveled toward him.

"Yes, I'm sorry. I can't stay." He squeezed her shoulder, then rushed out.

STEFAN SPED ALONG the highway toward Emona, his mind reeling. *Is there an actual temple to the Goddess Bendis? I have to find the cave so I know I'm not losing my mind.*

He stopped the vehicle at Peter's house. Maybe he could help him figure out how to find the golden edelweiss that was supposed to open the door to the temple.

From the hotel terrace, Maria hollered to him. "Peter's not there. He's still at the Old Beach with his goats. He should be back soon since it's almost dusk."

"Thank you." He gave her a hurried wave and opened the car door, still thinking about the clue. *In order to open the sacred door to our temple, he needs to find the golden edelweiss, our symbol. It's hidden in the maiden carrying the ...* Maiden? Carrying something? He looked over at the brass statue on the cheshma. The girl carried an amphora on her shoulder.

Closing the car door, he headed toward the cheshma. The cool breeze gusted around him and moaned, sending chills through his body. The water pouring from the brass pipes bellowed, as if sounding a warning. He looked up at the bronze girl. The fading light cast ethereal shadows around her figure. She appeared to smile at him.

He walked around the statue, looking for a golden edelweiss. Everything was made of bronze. He examined the cheshma itself, looking for a crevice where something could be hidden. Nothing. Not even in the marble basin. Everything was solid. He ran his hand along the base of the amphora. His fingers touched a small slot. Leaning in closer, he discovered a cross-shaped hole.

Wondering if a key might fit in it, he removed his keychain from his pocket. The Key of Life Kalyna had given him looked the right shape. His heart thudded as he inserted it into the slot. He twisted it to the right. Nothing happened. He tried again, twisting it to the left. Still nothing. Frustrated, he turned it back again to the right, then to the left, right, and left. A faint clicking sound like the opening of a bottle came from somewhere nearby.

He ran his fingers around the amphora, but it hadn't opened. Scowling, he returned the key to his pocket. About to walk away, he stopped when some rocks clattered down the slope behind the cheshma. He looked up. Nona lingered at the top of the hill. She waved to him, then pointed toward the statue before she darted off into the darkness. He glanced at the statue again. The girl's belt buckle had opened, revealing a small chamber. With shaking hands, he reached in with his thumb and forefinger and touched something the size of a half dollar. He removed it and closed the buckle.

"Stefan, what are you doing?" Peter called from across the street.

He hurried over to Peter's house. "I found the way to the cave."

Peter gestured for him to come in. Stefan told him about his meeting with the Keeper and his visit to the tomb where he found the key that opened the jewelry box. Then, he showed Peter the document the box had contained.

Peter scratched his beard. "Is this another dream you're telling me?"

"No. It's real. I know it sounds crazy, but look." He pointed to the map. "Lada said this is where the cave is."

"It's a small beach called Litos. I haven't been there since I was a boy."

"Will you go with me there tomorrow? It's too late now."

Peter paused. "Yes, I'll go. It's too dangerous for you to go alone. Come by in the morning. I have rock-climbing gear we can use to scale the steep cliffs."

Stefan left. He hadn't wanted to tell Peter about the translated legend, the ring, the belt, Kalyna, or the golden edelweiss. None of that still made sense. He would find the cave and prove his fears weren't true. Opening his palm, he looked at the object purported to open the door. The small golden disk, shaped like edelweiss, showed a woman with a crown of flowers in her braided hair. Turning it over, he swallowed the lump in his throat.

Three words created a circle inside the flower, the same words on Kalyna's tattoo.

Welcoming Arms

October 17

CARINA LAY ON her stomach, stretched out on the rocks, looking into her jubilant face reflected in the pool's emerald water. Much despair had filled her life, but soon she would reap the fruit of happiness. Her beloved neared the end of his journey while the door to his world remained open to her. Today, her arms would embrace the one lost to her for so long. Stefan had found the secret key to open the door to the temple.

The village woman, the devoted follower of the samodivi, had helped him along the way. She would receive her reward, what she had longed for since the day Carina had pulled her from the water, barely alive, so many years ago. Her silence had proven her faithfulness.

Even so, Carina's chest tightened. What if all her beloved's memories didn't return when he arrived? The goddess would be angry. No mortal, except Carina's true love, could enter the sanctuary, so the curse could be broken. The goddess would inflict punishment on all others. Carina's heart had captured Stefan's soul. He had power within him to embrace her immortal love without fear. He wouldn't fail.

She returned to the sanctuary above. It was time to await his arrival. Vedra and Morena, clothed in sacred ceremonial gowns, had already gathered by the goddess, who graced them with her presence on this fateful day.

Bendis summoned Carina to sit by the throne as well. Her slight smile wavered as her hand smoothed the hair of her favored maiden. "I fear I'm going to lose you, my beloved. You should not have given him the key so soon. He won't understand, and he'll betray you."

"He'll stand true." Carina clasped her hands together. "He loves me."

Smiling in agreement, Vedra shared her sister's excitement.

But Morena whispered to Carina, "Another plans to accompany your beloved. I must hinder him."

Carina cast a beseeching look at Morena. "Do not harm the mortal or the flock he loves. He has served us well many times."

Patting her sister's trembling hands, Morena replied, "He will suffer no more loss."

Bendis clapped her hands twice. Immediate silence ensured. "Begin the preparations for the sacrifice. The mortal shall arrive soon."

UNABLE TO SLEEP that night, Stefan finished Kalyna's portrait. Her mouth turned up in the same secret smile she had worn during the first dream he had of her. The one where she beckoned to him to follow her to the cave. He placed his hands on his temples. His dreams. The cave. Legends. Golden belts. Treasure. Samodivi. Nikola. Dushan. Carina. Would finding the cave solve any of these riddles?

The sun would be rising soon. He couldn't wait here any longer. Peter would be awake already. At least at his house, Stefan could talk to someone until they left. He filled his backpack with what he thought he needed to get to the cave—ropes, a hatchet, a lantern, and matches. Peter could supply the rest. Adding his camera and phone in one of the side pockets, he secured the straps. He tucked the golden token and map secure in his jacket pocket. After feeding Balkan and letting him out, Stefan headed to Peter's house. Balkan rushed over to the gate, whining and scratching at the door.

"Sorry, not this time." Stefan patted Balkan's nose through a crack in the door. "I'll be home soon."

The crisp air and changing foliage reminded him of his old home in Boston. Autumn remained his favorite season, with its red, gold, orange, and yellow leaves mixed with myriad shades of green not yet changed. He now belonged in this little corner of the world.

When he passed the church, something jumped off the gate and sailed over his head.

"Oh god." He jumped backward, almost falling. "Only a cat. Only a black cat." Its yellow eyes glowed in the darkness. Did the villagers believe a black cat crossing your path was a sign of bad luck the way Americans did? His hand involuntarily reached for his forehead. He laughed nervously, aware he had been about to cross himself to ward off evil.

He took a few more steps down the uneven gravel path, the rocks cracking beneath his feet. Feeling someone watching him, he looked back at the church. Nona leaned against the fence, holding a bouquet of flowers. She wore a white robe instead of her usual black dress. Stefan walked over, expecting she might run away again.

Instead, she handed him the spikes of burning bush. "Please give these to my patroness in her temple."

His eyes opened wide and his jaw dropped, but no words came out. Nona spoke. To him. And ... how did she know where he was going? He remained there a moment later as she disappeared into the darkness.

ALL THE LIGHTS of the houses Stefan passed were off, except Peter's. He raised his hand to tap on the door, but stopped. A note with his name on it was taped to the frame. Unfolding it, he read Peter's apologies. Someone had called him away on an emergency. The final line warned Stefan to be careful if he decided to go alone.

Shaking his head, he crumpled the note, stuffing it into the backpack. He couldn't wait until Peter returned. If he didn't do this today, he would drive himself crazy with all his unanswered questions. He headed toward the path that led to Litos Beach.

After he had walked a few miles, he stopped to look at the view. The bay in Elenite was full of yachts bobbing on the quiet sea. Taking out the map, he checked where the cutoff for Litos Beach was supposed to be. The trail should be somewhere nearby.

He continued his trek, and would have missed the cut-off if the fluttering of wings hadn't startled him. A white falcon—was it the same one that seemed to follow him around Emona?—sat where the branches of two trees intertwined, forming what looked like an arched doorway. A tiny, overgrown path lay at the base of the two trees.

The ground started shaking, and the rumbling soon grew in volume. He looked toward where the clatter of hooves originated. A herd of wild horses rushed toward him. He barely had time to duck into some bushes out of their direct path when they passed by like a hurricane, wrapped in a cloud of dust.

Shaking his head at how nearly he had missed being trampled, he looked for a sturdy stick to use as a staff for the rest of the hike. The trail soon became thick with wild blackberries. He removed the hatchet from the backpack to clear away some of the brush.

The dark path wound its way toward the rocky shore. The thicket gave testament no human had set foot on the path for years. The trail ended on a steep cliff above the shore. Waves slammed against the rocks below. This had to be the place.

Stefan put his backpack down and removed a rope. He tied it around the trunk of a sturdy tree. Scouring through the items, he searched for gloves, but didn't find them. Had he packed them? He looked over the edge. A landing wasn't that far below. He could make it there. Putting the backpack on again, he began the descent. He had gone several feet when the rope cut into his skin, leaving a thin trail of red. He looked down again. The ledge was a few feet lower. Soon his feet touched firm ground. He let out a deep breath and released the rope.

Easing his way along the narrow slate ledge, he came to an opening. He walked into its dark interior, shaking with curiosity and excitement. Removing his backpack, he took out and lit the lantern. Moss and wild berries covered the walls. A stone door in the center had a symbol carved into it.

His hands trembling, Stefan removed the golden edelweiss from his pocket and placed the token over the symbol. With a grating noise, the door slid open, stirring up dust. Was this another dream? Would he wake up in another moment back in Emona?

He retrieved his camera from the backpack. Ducking under the low doorway, he stepped inside the cave. Lit torches lined the passageway, illuminating paintings covering the rocky walls. He peered closer at a drawing of three women dancing, with their hair turning to flames. His eyes opened wide. He had seen it before in his dream. Continuing down the passage, he looked at the others—a woman riding a horse, several women at a sacrificial pillar. Each of them had been in his dream, exactly where they were now.

This must be another dream. He couldn't possibly be in the samodivi's cave.

Many more paintings lined the long hallway, revealing a tale of violence. Women fleeing from attacking soldiers. Valuables stolen. A village burning. A sword piercing a boy. And a tale of revenge. A goddess slaughtering the attackers. So much pain. His heart ached for the suffering the walls portrayed.

Soon the passageway of drawings opened into a large cavern. Stefan held his lantern in front of him and stood in awe of the beauty of the underground palace. On the marble floor, stalagmites rose to merge with sister stalactites suspended from the ceiling. They formed stunning sculptures, rivalling any created by master artists. Joining the stalactites, thousands of pink and blue crystals sparkled like diamonds amidst snow-white cave pearls. Where they ended, a stone waterfall began, flowing through a passage to some unknown place below. A steady stream poured down it, into a basin carved out of the stone. He walked over to it and listened to the muted sound of more water, perhaps a real waterfall far below.

In the middle of the cavern stood a marble column with a shining disk on top. He went closer to examine it. The metal disk with an inscription and a raised edelweiss in its center glittered in the light of his lantern. Surprised dust didn't cover the disk, he ran his fingers over it. Touching something wet and sticky, he withdrew his hand in a hurry. It felt like fresh blood.

As Stefan adjusted the settings on his camera to get a close-up of the disk, the air surrounding him grew heavy. The hairs on the back of his neck prickled when a green glow floated toward him from the back of the cave. Soon the profile of a woman appeared inside the glowing light. She wore a long white robe, and her blond hair appeared to be transparent. Approaching him with outstretched hands, she kept her head bent so low the curls covered her face. She didn't raise her head until she stepped almost in front of him.

Stefan looked into Kalyna's black eyes.

She smiled and called out to him in a soft, low voice. It echoed throughout the chamber, "Dushan, come to me." *Me, me, me ... me.*

No! I'm not Dushan! His heart pounded to bursting, the sound of her voice mesmerizing him, frightening him.

Step by step he backed away, unable to tear himself away from her gaze. He became trapped within her eyes, blind to his surroundings and found himself swimming in their blackness.

"Don't be afraid." *Fraid, fraid, fraid ... fraid.* She glided closer to him with each retreating step he took.

He bumped into a column and dropped his camera. *No! This can't be Kalyna!*

"Be mine." *Mine, mine, mine ... mine.*

No! He screamed in his mind, unable to speak.

Run! But he couldn't break the invisible bond between them. He couldn't look away. He couldn't move.

She reached her hand to touch his face. Sweat seeped out of his pores, drenching his clothes and his hair. It dripped into his eyes. He blinked, releasing him from his hypnotic state. Flying down the passageway, he tripped over loose rocks and fell. He pulled himself up and continued his flight, not daring to look back to see if she followed him. His adrenaline kept him going.

Light from the entrance of the cave was ahead. He rushed out onto the ledge. The crackling of rocks warned him too late. The slab collapsed. Unable to hold onto the branches of a bush, he tumbled down the cliff and a sharp pain tore through his leg. Then everything went black.

Victim of Fate

October 17

"THE MORTAL HAS failed!" The goddess screeched from her throne on the second level of the temple. "He must die."

The sound echoed to the mouth of the cave where Carina, tears streaming down her face, gazed at Stefan's broken body lying on the rocks. His moans rose over the roaring of the sea, wrapping themselves around her, constricting her throat and heart. Every excruciating pain wracking his body intensified a hundredfold in her. She drew more of his pain into herself, easing his own. He had succumbed to his fears. Mortals did not have the strength or knowledge of the samodivi.

She twirled, tiny feathers growing along her arms, as she prepared to go to him to heal his wounds and erase the memories. Arms reached into the whirling mass, wrapping around her. The transformation ceased.

Morena continued to embrace her trembling sister. She whispered, "Mother Bendis orders you to her side."

Vedra, too, hugged Carina. "Go. Her anger is directed at the mortal you love."

Carina looked over the cliff again. "No. I must help him now or he'll die."

Morena brushed back the hair plastered to Carina's tear-streaked cheeks. "He will surely die if you don't go to the goddess. Vedra and I will help him until you can heal him."

Placing her fingers to her lips, Carina sent a kiss toward Stefan. Even if she did help him now, Bendis would hunt him down. It would be impossible for him to escape the Goddess of Fate. She hugged and kissed her sisters. "Yes, help him, please. I must plead mercy for him."

Carina waited until her sisters disappeared in a whirlwind before she hastened to the throne. She bowed low, fearful of the fire blazing in the goddess' eyes.

With lips drawn tight, Bendis spoke, but her words were gentle. "Dearest one, I fear he is not your destiny." She laid her hand on Carina's head. "He failed the test of true love when he didn't recognize you. Now, the mortal must be punished for entering the sacred temple."

"Mother Goddess, please don't." Carina choked out the words and looked up, tears blurring her vision. She clung to the hands of the goddess. "He found the belt that restored Vedra to us. He has a good heart. So many other mortals love him. Please give him another chance to remember."

With sadness in her eyes, Bendis looked upon her favored guardian. "You have until the Winter Moon, when the door to the mortal world closes. If he does not remember, he must be punished or offer us a sacrifice."

Carina rose. "Thank you, Mother Goddess. Dushan's journey has been long. The centuries have erased his memories of the past and of me. I have done what I can to guide him back to me through his dreams, but it hasn't been enough."

"If he is not the one, you cannot change his fate or yours."

"I know he is my destiny. His soul is trapped. I will not let him die again. I now know the way to free him so he can complete his journey. I must wait a while longer, for the time is not yet nigh." Carina bowed to her Goddess and kissed the hand offered to her, then left the temple to help her sisters.

FORTY LASHES FROM a cat-of-nine-tails embedded with metal spikes and bone fragments couldn't have inflicted Stefan with more agonizing pain. His brain pummeled his skull as if someone had poured molten lead through his eye sockets. His raw, battered face burned from the sticky, coppery-tasting substance inching its way down his cheek and into his mouth. *Blood!*

He tried to move his legs, but couldn't feel them. His breathing shallow and his heart racing, he pushed himself up on his elbows. The excruciating pain in his head shattered into a myriad of bright, flashing lights, paralyzing him. His brain shrieked in agony, but his voice managed only a hoarse groan. He let his head fall back, his energy spent. Straining to suppress the pain, he squeezed his eyes shut and clenched his teeth, the muscles in his body tensing from the agony.

Remaining still until his breathing became regular, his heartbeat returned to normal, and the lightning flashes ceased, he finally opened his eyes to slits. He looked around the rocky beach. His head and neck rested in a pool of water. The rest of his body lay tangled around kelp-covered rocks. Mercifully, he was still alive.

How was he going to get out of here? He opened his mouth to shout for help, but no words emerged. The uproar of the crashing waves would swallow his voice even if he could cry out. His life was as flitting as a candle burning in the wind, ready to be doused at any moment.

The ringing in his ears made concentration difficult. Ringing? Of course, his cell phone. Wait. It was in his backpack, which he had set down when he went exploring.

What had he been searching for? Stefan closed his eyes and pressed his hands to his throbbing temples. He took long breaths to relax his mind, letting his consciousness wander back in time.

A cave.

His eyes shot open. A steep, rocky cliff loomed overhead, with the entrance to the cave about thirty-five to fifty feet above him. The ledge he'd been standing on had crumbled when he rushed out of the inky blackness.

Something had frightened him. No, more than frightened. Terrified. What had it been? He recalled ancient drawings on the cave walls, depicting women performing strange rituals. They astonished him, but hadn't frightened him. What else had he seen? The sacrificial altar, the one with sticky blood in its crevices. That hadn't terrified him, although it did make him uneasy.

The woman!

Stefan gasped. The beautiful blonde he had glimpsed in the darkness of the cave. Like a hallucination, a wraith surrounded by an eerie glow, she floated toward him, smiling, her hands outstretched. Was she the woman from his dreams? Had she said or done something to cause him to flee? Why couldn't he remember anything?

Rubbing his temples in a small circular motion with his fingertips, he tried to restore the memories, but couldn't remember anything more. His head light and his limbs tingling, he struggled to remain awake, fearing this sleep could be his last. Despite his effort, his eyelids drooped, and the noise of the sea faded away.

BARKING DOGS AND shouting voices woke Stefan. Lights flickered like fireflies farther along the coast.

They must be looking for me.

When he hadn't returned after going to the cave alone, Peter must have summoned the villagers to comb the shoreline.

He willed the search party to come his way. They were so close now. The wind carried their words to him.

"Stefan, are you here?" Peter's voice boomed over the roar of the waves.

I'm here. Please help me. Stefan's lips moved, but his mouth emitted no sound.

Peter had warned him of the danger. Now he regretted his impulsive behavior.

"Where could he be? We've searched everywhere along the coast," a voice Stefan didn't recognize said.

"We can't continue the search today. It's too rocky and dangerous here with night falling and the tide coming in."

Stefan searched for a stone. Perhaps he could throw it and make a noise. But then the lights, barking, and voices faded away, leaving only flashes of lightning and the rumble of the waves.

No! Come back!

He dreaded being trapped on the beach, bleeding to death like a wounded animal. He wasn't ready to die. Not now, when he was living the life he had dreamed of for so long. Not now, when he had fallen in love again.

The turbulent sea roiled nearby, sending the waxing tide closer to draw him into its watery depths. The misty drops gnawed at the gashes on his lips and buried their salt deep into his raw, sliced skin.

He drifted in and out of a sea of blackness as the sun sank below the horizon. The last image he saw before he lost consciousness was a white falcon with black, piercing eyes, staring at him from the edge of a boulder.

Have No Fear

October 20

STEFAN FELL IN and out of consciousness. Voices floated around him. Peter. Kalyna. Elena. Others. Gentle hands touched him. His pain receded. Darkness, light, and strange glows appeared before his eyes, dwindling moments later. The sea grew loud, then faded away. Softness replaced the hard ground.

Roused by a noise, he wondered if he would ever be rescued from the beach. How much time had passed? He opened his eyes to the piercing light of day. But it wasn't the sun. He looked around at his surroundings. The small white room smelled of alcohol and bleach. Beside him a table held a vase of red and white roses. Stefan raised both hands to his face. Nothing other than scratches from the rope marred them. He looked at his legs. No cast.

Fortune had given him a second chance at life. He wouldn't be foolish again.

Peter and Elena spoke in hushed tones by the window.

"Hello," he managed a hoarse whisper.

"Stefan!" Elena choked out the word. She dashed to his bed, kissing him on the cheek. "We were so worried. You've been unconscious for *three* days."

"Three days!" He struggled to sit up. Groaning, he fell back on the pillow. "I have to call Sonia. Take care of Balkan."

Peter walked over. "It's fine. Neda called your daughter. Sonia knows you're in the hospital in Varna. And I've taken care of the puppy."

"How did you find me? You were so close, but you walked away."

Pulling a chair close, Peter sat next to the bed. "A woman told the search party she had heard someone at the Old Beach. Even though we had already looked there, we returned and found you."

"The Old Beach?" He pursed his lips. "How did I end up there? I was on Litos Beach. That's a few miles away."

Peter shrugged. "Maybe you only thought you made it that far."

"Who was the woman?" Could it have been the one from the cave?

"She didn't say her name." Peter stood. "We should let you rest."

"Wait!" Stefan held his hand out. "Nona. Sh-she spoke to me yesterday. Or the last day I remember. She asked me to give flowers to her patroness."

Peter and Elena looked at each other, then Peter spoke. "Nona's missing. No one's seen her since you had your accident."

Stefan groaned.

Elena sat next to Stefan. "Don't upset yourself. People are looking for her. Do you remember anything about what happened?"

"No. I had a backpack." He tried to get up to look around. "Where's my camera? Did you find it?"

She put her hand on his arm. "Your backpack is here. Peter found it next to you on the beach, but he didn't find a camera. Now you need to rest."

Next to me? He had left it at the entrance to the cave. And he had dropped his camera inside the cave. Why would someone place the backpack by his body, but not his camera? Had he taken a picture of something that someone didn't want to see the light of day? Could it have been the ghostly woman from the cave? Had she been the one who brought him his backpack?

Peter and Elena stepped away from the bed and whispered to each other. She came back and gave him a light kiss on his cheek. "We're going to the cafeteria to get something to eat, so you can rest now. We'll come back later."

"Where's my phone? I want to call Sonia."

Elena retrieved it from his backpack and handed it to him. He dialed the number when they left.

"Daddy! I was so worried." She sounded close to tears.

"I'm okay now, sweetheart." He closed his eyes. "It's so good to hear your voice."

"Sh-she told me you would be okay."

"Who? Neda?"

"No, the samodiva." Sonia paused. "She said she didn't mean to frighten you."

"What?" He sat up. Regretting the action when his head throbbed, he eased back down. "Did she say anything else?" *Kalyna? Had she been the woman in the cave?* She looked so much like Kalyna. But those eyes. And she had called him Dushan.

"Only to trust her," she whispered. "And she loves you and me."

"Trust her. Loves us." Stefan yawned.

"Daddy, I learned some more stories in school."

"Tell me about them."

She chatted on, talking about elves, gnomes, and dwarfs. He listened to her voice, but couldn't concentrate on the words. "Sonia, sweetheart, I enjoy your stories, but I'm so tired. I'll call you tomorrow, okay?"

"Okay, Daddy. Love you the most."

He ended the call. Images of the nightmare floated through his mind. Had any of it happened? Did he imagine seeing Kalyna in the cave? He wanted to see her again and ask her. He tried to open his eyes, but they wouldn't move.

I'm so glad I'm alive.

A warm hand caressed his face. He managed to open his eyes to slits. *Kalyna.* She kissed him and left the room. He fell asleep, heavily medicated.

When he woke again, someone was moving in the room. *Kalyna's still here.*

He opened his eyes. A nurse hovered near him, adjusting his blanket.

"Did I have any visitors while I was asleep? A blond, slender woman?"

"No one has been here since your friends left. I told them not to come back tonight. You needed your rest." She looked at his chart, took the tray away, and closed the door behind her.

Stefan reached out to get a glass of water from the table next to him. A white flower like a dazzling star lay there.

DREAMS OF THE woman beckoning to him from the cave haunted Stefan for several days after he left the hospital. Each night, they increased in intensity, until he woke up in a feverish sweat. He had to return to the cave to discover the identity of the woman, if she even existed. He asked Peter to go with him, but he declined.

"Let the cave remain a mystery," he had said. "Search for happiness in your real life, and let the legend live."

Not heeding Peter's advice, Stefan set out early one morning a couple of weeks after his first trip there. He had to discover what secrets it hid. Finding the path, he headed down it, positive it led to the cave. At the end was a tree stripped of its bark. Broken branches lay around it.

As he reached behind him to remove his backpack, a sharp pain pierced his shoulders. Sliding the pack off, he rubbed the area. Maybe this wasn't such a good idea. He looked over the edge. The cave was so close. Why turn back now?

He removed a thick rope and tied it to the trunk of the tree. Below the cliff, raging waves crashed into the rocks. Lucky the first time to escape with nothing more serious than a few bruised ribs, why was he tempting fate again? Because he had to know.

All that remained was building up his nerve to descend the rope to what remained of the ledge. He put on his gloves. Taking a deep breath, he grabbed hold of the rope. Wrapping his legs around it, he stepped over the side. He clenched his teeth as the pain in his shoulders intensified. *Find the cave,* he ordered himself as he slid down the rope. In a short time, his feet touched a hard surface. Before letting go of the rope, he clutched some ivy to gain a secure hold. The ledge didn't give way.

Stefan held onto ivy as he walked along the narrow ledge to the cave opening. He removed a flashlight from his jacket pocket and shone it along the inside. Ivy covered the surface of the rock for as far as he could see.

"I know the door was here. I saw it."

He ripped at branches and leaves. The rock beneath the ivy was smooth. Not a single crack marred its surface. An image formed on the exposed rock. A circle first, then within it the shape of a three-headed snake emerged. A hissing came from beneath the ivy he had torn away. A black snake slithered out, staring at him with its glassy green eyes.

Breathe. Don't move suddenly.

Stefan backed away without taking his eyes off the snake. When he reached the tree, he grabbed the rope, hurrying up despite the unbearable pain in his shoulder. At the top, he collapsed onto the grass, breathing a sigh of relief. On the next ridge, the black stallion tossed its head in Stefan's direction before it galloped away.

Awakening

November 8

MUSIC FROM *TUPANS*, *gaidas*, and *zurlas* drifted to the outskirts of the village toward Stefan. The dreary, overcast day made the notes even more mournful. As he drew closer to the solemn ceremony, he passed a woman coating ashes on her face. They streaked down her cheeks from the tears overflowing her eyes. She kneeled on the ground, raising her hands and face to the sky in somber prayer.

"I'm sorry for your loss." He touched her shoulder.

She didn't respond, as if she neither saw, heard, nor felt him.

A crowd gathered around a man standing on a flat stone amidst piles of other stones. Twin striped rows of budding branches decorated his colorful *zeira*, a long woolen hooded cloak. A foxskin cap rested on his bowed head, and high deerskin boots covered his motionless feet.

As the beats on the *tupans* softened to a gentle roll, the crowd kneeled in reverence. A shaman, wearing a full-faced golden mask, appeared at the edge of the forest. In his hands he held a golden *rhyton*, a horned drinking vessel, shaped like a stag's head. Raising it toward the sky, he danced in a trance-like state around the man on the stone, all the while chanting low in an ancient language. The words and dance intensified. Lowering his hands, the shaman poured red wine into the top of the *rhyton*. It flowed out the open end at the base, onto the flat stone around the other man's feet. While the shaman continued to chant, a three-headed black snake with a crown-shaped marking on its center head slithered from a basket set at the edge of the stone. The snake wrapped itself around the man on the stone and began its ascent up his body.

The shaman's chanting reached a crescendo. He raised his hands once more to the sky. The sun emerged from behind thick black clouds, casting a shadow of the other man onto the stone. Two other villagers hurried over, piling rocks on top of the shadow, building a wall. Row after row, stone after stone it rose. Soon the outline for a door appeared.

The woman Stefan had seen praying rushed over and clung to the feet of the man on the stone. "Dushan, don't sacrifice yourself! Your Carina is gone, but you're young. You'll find a new love. Please stop this madness. Don't trap your shadow in the wall of the house. Please don't!"

The snake hissed, staring at the woman with its cold green eyes.

Dushan reached down, laying his hand on her head. "It is already done, Mother."

The snake coiled itself around his neck. All three heads drew back, tongues spitting, then jerked forward, biting Dushan. His mother screamed and fainted.

The builders finished the doorway. The shaman poured wine over its threshold. "Continue your journey, Dushan. One day, you will return with a different life for you have been chosen to be reborn."

The snake uncoiled its black body. It slithered beneath the threshold to become the guardian of the home.

Dushan turned pale as the poison seeped into his body. He placed his trembling hands onto the wall, swearing an oath. "This is the house for my beloved Carina. I have hidden my shadow within its wall to make sure I'll be here forever until she returns to me."

He dropped to his knees, collapsing over the threshold. The snake's poison had accomplished his desire. Soon his face relaxed into a peaceful smile, and his breath left his body.

As if in a trance, the crowd danced in a circle around the stone. The music once again played its sorrowful tune, and the shaman chanted. Amidst the noise was the flutter of wings. A white falcon landed on the branch of a young walnut tree next to the house. With an ear-splitting scream, the bird flew down toward Dushan's body lying prone over the hearth. The falcon laid its head next to his lifeless body.

Stefan walked among the crowd unobserved. His breath caught, his body shook, and his hands trembled when he reached Dushan. He stared into his own face.

IT'S BEEN THREE weeks! He continued to dream about Dushan and Carina after finding the cave, but still didn't have any answers. As with the other nightly journeys, this latest one had been vivid, as if he had relived the terrifying event. In all the others, he had envisioned events through Dushan's eyes, never realizing the man could have been his twin.

He understood the devotion he had for his bride. Kalyna had the same effect on him. Where was she? He had so many things he wanted to know, but unsure he wanted to ask the questions, afraid the answers might terrify him, like the dreams.

Uncovering her portrait, he imagined her dazzling smile, the warmth of her body, and the taste of raspberries on her lips. The portrait watched him, smiling, her eyes filled with flames of passion. He gazed at it with a desire of his own. As he ran his fingers over her face in a caress, warmth surged through his body. He loved her—body, soul, and mind. When would he see her again so he could hug her, make love with her, and share his life with her forever?

The cool air in the studio became oppressive instead of invigorating. In need of company, he headed to Peter's house, hoping he had some Turkish coffee. The cool

November morning sent chills through his body, as did the stares of the villagers. Some of them continued to make the sign of the cross when he approached. Every once in a while, he caught the word "cursed" in their whispered conversations. Peter, Maria, and Todor treated him no differently than before, continuing to welcome him.

At the village center, a crowd gathered outside the hotel. Many of them, including Maria, had dressed all in black. By the way she moved her hands, she appeared to be giving instructions to those around her.

When they headed down the road, Stefan approached her, blowing on his hands. "What's going on?"

"Today's the Day of Saint Michael the Archangel. We came from the church service this morning celebrating the lives of our loved ones who are no longer here. Now we're going to visit their graves. You're welcome to go with us if you want, even though you don't have family here."

"No, thank you. It's too cold to be standing around outside. I came to have some coffee with Peter, but I guess he'll be going, too." He looked around at everyone laughing and chatting with one another. They all had families here, past and present. Saddened and feeling the weight of the absence of his family, Stefan closed his eyes, remembering Katherine's happy face smiling at him. He would celebrate her life when he got home. He couldn't do it here with so many other people around.

"Are you sure? We're going to have a lunch afterwards."

He smiled at her. "Thanks, but no. I have a backlog of work to do."

As he walked home, a falcon circled above him. It swooped down and landed on a wooden fence to watch him. He shivered, remembering the falcon in the dream.

WITH HIS ARMS loaded with wood, Stefan entered the studio after returning from Peter's house. He lay the kindling down first, then the larger chunks on top. Before starting the fire, he lit the *kandilo* and said a silent prayer for Katherine, remembering with fondness their happy years together. He bent to strike a match in the fireplace, when someone tapped on the door.

Not feeling like socializing, he hesitated, thinking the person might go away. The knock came again. His mood brightened immediately when he opened the door. Kalyna was on the other side. He admired her colorful costume. Red, yellow, and white flowers had been embroidered along the neckline of her long-sleeved white cotton shirt. Over that she wore a V-necked dress. Its maroon skirt had blue and pink floral designs embroidered along the hem. The contrast of her pale skin to the black bodice made her look like an exotic flower herself.

"I was thinking about you. I have so many things I want to ask." He stood aside. "But, come in. I don't want to make you stand out there in the cold."

Kalyna hugged Stefan and kissed him on the cheek. "I know it's rather chilly today, but I've made a picnic lunch for us. I have a special place in mind where we can go. You'll love it." She grasped his hand and looked into his eyes. "Please say you have the time to go there with me."

"I have all the time in the world for you." His responsibility to his commitments vanished. She made him feel happy and secure, like entering the realm of another world, their own world where everything could be possible. He hugged and kissed her. "My beautiful nymph, I need to know if you were—"

Laughing, she pushed him away. "We'll have time for questions later. We should leave now, or we won't leave at all. I'd like to be there at noon for our feast. Get a warm jacket. I don't remember it being so bitter cold in November in ages."

Stefan got his jacket from the closet. "Won't you tell me—"

"Shh." She placed her finger on his lips. "Later."

He exhaled a long breath as he reached for the basket. "Would you like me to carry this?"

Kalyna hugged it close to her. "It's okay. It's light. I don't mind."

The stony path they walked down seemed familiar to Stefan. "Where are we going?"

"There's a place in the meadow I like to go to."

They soon stopped near an ancient walnut tree. Rocks scattered all around formed a circle. The villagers called such a place an *obrok*, a sacred place. He glanced around. This was the location he had first seen the mysterious woman with the horses.

Kalyna set the basket on a large flat rock and looked around with a painful longing in her eyes. "The view here is heavenly. It would be a wonderful place to build a house, spending a lifetime with a beloved one, raising children and growing old together."

At the mention of a house, he looked around again. Chills swept through his body, and he wiped sweat off his brow. His dream this morning had taken place here. Even the walnut tree remained, although now quite ancient. If he mentioned it to Kalyna, would his crazy dream frighten her?

To hide his discomfort, he scraped off some moss from the rock. He uncovered an inscription worn down so much he couldn't read it. Next to the writing, an image of a three-headed snake coming out of a circle had been carved into the stone. The same image had been on the door to the cave.

He spoke with a shaky voice. "Look at this. If stones could talk, I wonder what hidden stories this one would tell us."

She opened her mouth, but remained silent for a while. "This is a sacred place for me. I come here every year on this day. This is the first time I've brought anyone with me. I wanted to share it with you because it's a special day."

Taking the white cloth off the basket, she spread it out on the stone, setting a bowl on it. "This is boiled wheat with nuts and sugar." She added a loaf of bread, a bottle of wine, and two wine glasses. "It's not a fancy lunch, but I'm elated because of the place and the company. The grains of wheat symbolize the soul's journey, and the wine is a symbol of life."

She looked at him so forlorn, with her curls tumbling around her face, that he leaned over and kissed her. "With you around, it's a meal fit for a prince."

Breaking off a piece of the bread, she handed it to him. She poured wine first into the glasses, then a small amount on the ground. As the red liquid flowed into a crack in the stone, she made a toast. "Here's to love and happiness and the soul's journey."

They clinked glasses. Stefan took a sip with the sound of the crystal ringing in his ears. The fruity-flavored wine made him dizzy. Soon bright lights flashed all around. He travelled down a tunnel. Shadows and strange noises surrounded him. The stone house from his dream materialized, then someone touched his arm. He held his breath as he turned around. Kalyna wore a white wedding gown, with flowers in her hair.

Her eyes widened as a three-headed black snake with a golden crown on its center head wrapped itself around her neck. The reptile stared at him with cold green eyes as it tightened its hold. Frantic, Kalyna extended her hand toward him. He searched for the ring in his pockets. It was the key to destroying the snake, but he couldn't find the blue-star. He reached out to her, but she disappeared. His breath left him, and he fell to the ground. Two invisible hands lifted his body into the air.

The warp and weave of time became as one. He could neither move forward nor backward. He remained lost in that moment. Shadows formed into images, scenes of a life long ago.

Three young girls ran along the beach, laughing. One stopped abruptly. All three tumbled onto the sand, giggling and rolling around.

A youth and a maiden lay hand in hand among the wildflowers, looking at the night sky. The heavenly bodies were as bright as the stars in their own eyes. The youth gave her a ring with a shining blue stone. Tears of happiness streamed down the maiden's face.

Then Stefan became that youth, looking into the adoring eyes of his beloved. And the maiden became Kalyna. Had he always been that youth? Or had he become him the moment he bought the ring?

Like the grim reaper hourglass in the Salem shop where he bought the ring, death stood at his door, and yet life was endless. The sands of time flowed out, but did not grow less. Never running out, never overflowing. Always constant, always the same. Yesterday became today, and today turned into tomorrow.

"Stefan, Stefan!" Kalyna shook him.

He sat up. Everything around him was spinning. He closed his eyes, then opened them again. Slowly items came into focus. The walnut tree. The stones. Finally, Kalyna. "What happened? Where am I?"

"You're here with me. It's Kalyna. You must have passed out from the wine. It's made from black currant, so it's quite potent." She poured the rest of his drink onto the ground. "Are you okay? Do you want to leave?"

"No, no. I'm fine." A strange tingling crept over his body, as if awakening from a long sleep.

He looked over at Kalyna. Love for her, like none he had yet experienced, poured out from him. He touched her hair, her face, and her lips as if seeing her for the first time in ages. "Carina, my darling one, I love you. I've missed you so much." His voice did not sound like his own, but Kalyna's face became ecstatic.

Rejected Love

November 8

"DUSHAN REMEMBERED ME! He called me Carina!" She grabbed hands with her sisters and danced in the temple until all three toppled to the floor, giggling the way they had as children.

"Carina, my dear, come sit by me." Bendis' voice rose above their jubilation.

She obeyed, all traces of a smile removed when she looked into the expressionless face of her goddess.

"Dear one, he remembered only a moment. Time runs short before the Winter Moon."

Carina trembled at the words, their meaning clear. "Dushan is still weak from his long sleep."

"How can you be sure, dearest?"

"The moment I met Stefan on the beach, Dushan's power surged from within." Carina leaned closer, grasping Bendis' hands. She looked at the ring shining on her finger. "Now that Dushan has awakened, the blue-star has the power to give him strength."

"Be careful with your heart, Carina. Will you marry and become mortal if Dushan remains dormant?"

Did she love Stefan enough to make such a great sacrifice? "Yes, I'm ready to spend my life with him and his child. The curse of the ring must end."

Bendis held out her hand for Carina to kiss. "Wait a bit longer to ensure you haven't spoken in haste. If you still love the mortal on the eve of the Winter Moon, you may go to him. For now, I command you to remain here to consider your destiny."

STEFAN RUBBED HIS temples. Work on restoring the panels of the iconostasis required his full attention to details. Today, he couldn't master his art. Memories, no not memories—his imagination was clouding what he knew to be true. He was confusing himself with Dushan, and Kalyna with Carina. The way he had at the picnic earlier in the day. Why hadn't she corrected him when he called her Carina? The names did sound similar. Perhaps she had misunderstood. And her answer to his questions had been "Soon. Trust me." That, followed by her kisses, left him weak and confused.

Shaking his head, he opened a drawer on his workbench, replacing the photographs of the iconostasis. A paper fluttered to the floor. Kalyna's invitation to the exhibit in April. He picked it up, about to replace it in the drawer, then stopped. The edelweiss monogram at the top was the same as the image on the golden edelweiss he had used to open the cave door. Three words were written in a circle on the inside of the flower.

The design and words also matched Kalyna's tattoo. And the one on the hand of the woman at the boutique. As well as the one on Angelina's ankle. How had that escaped his notice before? What did the words mean? And were the three women actually the ones spoken of in the legend? That was ... impossible.

With his heart racing, Stefan wrote the words onto a piece of paper. He would ask Elena to give the paper to Lada to translate for him.

Someone knocked at the door, and Balkan scampered over, barking and wagging his tail. Right behind him, Stefan opened the door. Elena was shivering on the porch. The strong wind forced her to hold onto her unadorned black hat.

"What a pleasant surprise. Come in. I was just thinking about you." He ushered her in and took her jacket. "Would you like to join me in the studio for a glass of homemade red wine? Peter gave me some. The fire's going in there. It'll warm you in no time."

"I'd love a glass. Thank you." She followed him and sat on the couch.

He poured her drink and set it on the table, then sat on the other end of the couch. Leaning toward her, he extended the paper with the three words on it. "When you see Lada again, could you give her this and ask if she can translate it?"

"Of course." Taking the paper without looking at it, she stuffed it into her purse. "It's so comfortable in your house. It has a calming effect on me."

"You're always welcome to visit. Cheers." He raised his glass and took a sip.

She didn't touch hers. Her eyes remained fixed on the fire while it bathed the studio with soft light.

"Elena, is everything okay?" He set his glass down and slid closer.

She looked at him, her expression one of misery. Dark circles even her makeup couldn't conceal ringed her eyes. Her voice quavered. "I know my visit wasn't planned, but I hated being alone this evening. I-I have news about Nikola."

"Is everything okay? Have they found him?"

A sob escaped her throat, and a shimmer of tears swelled in her eyes. "No, not yet, but they found some of his clothing on the beach in Irakli."

Taking her hands in his, he held them firmly and spoke with sympathy and concern. "Well, it doesn't mean he still won't be found ... alive."

She squeezed his hand. Her eyes softened as she looked at him. "That's what I think, too. I'm sure they'll find him. The police are still looking. I won't allow myself to believe Nikola is dead." Her lips paled, and her eyes stared out at nothing. She moaned, "Noooooo."

"Elena?"

Her body shook from her weeping. He had never seen her so upset. What could he do? What should he say? He wrapped his arms around her, and she leaned into his shoulder. He held her until she stopped sobbing. If she didn't cry for Nikola, who would?

She looked up, her perfect makeup streaking down her face. Her eyes shining bright from the tears seemed to hold back some other emotion. Getting some tissues, he cleaned her face the best he could. Her lips parted, and she sighed. She reached out and ran her fingers along his.

Startled, he pulled his hand away. "I-I got most of it off."

The anguish in her eyes returned. "Stefan," she began, her voice cracking. Clearing her throat, she tried again. "Nikola's lawyer stopped by the museum today. He gave me shocking news." She took a deep breath. "He said Nikola had written a new will recently. If anything happened to him where he wasn't able to manage his business—d-dead or alive—h-he wanted me to inherit his estate and manage his company. He also left a sizable sum of money to Boyan. The lawyer wouldn't explain why Nikola left it to me rather than to his brother."

She paused, as if waiting for him to say something, anything, but he didn't know what to say. "But that's not all. Nikola was the anonymous buyer of my gallery. He stipulated I retain fifty percent ownership in it, but he never told me anything about it. Since he's missing, it reverts to me." Her lips trembled. "I-I don't know what to think. Why did he buy the gallery? As my friend, he should have told me he wanted to help. I would have found some way to repay him. He-he must not have wanted to burden me with that financial responsibility."

Stefan stood, then paced the room. Nikola had been antagonistic toward him since he returned, apparently thinking Stefan had stolen Katherine from him. But would Nikola have wanted to hurt Elena, too, to get back at him? He couldn't tell her that. She was in too much pain to believe Nikola meant to harm her.

He sat next to her again and held her hands. "Nikola loved you. I'm sure he had a good reason for keeping this from you."

Relief flooded her eyes. "Thank you," she whispered. Wiping her eyes, she stood and walked toward the fireplace. "What's this?" With shaking hands, she picked up a lighter, embossed with the letter "N."

He joined her. "That's something Balkan found the night of the church fire."

"I-I gave this to Nikola for his birthday." She stared at it, then turned her gaze to Stefan, her eyes confused. "Do you ... do you think he had something to do with the fire?"

Stefan took a step back. "Why do you ask that?"

"You once said you thought Nikola cancelled the restoration project, didn't you." She pressed her lips into a tight line.

He nodded.

"And I thought you were joking." She squeezed the lighter tight into a fist. "What do you know? Why would he do this? Why didn't you tell me?"

"I-I ... Let's sit on the couch." He touched her arm. "I'll tell you what I've suspected about him—and why."

He told her of Nikola's obsession with Katherine. Then, he explained how he suspected Nikola was trying to hurt him in any way possible—the episode in Nessebar, the boat ride, the project cancellation, the fire.

"If he could do all that, then he might have been responsible for my cancelled insurance and the theft of the paintings." She trembled. "That would have prevented you from advancing in your art career. If you didn't have the exhibit or the project, nobody would know anything about your abilities."

Stefan nodded.

"How could I have been so naïve! I trusted him. I thought he was my friend." She looked at Stefan with longing in her eyes. "But you ... you've always been there for me, have always been honest."

Silence blanketed the room. The sparks from the fire reflected in Elena's eyes. She put the lighter down on the table, placed one hand behind Stefan's neck, and drew his head toward her. Her lips were open. Radiating with a tenderness and subdued passion he had never seen in her before, she clung to him and kissed him.

Pulling back in confusion, he walked to the window, staring into the night without speaking, caught in a gap between truth and denial. Had he in any way encouraged her? If so, he cursed himself for his insensitivity. He didn't want to lose her friendship, but he loved Kalyna.

He looked back at her. Tears streamed down her face. How could he comfort her without encouraging her? He returned to the couch. "Elena, you're a beautiful and talented woman. You're my friend. I'm sorry if I gave you the wrong impression. Please forgive me. The wine and our emotions about Nikola are to blame."

"Of course." Her smile faltered, and her eyes spoke what her words could not, of sorrow and rejected love. She wiped her tear-stained face, outwardly composing herself. Inwardly, though, Stefan thought she remained a wreck. Without saying another word, she got up and headed to her car.

Stefan accompanied her. "Elena, I'm sorry."

His heart ached, but he didn't know how to handle this type of situation. He wished she would look at him, giving him absolution for whatever he may have done to make her believe he wanted more than friendship. What could he say? He spoke the only words he could, those of a concerned friend. "Call me if you need anything. Be careful driving. You're upset, and the roads are dangerous if you don't pay attention."

"I'll be careful." She got into her car, driving away without looking back or waving to him the way she normally did.

He remained at the side of the road until the taillights disappeared into the darkness. Returning to the studio, he pulled the cloth off Kalyna's painting. Her beautiful face looked at him from the canvas. Stefan had captured the magic of her personality. Her smiling eyes followed him across the studio.

Ties that Bind

December 14

THE RAYS OF the rising sun illuminated the church, piercing the stained-glass panels to cover the walls with a colorful palette of dancing light. The door opened. Sonia walked down the aisle toward him, strewing flower petals along the floor. Grinning, she waved at him, getting petals stuck in her hair. Behind her walked Kalyna, the ethereal beauty of her sparkling skin so surreal. A long, white dress as delicate as a moonbeam flowed around her. In her arms, she carried a bridal bouquet of wild white flowers. Another wreath of them crowned her head. Her dazzling blond hair cascaded down her shoulders like a waterfall.

Two women walked by her side—Angelina and another he didn't recognize. Kalyna stopped to look at the ring sparkling like a miniature blue star on her finger.

"Oh, let me see the ring, sister," Angelina said.

Kalyna held up her hand and waved it in front of the two women.

"It's beautiful. Fortune favors you. Your intended loves you so much," the other woman exclaimed.

"I love him. He's my one and true love. We are bound together for eternity." Her joyful laughter floated through the air like a chime, echoing throughout the dome.

KALYNA'S LAUGHTER ECHOED in his ears even after he woke up. A warm sensation lingered on his chest. Putting his hand over the spot, he touched an object. He sprang up in bed, staring at the ring he had bought for Katherine, the one the wolf carried off several months ago, the same one Kalyna wore in his dream. How had it gotten around his neck while he slept?

He scanned the room. No one was there. Sliding out of bed, he searched the house, checking all the doors and windows. Everything was locked. He returned to the bedroom to get dressed. Balkan yawned, stretched, and got out of his own bed.

"What about you, buddy? You didn't hear anyone come in?"

The dog stared at him, then trotted down the hall to the front door. Stefan let him out before he started a pot of coffee. Who could he talk to about the ring? Maria acted scared about such things. Elena would scoff at him. Peter told him to leave things alone. Sultana would again proclaim him the chosen one. And Kalyna, in her mysterious way, would say everything was going to be okay. That is, if or when he saw her again. Only one person would listen—Sonia.

When the coffee was done, he poured a cup and went to his studio. He sat on the couch and called his daughter.

"Good morning, sweetheart. How are you today?"

"Daddy! Are you getting married? You didn't tell me!"

"Wh-what?"

"I dreamed you were getting married to your samodiva." She giggled. "I got to throw flowers on the floor."

"I haven't asked my samodiva, anyone, to marry me." He drew a deep breath. He hadn't even seen Kalyna in five weeks. "Would it bother you if I did?"

"No, no, no!" She clapped her hands. "I saw a pretty dress I could wear."

"I have a secret to tell you," he whispered.

"What? I like secrets."

"I dreamed that I was getting married, too, and that you were the flower girl." He paused. "But that's not the secret."

"Tell me, pleeeease."

"I think she wants to get married to me. She even gave me the ring she wants to wear."

"The pretty blue one?"

"Yes, that one." He removed the ring from beneath his shirt. Surely it wasn't cursed.

"I like blue. It's like Bluei's nose."

"Maybe he can be the ring bearer. We can tie it around his neck."

Sonia giggled. "That's silly."

Balkan barked at the door.

"Sonia, sweetheart. Balkan wants to come in, then I have to go to the city. I'll call you later, okay."

"Yup. I have to get ready for school. Love you MOST!"

"Love you, too." Stefan ended the call and got up to let the puppy in. With Balkan on his heels, he opened a cupboard in the kitchen and poured the food into a dish. Picking up the water dish, he filled that and set it down.

He was happy Sonia would accept someone new. But he was uneasy at the same time. Had Sonia had the same dream that he did? How? Was his daughter psychic? She had always seemed in tune with his feelings, but this ... was a bit unsettling.

There was time enough to think about the mystery more on his way to Varna to go over the final details for his exhibit with Elena. Now that she had her gallery back, his show had been rescheduled for the following week.

He went out onto the porch and down the walkway. Elena pulled in the driveway as he walked out the gate.

Opening the car door for her, he helped her out. "I thought we were going to meet at the gallery, not here."

"Boyan helped me get everything ready last night." She put her hands on his shoulders. "So many things have happened recently. I wanted to tell you the news in person."

"Not more bad news, I hope."

"Not at all. You know my weakness is hats." She touched the wide-brimmed white one she wore.

He liked this one and thought it one of her most beautiful creations. It had large, soft feathers gathered together at one side like a blossoming flower. A transparent white ribbon behind the feathers looked like the flower's petals. And pearls had been sewn all around the brim.

He shuddered remembering one made out of red butterflies with black and white trim. Not real ones, of course, but so lifelike. At least fifty of them must have been piled high around her head. He could barely see her face because of them.

Elena touched his forearm. "After I sold my gallery, I entered a design competition in Paris. I came in second place."

"That's wonderful. You're quite talented. I'm so happy for you."

"But that's not the best part. I got an offer to work and study with a small company outside of Paris. I'll be leaving soon after the opening of your exhibit." She leaned closer to him. "Nothing's keeping me here, is it?" She looked at him, as if waiting for him to tell her not to leave.

"You deserve this chance, especially after all you've been through lately. Don't miss this opportunity. You'll be the best hat designer in the world."

Her shoulders slumped forward. "Boyan will assume my responsibility at the gallery. He's quite talented. I think this will work for him as well."

"Do you know where you'll be staying?"

"With a friend in Paris until I find a rental. He said he has something in mind, a castle. The gentleman who owns it is quite old and needs someone to live with him to help maintain the property."

"That sounds fantastic, Marquise Elena, your majesty." Stefan bowed low to her.

Elena's laughter lessened the tension between them. "Who knows what secrets are hidden in the walls of a castle. Maybe even more than in your house." She kissed him on the cheek. "I almost forgot. I have the translation from Lada. Here you go." She handed him a folded paper, then got in the car and drove off. This time, she waved goodbye.

He unfolded the paper. "Voda, Gora, Planina." Where had he heard those words before? Then he remembered; they were the names from the legend. He went inside and read it again.

Touching Vedra on the hand, Bendis said, "You are now 'Voda,' the keeper of the waters. I grant you power over the elements, to cause or withhold storms."

Touching Morena on the ankle, she said, "You are now 'Gora,' the keeper of the woodlands. I bestow upon you the gift of sight, to know what is to come."

And touching Carina on the shoulder, she said, "You are now 'Planina,' the keeper of the mountains. You shall have the gift of illusion, to reach into the minds of men."

Voda, Gora, Planina. Vedra, Morena, Carina. What did they have to do with Kalyna, Angelina, and the woman at the boutique? It wasn't possible they were the samodiva in the legend. That would mean everything else he feared was true. *Wait!* He read it again.

You shall have the gift of illusion, to reach into the minds of men.

His dreams. If this was true, was Kalyna manipulating his dreams? Why? Some of them had been terrifying.

Yesterday, Today, and Forever

December 20

ON THE NIGHT of the Winter Moon, Carina gazed at the expanse of stars sparkling like a million fireflies. She leaned her forehead against the gate to the mortal world. Soon it would close until Blagovets. Tonight she must leave behind either cherished ones she had known for so long or the mortal she had grown to love.

"Carina, it's time to begin." Morena's voice rose from below.

Heaving a deep sigh, she returned to the temple to inform the goddess and her sisters of her decision.

Bendis rose from her throne, taking Carina's hands in her own. "Look at me, child."

She raised her head, looking at her protectress through teary eyes. "I—"

"Not yet. Partake of the ceremony, then decide." Bendis released her hands. "Consecrate your body and soul. Your sisters await you."

Carina walked to the alcove. The final note of her sisters' chant hummed in the air.

Morena opened her eyes and grasped Carina's hand. "Hold fast to your choice, sister." Stepping aside, she held out a white candle for Carina.

Lighting the candle, Carina placed it amidst the others. She breathed in its sweet honey scent while she dipped the healing herbs into the basin of *aqua vitae*, then brushed them across her face and hands. After sipping the nectar, she sang the words recited moments ago by her sisters. "Oh light of the first Winter Moon, tonight we bid ye farewell. As you wane, let your darkness reside within the sacred temple in our stead. Envelop our home, protecting it while we sojourn in the temple of the sun."

Morena stood behind her, braiding Carina's hair and twisting the coils around her head. A thin, white veil drifted over her face, covering her sorrowful eyes.

Giving Morena's hand a quick squeeze, she picked up her candle to join the others in the sacrificial room above. She marveled at the site, ablaze with tiny, flickering lights. Fragrant herbs and incense intoxicated the air. Bendis stretched out her arms, a signal to Vedra to begin the ritual of the lighting of the triple goddess candles.

The eldest sister placed a golden box on the floor. Light gleamed off rubies, sapphires, and emeralds bordering a mosaic of white marble chips shaped like edelweiss. As Vedra lifted the cover, Morena glided her fingers over the strings of the *outi*. She poured forth ancient words forever to remain unknown to mortals, summoning the creature from within. Its scales glittering like diamonds, the three-headed snake slithered toward the goddess.

Carina poured wine from an amphora into *rhytons* positioned at each corner of the altar. The blood-red liquid swirled around the raised petals of the central disk, cleansing it of sacrificial blood. When it drained through the holes at each corner, she added the sacred anointing oil. Flames shot up to the ceiling, completing the purification.

She gestured to their newest member. With a shy smile, the girl covered the altar with a thin maple board, overlaid with a fine sheet of hammered gold. Upon it she laid a purple cloth. After sprinkling white rose petals around, she set on it three candle holders, a golden viper coiled along each stem.

The snake Vedra had released reached Bendis. It slid around her outstretched arm, creeping toward the crown of her head, where it coiled like a turban. Each head flicked its tongue in different directions. The sisters placed their lit candles within the open viper mouth on their holders. Facing the goddess in silence, they awaited their summons and blessing.

"Tonight is our final Moon. I share its power with you, the guardians of my temple." She stretched out her hands. "Vedra, come forth."

Bowing low, the eldest approached. She kneeled at the feet of the goddess and raised her candle.

"My daughter, you are like the light you hold. Blue, the symbol of the water of life, fills you with ever-flowing passion and desire. Once your downfall, it shall now become your strength. No more shall you choose unwisely." Bendis touched Vedra on her head. "Rise and resume your place with your sisters."

She stood and kissed the outstretched hand of the goddess.

Bendis called Morena to her. "Daughter of reason, your black candle nourishes your soul like the rains feed the earth, bringing forth its bounty. Constant and reliable one, you, too, shall one day understand the love you now scoff, but not before heartache clasps you in its grip." Touching her on the head, she said, "Rise and resume your place with your sisters."

The second sister kissed the hand offered to her.

"Carina, my dearest, come to me."

Her heart pounding, the youngest stepped forth. Bowing to her goddess, she kneeled at the royal feet.

"The white candle represents your spirit that flies free through the sky. Your pure, loving heart will not lead you astray. Fear not that your wings will be stilled if you choose the mortal. Your love is strong and true. It will prevail." Bendis stroked Carina's hair, then touched the shoulder of the youngest. "Rise and resume your place with your sisters."

Once more Bendis held out her hand. "Come to me, my newest child. Receive your blessing."

The girl hesitated, her eyes opening wide, darting from Vedra, to Morena, to Carina. The sisters led her forward, whispering encouraging words. She kissed the divine hand and kneeled, her body trembling.

"Raise your hands, child," the goddess commanded.

Into the shaking fingers, Bendis placed a holder identical to the others. A candle glowed from the mouth of the viper. "Red, the color of blood, is the symbol of life. Be bold now and live without fear." Bendis touched her on the shoulder. "Rise, Nona. Drink of the *aqua vitae* and join the sisterhood. Their strength shall be yours."

Nona handed her candle to Morena, took the goat-shaped *rhyton* from Bendis' hand, and drank. A green glow surrounded her and her trembling ceased. Her inward beauty now shone on the outside.

Vedra held out a bowl with anointing oil to the goddess. Holding her other hand over her heart, she closed her eyes. Bendis dipped a finger into the oil, touching Vedra's forehead with it. The goddess repeated the ceremony for each of the others. "You are blessed, my children. Feel the power of the moon."

A bright light flashed through the room. The snake uncoiled and slithered down toward its golden sanctuary.

Carina's heart pounded. She must declare her intent now.

Bendis placed her hands on Carina's shoulders. "Tell me what you have decided, dearest one."

Carina gazed into a face as sad as her own. "I will live my life with Stefan if he will accept me tonight."

Bendis sighed. "Don't forget about your guardian, your goddess. You have my blessing, dearest one. Seek your fate."

The maiden solemnly kissed the outstretched hand of the goddess. Then hugging her sisters, she left the temple that had been her sanctuary for centuries.

FRIENDS, STRANGERS, AND journalists filled the gallery to capacity, making it stifling hot and loud. Conversations, laughter, and clinking crystal rang throughout the evening. Stefan wandered around, amazed at the attention the exhibit had generated. Someone touched his shoulder and spoke in a sultry voice.

"Great show. Congratulations. It's such a success."

Kalyna.

He turned to face her. Her blond hair flowed around her bare shoulders and over her stylish red dress. A golden belt with an edelweiss buckle accented the outfit. Passionate emotions flooded through him. He gazed at her with love, not knowing what to say.

She had a twinkle in her eye as she held a business card out to him. "Call me when you have a chance so we can schedule an interview."

"What?" He stared at it, then looked back at her.

"Did you forget I work for a magazine?" She tucked the card into his shirt pocket. "I want to write an article about you."

"An interview?" He shook his head. "I have so many questions I need to ask *you.*"

"I'm in awe of all your work," a man to his side said.

Stefan looked over his shoulder toward the speaker. "Thank you. One moment, please." He turned back to ask Kalyna to wait in the alcove, but she had disappeared. *Not again.*

He turned his attention back to the gray-haired man. "Did you see where the woman I was speaking with went?"

"Sorry, I didn't. I was admiring your work. Your paintings are full of strength, freedom, and vitality. Why haven't we heard about you all these years?"

"I've been abroad."

The man examined the nearby paintings. "Wild horses galloping like a whirlwind. The sea thundering like an angry god. Amazing. I think the mythical woman is my favorite, with her body shrouded in long blond hair like sea foam. Something enigmatic and vibrant shines in her eyes."

"She's my muse." Like most of the art at the exhibit, Kalyna had been his inspiration.

Later that evening when the exhibition ended, Elena approached him. He had been so busy the entire night, talking with guests and reporters, answering their questions, he hadn't had time to thank her for everything she did.

"What a show. My success is all due to you. You've done a fabulous job."

"It was splendid. I think you'll be busy with all the publicity you've gotten." She laid her hand on his shoulder. "I'll leave instructions with Boyan. He can tell you what you need to do to continue this success." Someone called to her. "I'll catch up with you tomorrow. Go home now and rest. My assistants will clean up."

Stefan pulled out Kalyna's business card after Elena left. It would take about twenty minutes to get to the address listed on it. He had to talk to her again tonight, get answers to his questions.

The drive to her house seemed to take forever. His head became heavy and his eyes burned by the time he arrived at the small cottage.

He walked through the gate and knocked on the front door. A window lit up, then the door opened a crack. A quiet female voice broke the silence. "Who is it? How may I help you?"

"I'm sorry for stopping by at such a late hour. I want to talk with Kalyna. Is she home?"

A petite dark-haired woman opened the door. The moon shone on her face. She resembled the woman from the boutique, but was quite a bit younger. Her hand rested on the doorknob. She had an edelweiss tattoo on her hand. It must be her. He didn't know why he thought she was older.

From her startled look, she recognized him as well. "No. She isn't here. Do you want to leave her a message?"

"Yes. Tell her Stefan stopped by and will call her tomorrow."

"Of course. Good night."

As she started to close the door, a male voice spoke from the corridor. "Leana, who is it?"

"Someone looking for Kalyna," she told the voice.

Leana? Was she the woman the Keeper spoke about? She couldn't be. Leana would have to be nearly forty. What did it all mean?

A LIGHT SHONE out of the studio window when Stefan arrived home. Maybe Peter had stayed to visit when he came by to let Balkan out. He didn't really want company, but Peter never stayed long. Dragging his feet, he climbed the porch stairs and entered the house.

"Balkan, buddy, where are you?"

The puppy didn't come, but barked from the studio. Stefan went to tell Peter about the exhibit. "Peter, thanks for taking care of—" He stopped. Kalyna was lying on the sofa, patting the puppy.

"Kalyna!"

"Are you ready for your interview?" She got up and held out a notepad.

"I've been looking for you." He rushed over and twirled her around the room, then set her down. "You have to answer my questions. Too many crazy things need explanations. The ring. My dreams."

Her eyes twinkled. "Maybe we can interview each other."

He looked in the corner. The canvas remained covered. "First let me show you something. Close your eyes." He held her hand, leading her to the painting. After he uncovered it, he whispered in her ear, "Now open them."

She gasped in delight. "It's wonderful. When did you paint my portrait?"

"You're always in my mind, darling one. This is how I see you through my eyes, so beautiful." He hugged her. "I love you. Stay with me. Don't ever leave me again. I go crazy when you're not here."

"I love you, too, but I thought you wanted to talk." She pulled away slightly, tilting her head as she looked at him.

"I do, but I can't think when you're so close." He paced the room, finally turning back to her. "What can I do to convince you to stay this time?"

"Your true love and eternal devotion are the only sacrifices I require."

"They're yours. They've always been yours."

"Then accept this as a pledge of that love." Kalyna unbuckled her golden belt, holding it out to Stefan.

He took a step back. "Isn't this the belt you didn't want me to touch?"

"Yes." She came closer. "Now I'm offering it to you from my own free will as a symbol of my love for you."

"The last time I held it, it was as if I could read your thoughts." He looked from the belt to her.

"I promise this time it won't." She extended it to him. "It's a symbol of our everlasting true love if I give it to you freely."

"To beget eternal happiness?" He quoted the legend.

"Yes. Please don't be afraid. Trust me if you love me as much as I love you."

Stefan hesitated, then held his hand out for the belt. "You are my true love, Kalyna."

With all certainty, she was his soul mate. Being with her brought him joy, an exquisite high, a oneness and peace. She was part of him. Their love would go on for eternity even after their lives one day ended since all men are destined to die. But that unknown day had yet to arrive. His future stood beside him now. He wanted to be with her always, share passion and love with her, experience happiness and sorrow together. He could embrace every challenge life had in store for him as long as she remained by his side.

Kalyna placed the belt in his hand.

The window flew open with a bang. A cold wind gusted into the studio, scattering drawings and blowing Kalyna's hair around her shoulders. A green glow shone in the studio, leaving Stefan spellbound by the surreal scene. It had to be another dream.

Kissing him with wild desire, Kalyna smothered his lips with the familiar taste of raspberries. Her hands caressed the golden ring on the chain around his neck. She looked at him with longing.

He removed the chain, unclasped it, and slid off the ring. When he placed it on her finger, the rays in the stone shone as bright as a star. "Will you marry me, Kalyna? Will you be my bride?"

"Yes, I will." Her eyes filled with tears. "I've waited for this moment for so long." She removed the ring. Looking at the inscription, she read: "For my beloved, my one true love. Together forever."

The wind stopped as inexplicably as it had begun. A peaceful quiet enclosed Stefan as he embraced his beloved.

Soft words drifted through the air around them. "The soul begins its long journey alone in this world. We learn and we feel pain while we travel along the path of our lives. A few of us are fortunate enough to find our soul mate, the person with whom we can experience the beauty of humanity. Even more blessed are those who have lost their one true love, only to rediscover each other after centuries of being apart."

Stefan looked around for the person who spoke, but saw no one but Kalyna. "I-I don't understand any of this. The ring? The inscription? B-but I trust you. I love you." Stefan kissed her lips. "Please don't run away from me ever again. You've changed my universe, my life. I promise you, my love, if I've lived other lives, we'll get it right in this lifetime."

If she was a dream, she was his new reality, and he didn't want to wake up. He hugged her tight in his arms, afraid she would fly away like a falcon.

THE NEXT MORNING, Stefan woke in a sweat and his head tingled. Placing his fingers on his forehead, he felt a slight fever. He opened his eyes, but couldn't focus. Shadowy figures danced before him, and indistinguishable sounds played in his head.

Where was he? Closing his eyes, he concentrated. In Emona. At home with Kalyna. His beloved.

Upon opening his eyes again, his vision had cleared. He turned to his side. The space next to him was empty. Had she disappeared from his life once more? Last night had been strange to say the least. He still had questions to ask her, but now he wasn't afraid of the answers. Loving her was enough to overcome his fears.

"Good morning, my prince. Breakfast is ready." Kalyna carried in a tray of food.

He looked at her with a blissful smile. "I thought you were gone again."

"I'll be with you forever. I promised." She set the tray next to him. "Now eat, while it's still hot."

"Mmm." He sat up, and patted the bed for her to join him. "Honey, yogurt, coffee. What's this one?"

"It's a *printsessi*. It has a mixture of egg, white cheese, and spices baked onto a slice of bread." She picked up a piece and brought it to his mouth. "Take a bite."

"Delicious." He took the other piece. "Now, you."

She bit into it, then glanced at him with a mischievous look. "This is a nice way to spend our day. Perhaps we could—"

"Carina?" His head spun again. He closed his eyes and placed the back of his hand against his forehead. This time the images appeared more distinct—a girl skipping through a field of poppies, the sounds clearer—a shepherd playing a *kaval*. "Where are you?"

"Stefan, I'm here." Her voice anxious, she touched his arm.

He opened his eyes to slits, seeing double. "I'm not feeling well, Kalyna. Rather dizzy. Hot." Reaching for the tray with shaking hands, he knocked over his coffee. "Sorry. Must lie down."

She put her hand on his head. "You're burning!" She moved the tray off the bed.

After helping him to recline, she slid off the bed. Her eyes turned black and she murmured strange words. A green glow surrounded the two of them.

"Go away, Slava." He lashed out with his hand. "I want my Carina."

"It's me." She turned back. "What's wrong?"

"You, *rudas mezéna*, you fiend!" He glared at her. "How dare you attack Aemon? You're going to die this very day. You and your raiding hoards."

Her face paled, and she rushed from the room. A moment later, she returned with a bowl. She lifted a wet cloth from it, wrung it out, and placed it on his forehead.

Cool water dripped down his face. The swirling images faded, then one by one disappeared entirely, along with the screams and battle cries. Soft sobs replaced them, and gentle fingers caressed his cheeks. A hand removed the weight from his forehead, dipped it into the bowl, then replaced it again. Its coolness eased his throbbing head. Soon the room stopped spinning and objects came into focus. His eyes drooped, and he drifted off to sleep.

THE ROOM WAS too quiet and dark. Night had fallen, and the light in the bedroom was low. Stefan sat up and looked around. Kalyna slept on a chair by the bed, her hand resting by his side.

Where was his daughter? "Sonia?"

Kalyna jerked her head up. "You're finally awake!" She touched his forehead with the back of her hand, then let out a long breath of air. "How do you feel? You were burning up this morning."

"I'm fine now." He sat up. "Where's Sonia?"

"She's in Rouen, with her grandparents."

"Yes, right." He rubbed his temples. "I don't know what happened. So many strange dreams."

"I'm ready to try to explain things to you now. But first, I have something to give you. I'll be right back." She left the room, but returned in a few minutes. "Here, this is yours." She handed him a camera. "Do you remember anything?"

He looked at it, the one he had lost at the cave. "No. It's all a blur. So confusing." He patted the mattress. "Please sit by me. I need you close."

She sat on the edge of the bed and wrapped an arm around his waist. He grasped her hand in both of his. The stone on the ring warmed his palms.

Raising his head, he glanced at her, so beautiful with her mysterious smile, her eyes glistening. They were black and deep, the same ones he had seen in the cave.

His head spun again. He closed his eyes. A lifetime of visions passed before him. It was all true—the legend, everything the villagers had told him, all the stories he had told Sonia. He looked at her with awe and love, but no longer the fear he had shown in the cave.

"Yes, I remember, Carina, my love."

"Dushan, my beloved." Tears streaming down her face, she flung her arms around him. "I've waited so long to be with you. We are one."

He caressed her cheeks with the gentleness of Stefan, but kissed her with the passion of Dushan. His past and present became one.

Glossary

À ta santé: A toast meaning "to your health."

Anemoi: The gods of the winds.

Aqua vitae: Water of life. Used in this context for its literal meaning, not an alcoholic beverage.

Bendis: Thracian goddess of the moon and destiny.

Banitsa: A baked dish of whisked eggs and pieces of cheese layered between filo dough.

Blagodarya: Thank you.

Blagovets: March 25. The day samodivi return. Also the Annunciation of Mary, when she was told she would give birth to the Savior.

Boreas: God of the North wind and winter.

Cherga: A type of rug often made in stripes or geometrical shapes.

Cherpak: Ladle.

Cheshma: A fountain, often built into the side of a hill to draw water from springs.

Christos Voskrese: Christ is risen.

Day of Saint Michael the Archangel: November 8. Celebration of loved ones who have passed on.

Dobra dusha: Kind soul. Bread without yeast that's baked in a *podnitza*.

Dobre doshul (to males) or dobre doshla (to females): Welcome.

Emonska kavarma: A stew made with pork and several vegetables.

Eniovden: June 24. Midsummer's Day. A day to gather herbs.

Gaida: A type of bagpipe in the Balkans made of sheep or goat hide.

Gora: Woodland.

Kamoles: Beloved.

Kandilo: A vigil lamp set in front of an icon of a saint.

Karakachan: Bulgarian Shepherd dog.

Karakachka: A design of rug that has triangles representing a tree. Called a black-eyed bride.

Kaval: A long wooden flute-like instrument.

Kolo: Circle dance. Also called a horo.

Kozunak: Easter sweet bread decorated with eggs.

Kuker (plural: kukeri): Men dressed in furry costumes, and wearing scary wooden masks. The ritual is intended to scare away evil spirits.

Lamia: Female dragon.

Martenitsa (plural: martenitsi): Amulets made of red and white yarn worn on March 1 until spring.

Maenads: Female followers of Dionysus, god of wine.

Mémé: Grandmother.

Mon cher: My darling.

Name Day: A day when you celebrate your name the way you would celebrate a birthday.

Nazdrave: Cheers (a toast).

Ne se strakhuvaĭ ot cherniya zhrebets: Don't be afraid of the black stallion.

Nestinarstvo: Fire dance. Dancing on coals with bare feet.

Obrok: A sacred place.

Odiak: Type of fireplace popular in the nineteenth century.

Other side of the moon: Term used to describe where the mortals live.

Outi: A stringed, lute type of instrument played by Thracians.

Pépé: Grandfather.

Pitka: Bread eaten on holidays.

Planina: Mountain.

Podnitza: A special earthen baking dish used to bake bread on burning embers or ashes.

Pomada: Ointment.

Preroden otnovo: Reborn.

Printsessi: A slice of bread covered with a mixture of egg, cheese, and spices that is baked in an oven.

Prokopi Pchelar: July 8. Beekeeper's Day. Ritual loaves of bread are baked so bees will gather lots of honey.

Rhyton: A drinking goblet. Also used to pour ceremonial libations.

Rudas mezéna: Red horseman.

Saint Joseph: Patron saint of woodworkers.

Saint Luke: Patron saint of painters.

Saint Nicholas: Patron saint of fishermen.

Samodiva (plural: samodivi): Mystical nymphs in the Balkans. Known for shape-shifting and enchanting men with their beauty. Also called samovila, vila, or veela.

Samodivsko Tsvete: Rosen. Nymph's flower. Type of flowering plant. Also called *Dictamnus Alba* or Burning Bush.

Sharena sol: Colorful salt. A mixture of sea salt, paprika, and summer savory.

Sine, sine. Dobre li si?: Son, son, are you okay?

Tsigani: Gypsies.

Tzatza: Small fried fish that look like French fries.

Tupan: A double-headed drum used in the Balkans and played with mallets.

Uroki: Evil spirit.

Varna Day: August 15. A four-day celebration held in Varna. Also the Assumption of Mary.

Vizier: A high official.

Vo Istine Voskrese: He is risen indeed.

Voda: Water

Zeira: A long woolen hooded cloak worn by Thracians.

Zephryos: God of the West wind and Spring.

Zdravei: Hello.

Zemi: Male dragon.

Znahar: A person proficient with using herbs to heal.

Zurla: An oboe-like woodwind instrument used in the Balkans.

Acknowledgments

We would like to thank **Radio Bulgaria**, the Internet program of the Bulgarian National Radio, for their willingness to share the vast knowledge they have accumulated on Bulgarian history, culture, traditions, and folklore. Their materials have proven to be an invaluable resource for bringing to life the characters in this book. We especially want to thank Rossitsa Petcova, editor-in-chief English Section, for working with us to make this happen. There are hardly enough words of gratitude to thank the authors, translators and entire staff at Radio Bulgaria for all the wonderful material they have provided to the world and now to us. Visit them at http://bnr.bg/en to see what magic you can discover on your own.

Thanks to authors Albena Bezovska, Valia Bojilova, Vihra Baeva, Lina Ivanova, Associate Prof. Vihra Baeva, Associate Prof. Dr. Valentina Dineva, Rumiana Panayotova, and Darina Grigorova.

Thanks to English translators Vyara Popova, Rossitsa Petcova, Daniela Konstantinova, Kostadin Atanasov, Radostin Zhelev, and Alexander Markov.

Thanks to all those whose names we do not know.

We appreciate the efforts of everyone at **Scribophile.com**. To Alex Cabal for creating a great place for writers to help each other. To Jerry Quinn, Lord of The Ubergroup, for his dedication in herding cats. To the Spirit Warriors: Patrick Null, Monica Mynk, Viktor Steiner, Jordan Phillips, and Paylor. And to so many others who stuck with "Mystical Emona," as teams or individual contributors, offering advice and words of encouragement, especially Erica Madison-Youman, Alexander Key, Morgan Domini, Lindsay Reid, Jennifer Orth, Dawn Chapman, Noor Lek, Lea Grover, and others who wished to be anonymous or contributed in even a small way.

Thank you, **beta readers**: Mary Maniscalco, Diane Crusco, Aparna Challuri, Katie Kissel, Bobbie Hennessee, and Veronica Hitterman.

And special thanks to Violeta Jeliazkova, friend and founder of the Bulgarian-American Cultural Center Madara, for her support and unstoppable energy, smiles, and enthusiasm in bringing wonderful cultural Bulgarian rituals and celebrations to us throughout the years.

About the Author

Ronesa Aveela is "the creative power of two." Two authors that is. Nelly, the main force behind the work, the creative genius, was born in Bulgaria and moved to the US in the 1990s. She grew up with stories of wild Samodivi, Kikimora, the dragons Zmey and Lamia, Baba Yaga, and much more. She's a freelance artist and writer. She likes writing mystery romance inspired by legends and tales. In her free time, she paints. Her artistic interests include the female figure, Greek and Thracian mythology, folklore tales, and the natural world interpreted through her eyes. She is married and has two children.

Rebecca, her writing partner was born and raised in the New England area. She has a background in writing and editing, as well as having a love of all things from different cultures. She's learned so much about Bulgarian culture, folklore, and rituals, and writes to share that knowledge with others.

Connect with us at www.ronesaaveela.com.

Would you like to learn more about folklore and mythology? Visit our website and sign up for our newsletter and receive a FREE supplement to our "Spirits and Creatures" book series. Your free gift is all about a malicious water spirit, Vodyanoy or Vodnik.

Reviews

We hope you've enjoyed this book, and that it has inspired you. We would appreciate your gift of a review. Good or bad, we'd love to hear your honest thoughts.